THE **8**TH ANNUAL OF

THE YEAR'S BEST SF 1963

Edited by Judith Merril

SIMON AND SCHUSTER
NEW YORK   1963

Acknowledgments

"The Unsafe Deposit Box" by Gerald Kersh; © 1962 by the Curtis Publishing Company. By permission of the author and the Sterling Lord Agency.

"Seven-Day Terror" by R. A. Lafferty; © 1962 by Galaxy Publishing Company. By permission of the author and his agent, General Artists Corporation.

"The Toy Shop" by Harry Harrison; © 1962 by Condé Nast Publications, Inc. By permission of the author and his agent, Hans Stefan Santesson.

"The Face in the Photo" by Jack Finney; © 1962 by Jack Finney. Reprinted from *I Love Galesburg in the Springtime* by permission of the author, his agent, Harold Matson Company, Inc., and Simon and Schuster, Inc.

"The Circuit Riders" by R. C. FitzPatrick; © 1962 by Condé Nast Publications, Inc. By permission of the author.

"Such Stuff" by John Brunner; © 1962 by Mercury Press, Inc. By permission of the author and his agent, Hans Stefan Santesson.

"The Man Who Made Friends with Electricity" by Fritz Leiber; © 1962 by Mercury Press, Inc. By permission of the author and his agent, General Artists Corporation.

"Kings Who Die" by Poul Anderson; © 1962 by Digest Products Corporation. By permission of the author and his agent, Scott Meredith Literary Agency, Inc.

"The Unfortunate Mr. Morky" by Vance Aandahl; © 1962 by Mercury Press, Inc. By permission of the author and his agent, General Artists Corporation.

"Christmas Treason" by James White; © 1961 by Mercury Press, Inc. By permission of the author and his agent, E. J. Carnell.

"A Miracle of Rare Device" by Ray Bradbury; © 1961 by Ray Bradbury. By permission of the author and his agent, Harold Matson Company, Inc.

"All the Sounds of Fear" by Harlan Ellison; © 1962 by Harlan Ellison. Reprinted from *Ellison Wonderland* by permission of the author, his agent, General Artists Corporation, and Paperback Library, Inc.

"One of Those Days" by William F. Nolan; © 1962 by Mercury Press, Inc. Reprinted from *The Fiend in You* and *Impact 20*. By permission of the author and of Ballantine Books, Inc., and Paperback Library, Inc.

"The Day Rembrandt Went Public" by Arnold M. Auerbach; © 1962 by Harper & Row, Publishers, Inc. By permission of the author and his agent, Julian S. Bach, Jr.

"Ms. Found in a Bus" by Russell Baker; © 1962 by The New York Times Company. Reprinted by permission.

CONTENTS

THE UNSAFE DEPOSIT BOX

by Gerald Kersh

from the *Saturday Evening Post*

Fable and fantasy—imaginative fiction in general, from earliest myths and early moon voyages to *1984* and the *Eighth Annual SF*—have always served as vehicles for social criticism and for speculation on new ideas in science and philosophy. The most startling, heretical, extreme or radical new notions could always be explored in fairy tales when risk to personal reputation, or danger of public repression, made "serious" expositions seem unwise; or a hypothesis, as yet unproven, could be pre-tested, as it were, by building a story structure—an imaginary, but logical, "reality"—on the assumption of its validity.

The specialized variety of fantasy that we call "modern science fiction" had its beginnings in the first half of the nineteenth century with the literary discovery (by Mary Shelley, Poe, Hawthorne and Balzac, most notably) of the Wonderful Invention. It was a time of effervescent technological excitement: the beginning of man's consciousness of his capacity to create his own environment—to remake the actual physical world closer to his own desires. The Wonderful Invention (ordinarily, at the start, a machine or a formula) opened a whole new area of the imagination, with the basic question: *If* we can effect this change (mechanical, biological, etc.) in our world, what will the changed world be like for us?

It is this inquiry that constitutes the essence of "science fiction." And this volume begins, as it were, at the beginning of s-f, with an almost classically pure example of the Wonderful Invention—complete with a secret formula, an at least moderately mad scientist, a tricky intellectual puzzle, a clutch of comically inept civil authorities, and even the traditional, if somewhat cheeky-tongued, formalized style of first-person narration.

You have a sharp eye, sir, a very sharp eye indeed, if you recognize me by those photographs that used to appear in the newspapers and the sensational magazines about 1947. I fancy I must have changed somewhat since then; but yes, I am Peter Perfrement, and they did make a knight of me for some work I did in nuclear physics. I am glad, for once, to be recognized. You might otherwise mistake me for an escaped convict, or a lunatic at large, or something of that sort; for I am going to beg you to have the goodness to sit in this shadowy corner and keep your broad back between me and the door. Have an eye on the mirror over my head and you will in due course see the reflections of a couple of fellows who will come into this cozy little bar. Those men will be looking for me. You will perceive, by the complete vacuity of their expressions, that they are from Intelligence.

They'll spot me, of course, and then it will be, "Why, Sir Peter, how lucky to find you here!" Then, pleading business, they'll carry me off. And evading those two young men is one of the few pleasures left me in my old age. Once I got out in a laundry basket. Tonight I put on a workman's suit of overalls over my dinner suit and went to a concert. I intend to go back home to the Center after I've had my evening, but I want to be left alone a bit. Of course, I have nobody but myself to blame for any slight discomfort I may at present suffer. I retired once and for all, as I thought, in 1950. By then the inwardness of such atom bombs as we let off over, say, Hiroshima was public property. My work, as it seemed, was done.

So I withdrew to a pleasant little villa at the Cap des Fesses just outside that awful holiday resort Les Sables des Fesses in the south of France. Fully intended to end my days there, as a matter of fact—set up library and study there, and a compact but middling-comprehensive laboratory. I went to all the music festivals, drank my glass of wine on the *terrasse* of whatever café happened to take my fancy, and continued my academic battle with Doctor Frankenburg. This battle, which was in point of fact far less acrimonious than the average game of chess, had to do with the nature of the element fluorine. I take it that esoteric mathematics are, mercifully, beyond your comprehension; but perhaps you were told at school something of the nature of fluorine. This is the *enfant terrible* of the elements.

Fluorine, in temperament, is a prima donna and, in character, a born delinquent. You cannot keep it pure; it has such an affinity for practically everything else on earth, and what it has an affinity for, it tends to destroy. Now I had a theory involving what I can only describe to a layman as tame fluorine—fluorine housebroken and in harness. Doctor Frankenburg, whose leisure is devoted to reading the comic papers, used to say concerning this, "You might as well imagine Dennis the Menace as a breadwinner." However, I worked away not under pressure nor under observation, completely at my leisure, having access to the great computer at Assigny. And one day I found that I had evolved a substance which, for convenience, I will call fluorine 80+.

I do not mean that I made it merely in formula. The nature of the stuff, once comprehended, made the physical production of it really absurdly simple. So I made some— about six ounces of it, and it looked rather like a sheet of hard, lime-colored gelatin. And potentially this bit of gelatinous-looking stuff was somewhat more potent than a cosmic collision. Potentially, mark you—only potentially. As it lay in my hand, fluorine 80+ was, by all possible calculations, inert. You could beat it with a sledge hammer or burn it with a blowlamp, and nothing would happen. But under certain conditions—conditions which seemed to me at that time quite impossible of achievement—this morsel of matter could be unbelievably terrible. By unbelievably, I mean immeasurably. Quite beyond calculation.

The notebook containing my formula I wrapped in paper with the intention of putting it in the vault of the Banque Maritime des Sables des Fesses. The sheet of fluorine 80+ I placed between two pieces of cardboard; then I wrapped it likewise and put it in my pocket. You see, I had a friend in the town with whom I often had tea, and he had a liking for the weird and the wonderful. Like the fool that I am, I proposed to amuse myself by showing him my sample and telling him that this inoffensive little thing, in a suitable environment, might cause our earth to go *pssst!*—in about as long as it takes for a pinch of gunpowder to flash in a match flame. So in high spirits I went into town, paid my visit to the bank, first having got a pot of Gentlemen's Relish and a jar of Oxford Marmalade for tea, and so called on Doctor Raisin.

He was another old boy who had outlived his usefulness, although time was when he had some reputation as an architect specializing in steel construction. "Something special for tea," I said and tossed my little package of fluorine 80+ on the table.

"Smoked salmon?" he asked.

Then I brought out the marmalade and the relish, and said, "No," chuckling like an idiot.

He growled, "Evidently you have just paid a visit to the Café de la Guerre Froide," and sniffed at me.

"No, I've just come from the bank."

"So," he said, "that's a parcel of money, I suppose. What's it to me? Let's have tea."

I said, "I didn't go to the bank to take something out, Raisin. I put something in."

"Make me no mystifications, if you please. What's that?"

"That," I said, "is proof positive that Frankenburg is wrong and I am right, Raisin. What you see there is half a dozen ounces of absolutely stable fluorine eighty-plus and a critical mass, at that!"

Dry as an old bone, he said, "Jargon me no jargons. As I understand it, an atomic explosion takes place when certain quantities of radioactive material arrive, in certain circumstances, at what you call 'critical mass.' This being the case, that little packet may, I take it, be considered dangerous?"

I said, "Rather so. There's about enough fluorine eighty-plus there to vaporize a medium-sized planet."

Raisin said, "A fluorine bomb, an ounce of nitroglycerin —it's all the same to me." Pouring tea, he asked nonchalantly, "How do you make it go off? Not, I gather, by chucking it about on tables?"

I said, "You can't explode it—as you understand an explosion—except under conditions difficult to create and useless once created; although, perhaps, while valueless as a weapon, it could be put to peaceful uses."

"Perhaps me no perhapses. A fighting cock *could* be used to make chicken broth. What did you want to bring it here for, anyway?"

I was a little put out. Raisin was unimpressible. I told him, rather lamely, "Well, neither you nor anyone else will ever see fluorine eighty-plus again. In about fourteen hours that piece there will—as you would put it—have evaporated."

"Why as *I* would put it? How do you put it?"

"Why, you see," I explained, "in point of actual fact, that stuff is exploding now. Only it's exploding very, very gradually. Now, for this explosion to be effectual as an explosion, we should have to let that mass expand at a temperature of anything over sixty degrees Fahrenheit in a hermetically sealed bomb case of at least ten thousand cubic feet in capacity. At this point, given suitable pressure, up she'd go. But when I tell you that before we could get such a pressure under which my fluorine eighty-plus would undergo certain atomic alterations, the casing of our ten-thousand-cubic-foot bomb would need to be at least two or three feet thick."

Being a Russian, Raisin stirred marmalade into his tea and interrupted. "It is a chimera. So let it evaporate. Burn your formula. Pay no further attention to it. . . . Still, since you have brought it, let's have a look at it." He undid the little parcel, and said, "I knew all along it was a joke." The paper pulled away, there lay nothing but a notebook.

I cried, "Good heavens—that ought to be safe in the bank! That's the formula!"

"And the bomb?"

"Not a bomb, Raisin—I've just told you that fluorine eighty-plus can't possibly be a bomb of its own accord. Confound it! I must have left it at the grocer's shop."

He said, "Is it poisonous?"

"Toxic? I don't think so. . . . Now wait a minute, wait a

minute! I distinctly remember—when I left the house I put the formula in my right-hand coat pocket and the fluorine eighty-plus in the left. Now first of all I went to the Epicerie Internationale to get this marmalade and stuff, and so as not to crowd my left pocket I transferred.... Oh, it's quite all right, Raisin. There's nothing to worry about, except that this is not the kind of notebook I like to carry about with me. The sample is safe and sound in the bank. It was a natural mistake—the packages are very much alike in shape and weight. No cause for anxiety. Pass the Gentlemen's Relish, will you?"

But Raisin said, "This horrible little bit of fluorine—you left it in the bank, did you?"

"Fluorine eighty-plus. Well?"

"You bank at the Maritime?"

"Yes, why?"

"So do I. It is the safest bank in France. Its vaults—now follow me carefully, Perfrement—its vaults are burglarproof, bombproof, fireproof, and absolutely airtight. The safe deposit vault is forty feet long, thirty feet wide and ten feet high. This gives it a capacity of twelve thousand cubic feet. It is maintained at a low humidity and a constant temperature of sixty-five degrees Fahrenheit. The walls of this vault are of hard steel and reinforced concrete three feet thick. The door alone weighs thirty tons, but fits like a glass stopper in a medicine bottle. Does the significance of all this sink in?"

"Why," I said, "why—"

"Yes, why? You can say that again. What you have done, my irresponsible friend," said Doctor Raisin, "is put your mass of fluorine eighty-plus in its impossible casing. That's the way with the likes of you. It would never dawn on you that a bomb might be an oblong thing as big as a bank. Congratulations!"

I said, "I know the manager, M. le Queux, and he knows me. I'll go and see him at once."

"It's Saturday. The bank's closed by now."

"Yes, I know, but I'll ask him to come over with his keys."

Raisin said, "I wish you luck."

A telephone call to M. le Queux's house got me only the information that he was gone for the weekend to Laffert, about eighty miles inland, up the mountain, where he had a bungalow. So I looked about for a taxi. But it was carnival weekend, and there was nothing to be got except one of those essentially French machines that have run on coal gas and kerosene, and have practically no works left inside them, and yet, like certain extremely cheap alarm clocks, somehow continue to go, without accuracy, but with a tremendous noise. And the driver was a most objectionable man in a beret, who chewed whole cloves of raw garlic all the time and shouted into one's face as if one were a hundred yards distant.

After a disruptive and malodorous journey, during which the car had twice to be mended with bits of wire, we reached Laffert, and with some difficulty found M. le Queux.

He said to me, "For you—anything. But to open the bank? No, I cannot oblige you."

"You had better," I said to him, in a minatory tone.

"But Sir Peter," said he, "this is not merely a matter of turning a key and opening a door. I don't believe you can have read our brochure. The door of the vault is on a time lock. This means that after the lock is set and the door closed, nothing can open it until a certain period of time has elapsed. So, precisely at 7:45 on Monday morning—but not one instant before—I can open the vault for you."

I said, "Then as I see it, you had better send for the locksmith and have the lock picked."

M. le Queux laughed. He said, "You couldn't open our vault without taking the door down." He spoke with a certain pride.

"Then I'm afraid I'll have to trouble you to have the door taken down," I told him.

"That would necessitate practically taking down the bank," M. le Queux said; and evidently he thought that I was out of my mind.

"Then," I said, "there's nothing for it *but* to take down the bank. Of course, there'll be compensation, I suppose.

Still, the fact remains that, by the sheerest inadvertence, for which I hold myself greatly at fault, I have turned your bank-vault into a colossal bomb—a bomb compared with which your Russian multimegaton bombs are milk-and-water. Indeed, you would no more weigh or measure my fluorine eighty-plus in terms of mere megatons than you'd buy coal by the milligram or wine by the cubic centimeter."

"One of us is going crazy," said M. le Queux.

"Call a Hiroshima bomb a megaton," I said. "Dealing with my fluorine eighty-plus we have to make tables. So a million megatons equal one tyrrannoton. A million tyrranno-tons equal one chasmaton. A million chasmatons make one brahmaton. And after a million brahmatons we come to something I call an ultimon, because it is beyond even the scope of mathematical conjecture. In a certain number of hours from now—and we are wasting time talking, M. le Queux—if you don't get that vault of yours open, the universe will experience the shock of half a chasmaton. Please let me use your telephone."

So I called a certain branch of Security, and after that told a minister, who shall be nameless, to be so kind as to get a move on—referring him, of course, to several other nuclear experts, in case my own name was not enough for him. Thus I was able, within twenty minutes, to tell M. le Queux, "It's all arranged. Army and police are on the way. So are some colleagues of mine. The Custodia Safe Company, who installed your vault, are flying their best techni-cians into Fesses. We'll have your vault open in a couple of hours or so. I'm sorry if this inconveniences you, but it's got to be done, and you must put up with it."

He could only say, "Inconveniences me!" Then he shouted, "After this, Sir Peter Perfrement, you will kindly take your banking business elsewhere!"

I was sorry for him, but there was no time for sentiment just now, for I found myself caught in a sort of whirlpool of giddy activity. Accompanied by the usual quota of se-cret police from Security, four highly regarded nuclear physicists were rushed to Fesses. I was pleased to see among them my dear old enemy Frankenburg, who would have to admit that in the matter of fluorine he was totally confuted. There was also, of course, a swarm of policemen, both uniformed and in plain-clothes, and, goodness knows why, two doctors, one of whom kept talking and talking without rhyme or reason about fluorine being found in relatively high concentration in the human embryo and how good it was for children's teeth. An expert from the quiet old days of the high-explosive blitzes said that since one invariably evacuated the area surrounding an unexploded bomb until it was defused, it would be wise to evacuate Sables des Fesses.

At this the *maire* went into ecstasies of Gallicism. To evacuate this place at carnival weekend would be to ruin it —death rather than dishonor, and so forth. I said that if my fluorine 80+ blew, the problem of evacuation need not arise; for nobody anywhere, ever, would be any the wiser. The chief of police, giving me a suspicious look, said that the present danger was only hypothetical; but the panic that must attend a mass alarm would be inevitably disastrous. It would be necessary only to surround the block in which the bank was situated. This being in the business district of the town, and most of the offices shut up for the weekend, the matter might be accomplished—a hairsbreadth this side of impossibility.

So said the chief of police, filling a pipe as a pioneer fills his muzzle-loader with his last hard-bitten cartridge, and pointing it right at me. He made it clear, without speaking, that he thought this was all a put-up job, to get that bank vault open.

M. le Queux said, "But the armored car has been and gone, and the bank is just about empty of cash until Monday." Still the chief of police wasn't satisfied. Watching him tamp down the charge in his pipe, I could not help reciting a hunting proverb of my grandfather's: *Ram tight the powder, leave loose the lead, if you want to kill dead.* He made a note of that. Meanwhile, Frankenburg and the others were poring over my notes, which I had been compelled to hand over.

Frankenburg growled, "I want to check, and double-check. I want a computer. I want five days."

But little Doctor Imhof said, "Come, we must grant the possibility that what we read here is valid. Even for the sake of argument we must grant it."

"Well, for the sake of argument," said Frankenburg. "So?"

"So," said Imhof, "*any* relaxation of pressure must render Perfrement's so-called fluorine eighty-plus harmless, must it not? This being the case, a hole drilled in the vault door should be an ample measure of precaution. This hole made, why, let the matter wait until Monday."

"So be it," said I. "He talks sense."

So now the engineers from the Custodia Company, having come in by plane, unloaded their massive paraphernalia in the bank. And among the cylinders and eye shields and other gear I noticed a number of gas masks. "What are they for?" I asked le Queux.

Frankenburg, unwilling to be convinced, was complaining, "Yes, yes, bore holes—leave Perfrement's thing until Monday. But unless I misread this formula, his so-called fluorine eighty-plus will by that time have ceased to exist."

A certain Doctor Chiappe said in a glum voice, "Metaphysics: If we leave it, it ceases to exist; if we don't leave it, it ceases to exist; but, as I read Perfrement's notes, if we leave fluorine eighty-plus, we shall be involved with it in a state of co-nonexistence. Better bore holes."

I said, "I asked you, M. le Queux, what are those gas masks for?"

He said, "Why, when the door is in any way interfered with, the alarm automatically goes off. We omit no precautions, none whatsoever. As soon as the alarm goes off, the vault fills with tear gas from built-in containers."

"Did you say tear gas?" I asked.

"In a high concentration."

"Then," I cried, "get away from that door at once!" I appealed to Frankenburg. "You hate every word I say, old fellow, but you're an honest man. Conceding that my notes are right—and I swear they are—you'll see that my fluorine eighty-plus has one affinity. One only. That is with C_8H_7ClO

—chloroacetophenone. And that, damme, is the stuff tear gas is made of!"

Frankenburg nodded. Chiappe said, "Slice it as you like —we've had it!"

And old Raisin grumbled, "This, I believe, is what the dramatists call a perfectly damnable impasse. Correct me if I'm wrong."

It was little Imhof who asked, "Is there no part of this place at all that's not guarded by alarm, and what not?"

Le Queux said, "Technically, there is only one part of our vault that's reachable from the outside—if you can call it the outside. The back of our vault abuts on the back of the jeweler's, Monnickendam's, next door. His vault, you see, is itself two feet thick. Hence—"

"Aha!" said the chief of police.

"Get Monnickendam," said the minister of Security, and that famous jeweler and pawnbroker was duly produced.

He said, "I'd open my vault with pleasure, but I have a partner, Warmerdam. Our vault opens by two combination locks which must be operated simultaneously. These locks are so placed that no one can operate both at the same time. I have my own secret combination and Warmerdam has his. We must both be present to open the vault."

"That's how one gets rich," old Raisin muttered.

Monnickendam corrected him, "That is how one *stays* rich."

"Where's Warmerdam?" they asked.

"In London."

London was telephoned, and Secret Service agents dragged poor Warmerdam shrieking from a dinner table and rushed him to a jetport and fired him over to Sables des Fesses with such dispatch that he arrived in a state of semiobfuscation, with a napkin still tucked under his chin.

But now, by the the chief of police's expression, it was evident that the whole matter was an open-and-shut case to him. I was some sort of master criminal, a Moriarty, and my real objective was the jewelers' strong room. He strengthened the police cordon, and Monnickendam and

Warmerdam opened their vault.

The men from Custodia went to work—but not before the two jewelers had got a signed and witnessed indemnity from the president of the bank; they wouldn't trust the minister—and so the heavy steel and concrete of the strong room cut through, we began to bite into the back of the bank.

"Time runs out," I said.

Raisin irritated everybody by saying, "Imagination, my friends, and nothing but imagination, is making us all sweat. All things considered, do you think that a megaton, a tyrannoton, or an ultimon could do us—us personally— more harm than, let us say, a pound of dynamite?"

The chief of police said, "Ha! You know a lot about dynamite, it seems."

"I should hope so," said Raisin. "I was sabotaging Nazis, my friend, when you were swinging a truncheon for the *Deuxième Bureau.*"

I had better be brief, however. At about five in the morning we broke through.

I said, "Fine. You can take it easy now. Fluorine eighty-plus can't blow." And when I then suggested a hot cup of tea, M. le Queux tried to strangle me.

But the men worked on, until the hole was about two feet in diameter; and then one of the smallest of them took my key, wriggled through, and came back with the contents of my safe-deposit box—the little paper package of fluorine 80+.

I pointed out to Frankenburg how greatly it had diminished. "By George, we had a close call then!" I said.

And that, as you might think, was that. Ah, but you'd be wrong. For you see, in the course of that mad night, when every policeman in Sables des Fesses and its environs was mounting guard at the bank and at Monnickendam's, a gang of thieves broke into the Prince of Mamluk's Galleries, said to contain one of the four finest art collections in the world.

They stripped the place at their leisure. They took a priceless collection of antique jewels, three Rembrandts, four Holbeins, two Raphaels, a Titian, two El Grecos, a Vermeer, three Botticellis, a Goya and a Greuze. Greatest art burglary of all time, I'm told. They say that Lloyds would rather have lost a fleet of transatlantic liners than what they underwrote those pictures and things for.

Taking it by and large, I suppose it's for my own good that I was shipped back to England and put under guard.

If I'd had any sense, of course, I'd have kept quiet about that confounded fluorine 80+. As it is, I've made a prisoner of myself. They regard me—of all people!—as a compulsive chatterbox. As if fluorine 80+ is anything to chatter about. Why, you could make it yourself. Take 500 grams of fluorspar—

Oh-oh! Here come my two friends, I'm afraid. I will take my leave of you now, sir. . . . Good night to you.

Good evening, gentlemen!

SEVEN-DAY TERROR

by R. A. Lafferty

from *If*

And now, a truly Marvelous (not just Wonderful) Invention—combining in miniature the classic and the most casual contemporary, fantasy and technology, some kids, some cops (comic and otherwise), and what I guess you'd have to call a Mad Scientist's Apprentice. . . .

"Is there anything you want to make disappear?" Clarence Willoughby asked his mother.

"A sinkful of dishes is all I can think of. How will you do it?"

"I just built a disappearer. All you do is cut the other end out of a beer can. Then you take two pieces of red cardboard with peepholes in the middle and fit them in the ends. You look through the peepholes and blink. Whatever you look at will disappear."

"Oh."

"But I don't know if I can make them come back. We'd better try it on something else. Dishes cost money."

As always, Myra Willoughby had to admire the wisdom of her nine-year-old son. She would not have had such foresight herself. He always did.

"You can try it on Blanche Manners' cat outside there. Nobody will care if it disappears except Blanche Manners."

"All right."

He put the disappearer to his eye and blinked. The cat disappeared from the sidewalk outside.

His mother was interested. "I wonder how it works. Do you know how it works?"

"Yes. You take a beer can with both ends cut out and

put in two pieces of cardboard. Then you blink."

"Never mind. Take it outside and play with it. You hadn't better make anything disappear in here till I think about this."

But when he had gone his mother was oddly disturbed.

"I wonder if I have a precocious child. Why, there's lots of grown people who wouldn't know how to make a disappearer that would work. I wonder if Blanche Manners will miss her cat very much?"

Clarence went down to the Plugged Nickel, a pot house on the corner.

"Do you have anything you want to make disappear, Nokomis?"

"Only my paunch."

"If I make it disappear it'll leave a hole in you and you'll bleed to death."

"That's right, I would. Why don't you try it on the fire plug outside?"

This in a way was one of the happiest afternoons ever in the neighborhood. The children came from blocks around to play in the flooded streets and gutters, and if some of them drowned (and we don't say that they *did* drown) in the flood (and brother! it was a flood), why, you have to expect things like that. The fire engines (who ever heard of calling fire engines to put out a flood?) were apparatus-deep in the water. The policemen and ambulance men wandered around wet and bewildered.

"Resuscitator, resuscitator, anybody wanna resuscitator?" chanted Clarissa Willoughby.

"Oh, shut up," said the ambulance attendants.

Nokomis, the bar man in the Plugged Nickel, called Clarence aside.

"I don't believe, just for the moment, I'd tell anyone what happened to that fire plug," he said.

"I won't tell if you won't tell," said Clarence.

Officer Comstock was suspicious. "There's only seven possible explanations. One of the seven Willoughby kids did it. I dunno how. It'd take a bulldozer to do it, and then there'd be something left of the plug. But however they did it, one of them did it."

Officer Comstock had a talent for getting near the truth of dark matters. This is why he was walking a beat out here in the boondocks instead of sitting in a chair downtown.

"Clarissa!" said Officer Comstock in a voice like thunder.

"Resuscitator, resuscitator, anybody wanna resuscitator?" chanted Clarissa.

"Do you know what happened to that fire plug?" asked Officer C.

"I have an uncanny suspicion. As yet it is no more than that. When I am better informed I will advise you."

Clarissa was eight years old and much given to uncanny suspicions.

"Clementine, Harold, Corinne, Jimmy, Cyril," he asked the five younger Willoughby children. "Do you know what happened to that fire plug?"

"There was a man around yesterday. I bet he took it," said Clementine.

"I don't even remember a fire plug there. I think you're making a lot of fuss about nothing," said Harold.

"City Hall's going to hear about this," said Corinne.

"Pretty dommed sure," said Jimmy, "but I won't tell."

"Cyril!" cried Officer Comstock in a terrible voice. Not a terrifying voice, a terrible voice. He felt terrible now.

"Great green bananas," said Cyril, "I'm only three years old. I don't see how it's even my responsibility."

"Clarence," said Officer Comstock.

Clarence gulped.

"Do you know where that fire plug went?"

Clarence brightened. "No, sir. I don't know where it went."

A bunch of smart alecs from the water department came out and shut off the water for a few blocks around and put some kind of cap on in place of the fire plug. "This sure is going to be a funny-sounding report," said one of them.

Officer Comstock walked away discouraged. "Don't bother me, Miss Manners," he said. "I don't know where to look for your cat. I don't even know where to look for a fire plug."

"I have an idea," said Clarissa, "that when you find the cat you will find the fire plug the same place. As yet it is only an idea."

Ozzie Murphy wore a little hat on top of his head. Clarence pointed his weapon and winked. The hat was no longer there, but a little trickle of blood was running down the pate.

"I don't believe I'd play with that any more," said Nokomis.

"Who's playing?" said Clarence. "This is for real."

This was the beginning of the seven-day terror in the heretofore obscure neighborhood. Trees disappeared from the parkings; lamp posts were as though they had never been; Wally Waldorf drove home, got out, slammed the door of his car, and there was no car. As George Mullendorf came up the walk to his house his dog Pete ran to meet him and took a flying leap to his arms. The dog left the sidewalk but something happened; the dog was gone and only a bark lingered for a moment in the puzzled air.

But the worst were the fire plugs. The second plug was installed the morning after the disappearance of the first. In eight minutes it was gone and the flood waters returned. Another one was in by twelve o'clock. Within three minutes it had vanished. The next morning fire plug number four was installed.

The water commissioner was there, the city engineer was there, the chief of police was there with a riot squad, the president of the parent-teachers association was there, the president of the university was there, the mayor was there, three gentlemen of the FBI, a newsreel photographer, eminent scientists and a crowd of honest citizens.

"Let's see it disappear now," said the city engineer.

"Let's see it disappear now," said the police chief.

"Let's see it disa—it did, didn't it?" said one of the eminent scientists.

And it was gone and everybody was very wet.

"At least I have the picture sequence of the year," said the photographer. But his camera and apparatus disappeared from the midst of them.

"Shut off the water and cap it," said the commissioner. "And don't put in another plug yet. That was the last plug in the warehouse."

"This is too big for me," said the mayor. "I wonder that Tass doesn't have it yet."

"Tass has it," said a little round man. "I am Tass."

"If all of you gentlemen will come into the Plugged Nickel," said Nokomis, "and try one of our new Fire Hydrant Highballs you will all be happier. These are made of good corn whisky, brown sugar and hydrant water from this very gutter. You can be the first to drink them."

Business was phenomenal at the Plugged Nickel, for it was in front of its very doors that the fire plugs disappeared in floods of gushing water.

"I know a way we can get rich," said Clarissa several days later to her father, Tom Willoughby. "Everybody says they're going to sell their houses for nothing and move out of the neighborhood. Go get a lot of money and buy them all. Then you can sell them again and get rich."

"I wouldn't buy them for a dollar each. Three of them have disappeared already, and all the families but us have their furniture moved out in their front yards. There might be nothing but vacant lots in the morning."

"Good, then buy the vacant lots. And you can be ready when the houses come back."

"Come back? Are the houses going to come back? Do you know anything about this, young lady?"

"I have a suspicion verging on a certainty. As of now I can say no more."

Three eminent scientists were gathered in an untidy suite that looked as though it belonged to a drunken sultan.

"This transcends the metaphysical. It impinges on the quantum continuum. In some ways it obsoletes Boff," said Dr. Velikof Vonk.

"The contingence on the intransigence is the most mystifying aspect," said Arpad Arkabaranan.

"Yes," said Willy McGilly. "Who would have thought that you could do it with a beer can and two pieces of cardboard? When I was a boy I used an oatmeal box and red crayola."

"I do not always follow you," said Dr. Vonk. "I wish you would speak plainer."

So far no human had been injured or disappeared—except for a little blood on the pate of Ozzie Murphy, on the lobes of Conchita when her gaudy earrings disappeared from her very ears, a clipped finger or so when a house vanished as the front door knob was touched, a lost toe when a neighborhood boy kicked at a can and the can was not; probably not more than a pint of blood and three or four ounces of flesh all together.

Now, however, Mr. Buckle the grocery man disappeared before witnesses. This was serious.

Some mean-looking investigators from downtown came out to the Willoughbys. The meanest-looking one was the mayor. In happier days he had not been a mean man, but the terror had now reigned for seven days.

"There have been ugly rumors," said one of the mean investigators, "that link certain events to this household. Do any of you know anything about them?"

"I started most of them," said Clarissa. "But I didn't consider them ugly. Cryptic, rather. But if you want to get to the bottom of this just ask me a question."

"Did you make those things disappear?" asked the investigator.

"That isn't the question," said Clarissa.

"Do you know where they have gone?" asked the investigator.

"That isn't the question either," said Clarissa.

"Can you make them come back?"

"Why, of course I can. Anybody can. Can't you?"

"I cannot. If you can, please do so at once."

"I need some stuff. Get me a gold watch and a hammer. Then go down to the drugstore and get me this list of chemicals. And I need a yard of black velvet and a pound of rock candy."

"Shall we?" asked one of the investigators.

"Yes," said the mayor, "it's our only hope. Get her anything she wants."

And it was all assembled.

"Why does she get all the attention?" asked Clarence. "I was the one that made all the things disappear. How does she know how to get them back?"

"I knew it!" cried Clarissa with hate. "I knew he was the one that did it. He read in my diary how to make a disappearer. If I was his mother, I'd whip him for reading his little sister's diary. That's what happens when things like that fall into irresponsible hands."

She poised the hammer over the gold watch of the mayor on the floor.

"I have to wait a few seconds. This can't be hurried. It'll be only a little while."

The second hand swept around to the point that was preordained for it before the world began. Clarissa suddenly brought down the hammer with all her force on the beautiful gold watch.

"That's all," she said. "Your troubles are over. See, there is Blanche Manners' cat on the sidewalk just where she was seven days ago."

And the cat was back.

"Now let's go down to the Plugged Nickel and watch the fire plug come back."

They had only a few minutes to wait. It came from nowhere and clanged into the street like a sign and a witness.

"Now I predict," said Clarissa, "that every single object will return exactly seven days from the time of its disappearance."

The seven-day terror had ended. The objects began to reappear.

"How," asked the mayor, "did you know they would come back in seven days?"

"Because it was a seven-day disappearer that Clarence

made. I also know how to make a nine-day, a thirteen-day, a twenty-seven-day, and an eleven-year disappearer. I was going to make a thirteen-day one, but for that you have to color the ends with the blood from a little boy's heart, and Cyril cried every time I tried to make a good cut."

"You really know how to make all of these?"

"Yes. But I shudder if the knowledge should ever come into unauthorized hands."

"I shudder too, Clarissa. But tell me, why did you want the chemicals?"

"For my chemistry set."

"And the black velvet?"

"For doll dresses."

"And the pound of rock candy?"

"How did you ever get to be mayor of this town if you have to ask questions like that? What do you think I wanted the rock candy for?"

"One last question," said the mayor. "Why did you smash my gold watch with the hammer?"

"Oh," said Clarissa, "that was for dramatic effect."

THE TOY SHOP

by Harry Harrison

from *Analog*

. . . and right here, ladies and gentlemen, the Atomic Wonder Space Wave Tapper—which, in spite of its name, is not in quite the same category as the Disappearer. Every bit as Marvelous in its own way, the Tapper is a good solid laws-of-physics Machine. The only question is—Which laws?

Because there were few adults in the crowd, and Colonel "Biff" Hawton stood over six feet tall, he could see every detail of the demonstration. The children—and most of the parents—gaped in wide-eyed wonder. Biff Hawton was too sophisticated to be awed. He stayed on because he wanted to find out what the trick was that made the gadget work.

"It's all explained right here in your instruction book," the demonstrator said, holding up a garishly printed booklet opened to a four-color diagram. "You all know how magnets pick up things and I bet you even know that the earth itself is one great big magnet—that's why compasses always point north. Well . . . the Atomic Wonder Space Wave Tapper hangs on to those space waves. Invisible all about us, and even going right through us, are the magnetic waves of the earth. The Atomic Wonder rides these waves just the way a ship rides the waves in the ocean. Now watch . . ."

Every eye was on him as he put the gaudy model rocket-ship on top of the table and stepped back. It was made of stamped metal and seemed as incapable of flying as a can of ham—which it very much resembled. Neither wings, propellers, nor jets broke through the painted surface. It rested on three rubber wheels, and coming out through the bottom was a double strand of thin insulated wire. This white wire ran across the top of the black table and terminated in a control box in the demonstrator's hand. An indicator light, a switch and a knob appeared to be the only controls.

"I turn on the Power Switch, sending a surge of current to the Wave Receptors," he said. The switch clicked and the light blinked on and off with a steady pulse. Then the man began to turn the knob slowly. "A careful touch on the Wave Generator is necessary, as we are dealing with the powers of the whole world here . . ."

A concerted *ahhhh* swept through the crowd as the Space Wave Tapper shivered a bit, then rose slowly into the air. The demonstrator stepped back and the toy rose higher and higher, bobbing gently on the invisible waves of magnetic force that supported it. Ever so slowly the power was reduced and it settled back to the table.

"Only $17.95," the young man said, putting a large price sign on the table, "for the complete set of the Atomic Wonder, the Space Tapper control box, battery and instruction book . . ."

At the appearance of the price card the crowd broke up noisily and the children rushed away toward the operating model trains. The demonstrator's words were lost in their noisy passage, and after a moment he sank into a gloomy silence. He put the control box down, yawned and sat on the edge of the table. Colonel Hawton was the only one left after the crowd had moved on.

"Could you tell me how this thing works?" the colonel asked, coming forward. The demonstrator brightened up and picked up one of the toys.

"Well, if you will look here, sir . . ." he opened the hinged top, "you will see the Space Wave coils at each end of the ship." With a pencil he pointed out the odd shaped plastic forms about an inch in diameter that had been wound—apparently at random—with a few turns of copper wire. Except for these coils, the interior of the model was empty. The coils were wired together and other wires ran out through the hole in the bottom of the control box. Biff Hawton turned a very quizzical eye on the gadget and upon the demonstrator, who completely ignored this sign of disbelief.

"Inside the control box is the battery," the young man said, snapping it open and pointing to an ordinary flashlight battery. "The current goes through the Power Switch and Power Light to the Wave Generator..."

"What you mean to say," Biff broke in, "is that the juice from this fifteen-cent battery goes through this cheap rheostat to those meaningless coils in the model, and absolutely nothing happens. Now tell me what really flies the thing. If I'm going to drop eighteen bucks for six-bits' worth of tin, I want to know what I'm getting."

The demonstrator flushed. "I'm sorry, sir," he stammered. "I wasn't trying to hide anything. Like any magic trick this one can't be really demonstrated until it has been purchased." He leaned forward and whispered confidentially. "I'll tell you what I'll do though. This thing is way overpriced and hasn't been moving at all. The manager said I could let them go at three dollars if I could find any takers. If you want to buy it for that price..."

"Sold, my boy!" the colonel said, slamming three bills down on the table. "I'll give that much for it no matter *how* it works. The boys in the shop will get a kick out of it," he said, tapping the winged rocket on his chest. "Now *really*—what holds it up?"

The demonstrator looked around carefully, then pointed. "Strings!" he said. "Or rather a black thread. It runs from the top of the model, through a tiny loop in the ceiling, and back down to my hand—tied to this ring on my finger. When I back up—the model rises. It's as simple as that."

"All good illusions are simple," the colonel grunted, tracing the black thread with his eye. "As long as there is plenty of flimflam to distract the viewer."

"If you don't have a black table, a black cloth will do," the young man said. "And the arch of a doorway is a good site, just see that the room in back is dark."

"Wrap it up, my boy, I wasn't born yesterday. I'm an old hand at this kind of thing."

Biff Hawton sprang it at the next Thursday-night poker party. The gang were all missile men and they cheered and jeered as he hammed up the introduction.

"Let me copy the diagram, Biff. I could use some of those magnetic waves in the new bird!"

"Those flashlight batteries are cheaper than lox; this is the thing of the future!"

Only Teddy Kaner caught wise as the flight began. He was an amateur magician and spotted the gimmick at once. He kept silent with professional courtesy, and smiled ironically as the rest of the bunch grew silent one by one. The colonel was a good showman and he had set the scene well. He almost had them believing in the Space Wave Tapper before he was through. When the model had landed and he had switched it off he couldn't stop them from crowding around the table.

"A thread!" one of the engineers shouted, almost with relief, and they all laughed along with him.

"Too bad," the head project physicist said, "I was hoping that a little Space Wave Tapping could help us out. Let me try a flight with it."

"Teddy Kaner first," Biff announced. "He spotted it while you were all watching the flashing lights, only he didn't say anything."

Kaner slipped the ring with the black thread over his finger and started to step back.

"You have to turn the switch on first," Biff said.

"I know." Kaner smiled. "But that's part of illusion— the spiel and the misdirection. I'm going to try this cold first, so I can get it moving up and down smoothly, then go through it with the whole works."

He moved his hand back smoothly, in a professional manner that drew no attention to it. The model lifted from the table—then crashed back down.

"The thread broke," Kaner said.

"You jerked it, instead of pulling smoothly," Biff said as he knotted the broken thread. "Here, let me show you how to do it."

The thread broke again when Biff tried it, which got a good laugh that made his collar a little warm. Someone mentioned the poker game.

This was the only time that poker was mentioned or even remembered that night. Because very soon after this they found that the thread would lift the model only when the switch was on and two and a half volts were flowing through the joke coils. With the current turned off the model was too heavy to lift. The thread broke every time.

"I still think it's a screwy idea," the young man said. "One week getting fallen arches, demonstrating those toy ships for every brat within a thousand miles. Then selling the things for three bucks when they must have cost at least a hundred dollars apiece to make."

"But you *did* sell the ten of them to people who would be interested?" the older man asked.

"I think so. I caught a few air force officers and a colonel in missiles one day. Then there was one official I remembered from the Bureau of Standards. Luckily, he didn't recognize me. Then those two professors you spotted from the university."

"Then the problem is out of our hands and into theirs. All we have to do now is sit back and wait for results."

"*What* results? These people weren't interested when we were hammering on their doors with the proof. We've patented the coils and can prove to anyone that there is a reduction in weight around them when they are operating . . ."

"But a small reduction. And we don't know what is causing it. No one can be interested in a thing like that— a fractional weight decrease in a clumsy model, certainly not enough to lift the weight of the generator. No one wrapped up in massive fuel consumption, tons of lift and such, is going to have time to worry about a crackpot who thinks he has found a minor slip in Newton's laws."

"You think they will now?" the young man asked, cracking his knuckles impatiently.

"I *know* they will. The tensile strength of that thread is correctly adjusted to the weight of the model. The thread will break if you try to lift the model with it. Yet you can lift the model—after a small increment of its weight has been removed by the coils. This is going to bug these men. Nobody is going to ask them to solve the problem or concern themselves with it. But it will nag at them because they know this effect can't possibly exist. They'll see at once that the magnetic-wave theory is nonsense. Or perhaps true? We don't know. But they will all be thinking about it and worrying about it. Someone is going to experiment in his basement—just as a hobby of course—to find the cause of the error. And he or someone else is going to find out what makes those coils work, or maybe a way to improve them!"

"And we have the patents . . ."

"Correct. They will be doing the research that will take them out of the massive-lift-propulsion business and into the field of pure space flight."

"And in doing so they will be making us rich—whenever the time comes to manufacture," the young man said cynically.

"We'll all be rich, son," the older man said, patting him on the shoulder. "Believe me, you're not going to recognize this old world ten years from now."

THE FACE IN THE PHOTO

by Jack Finney

from the *Saturday Evening Post*

Here again are the pure classic elements: the professor, the secret experiments, the frustrated police—and this time the Invention is that perennial favorite, a time machine. Here again is the first-person narration—but it owes rather more in style to Dashiell Hammett than to Conan Doyle. The treatment is subjective rather than impersonal; the basic problem is not so much intellectual as ethical; the theme is concerned with the inventor's responsibility to other people, rather than to science; and insofar as it is *science* fiction at all, the science involved is sociology rather than mathematics.

This is, in short, a rendering of the classic components of s-f (meaning, science fantasy), in the completely contemporary style of s-f (meaning, speculative fiction).

On one of the upper floors of the new Hall of Justice I found the room number I was looking for, and opened the door. A nice-looking girl inside glanced up from her typewriter, switched on a smile, and said, "Professor Weygand?" It was a question in form only—one glance at me, and she knew—and I smiled and nodded, wishing I'd worn my have-fun-in-San-Francisco clothes instead of my professor's outfit. She said, "Inspector Ihren's on the phone; would you wait, please?" and I nodded and sat down, smiling benignly, the way a professor should.

My trouble is that, although I have the thin, intent professorial face, I'm a little young for my job, which is assistant professor of physics at a large university. Fortunately I've had some premature gray in my hair ever since I was nineteen, and on campus I generally wear those miserable permanently baggy tweeds that professors are supposed to wear, though a lot of them cheat and don't. These suits, together with round, metal-rimmed, professor-style glasses which I don't really need, and a careful selection of burlap neckties in diseased plaids of bright orange, baboon blue, and gang green (*de rigueur* for gap-pocketed professor suits) complete the image. That's a highly popular word meaning that if you ever want to become a full professor you've got to quit looking like an undergraduate.

I glanced around the little anteroom: yellow plaster walls; a big calendar; filing cabinets; a desk, typewriter, and girl. I watched her the way I inspect some of my more advanced girl students—from under the brows and with a fatherly smile in case she looked up and caught me. What I really wanted to do, though, was pull out Inspector Ihren's letter and read it again for any clue I might have missed about why he wanted to see me. But I'm a little afraid of the police—I get a feeling of guilt just asking a cop a street direction—and I thought rereading the letter just now would betray my nervousness to Miss Candyhips here who would somehow secretly signal the inspector. I knew exactly what it said, anyway. It was a formally polite three-line request, addressed to my office on the campus, to come here and see Inspector Martin O. Ihren, if I would, at my convenience, if I didn't mind, please, sir. I sat wondering what he'd have done if, equally politely, I'd refused, when a buzzer buzzed, the smile turned on again, and the girl said, "Go right in, Professor." I got up, swallowing nervously, opened the door beside me, and walked into the inspector's office.

Behind his desk he stood up slowly and reluctantly as though he weren't at all sure but what he'd be throwing me into a cell soon. He put out a hand suspiciously and without a smile saying, "Nice of you to come." I answered, sat down before his desk, and I thought I knew what would have happened if I'd refused this man's invitation. He'd simply have arrived in my classroom, clapped on the handcuffs, and dragged me here. I don't mean that his face was forbidding or in any way remarkable; it looked ordinary enough. So did his brown hair and so did his plain gray suit. He was a young-middle-aged man somewhat taller and heavier than I was, and his eyes looked absolutely uninterested in anything in the universe but his work. I had the certain conviction that, except for crime news, he read nothing, not even newspaper headlines; that he was intelligent, shrewd, perceptive, and humorless; and that he probably knew no one but other policemen and didn't think much of most of them. He was an undistinguished formidable man, and I knew my smile looked nervous.

He got right to the point; he was more used to arresting people than dealing with them socially. He said, "There's some people we can't find, and I thought maybe you could help us." I looked politely puzzled but he ignored it. "One of them worked in Haring's Restaurant; you know the place; been there for years. He was a waiter and he disappeared at the end of a three-day weekend with their entire receipts—nearly five thousand bucks. Left a note saying he liked Haring's and enjoyed working there but they'd been underpaying him for ten years and now he figured they were even. Guy with an oddball sense of humor, they tell me." Ihren leaned back in his swivel chair, and frowned at me. "We can't find that man. He's been gone over a year now, and not a trace of him."

I thought he expected me to say something, and I did my best. "Maybe he moved to some other city and changed his name!"

Ihren looked startled, as though I'd said something even more stupid than he expected. "That wouldn't help!" he said irritatedly.

I was tired of feeling intimidated. Bravely I said, "Why not?"

"People don't steal in order to hole up forever; they steal money to spend it. His money's gone now, he feels forgotten, and he's got a job again somewhere—as a waiter." I looked skeptical, I suppose, because Ihren said, "Certainly as a waiter; he won't change jobs. That's all he knows, all he can do. Remember John Carradine, the movie actor? Used to see him a lot. Had a face a foot long, all chin and long jaw; very distinctive." I nodded, and Ihren turned in his swivel chair to a filing cabinet. He opened a folder, brought out a glossy sheet of paper, and handed it to me. It was a police WANTED poster, and while the photograph on it did not really resemble the movie actor it had the same remarkable long-jawed memorability. Ihren said, "He could move and he could change his name, but he could never change that face. Wherever he is, he should have been found months ago; that poster went everywhere."

I shrugged, and Ihren swung to the file again. He brought out, and handed me, a large old-fashioned sepia photograph mounted on heavy gray cardboard. It was a group photo of a kind you seldom see any more—all the employees of a small business lined up on the sidewalk before it. There were a dozen mustached men in this and a woman in a long dress smiling and squinting in the sun as they stood before a small building which I recognized. It was Haring's Restaurant looking not too different than it does now. Ihren said, "I spotted this on the wall of the restaurant office; I don't suppose anyone has really looked at it in years. The big guy in the middle is the original owner who started the restaurant in 1885 when this was taken; no one knows who anyone else in the picture was, but take a good look at the other faces."

I did, and saw what he meant; a face in the old picture almost identical with the one in the WANTED poster. It had the same astonishing length, the broad chin seeming nearly as wide as the cheekbones, and I looked up at Ihren. "Who is it? His father? His grandfather?"

Almost reluctantly he said, "Maybe. It could be, of course. But he sure looks like the guy we're hunting for, doesn't he? And look how he's grinning! Almost as though he'd deliberately gotten a job in Haring's Restaurant again, and were back in 1885 laughing at me!"

I said, "Inspector, you're being extremely interesting, not to say downright entertaining. You've got my full attention, believe me, and I am in no hurry to go anywhere else. But I don't quite see . . ."

"Well, you're a professor, aren't you? And professors are smart, aren't they? I'm looking for help anywhere I can get it. We've got half a dozen unsolved cases like that —people that absolutely should have been found, and found easy! William Spangler Greeson is another one; you ever heard of him?"

"Sure. Who hasn't in San Francisco?"

"That's right, big society name. But did you know he didn't have a dime of his own?"

I shrugged. "How should I know? I'd have assumed he was rich."

"His wife is; I suppose that's why he married her, though they tell me she chased him. She's older than he is, quite a lot. Disagreeable woman; I've talked to her. He's a young, handsome, likable guy, they say, but lazy; so he married her."

"I've seen him mentioned in Herb Caen's column. Had something to do with the theater, didn't he?"

"Stage-struck all his life; tried to be an actor and couldn't make it. When they got married she gave him the money to back a play in New York, which kept him happy for a while; used to fly East a lot for rehearsals and out-of-town tryouts. Then he started getting friendly with some of the younger stage people, the good-looking female ones. His wife punished him like a kid. Hustled him back here, and not a dime for the theater from then on. Money for anything else but he couldn't even buy a ticket to a play any more; he'd been a bad boy. So he disappeared with a hundred and seventy thousand bucks of hers, and not a sign of him since, which just isn't natural. Because he can't— you understand, he *can't*—keep away from the theater. He should have shown up in New York long since—with a fake name, dyed hair, a mustache, some such nonsense. We should have had him months ago, but we haven't; he's gone, too." Ihren stood up. "I hope you meant it when you said you weren't in a hurry, because . . ."

"Well, as a matter of fact . . ."

". . . because I made an appointment for both of us. On Powell Street near the Embarcadero. Come on." He walked out from behind his desk, picking up a large Manila envelope lying on one corner of it. There was a New York

Police Department return address on the envelope, I saw, and it was addressed to him. He walked to the door without looking back, as though he knew I'd follow. Down in front of the building he said, "We can take a cab; with you along I can turn in a chit for it. When I went by myself I rode the cable car."

"On a day like this anyone who takes a cab when he can ride the cable car is crazy enough to join the police force."

Ihren said, "Okay, tourist," and we walked all the way up to Market and Powell in silence. A cable car had just been swung around on its turntable, and we got an outside seat, no one near us; presently the car began crawling and clanging leisurely up Powell. You can sit outdoors on the cable cars, you know, and it was nice out, plenty of sun and blue sky, a typical late summer San Francisco day. But Ihren might as well have been on the New York subway. "So where is William Spangler Greeson?" he said as soon as he'd paid our fares. "Well, on a hunch I wrote the New York police, and they had a man put in a few hours for me at the city historical museum." Ihren opened his Manila envelope, pulled out several folded sheets of grayish paper, and handed the top one to me. I opened it; it was a photostatic copy of an old-style playbill, narrow and long. "Ever hear of that play?" Ihren said, reading over my shoulder. The sheet was headed: TONIGHT & ALL WEEK! SEVEN GALA NIGHTS! Below that, in big type: MABLE'S GREENHORN UNCLE!

"Sure, who hasn't?" I said. "Shakespeare, isn't it?" We were passing Union Square and the St. Francis Hotel.

"Save the jokes for your students, and read the cast of characters."

I read it, a long list of names; there were nearly as many people in old-time plays as in the audiences. At the bottom of the list it said *Members of the Street Crowd,* followed by a dozen or more names in the middle of which appeared William Spangler Greeson.

Ihren said, "That play was given in 1906. Here's another from the winter of 1901." He handed me a second photostat, pointing to another listing at the bottom of the cast.

Onlookers at the Big Race, this one said, and it was followed by a half-inch of names in small type, the third of which was William Spangler Greeson. "I've got copies of two more playbills," Ihren said, "one from 1902, the other from 1904, each with his name in the cast."

The car swung off Powell, and we hopped off, and continued walking north on Powell. Handing back the photostat, I said, "It's his grandfather. Probably Greeson inherited his interest in the stage from him."

"You're finding a lot of grandfathers today, aren't you, Professor?" Ihren was replacing the stats in their envelopes.

"And what are you finding, Inspector?"

"I'll show you in a minute," he said, and we walked on in silence. We could see the Bay up ahead now, beyond the end of Powell Street, and it looked beautiful in the sun, but Inspector Ihren didn't look at it. We were beside a low concrete building, and he gestured at it with his chin; a sign beside the door read, STUDIO SIXTEEN: COMMERCIAL TV. We walked in, passed through a small office in which no one was present and into an enormous concrete-floored room in which a carpenter was building a set—the front wall of a little cottage. On through that room—the inspector had obviously been here before—then he pulled open a pair of double doors, and we walked into a tiny movie theater. There was a blank screen up front, a dozen seats, and a projection booth. From the booth a man's voice called, "Inspector?"

"Yeah. You ready?"

"Soon as I thread up."

"Okay." Ihren motioned me to a seat, and sat down beside me. Conversationally he said, "There used to be a minor character around town name of Tom Veeley, a sports fan, a nut. Went to every fight, every Giant and Forty-Niners game, every auto race, roller derby, and jai-alai exhibition that came to town—and complained about them all. We knew him because every once in a while he'd leave his wife. She hated sports, she'd nag him, he'd leave, and we'd have to pick him up on her complaint for desertion and nonsupport; he never got far away. Even when we'd nab him all he'd talk about was how sports were dead, the public didn't care any more and neither did the players, and he wished he'd been around in the really great days of sports. Know what I mean?"

I nodded. The tiny theater went dark, and a beam of sharp white light flashed out over our heads. Then a movie appeared on the screen before us. It was black and white, square in shape; the motion was somewhat more rapid and jerky than we're used to, and it was silent. There wasn't even any music, and it was eerie to watch the movement, hearing no sound but the whir of the projector. The picture was a view of Yankee Stadium taken from far back of third base, showing the stands, a man at bat, the pitcher winding up. Then it switched to a closeup—Babe Ruth at the plate, bat on shoulder, wire backstop in the background, fans behind it. He swung hard, hit the ball, and— chin rising as he followed its flight—he trotted forward. Grinning, his fists pumping rhythmically, he jogged around the bases. Type matter flashed onto the screen: *The Babe does it again!* it began, and went on to say that this was his fifty-first home run of the 1927 season, and that it looked as though Ruth would set a new record.

The screen went blank except for some meaningless scribbled numbers and perforations flying past, and Ihren said, "A Hollywood picture studio arranged this for me, no charge. Sometimes they film cops-and-crooks television up here, so they like to cooperate with us."

Jack Dempsey suddenly appeared on the screen, sitting on a stool in a ring corner, men working over him. It was a poor picture; the ring was outdoors and there was too much sun. But it was Dempsey, all right, maybe twenty-four years old, unshaven and scowling. Around the edge of the ring, the camera panning over them now between rounds, sat men in flat-topped straw hats and stiff collars; some had handkerchiefs tucked into their collars and others were mopping their faces. Then, in the strange silence, Dempsey sprang up and moved out into the ring, crouching very low, and began sparring with an enormous slow-moving opponent; Jess Willard, I imagined. Abruptly the picture ended, the screen illuminated with only a flickering white light. Ihren said, "I looked through nearly six hours of stuff like this; everything from Red Grange to Gertrude Ederle. I pulled out three shots; here's the last one."

On the screen the scratched flickering film showed a golfer sighting for a putt; spectators stood three and four deep around the edge of the green. The golfer smiled engagingly and began waggling his putter; he wore knickers well down below his knees and his hair was parted in the middle and combed straight back. It was Bobby Jones, one of the world's great golfers, at the height of his career back in the 1920s. He tapped the ball, it rolled, dropped into the cup, and Jones hurried after it as the crowd broke onto the green to follow him—all except one man. Grinning, one man walked straight toward the camera, then stopped, doffed his cloth cap in a kind of salute, and bowed from the waist. The camera swung past him to follow Jones who was stooping to retrieve his ball. Then Jones moved on, the man who had bowed to us hurrying after him with the crowd, across the screen and out of sight forever. Abruptly the picture ended and the ceiling lights came on.

Ihren turned to face me. "That was Veeley," he said, "and it's no use trying to convince me it was his grandfather, so don't try. He wasn't even born when Bobby Jones was winning golf championships, but just the same that was absolutely and indisputably Tom Veeley, the sports fan who's been missing from San Francisco for six months now." He sat waiting, but I didn't reply; what could I say to that? Ihren went on, "He's also sitting just back of home plate behind the screen when Ruth hit the home run, though his face is in shadow. And I think he's one of the men mopping his face at ringside during the Dempsey fight, though I'm not absolutely certain."

The projection-booth door opened, the projectionist came out, saying, "That all today, Inspector?" and Ihren said yeah. The projectionist glanced at me, said, "Hi, Professor," and left.

Ihren nodded. "Yeah, he knows you, Professor. He remembers you. Last week when he ran off this stuff for me, we came to the Bobby Jones film. He remarked that he'd run that one off for someone else only a few days before. I asked who it was, and he said a professor from the university named Weygand. Professor, we must be the only two people in the world interested in that one little strip of film. So I checked on you; you were an assistant professor of physics, brilliant and with a fine reputation, but that didn't help me. You had no criminal record, not with us, anyway, but that didn't tell me anything either; most people have no criminal record, and at least half of them ought to. Then I checked with the newspapers, and the *Chronicle* had a clipping about you filed in their morgue. Come on"—Ihren stood up—"let's get out of here."

Outside, he turned toward the Bay, and we walked to the end of the street, then out onto a wooden pier. A big tanker, her red-painted bottom high out of the water, was sailing past, but Ihren didn't glance at her. He sat down on a piling, motioning me to another beside him, and pulled a newspaper clipping from his breast pocket. "According to this, you gave a talk before the American-Canadian Society of Physicists in June, 1961, at the Fairmont Hotel."

"Is that a crime?"

"Maybe; I didn't hear it. You spoke on 'Some Physical Aspects of Time,' the clipping says. But I don't claim I understood the rest."

"It was a pretty technical talk."

"I got the idea, though, that you thought it might actually be possible to send a man back to an earlier time."

I smiled. "Lots of people have thought so, including Einstein. It's a widely held theory. But that's all, Inspector; just a theory."

"Then let's talk about something that's more than a theory. For over a year San Francisco has been a very good market for old-style currency; I just found that out. Every coin and stamp dealer in town has had new customers, odd ones who didn't give their names and who didn't care what condition the old money was in. The more worn, dirty and creased—and therefore cheaper—the better they liked it, in fact. One of these customers, about a year ago, was a man with a remarkably long thin face. He bought bills and a few coins; any kind at all suited him just as long as they were no later than 1885. Another customer was a young, good-looking, agreeable guy who wanted bills no later than the early 1900s. And so on. Do you know why I brought you out on this dock?"

"No."

He gestured at the long stretch of empty pier behind us. "Because there's no one within a block of us; no witnesses. So tell me, Professor—I can't use what you say, uncorroborated, as evidence—how the hell did you do it? I think you'd like to tell someone; it might as well be me."

Astonishingly, he was right; I *did* want to tell someone, very much. Quickly, before I could change my mind, I said, "I use a little black box with knobs on it, brass knobs." I stopped, stared for a few seconds at a white Coast Guard cutter sliding into view from behind Angel Island, then shrugged and turned back to Ihren. "But you aren't a physicist; how can I explain? All I can tell you is that it really *is* possible to send a man into an earlier time. Far easier, in fact, than any of the theorists had supposed. I adjust the knobs, the dials, focusing the black box on the subject like a camera, as it were. Then"—I shrugged again—"well, I switch on a very faint specialized kind of precisely directed electric current or beam. And while my current is on—how shall I put it? He is afloat, in a manner of speaking; he is actually free of time, which moves on ahead without him. I've calculated that he is adrift, the past catching up with him at a rate of twenty-three years and eleven weeks for each second my current is on. Using a stopwatch, I can send a man back to whatever time he wishes with a plus or minus accuracy of three weeks. I know it works because—well, Tom Veeley is only one example. They all try to do something to show me they arrived safely, and Veeley said he'd do his best to get into the newsreel shot when Jones won the Open Golf Championship. I checked the newsreel last week to make sure he had."

The inspector nodded. "All right; now, *why* did you do

it? They're criminals, you know; and you helped them escape."

I said, "No, I didn't know they were criminals, Inspector. And they didn't tell me. They just seemed like nice people with more troubles than they could handle. And I did it because I needed what a doctor needs when he discovers a new serum—volunteers to try it! And I got them; you're not the only one who ever read that news report."

"Where'd you do it?"

"Out on the beach not far from the Cliff House. Late at night when no one was around."

"Why out there?"

"There's some danger a man might appear in a time and place already occupied by something else, a stone wall or building, his molecules occupying the same space. He'd be all mixed in with the other molecules, which would be unpleasant and confining. But there've never been any buildings on the beach. Of course, the beach might have been a little higher at one time than another, so I took no chances. I had each of them stand on the lifeguard tower, appropriately dressed for whatever time he planned to enter, and with the right kind of money for the period in his pocket. I'd focus carefully around him so as to exclude the tower, turn on the current for the proper time, and he'd drop onto the beach of fifty, sixty, seventy, or eighty years ago."

For a while the inspector sat nodding, staring absently at the rough planks of the pier. Then he looked up at me again, vigorously rubbing his palms together. "All right, Professor, and now you're going to bring them all back!" I began shaking my head, and he smiled grimly and said, "Oh, yes you are, or I'll wreck your career! I can do it, you know. I'll bring out everything I've told you, and I'll show the connections. Each of the missing people visited you more than once. Undoubtedly some of them were seen. You may even have been seen on the beach. Time I'm through, you'll never teach again." I was still shaking my head, and he said dangerously, "You mean you won't?"

"I mean I can't, you idiot! How the hell can I reach them? They're back in 1885, 1906, 1927, or whatever; it's absolutely impossible to bring them back. They've escaped you, Inspector—forever."

He actually turned white. "No!" he cried. *"No;* they're criminals and they've got to be punished, *got* to be!"

I was astounded. "Why? None of them's done any great harm. And as far as we're concerned, they don't exist. Forget them."

He actually bared his teeth. "Never," he whispered, then he roared, "I *never* forget a wanted man!"

"Okay, Javert."

"Who?"

"A fictional policeman in a book called *Les Misérables*. He spent half his life hunting down a man no one else wanted any more."

"Good man; like to have him in the department."

"He's not generally regarded too highly."

"He is by me!" Inspector Ihren began slowly pounding his fist into his palm, muttering, "They've got to be punished, they've got to be punished," then he looked up at me. "Get *out* of here," he yelled, *"fast!"* and I was glad to, and did. A block away I looked back, and he was still sitting there on the dock slowly pounding his fist in his palm.

I thought I'd seen the last of him then but I hadn't; I saw Inspector Ihren one more time. Late one evening about ten days later he phoned my apartment and asked me—ordered me—to come right over with my little black box, and I did, even though I'd been getting ready for bed; he simply wasn't a man you disobeyed lightly. When I walked up to the big dark Hall of Justice he was standing in the doorway, and without a word he nodded at a car at the curb. We got in, and drove in silence out to a quiet little residential district.

The streets were empty, the houses dark; it was close to midnight. We parked just within range of a corner street light, and Ihren said, "I've been doing some thinking since I saw you last, and some research." He pointed to a mailbox beside the street lamp on the corner a dozen feet ahead. "That's one of the three mailboxes in the city of San Francisco that has been in the same location for almost ninety years. Not that identical box, of course, but always that location. And now we're going to mail some letters." From his coat pocket, Inspector Ihren brought out a little sheaf of envelopes, addressed in pen and ink, and stamped for mailing. He showed me the top one, shoving the others into his pocket. "You see who this is for?"

"The chief of police."

"That's right; the San Francisco chief of police—in 1885! That's his name, address, and the kind of stamp they used then. I'm going to walk to the mailbox on the corner, and hold this in the slot. You'll focus your little black box on the envelope, turn on the current as I let it go, and it will drop into the mailbox that stood here in 1885!"

I shook my head admiringly; it was ingenious. "And what does the letter say?"

He grinned evilly. "I'll tell you what it says! Every spare moment I've had since I last saw you, I've been reading old newspapers at the library. In December, 1884, there was a robbery, several thousand dollars missing; there isn't a word in the paper for months afterward that it was ever solved." He held up the envelope. "Well, this letter suggests to the chief of police that they investigate a man they'll find working in Haring's Restaurant, a man with an unusually long thin face. And that if they search his room, they'll probably find several thousand dollars he can't account for. And that he will absolutely *not* have an alibi for the robbery in 1884!" The inspector smiled, if you could call it a smile. "That's all they'll need to send him to San Quentin and mark the case closed; they didn't pamper criminals in those days!"

My jaw was hanging open. "But he isn't guilty! Not of that crime!"

"He's guilty of another just about like it! And he's got to be punished; I *will* not let him escape, not even to 1885!"

"And the other letters?"

"You can guess. There's one for each of the men you helped get away, addressed to the police of the proper time and place. And you're going to help me mail them all, one by one. If you don't I'll ruin you, and that's a promise, Professor." He opened his door, stepped out, and walked to the corner without even glancing back.

I suppose there are those who will say I should have refused to use my little black box no matter what the consequences to me. Well, maybe I should have, but I didn't. The inspector meant what he said and I knew it, and I wasn't going to have the only career I ever had or wanted be ruined. I did the best I could; I begged and pleaded. I got out of the car with my box; the inspector stood waiting at the mailbox. *"Please* don't make me do this," I said. *"Please!* There's no need! You haven't told anyone else about this, have you?"

"Of course not; I'd be laughed off the force."

"Then forget it! Why hound these poor people? They haven't done so much; they haven't really hurt anyone. Be humane! Forgiving! Your ideas are at complete odds with modern conceptions of criminal rehabilitation!"

I stopped for breath, and he said, "You through, Professor? I hope so, because nothing will ever change my mind. Now, go ahead and use that damn box!" Hopelessly I shrugged, and began adjusting the dials.

I am sure that the most baffling case the San Francisco Bureau of Missing Persons ever had will never be solved. Only two people—Inspector Ihren and I—know the answer, and we're not going to tell. For a short time there was a clue someone might have stumbled onto, but I found it. It was in the rare photographs section of the public library; they've got hundreds of old San Francisco pictures, and I went through them all and found this one. Then I stole it; one more crime added to the list I was guilty of hardly mattered.

Every once in a while I get it out, and look at it; it shows a row of uniformed men lined up in formation before a San Francisco police station. In a way it reminds me of an old movie comedy because each of them wears a tall helmet of felt with a broad turn-down brim, and a long uniform coat to the knees. Nearly every one of them wears a drooping mustache, and each holds a long nightstick poised at the shoulder as though ready to bring it down on Chester Conklin's head. Keystone Kops they look like at first glance, but study those faces closely and you change your mind about that. Look especially close at the face of the man at the very end of the row, wearing sergeant's stripes. It looks positively and permanently ferocious, glaring out (or so it always seems) directly at me. It is the implacable face of Martin O. Ihren of the San Francisco police force, back where he really belongs, back where I sent him with my little black box, in the year 1893.

"The Face in the Photo" is included in *I Love Galesburg in the Springtime*, a collection of Mr. Finney's stories, Simon and Schuster, 1962.

THE CIRCUIT RIDERS

by R. C. FitzPatrick

from *Analog*

This is FitzPatrick's first published story, and appropriately enough, it is almost a prototype of contemporary s-f (speculative/science fiction/fantasy), in subject matter as well as treatment.

The Wonderful Invention is still with us; but it is neither a secret formula nor a mysterious black box. Actually, it is a mechanism that would once have been considered usable only in the most Gothic of pseudo-scientific horror fiction: a "psychic" machine, an emotion-reader. Today, the concept seems less remote than space travel appeared to most people a scant ten years ago; and the handling of the idea is so quietly naturalistic that the reader almost feels the instruction manual for the gadget must be lying just out of sight.

And out of sight is where it stays. The author's concern is not with the inventor or the invention, as such, but with the functioning relationships of (comparatively) ordinary people adapting themselves to yet one more change in the physical and social environment.

He was an old man and very drunk. Very drunk or very sick. It was the middle of the day and the day was hot, but the old man had on a suit, and a sweater under the suit. He stopped walking and stood still, swaying gently on wide-spread legs, and tried to focus his eyes. He lived here . . . around here . . . somewhere around here. He continued on, stumbling up the street.

He finally made it home. He lived on the second floor and he dragged himself up the narrow staircase with both hands clutching the railing. But he was still very careful of the paper bag under his arm. The bag was full of beer.

Once in the room, he managed to take off his coat before

he sank down on the bed. He just sat there, vacant and lost and empty, and drank his beer.

It was a hot, muggy, August afternoon—Wednesday in Pittsburgh. The broad rivers put moisture in the air, and the high hills kept it there. Light breezes were broken up and diverted by the hills before they could bring more than a breath of relief.

In the East Liberty precinct station the doors and windows were opened wide to snare the vagrant breezes. There were eight men in the room; the desk sergeant, two beat cops waiting to go on duty, the audio controller, the deAngelis operator, two reporters, and a local book . . . businessman. From the back of the building, the jail proper, the voice of a prisoner asking for a match floated out to the men in the room, and a few minutes later they heard the slow, exasperated steps of the turnkey as he walked over to give his prisoner a light.

At 3:32 P.M., the deAngelis board came alive as half-a-dozen lights flashed red, and the needles on the dials below them trembled in the seventies and eighties. Every other light on the board showed varying shades of pink, registering in the sixties. The operator glanced at the board, started to note the times and intensities of two of the dials in his log, scratched them out, then went on with his conversation with the audio controller. The younger reporter got up and came over to the board. The controller and the operator looked up at him.

"Nothing," said the operator shaking his head in a negative. "Bad call at the ball game, probably." He nodded his head towards the lights on the deAngelis, "They'll be gone in five, ten minutes."

The controller reached over and turned up the volume on his radio. The radio should not have been there, but as long as everyone did his job and kept the volume low, the Captain looked the other way. The set belonged to the precinct.

The announcer's voice came on, ". . . ning up, he's fuming. Doak is holding Sterrett back. What a beef! Brutaugh's got his nose not two inches from Frascoli's face, and brother! is he letting him have it. Oh! Oh! Here comes Gilbert off the mound; he's stalking over. When Gil puts up a holler, you know he thinks it's a good one. Brutaugh keeps pointing at the foul line—you can see from here the chalk's been wiped away; he's insisting the runner slid out of the base path. Frascoli's walking away, but Danny's going right aft . . ." The controller turned the volume down again.

The lights on the deAngelis board kept flickering, but by 3:37 all but two had gone out, one by one. These two showed readings in the high sixties; one flared briefly to 78.2 then went out. Brutaugh was no longer in the ball game. By 3:41 only one light still glowed, and it was steadily fading.

Throughout the long, hot, humid afternoon the board held its reddish, irritated overtones, and occasional readings flashed in and out of the seventies. At four o'clock the new duty section came on; the deAngelis operator, whose name was Chuck Matesic, was replaced by an operator named Charlie Blaney.

"Nothing to report," Chuck told Charlie. "Rhubarb down at the point at the Forbes Municipal Field, but that's about all."

The new operator scarcely glanced at the mottled board, it was that kind of a day. He noted an occasional high in his log book, but most signals were ignored. At 5:14 he noted a severe reading of 87 which stayed on the board; at 5:16 another light came on, climbed slowly through the sixties, then soared to 77 where it held steady. Neither light was an honest red, their angry overtones chased each other rapidly.

The deAngelis operator called over to the audio controller, "Got us a case of crinkle fender, I think."

"Where?" the controller asked.

"Can't tell yet," Blaney said. "A hothead and a citizen with righteous indignation. They're clear enough, but not too sharp." He swiveled in his chair and adjusted knobs before a large circular screen. Pale streaks of light glowed briefly as the sweep passed over them. There were milky dots everywhere. A soft light in the lower left-hand corner of the screen cut an uncertain path across the grid, and two indeterminate splotches in the upper half of the scope flared out to the margin.

"Morningside," the operator said.

The splashes of light separated; one moved quickly off the screen, the other held stationary for several minutes, then contracted and began a steady, jagged advance toward the center of the grid. One inch down, half an inch over, two inches down, then four inches on a diagonal line.

"Like I said," said Blaney. "An accident."

Eight minutes later, at 5:32, a slightly pompous and thoroughly outraged young salesman marched through the doors of the station house and over to the desk sergeant.

"Some clown just hit me . . ." he began.

"With his fist?" asked the sergeant.

"With his car," said the salesman. "My car . . . with his car . . . he hit my car with his car."

The sergeant raised his hand. "Simmer down, young feller. Let me see your driver's license." He reached over the desk for the man's cards with one hand, and with the other he sorted out an accident form. "Just give it to me slowly." He started filling out the form.

The deAngelis operator leaned back in his chair and winked at the controller. "I'm a whiz," he said to the young reporter, "I'm a pheenom. I never miss." The reporter smiled and walked back to his colleague who was playing gin with the book . . . businessman.

The lights glowed on and off all evening, but only once had they called for action. At 10:34 two sharp readings of 92.2 and 94 even, had sent Blaney back to his dials and screen. He'd narrowed it down to a four block area when the telephone rang to report a fight at the Red Antler Grill. The controller dispatched a beat cop already in the area.

Twenty minutes later, two very large—and very obedient young toughs stumbled in, followed by an angry officer. In addition to the marks of the fight, both had a lumbering, off-balance walk that showed that the policeman had been prodding them with his riot club. It was called an "electronic persuader"; it also doubled as a carbine. Police no longer carried sidearms.

He pointed to the one on the left, "This one hit me." He pointed to the one on the right, "This one kicked me."

The one on the left was certain he would never hit another cop. The one on the right knew he would never kick another cop.

"Book 'em," the sergeant said. He looked at the two youths. "You're going in the can . . . you want to argue." The youths looked down. No one else said anything. The younger reporter came over and took down the information as the cop and the two toughs gave it to the sergeant. Then he went back to his seat at the card table and took a minityper from his pocket. He started sending to the paper.

"You ought to send that stuff direct," the card player said.

"I scribble too bad," the reporter answered.

"Bat crap," said the older man, "that little jewel can transcribe chicken scratches."

The cub scrunched over his minityper. A few minutes later he looked up at his partner. "What's a good word for hoodlum?"

The other reporter was irritated. He was also losing at gin. "What are you, a Steinbeck?" He laid down his cards. "Look, kid, just send it, just the way you get it. That's why they pay rewrite men. We're reporters. We report. Okay?" He went back to his cards.

At 11:40 a light at the end of the second row turned pinkish, but no reading showed on the dial below. It was only one of a dozen bulbs showing red. It was still pinkish when the watch was changed. Blaney was replaced by King.

"Watch this one," Blaney said to King, indicating an entry in the log. It was numbered 8:20:18:3059:78:4a. "I've had it on four times now, all in the high seventies. I got a feeling." The number indicated date, estimated area and relation to previous alerts in the month, estimated intent, and frequency of report. The "a" meant intermittent. Only the last three digits would change. "If it comes on again, I think I'd lock a circuit on it right away." The rules called for any continuous reading over 75 to be contacted and connected after its sixth appearance.

"What about that one?" King said, pointing to a 70.4 that was unblinking in its intensity.

"Some drunk," said Blaney. "Or a baby with a head cold. Been on there for twenty minutes. You can watch for it if you like." His tone suggested that to be a waste of time.

"I'll watch it," said King. His tone suggested that he knew how to read a circuit, and if Blaney had any suggestions he could keep them to himself.

Joe Millsop finally staggered home, exhausted. He was half-drunk, and worn out from being on his feet all day, but the liquor had finally done its work. He could think about the incident without flushing hot all over. He was too tired, and too sorry for himself to be angry at anyone. And with his new-found alcoholic objectivity he could see now where he had been in the wrong. Old Bloomgarten shouldn't have chewed him out in front of a customer like that, but what the hell, he shouldn't have sassed the customer, even if she was just a dumb broad who didn't know what she wanted. He managed to get undressed before he stumbled into bed. His last coherent thought before he fell into a drugged sleep was that he'd better apologize in the morning.

8:20:18:3059:78:4a stayed off the board.

At 1:18 A.M., the deAngelis flared to a 98.4, then started inching down again. The young reporter sat up, alert, from where he had been dozing. The loud clang of a bell had brought him awake.

The older reporter glanced up from his cards and waved him down. "Forget it," he said, "some wife just opened the door and saw lipstick on her husband's neck."

"Oh, Honey, how could you . . . fifty dollars . . ." She was crying.

"Don't, Mother. . . . I thought I could make some money . . . some real money." The youngster looked sick. "I had four nines . . . four nines. . . . How could I figure him for a straight flush, he didn't have a thing showing?"

". . . How could you," sobbed the mother. ". . . Oh, how could you?"

The book . . . businessman dealt the cards. The reporter picked his up and arranged them in his hand; he discarded one. The businessman ignored it and drew from the deck; he discarded. The reporter picked the discard and threw away a card from his hand; the businessman drew from the deck and discarded the same card he'd drawn; the reporter picked it up, tapped it slowly in place with his elbow, placed his discard face down, and spread his hand.

"Gin," he said.

"Arrrgh," said the businessman. "Damn it, you play good. You play real good."

A light on the deAngelis flashed red and showed a reading of 65.4 on the dial.

"Can't beat skill," said the reporter. "Count!"

"Fifty-six," said the businessman. "That's counting gin," he added.

"Game," the reporter announced. "I'll figure the damage."

"You play good," said the businessman in disgust.

"You only say that 'cause it's true," the reporter said. "But its sweet of you all the same."

"Shut up!" said the businessman.

The reporter looked up, concerned. "You stuck?" he asked solicitously. He seemed sincere.

"Certainly I'm stuck," the businessman snarled.

"Then stay stuck," said the reporter in a kindly tone. He patted the businessman on the cheek.

The same light on the deAngelis flashed red. This time the dial registered eighty-two. The operator chuckled and looked over at the gamblers, where the reporter was still adding up the score.

"How much you down, Bernie?" he asked the businessman.

"Four dollars and ninety-six cents," the reporter answered.

"You play good," Bernie said again.

The deAngelis went back to normal, and the operator

went back to his magazine. The bulb at the end of the second row turned from a light pink to a soft rose; the needle on its dial finally flickered on to the scale. There were other lights on the board, but none called for action. It was still just a quiet night in the middle of the week.

The room was filthy. It had a natural filth that clings to a cheap room, and a man-made, careless filth that would disfigure a Taj Mahal. It wasn't so much that things were dirty, it was more that nothing was clean. Pittsburgh was no longer a smoky city. That problem had been solved long before the mills had stopped belching smoke. Now, with atomics and filters on every stack in every home, the city was clean. Clean as the works of man could make it, yet still filthy as only the minds of man could achieve. The city might be clean, but there were people who were not, and the room was not. Overhead the ceiling light still burned, casting its harsh glare on the trashy room, and the trashy, huddled figure on the bed.

He was an old man, lying on the bed fully clothed, even to his shoes. He twisted fretfully in his sleep; the body tried to rise, anticipating nature even when the mind could not. The man gagged several times and finally made it up to a sitting position before the vomit came. He was still asleep, but his reaction was automatic; he grabbed the bottom of his sweater and pulled it out before him to form a bucket of sorts. When he finished being sick he sat still, swaying gently back and forth, and tried to open his eyes. He could not make it. Still asleep, he ducked out of the fouled sweater, made an ineffectual dab at his mouth, wadded the sweater in a ball, and threw it over in front of the bathroom door.

He fell back on the bed, exhausted, and went on with his fitful sleep.

At 4:15 in the morning a man walked into the station house. His name was Henry Tilton. He was a reporter for the *Evening Press*. He waved a greeting to the desk sergeant and went over to kibitz the card game.

Both players looked up, startled. The reporter playing cards said, "Hello, Henry." He looked at his watch. "Whoosh! I didn't realize it was that late." He turned to the businessman. "Hurry up, finish the hand. Got to get my beauty sleep."

"Whaddaya mean, hurry up," said Bernie, "you're into me for fifteen bucks."

"Get it back from Hank here," the reporter said. He nodded at the newcomer, "Want this hand? You're fourteen points down. Lover boy's got sixty-eight on game, but you're a box up."

"Sure," said Tilton. He took the cards.

The morning news reporters left. The businessman dealt a new hand. Tilton waited four rounds, then knocked with ten.

Bernie slammed down his cards. "You lousy reporters are all alike! I'm going home." He got up to put on his coat. "I'll be back about ten, you still be here?"

"Sure," said Tilton, ". . . with the score." He folded the paper and put it in his pocket.

The businessman walked out and Tilton went over to the deAngelis board. "Anything?" he asked.

"Nah," said King. He pointed to the lights. "Just lovers' quarrels tonight; all pale pink and peaceful."

Tilton smiled and ambled back to the cell block. The operator put his feet up on his desk, then frowned and put them down again. He leaned toward the board and studied the light at the end of the second row. The needle registered sixty-six. The operator pursed his lips, then flicked a switch that opened the photo file. Every five minutes an automatic camera photographed the deAngelis board, developed the film, and filed the picture away in its storage vault.

King studied the photographs for quite a while, then pulled his log book over and made an entry. He wrote: 8:20:19:3142:1x. The last three digits meant that he wasn't sure about the intensity, and the "x" signified a continuous reading.

King turned to the audio controller. "Do me a favor, Gus,

but strictly unofficial. Contact everybody around us: Oakland, Squirrel Hill, Point Breeze, Lawrenceville, Bloomfield . . . everybody in this end of town. Find out if they've got one low intensity reading that's been on for hours. If they haven't had it since before midnight, I'm not interested."

"Something up?" the controller asked.

"Probably not," said the operator. "I'd just like to pin this one down as close as I can. On a night like this my screen shows nothing but milk."

"Give you a lift home?" the older reporter asked.

"Thanks," said the cub, shaking his head, "but I live out by the Youghiogheny River."

"So?" The older man shrugged. "Half-hour flight. Hop in."

"I don't understand," the cub said.

"What? Me offering you a lift."

"No," said the cub. "Back there in the station house. You know."

"You mean the deAngelis?"

"Not that exactly," said the cub. "I understand a deAngelis board; everybody broadcasts emotions, and if they're strong enough they can be received and interpreted. It's the cops I don't understand. I thought any reading over eighty was dangerous and had to be looked into, and anything over ninety was plain murder and had to be picked up. Here they been ignoring eighties and nineties all night long."

"You remember that children's story you wrote last Christmas about an Irish imp named Sean O'Claus?" his companion asked him.

"Certainly," the cub said scowling. "I'll sell it some day."

"You remember the Fashion Editor killed it because she thought 'See-Ann' was a girl's name, and it might be sacrilegious."

"You're right, I remember," the cub said, his voice rising.

"Like to bet you didn't register over ninety that day? As a matter of fact, I'll head for the nearest precinct and bet

you five you're over eighty right now." He laughed aloud
and the young man calmed down. "I had that same idea
myself at first. About ninety being against the law. That's
one of the main troubles, the law. Every damn state in the
dominion has its own ideas on what's dangerous. The laws
are all fouled up. But what most of them boil down to is
this—a man has to have a continuous reading of over ninety
before he can be arrested. Not arrested really, detained. Just
a reading on the board doesn't prove a thing. Some people
walk around boiling at ninety all their lives—like editors.
But the sweet old lady down the block, who's never sworn in
her life, she may hit sixty-five and reach for a knife. And
that doesn't prove a thing. Ninety sometimes means murder,
but usually not; up to a hundred and ten usually means
murder, but sometimes not; and anything over one-twenty
always means murder. And it still doesn't prove a thing.
And then again, a psychotic or a professional gunsel may
not register at all. They kill for fun, or for business—they're
not angry at anybody.

"It's all up to the deAngelis operators. They're the king-
pins, they make the system work. Not Simon deAngelis who
invented it, or the technicians who install it, or the police
commissioner who takes the results to City Hall. The operators make it or break it. Sure, they have rules to follow—
if they want. But a good operator ignores the rules, and a
bad operator goes by the book, and he's still no damn good.
It's just like radar was sixty, seventy years ago. Some got
the knack, some don't."

"Then the deAngelis doesn't do the job," said the cub.

"Certainly it does," the older man said. "Nothing's perfect. It gives the police the jump on a lot of crime. Pre-
meditated murder, for one. The average citizen can't kill
anyone unless he's mad enough, and if he's mad enough,
he registers on the deAngelis. And ordinary robbers get
caught; their plans don't go just right, or they fight among
themselves. Or, if they just don't like society—a good
deAngelis operator can tell quite a bit if he gets a reading
at the wrong time of day or night, or in the wrong part of
town."

"But what about the sweet old lady who registers sixty-five and then goes berserk?"

"That's where your operator really comes in. Usually that kind of a reading comes too late. Grandma's swinging the knife at the same time the light goes on in the station house. But if she waits to swing, or builds herself up to it, then she may be stopped.

"You know those poor operators are supposed to log any reading over sixty, and report downtown with anything over eighty. Sure they are! If they logged everything over sixty they'd have writer's cramp the first hour they were on watch. And believe me, Sonny, any operator who reported downtown on every reading over eighty would be back pounding a beat before the end of the first day. They just do the best they can, and you'd be surprised at how good that can be."

The old man woke up, but kept his eyes closed. He was afraid. It was too quiet, and the room was clammy with an early morning chill. He opened his eyelids a crack and looked at the window. Still dark outside. He lay there trembling and brought his elbows in tight to his body. He was going to have the shakes; he knew he'd have the shakes and it was still too early. Too early. He looked at the clock. It was only a quarter after five. Too early for the bars to be open. He covered his eyes with his hands and tried to think.

It was no use; he couldn't think. He sobbed. He was afraid to move. He knew he had to have a drink, and he knew if he got up he'd be sick. "Oh Lord!" he breathed.

The trembling became worse. He tried to press it away by hugging his body with his arms. It didn't help. He looked wildly around and tried to concentrate. He thought about the bureau . . . no. The dresser . . . no. His clothes . . . he felt feverishly about his body . . . no. Under the bed . . . no . . . wait . . . maybe. He'd brought some beer home. Now he remembered. Maybe there was some left.

He rolled over on his stomach and groped under the bed. His tremulous fingers found the paper bag and he dragged it out. It was full of empty cans; the carton inside was ripped. He tore the sack open . . . empty cans . . . no! there was a full one . . . two full ones—

He staggered to his feet and looked for an opener. There was one on the bureau. He stumbled over and opened his first beautiful, lovely can of beer. He put his mouth down close to the top so that none of the foam could escape him. He'd be all right 'til seven, now. The bars opened at seven. He'd be all right 'til seven.

He did not notice the knife lying beside the opener. He did not own a knife and had no recollection of buying one.

It was a hunting knife and he was not a hunter.

The light at the end of the second row was growing gradually brighter. The needle traveled slowly across the dial, 68.2, 68.4, 68.6. . . .

King called over to the audio controller. "They all report in yet?"

The controller nodded. "Squirrel Hill's got your signal on, same reading as you have. Bloomfield thinks they have it. Oakland's not too sure. Everybody else is negative." The controller walked over. "Which one is it?"

King pointed to the end of the second row.

"Can't you get it on your screen?"

"Hell, yes, I've got him on my screen!" King swiveled in his chair and turned on the set. The scope was covered with pale dots. "Which one is he? There?" He pointed to the left. "That's a guy who didn't get the raise he wanted. There?" He pointed to the center. "That's a little girl with bad dreams. She has them every night. There? That's my brother! He's in the Veterans' Hospital and wanted to come home a week ago."

"So don't get excited," said the controller. "I only asked."

"I'm sorry, Gus," King apologized. "My fault. I'm a little edgy . . . probably nothing at all."

"Well, you've got it narrowed down, anyway," Gus said. "If you've got it, and Squirrel Hill's got it, then he's in Shadyside. If Oakland doesn't have him, then he's on this side of Aiken Avenue." The controller had caught King's fever; the "it" had become a "him." "And if Bloomfield doesn't have him, then he's on the other side of Baum Boulevard."

"Only Bloomfield might have him."

"Well what the hell, you've still got him located in the lower half of Shadyside. Tell you what, I'll send a man up Ellsworth, get Bloomfield to cruise Baum Boulevard in a scout car, and have Squirrel Hill put a patrol on Wilkens. We can triangulate."

"No," said King, "not yet. Thanks anyway, Gus, but there's no point in stirring up a tempest in a teapot. Just tell them to watch it. If it climbs over seventy-five we can narrow it down then."

"It's your show," said Gus.

The old man finished his second can of beer. The trembling was almost gone. He could stand and move without breaking out in a cold sweat. He ran his hand through his hair and looked at the clock. 6:15. Too early. He looked around the room for something to read. There were magazines and newspapers scattered everywhere; the papers all folded back to the sports section. He picked up a paper, not even bothering about the date, and tried to interest himself in the batting averages of the Intercontinental League. Yamamura was on top with .387; the old man remembered when Yamamura came up as a rookie. But right now he didn't care; the page trembled and the type kept blurring. He threw the paper down. He had a headache.

The old man got up and went over to the bathroom. He steadied himself against the door jamb and kicked the wadded sweater out of sight beneath the dresser. He went into the bathroom and turned on the water. He ran his hands over his face and thought about shaving, but he couldn't face the work involved. He managed to run a comb through his hair and rinse out his mouth.

He came back into the room. It was 6:30. Maybe Freddie's was open. If Freddie wasn't, then maybe the Grill. He'd have to take his chances, he couldn't stand it here any longer. He put on his coat and stumbled out.

At eight o'clock, the watch was changed; Matesic replaced King.

"Anything?" asked Matesic.

"Just this one, Chuck," said King. "I may be a fool, but this one bothers me." King was a diplomat where Blaney was not.

King showed him the entry. The dial now stood at 72.8. "It's been on there all night, since before I had the watch. And it's been climbing, just slow and steady, but all the time climbing. I locked a circuit on him, but I'll take it off if you want me to."

"No," said Matesic, "leave it on. That don't smell right to me neither."

The old man was feeling better. He'd been in the bar two hours, and he'd had two pickled eggs, and the bartender didn't bother him. Beer was all right, but a man needed whiskey when he was sick. He'd have one, maybe two more, and then he'd eat some breakfast. He didn't know why, but he knew he mustn't get drunk.

At nine o'clock the needle on the dial climbed past seventy-five. Matesic asked for coverage. That meant that two patrolmen would be tied up, doing nothing but searching for an echo. And it might be a wild goose chase. He was explaining to the Captain, but the Captain wasn't listening. He was looking at the photographs in the deAngelis file.

"You don't like this?" the Captain asked.

Matesic said he didn't like it.

"And King said he didn't like it?"

"King thinks the same way I do, he's been on there too damn long and too damn consistent."

"Pick him up." The Captain turned and ordered the audio controller. "If we can't hold him, we can at least get a look at him."

"It's not too clear yet," said Matesic, "it'll take a spread."

"I know what it'll take," the Captain roared. "Don't tell me my job! Put every available man on this, I want that guy brought in."

The old man walked back to his room. He was carrying a dozen cans of beer, but the load was light and he walked upright. He felt fine, like a million dollars. And he was beginning to remember.

When he entered the room he saw the knife and when he saw the knife he smiled. A man had to be smart and a man had to be prepared. They were smart . . . wicked and smart . . . but he was smarter. He'd bought the knife a long, long time ago, in a different world—they couldn't fool him that way. They were clever all right, they fooled the whole world.

He put his beer on the bureau, then walked into the bathroom and turned on the water in the tub. He came back out and started to undress. He was humming to himself. When he finished undressing he went over to the bureau and opened a can of beer. He carried it into the bathroom, put it beside the tub, and lowered himself into the water.

Ah . . . that was the ticket. Water and being clean. Clean and being water. Being water and being candy and being smart. They fooled the whole world, but not him. The whole, wide world, but they couldn't fool him. He was going to fool them. All pretty and innocent. Hah! Innocent! He knew. They were rotten, they were rotten all the way through. They fooled the whole world but they were rotten . . . rotten . . . and he was the only one who knew.

He finished the beer and stood up in the tub. The water ran off his body in greasy runlets. He didn't pull the plug. He stepped out of the tub and over to the bathroom mirror. His face looked fine, not puffy at all. He'd fool them. He sprinkled himself with lilac water, put the bottle to his lips, and swished some of it in his mouth. Oh yes, he'd fool them. A man couldn't be too clever; they were clever, so he had to be clever. He began to shave.

The Captain was on an audio circuit, talking to an Assistant Commissioner. "Yes, Sir, I know that—Yes, Sir, it could be, but it might be something else—Yes, Sir, I know Squirrel Hill has problems, but we need help—Yes, Commissioner, it's over ninety now (The Captain signaled wildly to Matesic; Matesic held up four fingers, then two) 94.2 and still going up—No, Sir, we don't know. Some guy gonna quit his job . . . or kill his boss. Maybe he found out his wife is cheating on him. We can't tell until we pick him up— Yes, Sir—Yes, Sir—Thank you, Sir."

The Captain hung up. "I hate politicians," he snarled.

"Watch it, Captain," said Matesic, "I'll get you on my board."

"Get me on it, hell," the Captain said, "I've never been off."

The old man finished dressing. He knotted his tie and brushed off the front of his suit with his hand. He looked fine. He'd fool them, he looked just like anybody else. He crossed to the bureau and picked up the knife. It was still in the scabbard. He didn't take it out, he just put it in his pocket. Good. It didn't show.

He walked out on the street. The sun was shining brightly and heat waves were coming up from the sidewalk. Good. Good. This was the best time. People, the real people, would be working or lying down asleep. But they'd be out. They were always out. Out all sweet and innocent in the hot sun.

He turned down the street and ambled toward the drugstore. He didn't want to hurry. He had lots of time. He had to get some candy first. That was the ticket, candy. Candy worked. Candy was good but candy was wicked. He was good, but they were wicked. Oh, you had to be smart.

"That has to be him," Matesic said. The screen was blotched and milky, but a large splash of light in the lower left-hand corner outshone everything else. "He's somewhere around Negley Avenue." He turned to the Captain. "Where do you have your men placed?"

"In a box," the Captain said. "Fifth and Negley, Aiken

and Negley, Center and Aiken, and Center and Negley. And three scout cars overhead."

The old man walked up Ellsworth to the Liberty School. There were always lots of young ones around Liberty School. The young ones were the worst.

"I'm losing him."
"Where are you?"
"Center and Aiken."
"Anybody getting him stronger?"
"Yeah. Me. Negley and Fifth."
"Never mind. Never mind, we've got him. We see him now."
"Where?"
"Bellefonte and Ivy. Liberty School."

She was a friendly little thing, and pretty. Maybe five, maybe six, and her Mommy had told her not to talk to strangers. But the funny old man wasn't talking, he was sitting on the curb, and he was eating candy, and he was offering some to her. He smiled at the little girl and she smiled back.

The scout car settled to earth on automatic. Two officers climbed out of the car and walked quietly over to the old man, one on either side. They each took an arm and lifted him gently to his feet.

"Hello there, Old Timer."
"Hi, little girl."
The old man looked around bewildered. He dropped his candy and tried to reach his knife. They mustn't interfere. It was no use. The officers were very kind and gentle, and they were very, very firm. They led him off as though he were an old, old friend.

One of the officers called back over his shoulder, "Bye, bye, little girl."
The little girl dutifully waved bye.
She looked at the paper sack on the sidewalk. She didn't

know what to do, but the nice old man was gone. She looked around, but no one was paying any attention, they were all watching the softball game. Suddenly she made a grab and clutched the paper bag to her body. Then she turned and ran back up the street to tell her Mommy how wonderful, wonderful lucky she was.

"The Circuit Riders" will also appear soon in *Analog II*, edited by John W. Campbell, Jr., and published by Doubleday & Company, Inc.

SUCH STUFF

by John Brunner

from *Fantasy and Science Fiction*

The more we know, the less we know for sure. The once-glorious certainties of "natural law" have dimmed to shaky "statistical probabilities." Modern medicine continues to retrieve new "scientific miracles" from the old pharmacopoeia of witchcraft. Men build machines to think for them, and "human engineering" institutes design electronic-linguistic-visual circuits for the mechanical manipulation of men's minds.

And now, across a broad frontier in which the most sophisticated "hardware" and "know-how" is urgently employed (from cybernetics and electronics, through bio-chemistry, over to semantics), the latest, greatest explorations and discoveries are being made *into* the mind of man, seeking to separate, define and analyze the entire spectrum of the purely "subjective." (One visualizes an examination paper in some future university with such questions as: "Give the respective electro-chemical equivalents for the following concepts: (1) falsehood, (2) fiction, (3) fantasy, (4) creative, visualization, (5) dream.")

This is the research frontier to which, more and more, the most thoughtful and thought-provoking writers of s(science? speculation?)-f are turning now.

With the leads of the electroencephalograph stringing out from his skull like webs spun by a drunken spider, the soft adhesive pads laid on his eyes like pennies, Starling resembled a corpse which time had festooned with its musty garlands. But a vampire-corpse, plump and rosy in its state of not-quite-death. The room was as still as any mausoleum, but it smelt of floor polish, not dust; his coffin was a hospital bed and his shroud a fluffless cotton blanket.

Except for the little yellow pilot lights in the electronic

equipment beside the bed, which could just be seen through the ventilation holes in the casing, the room was in darkness. But when Wills opened the door from the corridor the shaft of light which came over his shoulder enabled him to see Starling clearly.

He would rather not have seen him at all—laid out thus, lacking candles only because he was not dead. That could be remedied, given the proper tools: a sharpened stake, a silver bullet, crossroads at which to conduct the burial—

Wills checked himself, his face prickly with new sweat. It had hit him again! The insane idea kept recurring, like reflex, like pupils expanding under belladonna, for all he could do to drive it down. Starling lay like a corpse because he had grown used to not pulling loose the leads taped to his head—*that's all! That's all! That's all!*

He used the words like a club to beat his mind into submission. Starling had slept like this for months. He lay on one side, in a typical sleeper's attitude, but because of the leads he barely moved enough in the course of a night to disturb the bedclothes. He breathed naturally. Everything was normal.

Except that he had done it for months, which was incredible and impossible and not in the least natural.

Shaking from head to foot, Wills began to step back through the door. As he did so, it happened again—now it was happening dozens of times a night. A dream began.

The electroencephalograph recorded a change in brain activity. The pads on Starling's eyes sensed eye movements and signaled them. A relay closed. A faint but shrill buzzer sounded.

Starling grunted, stirred, moved economically as though to dislodge a fly that had settled on him. The buzzer stopped. Starling had been woken; the thread of his dream was snapped.

And he was asleep again.

Wills visualized him waking fully and realizing he was not alone in the room. Cat-silent, he crept back into the corridor and closed the door, his heart thundering as though he had had a narrow escape from disaster.

Why? In daytime he could talk normally with Starling, run tests on him as impersonally as on anyone else. Yet at night—

He slapped down visions of Starling by day, Starling corpselike in his bed at night, and moved down the long corridor with his teeth set to save them from chattering. He paused at other doors, pressing his ear to them or glancing inside for a moment. Some of those doors led to private infernos which ought to have jarred on his own normality with shocking violence, as they always used to. But none affected him like Starling's passiveness—not even the moaning prayers of the woman in Room 11, who was being hounded to death by imaginary demons.

Conclusion: his normality had gone.

That thought also recurred in spite of attempts to blank it out. In the long corridor which framed his aching mind like a microwave guide tube, Wills faced it. And found no grounds for rejecting it. They were in the wards; he in the corridor. So what? Starling was in a ward, and he was not a patient. He was sane, free to leave whenever he wished. In remaining here he was simply being co-operative.

And telling him to go away would solve nothing at all.

His rounds were over. He went back toward the office like a man resolutely marching toward inevitable doom. Lambert—the duty nurse—was snoring on the couch in the corner; it was against regulations for the duty nurse to sleep, but Wills had had more than he could bear of the man's conversation about drink and women and what he was missing tonight on television and had told him to lie down.

He prodded Lambert to make him close his mouth and sat down at the desk, drawing the night report toward him. On the printed lines of the form his hand crawled with its shadow limping behind, leaving a trail of words contorted like the path of a crazy snail.

5 a.m. All quiet except Room 11. Patient there normal.

Then he saw what he had written. Angrily, he slashed a line through the last word, another and another till it was illegible, and substituted "much as usual." Normal!

I am in the asylum of myself.

He tilted the lamp on the desk so it shone on his face and turned to look at himself in the wall mirror provided for the use of female duty nurses. He was a little haggard after the night without sleep, but nothing else was visibly wrong with him. Much as usual, like the patient in Room 11.

And yet Starling was sleeping the night away without dreams, undead.

Wills started, fancying that something black and thread-like had brushed his shoulder. A picture came to him of Starling reaching out from his bed with the tentacle leads of the e.e.g., as if he were emitting them from spinnerets, and weaving the hospital together into a net of his own, trapping Wills in the middle like a fly.

He pictured himself being drained of his juices, like a fly.

Suddenly Lambert was sitting up on the couch, his eyes flicking open like the shutters of a house being aired for a new day. He said, "What's the matter, doc? You're as white as a flaming sheet!"

There was no black threadlike thing on his shoulder. Wills said with an effort, "Nothing. Just tired, I think."

He thought of sleeping, and wondered what he would dream.

The day was bright and warm. He was never good at sleeping in the daytime; when he woke for the fourth or fifth time, unrested, he gave up. It was Daventry's day for coming here, he remembered. Maybe he should go and talk to him.

He dressed and went out of doors, his eyes dark-ringed. In the garden a number of the less ill patents were working listlessly. Daventry and the matron moved among them, complimenting them on their flowers, their thorough weeding, the lack of aphis and blackfly. Daventry had no interest in gardening except insofar as it was useful for therapy. The patients, no matter how twisted their minds were, recognized this, but Daventry apparently didn't know they knew.

Wills might have laughed, but he felt laughter was receding from him. Unused faculties, like unused limbs, atrophy.

Daventry saw him approach. The bird eyes behind his glasses flicked poultry-wise over him, and a word passed from the thin-lipped mouth to the matron, who nodded and moved away. The sharp face was lit by a smile; brisk legs began to carry him over the tiny lawn, which was not mown by the patients because mowers were too dangerous.

"Ah, Harry!" in Daventry's optimistic voice. "I want a word with you. Shall we go to the office?" He took Wills's arm as he turned, companionably; Wills, who found the habit intolerable, broke the grip before it closed.

He said, "As it happens, I want a word with you, too."

The edginess of his tone sawed into Daventry's composure. The bird eyes scanned his face, the head tipped a little on one side. The list of Daventry's mannerisms was a long one, but he knew the reasons for all of them and often explained them.

"Hah!" he said. "I can guess what this will be about!"

They passed into the building and walked side by side with their footsteps beating irregularly like two palpitating hearts. In the passageway Daventry spoke again.

"I presume there's been no change in Starling, or you'd have left a note for me—you were on night duty last night, weren't you? I didn't see him today, unfortunately; I was at a conference and didn't get here till lunchtime."

Wills looked straight ahead, to the looming door of Daventry's office. He said, "No—no change. But that's what I wanted to talk about. I don't think we should go on."

"Ah!" said Daventry. It was automatic. It meant something altogether different, like "I'm astonished"—but professionally Daventry disavowed astonishment. The office accepted them, and they sat down to the idiot noise of a bluebottle hammering its head on the window.

"Why not?" Daventry said abruptly.

Wills had not yet composed his answer. He could hardly speak of the undead Starling with pads on his eyes like pennies, of the black tentacles reaching out through the hospital night, of the formulated but suppressed notion that he must be treated with sharp stakes and silver bullets, and soon. He was forced to throw up improvisation like an emergency earthwork, knowing it could be breached at a dozen points.

"Well—all our other cases suggest that serious mental disturbance results from interference with the dreaming process. Even the most resistant of our other volunteers broke down after less than two weeks. We've prevented Starling from dreaming every night for five months now, and even if there are no signs of harm yet it's probable that we *are* harming him."

Daventry had lit a cigarette while Wills talked. Now he waved it in front of him, as though to ward off Wills's arguments with an adequate barrier—a wisp of smoke.

"Good gracious, Harry!" he said affably. "What damage are we doing? Did you detect any signs of it last time you ran Starling through the tests?"

"No—that was last week and he's due for another run tomorrow—no, what I'm saying is that everything points to dreaming being essential. We may not have a test in the battery which shows the effect of depriving Starling of his dreams, but the effect must be there."

Daventry gave a neutral nod. He said, "Have you asked Starling's own opinion on this?"

Again, concede defeat from honesty: "Yes. He said he's perfectly happy to go on. He said he feels fine."

"Where is he at the moment?"

"Today's Tuesday. He goes to see his sister in the town on Tuesday afternoons. I could check if you like, but—"

Daventry shrugged. "Don't bother. I have good news for you, you see. In my view, six months is quite long enough to establish Starling's tolerance of dream deprivation. What's next of interest is the nature of his dreams when he's allowed to resume. So three weeks from now I propose to end the experiment and find out."

"He'll probably wake himself up reflexively," Wills said.

Daventry was prepared to take the words with utmost seriousness. He said, "What makes you think that?"

Wills had meant it as a bitter joke; when he reconsidered, he found reason after all. He said, "The way he's stood the treatment when no one else could. Like everyone else we tested, his dreaming frequency went up in the first few days; then it peaked at about thirty-four times a night, and dropped back to its current level of about twenty-six, which has remained constant for about four months now. Why? His mind seems to be malleable, and I can't believe that. People need dreams; a man who can manage without them is as unlikely as one who can do without food or water."

"So we thought," Daventry said briskly. Wills could see the conference papers being compiled in his mind, the reports for the *Journal of Psychology* and the four pages in *Scientific American,* with photographs. And so on. "So we thought. Until we happened across Starling, and he just proved we were wrong."

"I—" began Wills. Daventry took no notice and went on.

"Dement's work at Mount Sinai wasn't utterly definitive, you know. Clinging to first findings is a false attitude. We're now compelled to drop the idea that dreaming is indispensable, because Starling has gone without dreams for months and so far as we can tell—oh, I grant that: so far and no further—he hasn't suffered under the experience."

He knocked ash into a bowl on his desk. "Well, that was my news for you, Harry: that we finish the Starling series at the six-month mark. Then we'll see if he goes back to normal dreaming. There was nothing unusual about his dreaming before he volunteered; it will be most interesting . . ."

It was cold comfort, but it did give him a sort of deadline to work to. It also rid him of part of the horror he had suffered from having to face the presence in his mind of the vampire-corpse like a threat looming down the whole length of his future life-path. It actually heartened him till the time came to retest Starling.

He sat waiting in his office for half an hour beforehand, because everything was otherwise quiet and because before he came up for psychological examination Starling always underwent a physical examination by another member of the staff. Not that the physicals ever turned anything up. But the psychologicals hadn't either. It was all in Wills's mind. Or in Starling's. But if it was in Starling's, he himself didn't know.

He knew the Starling file almost by heart now—thick, much thumbed, annotated by himself and by Daventry. Nonetheless, he turned back to the beginning of it, to the time five months and a week ago when Starling was just one volunteer among six men and six women engaged in a follow-up to check on Dement's findings of 1960 with superior equipment.

There were transcripts of dreams with Freudian commentary, in their limited way extraordinarily revealing, but not giving a hint of the most astonishing secret—that Starling could get by without them.

I am in a railway station. People are going to work and coming home at the same time. A tall man approaches and asks for my ticket. I try to explain that I haven't bought one yet. He grows angry and calls a policeman, but the policeman is my grandfather. I cannot understand what he says.

I am talking to one of my schoolteachers, Mr. Bullen. I am very rich and I have come to visit my old school. I am very happy. I invite Mr. Bullen to ride in my car, which is big and new. When he gets in the door handle comes off in his hand. The door won't lock. I cannot start the engine. The car is old and covered with rust. Mr. Bullen is very angry but I do not care very much.

I am in a restaurant. The menu is in French and I order something I don't know. When it comes I can't eat it. I call the manager to make a complaint and he arrives in a sailor's uniform. The restaurant is on a boat and rocks so that I feel ill. The manager says he will put me in irons. People in the restaurant laugh at me. I break the plates on which the food is served, but they make no noise and no one notices. So I eat the food after all.

That last one was exactly what you would expect from Starling, Wills thought. He ate the food after all, and liked it.

These were records extracted from the control period—

the week during which his dreams and those of the other volunteers were being noted for comparison with later ones, after the experiment had terminated. In all the other eleven cases that was from three days to thirteen days later. But in Starling's—!

The dreams fitted Starling admirably. Miserable, small-minded, he had gone through life being frustrated, and hence the dreams went wrong for him, sometimes through the intervention of figures of authority from childhood, such as his hated grandfather and the schoolteacher. It seemed that he never fought back; he—ate the food after all.

No wonder he was content to go on co-operating in Daventry's experiment, Wills thought bleakly. With free board and lodging, no outside problems involved, he was probably in paradise.

Or a kind of gratifying hell.

He turned up the dreams of the other volunteers—the ones who had been driven to quit after a few nights. The records of their control week showed without exception indications of sexual tension, dramatized resolutions of problems, positive attacks on personal difficulties. Only Starling provided continual evidence of total surrender.

Not that he was outwardly inadequate. Considering the frustration he had endured first from his parents, then from his tyrannical grandfather and his teachers, he had adjusted well. He was mild-mannered and rather shy, and he lived with his sister and her husband, but he held down a fairly good job, and he had a small, constant circle of acquaintances mainly met through his sister's husband, on whom he made no great impression but who all "quite liked" him.

Quite was a word central to Starling's life. Hardly any absolutes. Yet—his dreams to the contrary—he could never have surrendered altogether. He'd made the best of things.

The volunteers were a mixed bag: seven students, a teacher on sabbatical leave, an out-of-work actor, a struggling writer, a beatnik who didn't care, and Starling. They were subjected to the process developed by Dement at New York's Mount Sinai Hospital, as improved and automatized by Daventry—the process still being applied to Starling even now, which woke him with a buzzer whenever the signs indicating dreaming occurred. In the eleven other cases, the effect found was the same as what Dement established: interrupting the subjects' dreaming made them nervous, irritable, victims of uncontrolled nervous tension. The toughest quit after thirteen days.

Except for Starling, that was to say.

It wasn't having their sleep disturbed that upset them; that could be proved by waking them between, instead of during, dreams. It was not being *allowed* to dream that caused trouble.

In general, people seemed to spend about an hour a night dreaming, in four or five "installments." That indicated that dreaming served a purpose: what? Dissipation of antisocial tensions? A grooming of the ego as repressed desires were satisfied? That was too glib an answer. But without Starling to cock a snook in their faces, the experimenters would have accepted a similar generalization and left the matter there till the distant day when the science of mind was better equipped to weigh and measure the impalpable stuff of dreams.

Only Starling *had* cropped up. At first he reacted predictably. The frequency of his dreaming shot up from five times a night to twenty, thirty and beyond, as the buzzer aborted each embryo dream, whirling into nothing his abominable grandfather, his tyrannical teachers—

Was there a clue there? Wills had wondered that before. Was it possible that, whereas other people *needed* to dream, Starling hated it? Were his dreams so miserable that to go without them was a liberation to him?

The idea was attractive because straightforward, but it didn't hold water. In the light of previous experiments, it was about equivalent to saying that a man could be liberated from the need to excrete by denying him food and water.

But there was no detectable effect on Starling! He had not lost weight, nor grown more irritable; he talked lucidly, he responded within predictable limits to IQ tests and Rorschach tests and every other test Wills could find.

It was purely unnatural.

Wills checked himself. Facing his own reaction squarely, he saw it for what it must be—an instinctive but irrational fear, like the fear of the stranger who comes over the hill with a different accent and different table manners. Starling was human; *ergo,* his reactions were natural; *ergo,* either the other experiments had agreed by coincidence and dreaming wasn't indispensable, or Starling's reactions were the same as everyone's and were just being held down until they blew like a boiler straining past its tested pressure.

There were only three more weeks to go, of course.

The habitual shy knock came to the door. Wills grunted for Starling to come in, and wondered as he looked at him how the sight of him passive in bed could inspire him to thoughts of garlic, sharpened stakes and burial at crossroads.

The fault must be in his own mind, not in Starling's.

The tests were exactly as usual. That wrecked Wills's tentative idea about Starling welcoming the absence of his dreams. If indeed he was liberated from a burden, that should show up in a trend toward a stronger, more assured personality. The microscopic trend he actually detected could be assigned to the fact that for several months Starling had been in this totally undemanding and restful environment.

No help there.

He shoved aside the pile of test papers. "Mr. Starling," he said, "what made you volunteer for these experiments in the first place? I must have asked you before, but I've forgotten."

It was all on the file, but he wanted to check.

"Why, I don't really know, doctor," Starling's mild voice said. Starling's cowlike eyes rested on his face. "I think my sister knew someone who had volunteered, and my brother-in-law is a blood donor and kept saying that everyone should do something to benefit society, and while I didn't like the idea of being bled, because I've never liked injections and things like that, this idea seemed all right, so I said I'd do it. Then, of course, when Dr. Daventry said I was unusual and would I go on with it, I said I hadn't suffered by it and I didn't see why I shouldn't, if it was in the cause of science—"

· The voice droned on, adding nothing new. Starling was very little interested in new things. He had never asked Wills the purpose of any test he submitted to; probably he had never asked his own doctor what was on a prescription form filled out for him, being content to regard the medical abbreviations as a kind of talisman. Perhaps he was so used to being snubbed or choked off if he showed too much interest that he felt he was incapable of understanding the pattern of which Wills and the hospital formed part.

He *was* malleable. It was the galling voice of his brother-in-law, sounding off about his uselessness, which pushed him into this. Watching him, Wills realized that the decision to offer himself for the experiment was probably the biggest he had ever taken, comparable in the life of anyone else with a decision to marry, or to go into a monastery. And yet that was wrong, too. Starling didn't take decisions on such a level. Things like that would merely happen to him.

Impulsively, Wills said, "And how about when the experiment is over, Mr. Starling? I suppose it can't go on forever."

Placid, the voice shaped inevitable words. "Well, you know, doctor, I hadn't given that very much thought."

No, it wasn't a liberation to him to be freed of his dreaming. It was nothing to him. Nothing was anything to him. Starling was undead. Starling was neuter in a human scale of values. Starling was the malleable thing that filled the hole available for it, the thing without will of its own which made the best of what there was and did nothing more.

Wills wished he could punish the mind that gave him such thoughts, and asked their source to go from him. But though his physical presence went, his nonexistent existence stayed, and burned and loomed and was impassive and cocked snooks in every hole and corner of Wills's chaotic brain.

Those last three weeks were the worst of all. The silver bullet and the sharpened stake, the crossroads for the burial —Wills chained the images down in his mind, but he ached from the strain of hanging on to the chains. *Horror, horror, horror,* sang an eldritch voice somewhere deep and dark within him. *Not natural,* said another in a professionally judicious tone. He fought the voices and thought of other things.

Daventry said—and was correct according to the principles of the experiment, of course—that so as to have a true control for comparison they must simply disconnect the buzzer attached to the e.e.g. when the time came, and not tell Starling what they had done, and see what happened. He would be free to finish his dreams again. Perhaps they would be more vivid, and he would remember more clearly after such a long interruption. He would—

But Wills listened with only half an ear. They hadn't predicted Starling's reaction when they deprived him of dreams; why should they be able to predict what would happen when he received them back? A chill premonition iced solid in his mind, but he did not mention it to Daventry. What it amounted to was this: whatever Starling's response was, it would be the wrong one.

He told Daventry of his partial breaking of the news that the experiment was to end, and his chief frowned.

"That's a pity, Harry," he said. "Even Starling might put two and two together when he realizes six months have gone by. Never mind. We'll let it run for another few days, shall we? Let him think that he was wrong about the deadline."

He looked at the calendar. "Give him three extra days," he said. "Cut it on the fourth. How's that?"

By coincidence—or not?—Wills's turn for night duty came up again on that day; it came up once in eight days, and the last few times had been absolutely unbearable. He wondered if Daventry had selected the date deliberately. Maybe. What difference did it make?

He said, "Will you be there to see what happens?"

Daventry's face set in a reflex mask of regret. "Unfortunately, no—I'm attending a congress in Italy that week.

But I have absolute confidence in you, Harry, you know that. By the way, I'm doing up a paper on Starling for *Journ. Psych.*"—mannerisms, as always: he made it into the single word "jurnsike"—"and I think you should appear as co-author."

Cerberus duly sopped, Daventry went on his way.

That night the duty nurse was Green, a small clever man who knew judo. In a way that was a relief; Wills usually didn't mind Green's company, and had even learned some judo holds from him, useful for restraining but not harming violent patients. Tonight, though . . .

They spoke desultorily together for the first half-hour of the shift, but Wills sometimes lost track of the conversation because his mind's eye was distracted by a picture of what was going on in that room along the corridor where Starling held embalmed court among shadows and pilot lights. No one breached his privacy now as he went to bed; he did everything for himself, attached the leads, planted the penny-pads on his eyes, switched on the equipment. There was some risk of his discovering that the buzzer was disconnected, but it had always been set to sound only after thirty minutes or more of typical simple sleep-readings.

Starling, though he never did anything to tire himself out, always went to sleep quickly. Another proof of his malleable mind, Wills thought sourly. To get into bed suggested going to sleep, and he slept.

Usually it was three-quarters of an hour before the first attempted dream would burgeon in his round skull. For six months and a couple of days the buzzer had smashed the first and all that followed; the sleeper had adjusted his position without much disturbing the bedding, and—

But not tonight.

After forty minutes Wills got up, dry-lipped. "I'll be in Starling's room if you want me," he said. "We've turned off his buzzer, and he's due to start dreaming again—normally." The word sounded unconvincing.

Green nodded, picking up a magazine from the table. "On to something pretty unusual there, aren't we, doc?" he said.

"God only knows," Wills said, and went out.

His heart was pumping so loudly he felt it might waken the sleepers around him; his footsteps sounded like colossal hammer blows and his blood roared in his ears. He had to fight a dizzy, tumbling sensation which made the still lines of the corridor—floor-with-wall a pair of lines, wall-with-ceiling another pair—twist like a four-strand plait, like the bit of a hand drill or a stick of candy turned mysteriously and topologically outside-in. Swaying as though drunk, he came to Starling's door and watched his hand go to the handle.

I refuse the responsibility. I'll refuse to co-author the paper on him. It's Daventry's fault.

Nevertheless he acquiesced in opening the door, as he had acquiesced all along in the experiment.

He was intellectually aware that he entered soundlessly, but he imagined himself going like an elephant on broken glass. Everything was as usual, except, of course, the buzzer.

He drew a rubber-shod chair to a position from which he could watch the paper tapes being paid out by the e.e.g., and sat down. As yet there were only typical early sleep rhythms—Starling had not yet started his first dream of the night. If he waited till that dream arrived, and saw that all was going well, perhaps it would lay the phantoms in his mind.

He put his hand in the pocket of his jacket and closed it around a clove of garlic.

Startled, he drew the garlic out and stared at it. He had no memory of putting it there. But the last time he was on night duty and haunted by the undead appearance of Starling as he slept, he had spent most of the silent hours drawing batwing figures, stabbing their hearts with the point of his pencil, sketching crossroads around them, throwing the paper away with the hole pierced in the center of the sheet.

Oh, God! It was going to be such a relief to be free of this obsession!

But at least providing himself with a clove of garlic was a harmless symptom. He dropped it back in his pocket. He noticed two things at the same time directly afterward. The first was the alteration in the line on the e.e.g. tapes which indicated the beginning of a dream. The second was that he had a very sharp pencil in his pocket, as well as the clove of garlic—

No, not a pencil. He took it out and saw that it was a piece of rough wood, about eight inches long, pointed at one end. That was all he needed. That, and something to drive it home with. He fumbled in all his pockets. He was carrying a rubber hammer for testing reflexes. Of course, that wouldn't do, but anyway . . .

Chance had opened a gap in Starling's pajama jacket. He poised the stake carefully over his heart and swung the hammer.

As though the flesh were soft as cheese, the stake sank home. Blood welled up around it like a spring in mud, trickled over Starling's chest, began to stain the bed. Starling himself did not awaken, but simply went more limp—naturally, for he was undead and not asleep. Sweating, Wills let the rubber hammer fall and wondered at what he had done. Relief filled him as the unceasing stream of blood filled the bed.

The door behind him was ajar. Through it he heard the cat-light footfalls of Green, and his voice saying urgently, "It's Room 11, doc! I think she's—"

And then Green saw what had been done to Starling.

His eyes wide with amazement, he turned to stare at Wills. His mouth worked, but for a while his expression conveyed more than the unshaped words he uttered.

"Doc!" Green said finally, and that was all.

Wills ignored him. He looked down at the undead, seeing the blood as though it were luminous paint in the dim-lit room—on his hands, his coat, the floor, the bed, flooding out now in a river, pouring from the pens that waggled the traces of a dream on the paper tapes, making his feet squelch stickily in his wet shoes.

"You've wrecked the experiment," Daventry said coldly as he came in. "After I'd been generous enough to offer you co-authorship of my paper in *Journ. Psych.*, too! How could you?"

Hot shame flooded into Wills's mind. He would never be able to face Daventry again.

"We must call a policeman," Daventry said with authority. "Fortunately, he always said he thought he ought to be a blood donor."

He took up from the floor a gigantic syringe, like a hypodermic for a titan, and after dipping the needle into the river of blood hauled on the plunger. The red level rose inside the glass.

And *click*.

Through a crack in Wills's benighted skull a fact dropped. Daventry was in Italy. Therefore he couldn't be here. Therefore he wasn't. Therefore—

Wills felt his eyes creak open like old heavy doors on hinges stiff with rust, and found that he was looking down at Starling in the bed. The pens tracing the activity of his brain had reverted to a typical sleep-rhythm. There was no stake. There was no blood.

Weak with relief, Wills shuddered at remembered horror. He leaned back in his chair, struggling to understand.

He had told himself that whatever Starling's reaction to being given back his dreams might be, it would be the wrong one. Well, here it was. He couldn't have predicted it. But he could explain it now—more or less. Though the mechanics of it would have to wait a while.

If he was right about Starling, a lifetime of frustration and making the best of things had sapped his power of action to the point at which he never even considered tackling an obstacle. He would just meekly try and find a way around it. If there wasn't one—well, there wasn't, and he left it at that.

Having his dreams stopped was an obstacle. The eleven other volunteers, more aggressive, had developed symptoms which expressed their resentment in manifold ways: irritability, rage, insulting behavior. But not Starling. To Starling it was unthinkable to express resentment.

Patiently, accustomed to disappointment because that was the constant feature of his life, he had sought a way around the obstacle. And he had found it. He had learned how to dream with someone else's mind instead of his own.

Of course, until tonight the buzzer had broken off every dream he attempted, and he had endured that like everything else. But tonight there was no buzzer, and he had dreamed *in* and *with* Wills. The driving of the stake, the blood, the intrusion of Green, the appearance of Daventry, were part of a dream to which Wills contributed some images and Starling contributed the rest, such as the policeman who didn't have time to arrive, and the giant hypodermic. He feared injections.

Wills made up his mind. Daventry wouldn't believe him—not unless he experienced the phenomenon himself—but that was a problem for tomorrow. Right now he had had enough, and more than enough. He was going to reconnect the buzzer and get to hell out of here.

He tried to lift his arm toward the boxes of equipment on the bedside table, and was puzzled to find it heavy and sluggish. Invisible weights seemed to hang on his wrist. Even when, sweating, he managed to force his hand toward the buzzer, his fingers felt like sausages and would not grip the delicate wire he had to attach to the terminal.

He had fought for what seemed like an eternity, and was crying with frustration, when he finally understood.

The typical pattern of all Starling's dreams centered on failure to achieve what he attempted; he expected his greatest efforts to be disappointed. Hence Wills, his mind somehow linked to Starling's and his consciousness seeming to Starling to be a dream, would never be able to reconnect that buzzer.

Wills let his hands fall limp on his dangling arms. He looked at Starling, naked fear rising in his throat. How much dreaming could a man do in a single night when he had been deprived for six mortal months?

In his pocket was a sharp wooden stake and a hammer. He was going to put an end to Starling's dreaming once for all.

He was still in the chair, weeping without tears, tied by invisible chains, when Starling awoke puzzled in the morning and found him.

THE MAN WHO MADE FRIENDS WITH ELECTRICITY

by Fritz Leiber

from *Fantasy and Science Fiction*

The problem, obviously, is to distinguish myth from matter—or at least intellect from imagination, reason from rationale. The more we learn about behavior (whether of atoms or persons, nations or galaxies), the more conscious we become of our real ignorance about character and composition.

Electricity (I mean simple, old-fashioned, wire-circuit electric power; none of your fancy tube or transistor electronic stuff) is almost as comfortably familiar as the steam engine: something we all understand pretty well, one part of our technological environment we *have* learned to live with.

Haven't we?

When Mr. Scott showed Peak House to Mr. Leverett, he hoped he wouldn't notice the high-tension pole outside the bedroom window, because it had twice before queered promising rentals—so many elderly people were foolishly nervous about electricity. There was nothing to be done about the pole except try to draw prospective tenants' attention away from it—electricity follows the hilltops and these lines supplied more than half of the juice used in Pacific Knolls.

But Mr. Scott's prayers and suave misdirections were in vain—Mr. Leverett's sharp eyes lit on the "negative feature" the instant they stepped out on the patio. The old New Englander studied the rather short thick wooden column, the 18-inch ridged glass insulators, the black transformer box that stepped down voltage for this house and a few others lower on the slope. His gaze next followed the heavy wires swinging off rhythmically four abreast across the empty gray-green hills. Then he cocked his head as his ears caught the low but steady frying sound, varying from a crackle to a buzz, of electrons leaking off the wires through the air.

"Listen to that!" Mr. Leverett said, his dry voice betraying excitement for the first time in the tour. "Fifty thousand volts if there's five! A power of power!"

"Must be unusual atmospheric conditions today—normally you can't hear a thing," Mr. Scott responded lightly, twisting the truth a little.

"You don't say?" Mr. Leverett commented, his voice dry again, but Mr. Scott knew better than to encourage conversation about a negative feature. "I want you to notice this lawn," he launched out heartily. "When the Pacific Knolls Golf Course was subdivided, the original owner of Peak House bought the entire eighteenth green and—"

For the rest of the tour Mr. Scott did his state-certified real-estate broker's best, which in Southern California is no mean performance, but Mr. Leverett seemed a shade perfunctory in the attention he accorded it. Inwardly Mr. Scott chalked up another defeat by the damn pole.

On the quick retrace, however, Mr. Leverett insisted on their lingering on the patio. "Still holding out," he remarked about the buzz with an odd satisfaction. "You know, Mr. Scott, that's a restful sound to me. Like wind or a brook or the sea. I hate the clatter of machinery—that's the *other* reason I left New England—but this is like a sound of nature. Downright soothing. But you say it comes seldom?"

Mr. Scott was flexible—it was one of his great virtues as a salesman.

"Mr. Leverett," he confessed simply, "I've never stood on this patio when I didn't hear that sound. Sometimes it's softer, sometimes louder, but it's always there. I play it down, though, because most people don't care for it."

"Don't blame you," Mr. Leverett said. "Most people are a pack of fools or worse. Mr. Scott, are any of the people in the neighboring houses Communists to your knowledge?"

"No, sir!" Mr. Scott responded without an instant's hesitation. "There's not a Communist in Pacific Knolls. And that's something, believe me, I'd never shade the truth on."

"Believe you," Mr. Leverett said. "The East's packed with Communists. Seem scarcer out here. Mr. Scott, you've made yourself a deal. I'm taking a year's lease on Peak House as furnished and at the figure we last mentioned."

"Shake on it!" Mr. Scott boomed. "Mr. Leverett, you're the kind of person Pacific Knolls wants."

They shook. Mr. Leverett rocked on his heels, smiling up at the softly crackling wires with a satisfaction that was already a shade possessive.

"Fascinating thing, electricity," he said. "No end to the tricks it can do or you can do with it. For instance, if a man wanted to take off for elsewhere in an elegant flash, he'd only have to wet down the lawn good and take twenty-five foot of heavy copper wire in his two bare hands and whip the other end of it over those lines. Whango! Every bit as good as Sing Sing and a lot more satisfying to a man's inner needs."

Mr. Scott experienced a severe though momentary sinking of heart and even for one wildly frivolous moment considered welshing on the verbal agreement he'd just made. He remembered the gray-haired lady who'd rented an apartment from him solely to have a quiet place in which to take an overdose of barbiturates. Then he reminded himself that Southern California is, according to a wise old saw, the home (actual or aimed-at) of the peach, the nut and the prune; and while he'd had few dealings with real or would-be starlets, he'd had enough with crackpots and retired grouches. Even if you piled fanciful death wishes and a passion for electricity atop rabid anti-communist and anti-machine manias, Mr. Leverett's personality was no more than par for the S. Cal. course.

Mr. Leverett said shrewdly, "You're worrying now, aren't you, I might be a suicider? Don't. Just like to think my thoughts. Speak them out too, however peculiar."

Mr. Scott's last fears melted and he became once more

his pushingly congenial self as he invited Mr. Leverett down
to the office to sign the papers.

Three days later he dropped by to see how the new ten-
ant was making out and found him in the patio ensconced
under the buzzing pole in an old rocker.

"Take a chair and sit," Mr. Leverett said, indicating
one of the tubular modern pieces. "Mr. Scott, I want to tell
you I'm finding Peak House every bit as restful as I hoped.
I listen to the electricity and let my thoughts roam. Sometimes I hear voices in the electricity—the wires talking, as
they say. You've heard of people who hear voices in the
wind?"

"Yes, I have," Mr. Scott admitted a bit uncomfortably;
then, recalling that Mr. Leverett's check for the first quarter's rent was safely cleared, he was emboldened to speak
his own thoughts. "But wind is a sound that varies a lot.
That buzz is pretty monotonous to hear voices in."

"Pshaw," Mr. Leverett said with a little grin that made
it impossible to tell how seriously he meant to be taken.
"Bees are highly intelligent insects, entomologists say they
even have a language, yet they do nothing but buzz. I hear
voices in the electricity."

He rocked silently for a while after that and Mr. Scott
sat.

"Yep, I hear voices in the electricity," Mr. Leverett said
dreamily. "Electricity tells me how it roams the forty-eight
states—even the forty-ninth by way of Canadian power
lines. It's sort of pioneer-like: the power wires are its trails,
the hydro-stations are its waterholes. Electricity goes everywhere today—into our homes, every room of them, into
our offices, into government buildings and military posts.
And what it doesn't learn that way it overhears by the trace
of it that trickles through our phone lines and over our air
waves. Phone electricity's the little sister of power electricity,
you might say, and little pitchers have big ears. Yep, electricity knows everything about us, our every last secret.
Only it wouldn't think of telling most people what it knows,

because they believe electricity is a cold mechanical force. It isn't—it's warm and pulsing and sensitive and friendly underneath, like any other live thing."

Mr. Scott, feeling a bit dreamy himself now, thought what good advertising copy that would make—imaginative stuff, folksy but poetic.

"*And* electricity's got a mite of viciousness, too," Mr. Leverett continued. "You've got to tame it. Know its ways, speak to it fair, show no fear—make friends with it. Well now, Mr. Scott," he said in a brisker voice, standing up, "I know you've come here to check up on how I'm caring for Peak House. So let me give *you* the tour."

And in spite of Mr. Scott's protests that he had no such inquisitive intention, Mr. Leverett did just that.

Once he paused for an explanation: "I've put away the electric blanket and the toaster. Don't feel right about using electricity for menial jobs."

As far as Mr. Scott could see, he had added nothing to the furnishings of Peak House beyond the rocking chair and a large collection of Indian arrowheads.

Mr. Scott must have talked about the latter when he got home, for a week later his nine-year-old son said to him, "Hey, Dad, you know that old guy you unloaded Peak House onto?"

"Rented is the proper expression, Bobby."

"Well, I went up to see his arrowheads. Dad, it turns out he's a snake charmer!"

Dear God, thought Mr. Scott, *I knew there was going to be something really impossible about Leverett. Probably likes hilltops because they draw snakes in hot weather.*

"He didn't charm a real snake, though, Dad, just an old extension cord. He squatted down on the floor—this was after he showed me those crumby arrowheads—and waved his hands back and forth over it and pretty soon the end with the little box on it started to move around on the floor and all of a sudden it lifted up, like a cobra out of a basket. It was real spooky!"

"I've seen that sort of trick," Mr. Scott told Bobby.

"There was a fine thread attached to the end of the cord pulling it up."

"I'd have seen a thread, Dad."

"Not if it were the same color as the background," Mr. Scott explained. Then he had a thought. "By the way, Bobby, was the other end of the cord plugged in?"

"Oh it was, Dad! He said he couldn't work the trick unless there was electricity in the cord. Because you see, Dad, he's really an electricity charmer. I just said snake charmer to make it more exciting. Afterward we went outside and he charmed electricity down out of the wires and made it crawl all over his body. You could see it crawl from part to part."

"But how could you see that?" Mr. Scott demanded, struggling to keep his voice casual. He had a vision of Mr. Leverett standing dry and sedate, entwined by glimmering blue serpents with flashing diamond eyes and fangs that sparked.

"By the way it would make his hair stand on end, Dad. First on one side of his head, then on the other. Then he said, 'Electricity, crawl down my chest,' and a silk handkerchief hanging out of his top pocket stood out stiff and sharp. Dad, it was almost as good as the Museum of Science and Industry!"

Next day Mr. Scott dropped by Peak House, but he got no chance to ask his carefully thought-out questions, for Mr. Leverett greeted him with, "Reckon your boy told you about the little magic show I put on for him yesterday. I like children, Mr. Scott. Good Republican children like yours, that is."

"Why yes, he did," Mr. Scott admitted, disarmed and a bit flustered by the other's openness.

"I only showed him the simplest tricks, of course. Kid stuff."

"Of course," Mr. Scott echoed. "I guessed you must have used a fine thread to make the extension cord dance."

"Reckon you know all the answers, Mr. Scott," the other said, his eyes flashing. "But come across to the patio and sit for a while."

The buzzing was quite loud that day, yet after a bit Mr. Scott had to admit to himself that it *was* a restful sound. And it had more variety than he'd realized—mounting crackles, fading sizzles, hisses, hums, clicks, sighs. If you listened to it long enough, you probably would begin to hear voices.

Mr. Leverett, silently rocking, said, "Electricity tells me about all the work it does and all the fun it has—dances, singing, big crackling band concerts, trips to the stars, foot races that make rockets seem like snails. Worries, too. You know that electric breakdown they had in New York? Electricity told me why. Some of its folks went crazy— overwork, I guess—and just froze. It was a while before they could send others in from outside New York and heal the crazy ones and start them moving again through the big copper web. Electricity tells me it's fearful the same thing's going to happen in Chicago and San Francisco. Too much pressure.

"Electricity doesn't *mind* working for us. It's generous- hearted and it loves its job. But it would be grateful for a little more consideration—a little more recognition of its special problems.

"It's got its savage brothers to contend with, you see—the wild electricity that rages in storms and haunts the moun- taintops and comes down to hunt and kill. Not civilized like the electricity in the wires, though it will be some day.

"For civilized electricity's a great teacher. Shows us how to live clean and in unity and brother-love. Power fails one place, electricity's rushing in from everywhere to fill the gap. Serves Georgia same as Vermont, Los Angeles same as Boston. Patriotic, too—only revealed its greatest secrets to true-blue Americans like Edison and Franklin. Did you know it killed a Swede when he tried that kite trick? Yep, electricity's the greatest power for good in all the U.S.A."

Mr. Scott thought sleepily of what a neat little electricity cult Mr. Leverett could set up, every bit as good as Mind Science or the swami that got blown up with dynamite. He could imagine the patio full of earnest seekers while Krishna Leverett—or maybe High Electro Leverett—dispensed wisdom from his rocker, interpreting the words of the humming wires. Better not suggest it, though—in Southern California such things sometimes have a way of coming true.

Mr. Scott felt quite easy at heart as he went down the hill, though he did make a point of telling Bobby not to bother Mr. Leverett any more. The old man seemed harmless enough, still . . .

But the prohibition didn't apply to himself. During the next months Mr. Scott made a point of dropping in at Peak House from time to time for a dose of "electric wisdom." He came to look forward to these restful, amusingly screwy breaks in the hectic round. Mr. Leverett appeared to do nothing whatever except sit in his rocker in the patio, yet stayed happy and serene. There was a lesson for anybody in that, if you thought about it.

Occasionally Mr. Scott spotted amusing side effects of Mr. Leverett's eccentricity. For instance, although he sometimes let the gas and water bills go, he always paid up phone and electricity on the dot.

And the newspapers eventually did report short but severe electric breakdowns in Chicago and San Francisco. Smiling a little frowningly at the coincidences, Mr. Scott decided he could add fortune-telling to the electricity cult he'd imaged for Mr. Leverett. "Your life's story foretold in the wires!"—more novel, anyway, than crystal balls or Talking with God.

Only once did the touch of the gruesome, that had troubled Mr. Scott on his first conversation with Mr. Leverett, come briefly back, when the old man chuckled and observed, "Recall what I told you about whipping a copper wire up there? I've thought of a simpler way, just squirt the hose at those H-T lines in a hard stream, gripping the metal nozzle. Might be best to use the hot water and throw a box of salt in the heater first." When Mr. Scott heard that, he was glad that he'd warned Bobby against coming around.

But for the most part Mr. Leverett maintained his mood of happy serenity.

When the break in that mood came, it was sudden, though afterward Mr. Scott realized there had been one warning note sounded when Mr. Leverett had added onto a rambling discourse, "By the way, I've learned that U.S. power electricity goes all over the world, just like the ghost electricity in radios and phones. It travels to foreign shores in batteries and condensers. Roams the lines in Europe and Asia. Some of it even slips over into Soviet territory. Wants to keep tab on the Communists, I guess. Electric freedom fighters."

On his next visit, Mr. Scott found a great change. Mr. Leverett had deserted his rocking chair to pace the patio on the side away from the pole, though every now and then he would give a quick funny look up over his shoulder at the dark muttering wires.

"Glad to see you, Mr. Scott. I'm real shook up. Reckon I'd better tell someone about it so if something happens to me they'll be able to tell the FBI. Though I don't know what *they'll* be able to do.

"Electricity just told me this morning it's got a world government—it had the nerve to call it that—and that there's Russian electricity in our wires and American electricity in the Soviets'—it shifts back and forth with never a quiver of shame. It doesn't have a spark of feeling for the U.S.A. *or* for Russia. It thinks only of itself.

"When I heard that, you could have knocked me down with a paper dart.

"What's more, electricity's determined to stop any big war that may come, no matter how rightful that war be or how much in defense of America. It doesn't care a snap about us—it just doesn't want its webs and waterholes destroyed. If the buttons are pushed for the atomic missiles— here *or* in Russia—it'll flash out and kill anybody who tries to set them off another way.

"I pleaded with electricity, I told it I'd always thought of it as American and true—reminded it of Franklin and Edison—finally I commanded it to change its ways and behave decent, but it just chuckled.

"Then it threatened me back! It told me if I tried to stop

it, if I revealed its plans, it would summon down its savage brothers from the mountains and with their help it would seek me out and kill me! Mr. Scott, I'm all alone up here with electricity on my window sill. What am I going to do?"

' Mr. Scott had considerable difficulty soothing Mr. Leverett enough to make his escape. In the end he had to promise to come back in the morning bright and early—silently vowing to himself that he'd be damned if he would.

His task was not made easier when the electricity overhead, which had been especially noisy this day, rose in a growl and Mr. Leverett turned and said harshly, "Yes, I hear!"

That night the Los Angeles area had one of its rare thunderstorms, accompanied by gales of wind and torrents of rain. Palms and pines and eucalypti were torn down, earth cliffs crumbled and sloshed, and the great square concrete spillways ran brimful from the hills to the sea.

The lightning was especially fierce. Several score Angelinos, to whom such a display was a novelty, phoned civil defense numbers to report or inquire fearfully about atomic attacks.

Numerous freak accidents occurred. To the scene of one of these Mr. Scott was summoned next morning bright and early by the police, because it had occurred on a property he rented and because he was the only person known to be acquainted with the deceased.

The previous night Mr. Scott had awakened at the height of the storm when the lightning had been blinding as a photoflash and the thunder had cracked like a mile-long whip just above the roof. At that time he had remembered vividly what Mr. Leverett had said about electricity threatening to summon its wild giant brothers from the hills. But now, in the bright morning, he decided not to tell the police about that or say anything to them at all about Mr. Leverett's electricity mania—it would only complicate things to no purpose and perhaps make the fear at his heart more crazily real.

Mr. Scott saw the scene of the freak accident before anything was moved, even the body—except there was now, of course, no power in the heavy corroded wire wrapped tight as a bullwhip around the skinny shanks with only the browned and blackened fabric of cotton pajamas between.

The police and the power-and-light men reconstructed the accident this way: At the height of the storm one of the high-tension lines had snapped a hundred feet away from the house, and the near end, whipped by the wind and its own tension, had struck back freakishly through the open bedroom window of Peak House and curled once around the legs of Mr. Leverett, who had likely been on his feet at the time. He had been killed instantly.

One had to strain that reconstruction, though, to explain the additional freakish elements in the accident—the fact that the high tension wire had struck not only through the bedroom window, but then through the bedroom door to catch the old man in the hall, and that the black shiny cord of the phone was wrapped like a vine twice around the old man's right arm, as if to hold him back from escaping until the big wire had struck.

KINGS WHO DIE

by Poul Anderson

from *If*

Leiber's Modern Gothic was composed of the most ordinary daylight-and-commonsense-and-better-business elements. Anderson now utilizes traditional Gothic components—darkness and isolation, treachery and imprisonment, Frankenstein and Svengali—in a solidly "science—fictional" space adventure set in an almost too-plausible future, whose dubiously Wonderful Inventions are rather less fantastic than one might wish.

Luckily, Diaz was facing the other way when the missile exploded. It was too far off to blind him permanently, but the retinal burns would have taken a week or more to heal. He saw the glare reflected in his view lenses. As a ground soldier he would have hit the rock and tried to claw himself a hole. But there was no ground here, no up or down, concealment or shelter, on a slice of spaceship orbiting through the darkness beyond Mars.

Diaz went loose in his armor. Countdown: brow, jaw, neck, shoulders, back, chest, belly . . . No blast came, to slam him against the end of his lifeline and break any bones whose muscles were not relaxed. So it had not been a shaped-charge shell, firing a cone of atomic-powered concussion through space. Or if it was, he had not been caught in the danger zone. As for radiation, he needn't worry much about that. Whatever particles and gamma photons he got at this distance should not be too big a dose for the anti-X in his body to handle the effects.

He was alive.

He drew a breath which was a good deal shakier than the

Academy satorist would have approved of. ("If your nerves twitch, cadet-san, then you know yourself alive and they need not twitch. Correct?" To hell with that, except as a technique.) Slowly, he hauled himself in until his boots made magnetic contact and he stood, so to speak, upon his raft.

Then he turned about for a look.

"Nombre de Dios," he murmured, a hollow noise in the helmet. Forgotten habit came back, with a moment's recollection of his mother's face. He crossed himself.

Against blackness and a million wintry stars, a gas cloud expanded. It glowed in many soft hues, the center still bright, edges fading into vacuum. Shaped explosions did not behave like that, thought the calculator part of Diaz; this had been a standard fireball type. But the cloud was nonspherical. Hence a ship had been hit. A big ship. But whose?

Most of him stood in wonder. A few years ago he'd spent a furlough at Antarctic Lodge. He and some girl had taken a snowcat out to watch the aurora, thinking it would make a romantic background. But then they saw the sky and forgot about each other for a long time. There was only the aurora.

The same awesome silence was here, as that incandescence which had been a ship and her crew swelled and vanished into space.

The calculator in his head proceeded with its business. Of those American vessels near the *Argonne* when first contact was made with the enemy, only the *Washington* was sufficiently massive to go out in a blast of yonder size and shape. If that was what had happened, Captain Martin Diaz of the United States Astromilitary Corps was a dead man. The other ships of the line were too distant, traveling on vectors too unlike his own, for their scoutboats to come anywhere close to where he was.

On the other hand, it might well have been a Unasian battlewagon. Diaz had small information on the dispositions of the enemy fleet. He'd had his brain full just directing the torp launchers under his immediate command. If that had indeed been a hostile dreadnaught which got clobbered, surely none but the *Washington* could have delivered the blow, and its boats would be near—

There!

For half a second Diaz was too stiffened by the sight to react. The boat ran black across waning clouds, accelerating on a streak of its own fire. The wings and sharp shape that were needed in atmosphere made him think of a marlin he had once hooked off Florida, blue lightning under the sun. . . . Then a flare was in his hand; he squeezed the igniter and radiance blossomed.

Just an attention-getting device, he thought, and laughed unevenly as he and Bernie Sternthal had done, acting out the standard irreverences of high school students toward the psych course. But Bernie had left his bones on Ganymede, three years ago, and in this hour Diaz's throat was constricted and his nostrils full of his own stench.

He skyhooked the flare and hunkered in its harsh illumination by his radio transmitter. Clumsy in their gauntlets, his fingers adjusted controls, set the revolving beams on SOS. If he had been noticed, and if it was physically possible to make the velocity changes required, a boat would come for him. The Corps looked after its own.

Presently the flare guttered out. The pyre cloud faded to nothing.

The raft deck was between Diaz and the shrunken sun, but the stars that crowded on every side gave ample soft light. He allowed his gullet, which felt like sandpaper, a suck from his one water flask. Otherwise he had several air bottles, an oxygen reclaim unit and a ridiculously large box of Q rations. His raft was a section of inner plating, torn off when the *Argonne* encountered the ball storm. She was only a pursuit cruiser, unarmored against such weapons. At thirty miles per second, relative, the little steel spheres tossed in her path by some Unasian gun had not left much but junk and corpses. Diaz had found no other survivors. He'd lashed what he could salvage onto this raft, including a shaped torp charge that rocketed him clear of the ruins. This far spaceward, he didn't need screen fields against solar-particle radiation. So he had had a small hope of rescue. Maybe bigger than small, now.

Unless an enemy craft spotted him first.

His scalp crawled with that thought. His right arm, where the thing lay buried which he might use in the event of capture, began to itch.

But no, he told himself, don't be sillier than regulations require. That scoutboat was positively American. The probability of a hostile vessel being in detection range of his flare and radio—or able to change vectors fast enough— or giving a damn about him in any event—approached so close to zero as to make no difference.

"Wish I'd found our bottle in the wreckage," he said aloud. He was talking to Carl Bailey, who'd helped him smuggle the Scotch aboard at Shepard Field when the fleet was alerted for departure. The steel balls had chewed Carl to pieces, some of which Diaz had seen. "It gripes me not to empty that bottle. On behalf of us both, I mean. Maybe," his voice wandered on, "a million years hence, it'll drift into another planetary system and owl-eyed critters will pick it up in boneless fingers, eh, Carl, and put it in a museum."

He realized what he was doing and snapped his mouth shut. But his mind continued. *The trouble is, those critters won't know about Carl Bailey, who collected antique jazz tapes, and played a rough game of poker, and had a D.S.M. and a gimpy leg from rescuing three boys whose patroller crashed on Venus, and went on the town with Martin Diaz one evening not so long ago when— What did happen that evening, anyhow?*

He dreamed . . .

There was a joint down in the Mexican section of San Diego which Diaz remembered was fun. So they caught a giro outside the Hotel Kennedy, where the spacemen were staying—they could afford swank, and felt they owed it to the Corps—and where they had bought their girls dinner. Diaz punched the cantina's name. The autopilot searched its directory and swung the cab onto the Embarcadero-Balboa skyrail.

Sharon sighed and snuggled into the curve of his arm. "How beautiful," she said. "How nice of you to show me this." He felt she meant a little more than polite banality. The view through the bubble really was great tonight. The city winked and blazed, a god's hoard of jewels, from horizon to horizon. Only in one direction was there anything but light: westward, where the ocean lay aglow. A nearly full moon stood high in the sky. He pointed out a tiny distant glitter on its dark edge.

"Vladimir Base."

"Ugh," said Sharon. "Unasians." She stiffened a trifle.

"Oh, they're decent fellows," Bailey said from the rear seat.

"How do you know?" asked his own date, Naomi, a serious-looking girl and quick on the uptake.

"I've been there a time or two." He shrugged.

"What?" Sharon exclaimed. "When we're at *war?*"

"Why not?" Diaz said. "The Ambassador of United Asia gave a party for our President just yesterday. I watched on the newscreen. Big social event."

"But that's different," Sharon protested. "The war goes on in space, not on Earth and—"

"We don't blow up each other's lunar bases either," Bailey said. "Too close to home. So once in a while we have occasion to, uh, 'parley' is the official word. Actually, the last time I went over—couple years ago now—it was to return a craterbug we'd borrowed and bring some algablight antibiotic they needed. They poured me full of very excellent vodka."

"I'm surprised you admit this so openly," said Naomi.

"No secret, my dear," purred Diaz in his best grandee manner, twirling an imaginary mustache. "The newscreens simply don't mention it. Wouldn't be popular, I suppose."

"Oh, people wouldn't care, seeing it was the Corps," Sharon said.

"That's right," Naomi smiled. "The Corps can do no wrong."

"Why, thankee kindly." Diaz grinned at Sharon, chucked her under the chin and kissed her. She held back an instant, having met him only this afternoon. But of course she knew what a date with a Corpsman usually meant, and he knew she knew, and she knew he knew, so before long she relaxed and enjoyed it.

The giro stopped those proceedings by descending to the street and rolling three blocks to the cantina. They entered a low, noisy room hung with bullfight posters and dense with smoke. Diaz threw a glance around and wrinkled his nose. "*Sanabiche!*" he muttered. "The tourists have discovered this place."

"Uh-huh," Bailey answered in the same disappointed *sotto voce*. "Loud tunics, lard faces, 3V and a juke wall. But let's have a couple drinks, at least, seeing we're here."

"That's the trouble with being in space two or three years at a time," Diaz said. "You lose track. Well—" They found a booth.

The waiter recognized him, even after so long a lapse, and called the proprietor. The old man bowed nearly to the floor and begged they accept tequila from his private stock. "*No, no, Señor Capitán, conserva el dinero, por favor.*" The girls were delighted. Picturesqueness seemed harder to come by each time Diaz made Earthfall. The evening was off to a good start in spite of everything.

But then someone paid the juke.

The wall came awake with a scrawny blonde fourteen-year-old, the latest fashion in sex queens, wearing a grass skirt and three times life size:

Bingle-jingle-jungle-bang-POW!
Bingle-jingle-jangle-bang-UGH!
Uh'm uh red-hot Congo gal an' Uh'm lookin' fuh a pal
Tuh share mah bingle-jingle-bangle-jungle-ugh-YOW!

"What did you say?" Sharon called through the saxophones.

"Never mind," Diaz grunted. "They wouldn't've included it in your school Spanish anyway."

"Those things make me almost wish World War Four would start," Naomi said bitterly.

Bailey's mouth tightened. "Don't talk like that," he said. "Wasn't Number Three a close enough call for the race? Without even accomplishing its aims, for either side. I've seen . . . Any war is too big."

Lest they become serious, Diaz said thoughtfully above the racket: "You know, it should be possible to do something about those Kallikak walls. Like, maybe, an oscillator. They've got oscillators these days which'll even goof a solid-state apparatus at close range."

"The FCC wouldn't allow that," Bailey said. "Especially since it'd interfere with local 3V reception."

"That's bad? Besides, you could miniaturize the oscillator so it'd be hard to find. Make it small enough to carry in your pocket. Or even in your body, if you could locate a doctor who'd, uh, perform an illegal operation. I've seen uplousing units no bigger than—"

"You could strew 'em around town," Bailey said, getting interested. "Hide 'em in obscure corners and—"

"*Ugga-wugga-wugga, hugga me, do!*"

"I *wish* it would stop," Naomi said. "I came here to get to know you, Carl, not that thing."

Bailey sat straight. One hand, lying on the table, shaped a fist. "Why not?" he said.

"Eh?" Diaz asked.

Bailey rose. "Excuse me a minute." He bowed to the girls and made his way through the dancers to the wall control. There he switched the record off.

Silence fell like a meteor. For a moment, voices were stilled too. Then a large tourist came barreling off his bar stool and yelled, "Hey, wha' d'yuh think you're—"

"I'll refund your money, sir," Bailey said mildly. "But the noise bothers the lady I'm with."

"Huh? Hey, who d'yuh think yuh are, you—"

The proprietor came from around the bar. "If the lady weeshes it off," he declared, "off it stays."

"What kinda discrimination is this?" roared the tourist.

Several other people growled with him.

Diaz prepared to go help, in case things got rough. But his companion pulled up the sleeve of his mufti tunic. The ID bracelet gleamed into view. "First Lieutenant Carl H. Bailey, United States Astromilitary Corps, at your service," he said; and a circular wave of quietness expanded around him. "Please forgive my action. I'll gladly stand the house a round."

But that wasn't necessary. The tourist fell all over himself apologizing and begged to buy the drinks. Then someone else bought them, and someone after him. Nobody ventured near the booth, where the spacemen obviously wanted privacy. But from time to time, when Diaz glanced out, he got many smiles and a few shy waves. It was almost embarrassing.

"I was afraid for a minute we'd have a fight," he said.

"N-no," Bailey answered. "I've watched our prestige develop exponentially, being stateside while my leg healed. I doubt if there's an American alive who'd lift a finger against a Corpsman these days. But I admit I was afraid of a scene. That wouldn't've done the name of the Corps any good. As things worked out, though—"

"We came off too bloody well," Diaz finished. "Now there's not even any pseudo life in this place. Let's haul mass. We can catch the transpolar shuttle to Paris if we hurry."

But at that moment the proprietor's friends and relations, who also remembered him, began to arrive. They must have been phoned the great news. Pablo was there, Manuel, Carmen with her castanets, Juan with his guitar, Tío Rico waving a bottle in each enormous fist; and they welcomed Diaz back with embraces, and soon there was song and dancing, and the fiesta ended in the rear courtyard watching the moon set before dawn, and everything was just like the old days, for Señor Capitán Diaz's sake.

That had been a hell of a good furlough. . . .

Another jet splashed fire across the Milky Way. Closer this time, and obviously reducing relative speed.

Diaz croaked out a cheer. He had spent weary hours waiting. The hugeness and aloneness had eaten further into his defenses than he wished to realize. He had begun to understand what some people told him, that it disturbed them to see the stars on a clear mountain night. (Where wind went soughing through pines whose bark smelled like vanilla if you laid your head close, and a river flowed cold and loud over stones—oh, Christ, how beautiful Earth was!) He shoved such matters aside and reactivated his transmitter.

The streak winked out and the stars crowded back into his eyes. But that was all right. It meant the boat had decelerated as much as necessary, and soon there would be a scooter homing on his beam, and water and food and sleep, and a new ship and eventually certain letters to write. That would be the worst part. But not for months or years yet, not till one side or the other conceded the present phase of the war. Diaz found himself wishing most for a cigarette.

He hadn't seen the boat's hull this time, of course; there had been no rosy cloud to silhouette its blackness. Nor did he see the scooter until it was almost upon him. That jet was very thin, since it need only drive a few hundred pounds of mass on which two spacesuited men sat. They were little more than a highlight and a shadow. Diaz's pulse filled the silence. "Hallo!" he called in his helmet mike. "Hallo, there!"

They didn't answer. The scooter matched velocities a few yards off. One man tossed a line with a luminous bulb at the end. Diaz caught it and made fast. The line was drawn taut. Scooter and raft bumped together and began gently rotating.

Diaz recognized those helmets.

He snatched for a sidearm he didn't have. A Unasian sprang to one side, lifeline unreeling. His companion stayed mounted, a chucker gun cradled in his arms. The sun rose blindingly over the raft edge.

There was nothing to be done. Yet. Diaz fought down a physical nausea of defeat, "raised" his hands and let them hang free. The other man came behind him and deftly wired his wrists together. Both Unasians spent a few minutes inspecting the raft. The man with the gun tuned in on the American band.

"You make very clever salvage, sir," he said.

"Thank you," Diaz whispered, helpless and stunned.

"Come, please." He was lashed to the carrier rack. Weight tugged at him as the scooter accelerated.

They took an hour or more to rendezvous. Diaz had time to adjust his emotions. The first horror passed into numbness; then there was a sneaking relief, that he would get a reasonably comfortable vacation from war until the next prisoner exchange; and then he remembered the new doctrine, which applied to all commissioned officers whom there had been time to operate on.

I may never get the chance, he thought frantically. *They told me not to waste myself on anything less than a cruiser; my chromosomes and several million dollars spent in training me make me that valuable to the country, at least. I may go straight to Pallas, or wherever their handiest prison base is, in a lousy scoutboat or cargo ship.*

But I may get a chance to strike a blow that'll hurt. Have I got the guts? I hope so. No, I don't even know if I hope it. This is a cold place to die.

The feeling passed. Emotional control, drilled into him at the Academy and practiced at every refresher course, took over. It was essentially psychosomatic, a matter of using conditioned reflexes to bring muscles and nerves and glands back toward normal. If the fear symptoms, tension, tachycardia, sweat, decreased salivation and the rest, were alleviated, then fear itself was. Far down under the surface, a four-year-old named Martin woke from nightmare and screamed for his mother, who did not come; but Diaz grew able to ignore him.

The boat became visible, black across star clouds. No, not a boat. A small ship . . . abnormally large jets and light guns, a modified *Panyushkin* . . . what had the enemy been up to in his asteroid shipyards? Some kind of courier vessel, maybe. Recognition signals must be flashing back and forth. The scooter passed smoothly through a lock that closed again behind. Air was pumped in. Diaz went blind as frost condensed on his helmet. Several men assisted him out of the armor. They hadn't quite finished when an alarm rang, engines droned and weight came back. The ship was starting off at about half a gee.

Short bodies in green uniforms surrounded Diaz. Their immaculate appearance reminded him of his own unshaven filthiness, how much he ached and how sandy his brain felt. "Well," he mumbled, "where's your interrogation officer?"

"You go more high, Captain," answered a man with colonel's insignia. "Forgive us we do not attend your needs at once, but he says very important."

Diaz bowed to the courtesy, remembering what had been planted in his arm and feeling rather a bastard. Though it looked as if he wouldn't have occasion to use the thing. Dazed by relief and weariness, he let himself be escorted along corridors and tubes, until he stood before a door marked with great black Cyrillic warnings and guarded by two soldiers. Which was almost unheard of aboard a spaceship, he thought joltingly.

There was a teleye above the door. Diaz barely glanced at it. Whoever sat within the cabin must be staring through it at him. He tried to straighten his shoulders. "Martin Diaz," he husked, "Captain, U.S.A.C., serial number—"

Someone yelled from the loudspeaker beside the pick-up. Diaz half understood. He whirled about. His will gathered itself and surged. He began to think the impulses that would destroy the ship. A guard tackled him. A rifle butt came down on his head. And that was that.

They told him forty-eight hours passed while he was in sick bay. "I wouldn't know," he said dully. "Nor care." But he was again in good physical shape. Only a bandage sheathing his lower right arm, beneath the insigneless uniform given him, revealed that surgeons had been at work. His mind was sharply aware of its environment—muscle play beneath his own skin, pastel bulkheads and cold fluorescence, faint machine-quiver underfoot, gusts from ventilator grilles, odors of foreign cooking. And always the men, with alien faces and carefully expressionless voices, who had caught him.

At least there was no abuse. They might have been justified in resenting his attempt to kill them. Some would call it treacherous. But they gave him the treatment due an officer and, except for supplying his needs, left him alone in his tiny bunk cubicle. Which in some respects was worse than punishment. Diaz was actually glad when he was at last summoned for an interview.

They brought him to the guarded door and gestured him through. It closed behind him.

For a moment Diaz noticed only the suite itself. Even a fleet commander didn't get this much space and comfort. The ship had long ceased accelerating, but spin provided a reasonable weight. The suite was constructed within a rotatable shell, so that the same deck was "down" as when the jets were in operation. Diaz stood on a Persian carpet, looking past low-legged furniture to a pair of arched doorways. One revealed a bedroom, lined with microspools—ye gods, there must be ten thousand volumes! The other showed part of an office, a desk and a great enigmatic control panel and—

The man seated beneath the Monet reproduction got up and made a slight bow. He was tall for a Unasian, with a lean mobile face whose eyes were startlingly blue against a skin as white as a Swedish girl's. His undress uniform was neat, but carelessly worn. No rank insignia was visible, for a gray hood, almost a coif, covered his head and fell over the shoulders.

"Good day, Captain Diaz," he said, speaking English with little accent. "Permit me to introduce myself: General Leo Ilyitch Rostock, Cosmonautical Service of the People of United Asia."

Diaz went through the rituals automatically. Most of him was preoccupied with how quiet this place was. How very quiet. But the layout was serene. Rostock must be fantastically important if his comfort rated this much mass. Diaz's gaze flickered to the other man's waist. Rostock bore a side-arm. More to the point, though, one loud holler would doubtless be picked up by the teleye mike and bring in the guards outside.

Diaz tried to relax. *If they haven't kicked my teeth in so far, they don't plan to. I'm going to live.* But he couldn't believe that. Not here, in the presence of this hooded man. Even more so, in his drawing room. Its existence beyond Mars was too eerie. "No, sir, I have no complaints," he heard himself saying. "You run a good ship. My compliments."

"Thank you." Rostock had a charming, almost boyish smile. "Although this is not my ship, actually. Colonel Sumoro commands the *Ho Chi Minh*. I shall convey your appreciation to him."

"You may not be called the captain," Diaz said bluntly, "but the vessel is obviously your instrument."

Rostock shrugged. "Will you not sit down?" he invited, and resumed his own place on the couch. Diaz took a chair across the table from him, feeling knobby and awkward. Rostock pushed a box forward. "Cigarettes?"

"Thank you." Diaz struck and inhaled hungrily.

"I hope your arm does not bother you."

Diaz's belly muscles tightened. "No. It's all right."

"The surgeons left the metal ulnar bone in place, as well as its nervous and muscular connections. Complete replacement would have required more hospital equipment than a spaceship can readily carry. We did not want to cripple you by removing the bone. After all, we were only interested in the cartridge."

Diaz gathered courage and snapped: "The more I see of you, General, the sorrier I am that it didn't work. You're big game."

Rostock chuckled. "Perhaps. I wonder, though, if you are as sorry as you would like to feel you are. You would have died too, you realize."

"Uh-huh."

"Do you know what the weapon embedded in you was?"

"Yes. *We* tell our people such things. A charge of iso-

topic explosive, with a trigger activated by a particular series of motor nerve pulses. Equivalent to about ten tons
of TNT." Diaz gripped the chair arms, leaned forward and
said harshly: "I'm not blabbing anything you don't now
know. I daresay you consider it a violation of the customs
of war. Not me! I gave no parole—"

"Certainly, certainly." Rostock waved a deprecating
hand. "There are—what is your idiom?—no hard feelings.
The device was ingenious. We have already dispatched a
warning to our Central, whence the word can go out through
the fleet, so your effort, the entire project, has gone for
nothing. But it was a rather gallant attempt."

He leaned back, crossed one leg over the other, and regarded the American candidly. "Of course, as you implied,
we would have proceeded somewhat differently," he said.
"Our men would not have known what they carried, and
the explosion would have been triggered posthypnotically,
by some given class of situations, rather than consciously.
In that way, there would be less chance of betrayal."

"How did you know, anyway?" Diaz sighed.

Rostock gave him an impish grin. "As the villain of this
particular little drama, I shall only say that I have my
methods." Suddenly he was grave. "One reason we made
such an effort to pick you up before your own rescue party
arrived, was to gather data on what you have been doing,
you people. You know how comparatively rare it is to get a
prisoner in space warfare; and how hard to get spies into an
organization of high morale which maintains its own laboratories and factories off Earth. Divergent developments
can go far these days, before the other side is aware of
them. The miniaturization involved in your own weapon,
for example, astonished our engineers."

"I can't tell you anything else," Diaz said.

"Oh, you could," Rostock answered gently. "You know
as well as I what can be done with a shot of babble juice.
Not to mention other techniques—nothing melodramatic,
nothing painful or disabling, merely applied neurology—in
which I believe Unasia is ahead of the Western countries.

But don't worry, Captain, I shall not permit any such breach of military custom.

"However, I do want you to understand how much trouble we went to, to get you. When combat began, I reasoned that the ships auxiliary to a dreadnaught would be the likeliest to suffer destruction of the type which leaves a few survivors. From the pattern of action in the first day, I deduced the approximate orbits and positions of several American capital ships. Unasian tactics throughout the second day were developed with two purposes: to inflict damage, of course, but also to get the *Ho* so placed that we would be likely to detect any distress signals. This cost us the *Genghis*—a calculated risk which did not pay off—I am not omniscient. But we did hear your call.

"You are quite right about the importance of this ship here. My superiors will be horrified at my action. But of necessity, they have given me *carte blanche*. And since the *Ho* itself takes no direct part in any engagement, if we can avoid it, the probability of our being detected and attacked was small."

Rostock's eyes held Diaz's. He tapped the table, softly and repeatedly, with one fingernail. "Do you appreciate what all this means, Captain?" he asked. "Do you see how badly you were wanted?"

Diaz could only wet his lips and nod.

"Partly," Rostock said, smiling again, "there was the desire I have mentioned, to—er—check up on American activities during the last cease-fire period. But partly, too, there was a wish to bring you up to date on what we have been doing."

"*Huh?*" Diaz half scrambled from his chair, sagged back and gaped.

"The choice is yours, Captain," Rostock said. "You can be transferred to a cargo ship when we can arrange it, and so to an asteroid camp, and in general receive the normal treatment of a war prisoner. Or you may elect to hear what I would like to discuss with you. In the latter event, I can guarantee nothing. Obviously, I can't let you go home in a

routine prisoner exchange with a prime military secret of
ours. You will have to wait until it is no longer a secret.
Until American Intelligence has learned the truth, and we
know that they have. That may take years. It may take
forever: because I have some hope that the knowledge will
change certain of your own attitudes.

"No, no, don't answer now. Think it over. I will see you
again tomorrow. In twenty-four hours, that is to say."

Rostock's eyes shifted past Diaz, as if to look through
the bulkheads. His tone dropped suddenly to a whisper.
"Have you ever wondered, like me, why we carry Earth's
rotation period to space with us? Habit; practicality; but
is there not also an element of magical thinking? A hope
that somehow we can create our own sunrises? The sky is
very black out there. We need all the magic we can invent.
Do we not?"

Some hours later, alarms sounded, voices barked over
the intercoms, spin was halted but weight came quickly back
as the ship accelerated.

Diaz knew just enough Mandarin to understand from
what he overheard that radar contact had been made with
American units and combat would soon resume. The guard
who brought him dinner in his cubicle confirmed it, with
many a bow and hissing smile. Diaz had gained enormous
face by his audience with the man in the suite.

He couldn't sleep, though the racket soon settled down
to a purposeful murmur with few loud interruptions. Rest-
less in his bunk harness, he tried to reconstruct a total
picture from what clues he had. The primary American
objective was the asteroid base system of the enemy. But
astromilitary tactics were too complicated for one brain to
grasp. A battle might go on for months, flaring up whenever
hostile units came near enough in their enormous orbitings
to exchange fire. Eventually, Diaz knew, if everything went
well—that is, didn't go too badly haywire—Americans
would land on the Unasian worldlets. That would be the
rough part. He remembered ground operations on Mars
and Ganymede much too well.

As for the immediate situation, though, he could only make an educated guess. The leisurely pace at which the engagement was developing indicated that ships of dreadnaught mass were involved. Therefore no mere squadron was out there, but an important segment of the American fleet, perhaps the task force headed by the *Alaska*. But if this was true, then the *Ho Chi Minh* must be directing a flotilla of comparable size.

Which wasn't possible! Flotillas and subfleets were bossed from dreadnaughts. A combat computer and its human staff were just too big and delicate to be housed in anything less. And the *Ho* was not even as large as the *Argonne* had been.

Yet what the hell was this but a command ship? Rostock had hinted as much. The activity aboard was characteristic, the repeated sound of courier boats coming and going, intercom calls, technicians hurrying along the corridors, but no shooting.

Nevertheless—

Voices jabbered beyond the cell door. Their note was triumphant. Probably they related a hit on an American vessel. Diaz recalled brushing aside chunks of space-frozen meat that had been his Corps brothers. Sammy Yoshida was in the *Utah Beach*, which was with the *Alaska*—Sammy who'd covered for him back at the Academy when he crawled in dead drunk hours after taps, and some years later had dragged him from a shell-struck foxhole on Mars and shared oxygen till a rescue squad happened by. Had the *Utah Beach* been hit? Was that what they were giggling about out there?

Prisoner exchange, in a year or two or three, will get me back for the next round of the war, Diaz thought in darkness. *But I'm only one man. And I've goofed somehow, spilled a scheme which might've cost the Unies several ships before they tumbled. It's hardly conceivable I could smuggle out whatever information Rostock wants to give me. But there'd be some tiny probability that I could, somehow, sometime. Wouldn't there?*

I don't want to. Dios mio, how I don't want to! Let me rest a while, and then be swapped, and go back for a long

*furlough on Earth, where anything I ask for is mine and
mainly I ask for sunlight and ocean and flowering trees.
But Carl liked those things too, didn't he? Liked them and
lost them forever.*

There came a lull in the battle. The fleets had passed each
other, decelerating as they fired. They would take many
hours to turn around and get back within combat range. A
great quietness descended on the *Ho*. Walking down the
passageways, which thrummed with rocketblast, Diaz saw
how the technicians slumped at their posts. The demands
on them were as hard as those on a pilot or gunner or missile chief. Evolution designed men to fight with their hands,
not with computations and push buttons. Maybe ground
combat wasn't the worst kind.

The sentries admitted Diaz through the door of the warning. Rostock sat at the table again. His coifed features
looked equally drained, and his smile was automatic. A
samovar and two teacups stood before him.

"Be seated, Captain," he said tonelessly. "Pardon me if
I do not rise. This has been an exhausting time."

Diaz accepted a chair and a cup. Rostock drank noisily,
eyes closed and forehead puckered. There might have been
an extra stimulant in his tea, for before long he appeared
more human. He refilled the cups, passed out cigarettes and
leaned back on his couch with a sigh.

"You may be pleased to know," he said, "that the third
pass will be the final one. We shall refuse further combat
and proceed instead to join forces with another flotilla near
Pallas."

"Because that suits your purposes better," Diaz said.

"Well, naturally. I compute a higher likelihood of ultimate success if we follow a strategy of— No matter now."

Diaz leaned forward. His heart slammed. "So this *is* a
command ship," he exclaimed. "I thought so."

The blue eyes weighed him with care. "If I give you any
further information," Rostock said—softly, but the muscles
tightened along his jaw—"you must accept the conditions
I set forth."

"I do," Diaz got out.

"I realize that you do so in the hope of passing on the secret to your countrymen," Rostock said. "You may as well forget about that. You won't get the chance."

"Then why do you want to tell me? You won't make a Unie out of me, General." The words sounded too stuck-up, Diaz decided. "That is, I respect your people and, and so forth, but, uh, my loyalties lie elsewhere."

"Agreed. I don't hope or plan to change them. At least, not in an easterly direction." Rostock drew hard on his cigarette, let smoke stream from his nostrils and squinted through it. "The microphone is turned down," he remarked. "We cannot be overheard unless we shout. I must warn you, if you make any attempt to reveal what I am about to say to you to any of my own people, I shall not only deny it but order you sent out the airlock. It is that important."

Diaz rubbed his hands on his trousers. The palms were wet. "Okay," he said.

"Not that I mean to browbeat you, Captain," said Rostock hastily. "What I offer is friendship. In the end, maybe, peace." He sat a while longer looking at the wall, before his glance shifted back to Diaz's. "Suppose you begin the discussion. Ask me what you like."

"Uh—" Diaz floundered about, as if he'd been leaning on a door that was thrown open. "Uh . . . well, was I right? Is this a command ship?"

"Yes. It performs every function of a flag dreadnaught, except that it seldom engages in direct combat. The tactical advantages are obvious. A smaller, lighter vessel can get about much more readily, hence be a correspondingly more effective directrix. Furthermore, if due caution is exercised, we are not likely to be detected and fired at. The massive armament of a dreadnaught is chiefly to stave off the missiles which can annihilate the command post within. Ships of this class avoid that whole problem by avoiding attack in the first place."

"But your computer! You, uh, you must have developed a combat computer as . . . small and rugged as an autopilot—I thought miniaturization was our specialty."

Rostock laughed.

"And you'd still need a large human staff," Diaz protested. "Bigger than the whole crew of this ship!

"Wouldn't you?" he finished weakly.

Rostock shook his head. "No." His smile faded. "Not under this new system. I am the computer."

"What?"

"Look." Rostock pulled off his hood.

The head beneath was hairless, not shaved but depilated. A dozen silvery plates were set into it, flush with the scalp; there were outlets in them. Rostock pointed toward the office. "The rest of me is in there," he said. "I need only plug the jacks into the appropriate points of myself, and I become—no, not part of the computer. *It* becomes part of *me.*"

He fell silent again, gazing now at the floor. Diaz hardly dared move, until his cigarette burned his fingers and he must stub it out. The ship pulsed around them. Monet's picture of sunlight caught in young leaves was like something seen at the far end of a tunnel.

"Consider the problem," Rostock said at last, low. "In spite of much loose talk about giant brains, computers do not think, except perhaps on an idiot level. They merely perform logical operations, symbol-shuffling, according to instructions given them. It was shown long ago that there are infinite classes of problems which no computer can solve: the classes dealt with in Godel's theorem, that can only be solved by the nonlogical process of creating a metalanguage. Creativity is not logical and computers do not create.

"In addition, as you know, the larger a computer becomes, the more staff it requires to perform such operations as data coding, programming, retranslation of the solutions into practical terms, and adjustment of the artificial answer to the actual problem. Yet your own brain does this sort of thing constantly . . . because it is creative. Moreover, the advanced computers are heavy, bulky, fragile things. They use cryogenics and all the other tricks, but that involves elaborate ancillary apparatus. Your brain weighs a kilogram or so, is very adequately protected in the skull and needs less than a hundred kilos of outside equipment—your body.

"I am not being mystical. There is no reason why creativity cannot someday be duplicated in an artificial structure. But I think that structure will look very much like a living organism; will, indeed, be one. Life has had a billion years to develop these techniques.

"Now, if the brain has so many advantages, why use a computer at all? Obviously, to do the uncreative work, for which the brain is not specifically designed. The brain visualizes a problem of, say, orbits, masses and tactics, and formulates it as a set of matrix equations. Then the computer goes swiftly through the millions of idiot counting operations needed to produce a numerical solution. What we have developed here, we Unasians, is nothing but a direct approach. We eliminate the middle man, as you Americans would say.

"In yonder office is a highly specialized computer. It is built from solid-state units, analogous to neurones, but in spite of being able to treat astromilitary problems, it is a comparatively small, simple and sturdy device. Why? Because it is used in connection with my brain, which directs it. The normal computer must have its operational patterns built in. Mine develops synapse pathways as needed, just as a man's lower brain can develop skills under the direction of the cerebral cortex. And these pathways are modifiable by experience; the system is continually restructuring itself. The normal computer must have elaborate failure detection systems and arrangement for re-routing. I, in the hookup here, sense any trouble directly, and am no more disturbed by the temporary disability of some region than you are disturbed by the fact that most of your brain cells at any given time are resting.

"The human staff becomes superfluous here. My technicians bring me the data, which need not be reduced to standardized format. I link myself to the machine and—think about it—there are no words. The answer is worked out in no more time than any other computer would require. But it comes to my consciousness not as a set of figures, but in practical terms, decisions about what to do. Furthermore, the solution is modified by my human awareness of those factors too complex to go into physical condition—men and equipment, morale, long-range questions of logistics and strategy and ultimate goals. You might say this is a computer system with common sense. Do you understand, Captain?"

Diaz sat still for a long time before he said, "Yes. I think I do."

Rostock had gotten a little hoarse. He poured himself a fresh cup of tea and drank half, struck another cigarette and said earnestly: "The military value is obvious. Were that all, I would never have revealed this much to you. But something else developed as I practiced and increased my command of the system. Something quite unforeseen. I wonder if you will comprehend." He finished his cup. "That repeated experience changed me. I am no longer human. Not really."

The ship whispered, driving through darkness.

"I suppose a hookup like that would affect the emotions," Diaz ventured. "How does it feel?"

"There are no words," Rostock repeated, "except those I have made for myself." He rose and walked restlessly across the subdued rainbows in the carpet, hands behind his back, eyes focused on nothing Diaz could see. "As a matter of fact, the only emotional effect may be a simple intensification. Although . . . there are myths about mortals who became gods. How did it feel to them? I think they hardly noticed the palaces and music and feasting on Olympus. What mattered was how, piece by piece, as he mastered his new capacities, the new god won a god's understanding. His perception, involvement, detachment, totalness . . . there *are* no words."

Back and forth he paced, feet noiseless but metal and energies humming beneath his low and somehow troubled voice. "My cerebrum directs the computer," he said, "and the relationship becomes reciprocal. True, the computer part has no creativity of its own but it endows mine with a speed and sureness you cannot imagine. After all, a great part of original thought consists merely in proposing trial solutions. The scientist hypothesizes, the artist draws a charcoal line, the poet scribbles a phrase. Then they test them to see if they work. By now, to me, this mechanical aspect of imagination is back down on the subconscious level where it belongs. What my awareness senses is the final answer, springing to life almost simultaneously with the question, and yet with a felt reality to it such as comes only from having pondered and tested the issue for thousands of times.

"Also, the amount of sense data I can handle is fantastic. Oh, I am blind and deaf and numb away from my machine half! So you will realize that over the months I have tended to spend more and more time in the linked state. When there was no immediate command problem to solve, I would sit and savor it."

In a practical tone: "That is how I perceived that you were about to sabotage us, Captain. Your posture alone betrayed you. I guessed the means at once and ordered the guards to knock you unconscious. I think, also, that I detected in you the potential I need. But that demands closer examination. Which is easily given. When I am linked, you cannot lie to me. The least insincerity is written across your whole organism."

He paused, to stand a little slumped, looking at the bulkhead. For a moment Diaz's legs tensed. *Three jumps and I can be there and get his gun!* But no, Rostock wasn't any brain-heavy dwarf. The body in that green uniform was young and trained. Diaz took another cigarette. "Okay," he said. "What do you propose?"

"First," Rostock said, turning about—and his eyes kindled—"I want you to understand what you and I are. What the spacemen of both factions are."

"Professional soldiers," Diaz grunted uneasily. Rostock waited. Diaz puffed hard and plowed on, since he was plainly expected to: "The only soldiers left. You can't count those ornamental regiments on Earth, nor the guys sitting by the big missiles. Those missiles will never be

fired. World War Three was a large enough dose of nucleonics. Civilization was lucky to survive. Terrestrial life
would be lucky to survive, next time around. So war has
moved into space. Uh . . . professionalism . . . the old
traditions of mutual respect and so forth have naturally
revived." He made himself look up. "What more cliches
need I repeat?"

"Suppose your side completely annihilated our ships,"
Rostock said. "What would happen?"

"Why . . . that's been discussed theoretically . . . by
damn near every political scientist, hasn't it? The total
command of space would not mean total command of Earth.
We could destroy the whole eastern hemisphere without
being touched. But we wouldn't because Unasia would fire
its cobalt weapons while dying, and there'd be no western
hemisphere to come home to either. Not that that situation will ever arise. Space is too big. There are too many
ships and fortresses scattered around; combat is too slow a
process. Neither fleet can wipe out the other."

"Since we have this perpetual stalemate, then," Rostock
pursued, "why is there perpetual war?"

"Well, uh, partial victories are possible. Like our capture
of Mars, or your destruction of three dreadnaughts in one
month, on different occasions. The balance of power shifts.
Rather than let its strength continue being whittled down,
the side which is losing asks for a parley. There are negotiations, which end to the relative advantage of the
stronger side. Meanwhile the arms race continues. Pretty
soon a new dispute arises, the cease-fire ends, and maybe
the other side is lucky that time."

"Is this situation expected to be eternal?"

"No!" Diaz stopped, thought a minute, and grinned with
one corner of his mouth. "That is, they keep talking about
an effective international organization. Trouble is, the two
cultures are too far apart by now. They can't live together."

"I used to believe that myself," Rostock said. "Lately I
have not been sure. A world federalism could be devised
which would let both civilizations keep their identities.
There have in fact been many such proposals, as you know.

None has gotten beyond the talking stage. None ever will. Because you see, what maintains the war is not the difference between our two cultures, but their similarity."

"Whoa, there!" Diaz bristled. "I resent that."

"Please," Rostock said. "I pass no moral judgments. For the sake of argument, at least, I can concede you the moral superiority, remarking only in parenthesis that Earth holds billions of people who not only fail to comprehend what you mean by freedom but would not like it if you gave it to them. The similarity I am talking about is technological. Both civilizations are based on the machine, with all the high organization and dynamism which this implies."

"So?"

"So war is a necessity— Wait! I am not talking about 'merchants of death,' or 'dictators needing an outside enemy,' or whatever the current propaganda lines are. I mean that conflict is built into the culture. There *must* be an outlet for the destructive emotions generated in the mass of the people by the type of life they lead. A type of life for which evolution never designed them.

"Have you ever heard about L. F. Richardson? No? He was an Englishman in the last century, a Quaker, who hated war but, being a scientist, realized the phenomenon must be understood clinically before it can be eliminated. He performed some brilliant theoretical and statistical analyses which showed, for example, that the rate of deadly quarrels was very nearly constant over the decades. There could be many small clashes or a few major ones, but the result was the same. Why were the United States and the Chinese Empire so peaceful during the nineteenth century? The answer is that they were not. They had their Civil War and Taiping Rebellion, which devastated them as much as required. I need not multiply examples. We can discuss this later in detail. I have carried Richardson's work a good deal further and have studied the problem more rigorously. I say to you now only that civilized societies must have a certain rate of immolations."

Diaz listened to silence for a minute before he said: "Well, I've sometimes thought the same. I suppose you mean we spacemen are the goats these days?"

"Exactly. War fought out here does not menace the planet. By our deaths we keep Earth alive."

Rostock sighed. His mouth drooped. "Magic works, you know," he said: "works on the emotions of the people who practice it. If a primitive witch doctor told a storm to go away, the storm did not hear, but the tribe did and took heart. The ancient analogy to us, though, is the sacrificial king in the early agricultural societies: a god in mortal form, who was regularly slain that the fields might bear fruit. This was not mere superstition. You must realize that. It worked—on the people. The rite was essential to the operation of their culture, to their sanity and hence to their survival.

"Today the machine age has developed its own sacrificial kings. We are the chosen of the race. The best it can offer. None gainsays us. We may have what we choose, pleasure, luxury, women, adulation—only not the simple pleasures of wife and child and home, for we must die that the people may live."

Again silence, until: "Do you seriously mean that's why the war goes on?" Diaz breathed.

Rostock nodded.

"But nobody—I mean, people wouldn't—"

"They do not reason these things out, of course. Traditions develop blindly. The ancient peasant did not elaborate logical reasons why the king must die. He merely knew this was so, and left the syllogism for modern anthropologists to expound. I did not see the process going on today until I had had the chance to . . . to become more perceptive than I had been," Rostock said humbly.

Diaz couldn't endure sitting down any longer. He jumped to his feet. "Assuming you're right," he snapped, "and you may be, what of it? What can be done?"

"Much," Rostock said. Calm descended on his face like a mask. "I am not being mystical about this, either. The sacrificial king has reappeared as the end product of a long chain of cause and effect. There is no reason inherent in natural law why this must be. Richardson was right in his basic hope, that when war becomes understood, as a phenomenon, it can be eliminated. This would naturally involve restructuring the entire terrestrial culture. Gradually, subtly. Remember—" His hand shot out, seized Diaz's shoulder and gripped painfully hard. "There is a new element in history today. Us. The kings. We are not like those who spend their lives under Earth's sky. In some ways we are more, in other ways less, but always we are different. You and I are more akin to each other than to our planet-dwelling countrymen. Are we not?

"In the time and loneliness granted me, I have used all my new powers to think about this. Not only think; this is so much more than cold reason. I have tried to feel. To love what is, as the Buddhists say. I believe a nucleus of spacemen like us, slowly and secretly gathered, wishing the good of everyone on Earth and the harm of none, gifted with powers and insights they cannot really imagine at home—I believe we may accomplish something. If not us, then our sons. Men ought not to kill each other, when the stars are waiting."

He let go, turned away and looked at the deck. "Of course," he mumbled, "I, in my peculiar situation, must first destroy a number of your brothers."

They had given Diaz a whole pack of cigarettes, an enormous treasure out here, before they locked him into his cubicle for the duration of the second engagement. He lay in harness, hearing clang and shout and engine roar through the vibrating bulkheads, stared at blackness and smoked until his tongue was foul. Sometimes the *Ho* accelerated, mostly it ran free and he floated. Once a tremor went through the entire hull, near miss by a shaped charge. Doubtless gamma rays, ignoring the magnetic force screens, sleeted through the men and knocked another several months off their life expectancies. Not that that mattered. Spacemen rarely lived long enough to worry about degenerative diseases. Diaz hardly noticed.

He's not lying, Rostock. Why should he? What could he gain? He may be a nut, of course. But he doesn't act like a nut either. He wants me to study his statistics and equations, satisfy myself that he's right. And he must be damn sure I will be convinced, to tell me as much as he has.

How many are there like him? Only a very few, I'm sure. The man-machine symbiosis is obviously new, or we'd've had some inkling ourselves. This is the first field trial of the system. I wonder if the others have reached the same conclusions as Rostock. No, he said he doubts that. Their psychology impressed him as being more deeply channeled than his. He's a lucky accident.

Lucky? Now how can I tell? I'm only a man. I've never experienced an IQ of 1,000, or whatever the figure may be. A god's purposes aren't necessarily what a man would elect.

The eventual end to war? Well, other institutions had been ended, at least in the Western countries; judicial torture, chattel slavery, human sacrifice— No, wait, according to Rostock human sacrifice had been revived.

"But is our casualty rate high enough to fit your equations?" Diaz had argued. "Space forces aren't as big as old-time armies. No country could afford that."

"Other elements than death must be taken into account," Rostock answered. "The enormous expense is one factor. Taxpaying is a form of symbolic self-mutilation. It also tends to direct civilian resentments and aggressions against their own government, thus taking some pressure off international relations.

"Chiefly, though, there is the matter of emotional intensity. A spaceman not only dies, he usually dies horribly; and that moment is the culmination of a long period under grisly conditions. His groundling brothers, administrative and service personnel, suffer vicariously: 'sweat it out,' as your idiom so well expresses the feeling. His kinfolk, friends, women, are likewise racked. When Adonis dies— or Osiris, Tammuz, Baldur, Christ, Tlaloc, whichever of his hundred names you choose—the people must in some degree share his agony. That is part of the sacrifice."

Diaz had never thought about it just that way. Like most Corpsmen, he had held the average civilian in thinly disguised contempt. But . . . from time to time, he remembered, he'd been glad his mother died before he enlisted. And why did his sister hit the bottle so hard? Then there had been Lois, she of the fire-colored hair and violet eyes, who wept as if she would never stop weeping when he left for duty. He'd promised to get in touch with her on his return, but of course he knew better.

Which did not erase memories of men whose breath and blood came exploding from burst helmets; who shuddered and vomited and defecated in the last stages of radiation sickness; who stared without immediate comprehension at a red spurt which a second ago had been an arm or a leg; who went insane and must be gassed because psychoneurosis is catching on a six months' orbit beyond Saturn; who—

Yeah, Carl had been lucky.

You could talk as much as you wished about Corps brotherhood, honor, tradition, and gallantry. It remained sentimental guff . . .

No, that was unjust. The Corps had saved the people, their lives and liberties. There could be no higher achievement—for the Corps. But knighthood had once been a noble thing, too. Then, lingering after its day, it became a yoke and eventually a farce. The warrior virtues were not ends in themselves. If the warrior could be made obsolete—

Could he? How much could one man, even powered by a machine, hope to do? How much could he even hope to understand?

The moment came upon Diaz. He lay as if blinded by shellburst radiance.

As consciousness returned, he knew first, irrelevantly, what it meant to get religion.

"By God," he told the universe, "we're going to try!"

The battle would resume very shortly. At any moment, in fact, some scoutship leading the American force might fire a missile. But when Diaz told his guard he wanted to speak with General Rostock, he was taken there within minutes.

The door closed behind him. The living room lay empty, altogether still except for the machine throb, which was not loud since the *Ho* was running free. Because acceleration might be needful on short notice, there was no spin. Diaz hung weightless as fog. And the Monet flung into his eyes all Earth's sunlight and summer forests.

"Rostock?" he called uncertainly.

"Come," said a voice, almost too low to hear. Diaz gave a shove with his foot and flew toward the office.

He stopped himself by grasping the doorjamb. A semicircular room lay before him, the entire side taken up by controls and meters. Lights blinked, needles wavered on dials, buttons and switches and knobs reached across black paneling. But none of that was important. Only the man at the desk mattered, who free-sat with wires running from his head to the wall.

Rostock seemed to have lost weight. Or was that an illusion? The skin was drawn taut across his high cheekbones and gone a dead, glistening white. His nostrils were flared and the colorless lips held tense. Diaz looked into his eyes, once, and then away again. He could not meet them. He could not even think about them. He drew a shaken breath and waited.

"You made your decision quickly," Rostock whispered. "I had not awaited you until after the engagement."

"I . . . I didn't think you would see me till then."

"This is more important." Diaz felt as if he were being probed with knives. He could not altogether believe it was his imagination. He stared desperately at the paneled instruments. Their nonhumanness was like a comforting hand. *They must only be for the benefit of maintenance techs,* he thought in a very distant part of himself. *The brain doesn't need them.*

"You are convinced," Rostock said in frank surprise.

"Yes," Diaz answered.

"I had not expected that. I only hoped for your reluctant agreement to study my work." Rostock regarded him for a still century. "You were ripe for a new faith," he decided. "I had not taken you for the type. But then, the mind can only use what data are given it, and I have hitherto had little opportunity to meet Americans. Never since I became what I am. You have another psyche from ours."

"I need to understand your findings, sir," Diaz said. "Right now I can only believe. That isn't enough, is it?"

Slowly, Rostock's mouth drew into a smile of quite human warmth. "Correct. But given the faith, intellectual comprehension should be swift."

"I . . . I shouldn't be taking your time . . . now, sir," Diaz stammered. "How should I begin? Should I take some books back with me?"

"No." Acceptance had been reached. Rostock spoke resonantly, a master to his trusted servant. "I need your help here. Strap into yonder harness. Our first necessity is to survive the battle upon us. You realize that this means sacrificing many of your comrades. I know how much that will hurt you. Afterward we shall spend our lives repaying our people—both our peoples. But today I shall ask you questions about your fleet. Any information is valuable, especially details of construction and armament which our intelligence has not been able to learn."

Doña mia. Diaz let go the door, covered his face and fell free, endlessly. *Help me.*

"It is not betrayal," said the superman. "It is the ultimate loyalty you can offer."

Diaz made himself look at the cabin again. He shoved against the bulkhead and stopped by the harness near the desk.

"You cannot lie to me," said Rostock. "Do not deny how much pain I am giving you." Diaz glimpsed his fists clamping together. "Each time I look at you, I share what you feel."

Diaz clung to his harness. There went an explosion through him.

NO, BY GOD!

Rostock screamed.

"Don't," Diaz sobbed. "I don't want—" But wave after wave ripped outward. Rostock flopped about in his harness and shrieked. The scene came back, ramming home like a bayonet.

"We like to put an extra string on our bow," the psych officer said. Lunar sunlight, scarcely softened by the dome, blazed off his bronze eagles, wings and beaks. "You know that your right ulna will be replaced with a metal section in which there is a nerve-triggered nuclear cartridge. But that may not be all, gentlemen."

He bridged his fingers. The young men seated on the other side of his desk stirred uneasily. "In this country," the psych officer said, "we don't believe humans should be turned into puppets. Therefore you will have voluntary control of your bombs; no posthypnosis, Pavlov reflex or any such insult. However, those of you who are willing will receive a rather special extra treatment, and that fact will be buried from the consciousness of all of you.

"Our reasoning is that if and when the Unasians learn about the prisoner weapon, they'll remove the cartridge by surgery but leave the prosthetic bone in place. And they will, we hope, not examine it in microscopic detail. Therefore they won't know that it contains an oscillator, integrated with the crystal structure. Nor will you; because what you don't know, you can't babble under anesthesia.

"The opportunity may come, if you are captured and lose your bomb, to inflict damage by this reserve means. You may find yourself near a crucial electronic device, for example a spaceship's autopilot. At short range, the oscillator will do an excellent job of bollixing it. Which will at least discomfit the enemy, and may even give you a chance to escape.

"The posthypnotic command will be such that you'll remember about this oscillator when conditions seem right for using it. Not before. Of course, the human mind is a damned queer thing, that twists and turns and bites its own tail. In order to make an opportunity to strike this blow, your subconscious may lead you down strange paths. It may even have you seriously contemplating treason, if treason seems the only way of getting access to what you can wreck. Don't let that bother you afterward, gentlemen. Your superiors will know what happened.

"Nevertheless, the experience may be painful. And posthypnosis is, at best, humiliating to a free man. So this aspect of the program is strictly volunteer. Does anybody want to go for broke?"

The door flung open. The guards burst in. Diaz was already behind the desk, next to Rostock. He yanked out the general's sidearm and fired at the soldiers. Free fall recoil sent him back against the computer panel. He braced himself, fired again and used his left elbow to smash the nearest meter face.

Rostock clawed at the wires in his head. For a moment Diaz guessed what it must be like to have random oscillations in your brain, amplified by an electronic engine that was part of you. He laid the pistol to the screaming man's temple and fired once more.

Now to get out! He shoved hard, arrowing past the sentries, who rolled through the air in a crimson galaxy of blood globules. Confusion boiled in the corridor beyond. Someone snatched at him. He knocked the fellow aside and dove along a tubeway. Somewhere hereabouts should be a scooter locker—there, and nobody around!

He didn't have time to get on a spacesuit, even if a Unasian one would have fitted, but he slipped on an air dome over the scooter. That, with the heater unit and oxy reclaim, would serve. He didn't want to get off anywhere en route; not before he'd steered the machine through an American hatch.

With luck, he'd do that. Their command computer gone, the enemy were going to get smeared. American ships would close in as the slaughter progressed. Eventually one should come within range of the scooter's little radio.

He set the minilock controls, mounted the saddle, dogged the air dome and waited for ejection. It came none too soon. Three soldiers had just appeared down the passageway. Diaz applied full thrust and jetted away from the *Ho.* Its blackness was soon lost among the star clouds.

Battle commenced. The first Unasian ship to be destroyed must have been less than fifty miles distant. Luckily, Diaz was facing the other way when the missile exploded.

THE UNFORTUNATE MR. MORKY

by Vance Aandahl

from *Fantasy and Science Fiction*

A swift reflection (literally) on science, society, psychology and the infinity of custard pie—by a young writer of remarkable ability.

When the unfortunate Mr. Morky met the carny-man, great things were bound to happen. He was the perfect object for a carny-man's intentions: unadulterated custard pie from the vulcanized soles of his shoes to the fuzzy apex of his crewcut. This is the way it occurred:

Mr. Morky was shuffling through the sawdust, beneath the hot neon lights, surrounded by the jolly sounds and sour-sweat smells of a carnival which was not really a carnival, but rather the wavering image of a carnival, when he found himself standing in the shade of a secluded tent.

"Hey, boy! You wantta come see the Museum of Mirrors?"

The unfortunate Mr. Morky entered the tent, shuffling cautiously behind the carny-man, in the manner in which all custard-pie people are cautious.

"Com'on now, boy. This is one plenty good deal for two bits, you betcha life."

Twenty-five cents was the price, and the unfortunate Mr. Morky suddenly was standing in the Museum of Mirrors, standing, by chance, on a plane mirror, while the carny-man scuttled off to the control room, his quarter clutched tightly between two rows of yellow teeth.

The unfortunate Mr. Morky was surrounded by mirrors —they coated the ceiling, the walls, and the floor. Plane mirrors, convex mirrors, concave mirrors. All shapes and all colors. They glittered in mad jest at their visitor.

The largest mirror in the room rested directly in front of the unfortunate Mr. Morky. The master mirror it was, and into its flat circularity stared the unfortunate Mr. Morky, gazing at one thousand jumbled images of his good friend, the unfortunate Mr. Morky, who was reflected by millions of mirrors from all sides, all of which reflected their images upon the master mirror, reflected and re-reflected and re-re-reflected into an infinite multiple reflection. It was indeed a murgled maze of Mr. Morkys. But lo! seated in his control room, where he chewed happily on his quarter, the carny-man touched a switch, adjusted a few mirrors the slightest fraction of an inch, and focused the million images into one ten-foot image of the unfortunate Mr. Morky.

"My, my," said Mr. Morky, staring at this marvelous sight. "My, my."

The carny-man touched another switch; the mirrors moved another fraction of an inch; and suddenly the image of the unfortunate Mr. Morky shrank from a gigantic custard pie to a three-inch custard pie. Then the image ran forward in the mirror until it was large again. It winked at Mr. Morky, clicked its heels, and stood on its head.

"My, my," said Mr. Morky. "My, my."

Then the image began to shrink. It shrank once more to three inches. It shrank to one third of an inch. It shrank to a point—a mere point of custard pie. And then—it disappeared into negative infinity.

Like a good custard pie, the unfortunate Mr. Morky disappeared into positive infinity.

It was novel to travel through time. A few fluttery inversions, a tickling sensation inside his stomach, and Mr. Morky suddenly had warm bones. Color kept coming and going (or perhaps he kept coming and going). He garked the bip and got past the first moebius cul-de-sac.

Unfortunately, there is at least one force in the universe which can overcome the laws of mathematics: the desire for security. The better half (purest custard) of Mr. Morky thwarted logic and went scrambling fearfully back to the time from which he had come. The weaker half was carried on toward positive infinity.

The unfortunate Mr. Morky who was struggling backwards did not make very rapid progress against the current, so we may forget him for the present. The other unfortunate Mr. Morky reached positive infinity in no time at all, hopped over to negative infinity, and popped back into the enclosure which surrounded the carnival grounds. He shuffled curiously through the sawdust, stopped in the dank shade of a secluded tent, followed a carny-man therein, paid his quarter, found himself facing a flat mirror, watched his image perform, and suddenly, as it disappeared, discovered that he was hurtling toward positive infinity.

On the way, he met the other Mr. Morky, who was still struggling to get back, and there was a collision. He fused with himself. Unfortunately, it was an abnormal fusion, quite cancerous; all that custard pie started dividing and re-dividing and re-re-dividing into an infinite multiple division. When the unfortunate Mr. Morkys had filled all the moebius cul-de-sacs, they started overflowing—dropping into this or that time strata.

The unfortunate Mr. Morkys are still coming.

It's a damn conformist world.

CHRISTMAS TREASON

by James White

from *Fantasy and Science Fiction*

Long before the advent of the Wonderful Invention story, speculative fiction had a favorite theme in the Wonderful Voyage. So far, the voyagers in this volume have made their way (into time, space or wherever) by way of beer-can Disappearers, black-box time machines and space ships—plus, of course, Morky, who did it with mirrors.

This time, all it takes is talent, highly specialized talent.

Richard sat on the woolly rug beside his brother's cot and watched the gang arrive one by one.

Liam came first wearing a thick sweater over pajamas too tight for him—his parents didn't have central heating. Then Mub, whose folks did not need it, in a nightie. When Greg arrived he fell over a truck belonging to Buster, because he was coming from the daytime, and the moonlight coming into the room was too dim for him to see properly. The noise he made did not disturb the sleeping grownups, but Buster got excited and started rattling the bars of his cot and had to be shushed. Loo arrived last, with one of her long, funny dresses on, and stood blinking for a while, then sat on the side of Richard's bed with the others.

Now the meeting could begin.

For some reason Richard felt worried even though the Investigation was going fine, and he hoped this was just a sign that he was growing up. His Daddy and the other big people worried nearly all the time. Richard was six.

"Before hearing your reports," he began formally, "we will have the Minutes of the last—".

"Do we *hafta* . . . ?" whispered Liam angrily. Beside him

Greg said a lot of nonsense words, louder than a whisper, which meant the same thing. Mub, Loo and his three-year-old brother merely radiated impatience.

"Quiet!" Richard whispered, then went on silently, "There has got to be Minutes, that book of my Daddy's says so. And talk without making a noise, I can hear you just as well. . . . "

That was his only talent, Richard thought enviously. Compared with the things the others could do it wasn't much. He wasn't able to go to Loo's place, with its funny shed that had no sides and just a turned up roof, or play pirates on the boat Liam's Daddy had given him. There was a big hole in the boat and the engine had been taken out, but there was rope and nets and bits of iron in it, and sometimes the waves came so close it seemed to be floating. Some of the gang were frightened when the big waves turned white and rushed at them along the sand, but *he* wouldn't have been scared if he had been able to go there. Nor had he been to Mub's place, which was noisy and crowded and not very nice, or climbed the trees beside Greg's farm.

Richard couldn't go *anywhere* unless a grown-up took him in a train or a car or something. Whereas if the others wanted to go somewhere they just went—even Buster could do it now. All he could do was listen and watch through their minds when they were playing and, if one of them wanted to say something complicated to the others, he would take what they were thinking and repeat it so everybody could hear it. And it was only his friends' minds he could get into—if only he could see what *Daddy* was thinking!

He was the oldest and the leader of the gang, but by itself that wasn't much fun. . . .

"I want my train set!" Greg broke in impatiently. A bright but indistinct picture of the promised model railway filled Richard's mind, to be overlaid rapidly by pictures of Mub's dolly, Loo's blackboard, Liam's cowboy suit and Buster's machine-gun. His head felt like bursting.

"Stop thinking so loud!" Richard ordered sharply. "You'll get them, you'll all get them. We were promised."

"I know, but . . ." began Greg.

". . . How?" ended the others, in unison.

"That's what the Investigation is for, to find out," Richard replied crossly. "And we'll never find out if you keep rushing things. Quiet, gang, and listen!"

The room was already silent and then even the thinking noises died down. Richard began to speak in a whisper— he had found that talking while he was thinking kept his mind from wandering onto something else. And besides, he had learned some new grown-up words and wanted to impress the gang with them.

He said, "Two weeks ago Daddy asked Buster and me what we wanted for Christmas and told us about Santa. Santa Claus will bring you anything you want. Or any two things, or even three things, within reason, my Daddy says. Buster doesn't remember last Christmas, but the rest of us do and that's the way it happens. You hang up your stocking and in the morning there's sweets and apples and things in it, and the *big* stuff you asked for is on the bed. But the grown-ups don't seem to know for sure how they got there . . ."

"S-sleigh and reindeer," Greg whispered excitedly.

Richard shook his head. "None of the grown-ups can say how exactly it happens, they just tell us that Santa will come all right, that we'll get our toys in time and not to worry about it. But we can't help worrying about it. That's why we're having an Investigation to find out what really happens.

"We can't see how one man, even when he has a sleigh and magic reindeer that fly through the air, can bring everybody their toys all in one night . . ." Richard took a deep breath and got ready to use his new, grown-up words. "Delivering all that stuff during the course of a single night is a logistical impossibility."

Buster, Mub and Greg looked impressed. Loo thought primly, "Richard is showing off," and Liam said, "I think he's got a jet."

Feeling annoyed at the mixed reception to his big words, Richard was getting ready to whisper "Yah, Slanty-Eyes!" at Loo when he thought better of it and said instead, "Jets make a noise and we'd remember if we heard one last Christmas. But what we're supposed to do in an Investigation is get the facts and then find the answer—" he glared at Loo—"by a process of deductive reasoning."

Loo didn't say or think a word.

"All right then," Richard went on briskly, "this is what we know . . ."

His name was Santa Claus. Description: a man, big even for a grown-up, fresh complexion, blue eyes, white hair and beard. He dressed in a red cap, coat and trousers, all trimmed with white fur, also black shiny belt and knee-boots. Careful questioning of grown-ups showed that they were all in agreement about his appearance, although none of them had admitted to actually seeing him. Liam's Daddy had been questioned closely on this point and had said that he knew because Liam's Grandad had told *him*. It was also generally agreed that he lived somewhere at the North Pole in a secret cavern under the ice. The cavern was said to contain his toy workshops and storage warehouses.

They knew quite a lot about Santa. The major gap in their knowledge was his methods of distribution. On Christmas Eve, did he have to shoot back and forth to the North Pole when he needed his sleigh refilled? If so it was a very chancy way of doing things and the gang had good cause to be worried. They didn't want any hitches on Christmas Eve, like toys coming late or getting mixed up. If anything they wanted them to come early.

Two weeks ago Richard had seen his mother packing some of his old toys in a box. She had told him that they were going to the orphans because Santa never came to orphans.

The gang had to be *sure* everything would be all right. Imagine wakening on Christmas morning to find you were an *orphan!*

". . . We can't get any more information at this end," Richard continued, "so we have to find the secret cavern and then see how he sends the stuff out. That was your last assignment, gang, and I'll take your reports now.

"You first, Mub."

Mub shook her head, she had nothing to report. But there was a background picture of her Daddy's face looking angry and shiny and sort of loose, and a smack from her Daddy's large, pink-palmed hand which had hurt her dignity much more than her bottom. Sometimes her Daddy would play with her for hours and she could ask him questions all the time, but other times he would come into the house talking funny and bumping into things the way Buster had done when he was just learning to walk, and then he would smack her if she asked questions all the time. Mub didn't know what to make of her Daddy sometimes.

Still without a word she floated up from the bed and drifted to the window. She began staring out at the cold, moonlit desert and the distant buildings where Richard's Daddy worked.

"Loo?" said Richard.

She had nothing to report either.

"Liam."

"I'll wait to last," said Liam smugly. It was plain that he knew something important, but he was thinking about seagulls to stop Richard from seeing what it was.

"All right, Greg then."

"I found where some of the toys are stored," Greg began. He went on to describe a trip with his mother and father into town to places called shops, and two of them had been full of toys. Then when he was home again his father gave him a beating and sent him to bed without his supper . . .

"O-o-oh," said Loo and Mub sympathetically.

This was because, Greg explained, he had seen a dinky little tractor with rubber treads on it that could climb over piles of books and things. When he got home he thought about it a lot, and then thought that he would try reaching for it the way they all did when they were somewhere and had left things they wanted to play with somewhere else. His Daddy had found him playing with it and smacked him, four times with his pants down, and told him it was wrong to take things that didn't belong to him and that the tractor was going right back to the shop.

But the beating had only hurt him for a short time and he was nearly asleep when his mother came and gave him a hug and three big chocolates with cream in the middle. He had just finished eating them when his father brought in some more . . .

"O-h-h," said Loo and Mub, enviously.

"Feeties for *me?*" asked Buster, aloud. When excited he was apt to slip back into baby talk. Greg whispered "Night" —a nonsense word he used when he was thinking "No"— and added silently, "I ate them all."

"Getting back to the Investigation," Richard said firmly, "Dad took Buster and me to a shop the day before yester-day. I've been to town before but this time I was able to ask questions, and this is the way they work. Everybody doesn't always know exactly what they want for Christmas, so the stores are meant to show what toys Santa has in stock so they'll know what to ask for. But the toys in the shops can't be touched until Christmas, just like the ones at the North Pole. Daddy said so, and when we were talk-ing to Santa he said the same thing . . ."

"Santa!!!"

A little awkwardly Richard went on, "Yes, Buster and I spoke to Santa. We . . . I asked him about his sleigh and reindeer, and then about what seemed to us to be a logisti-cally insoluble problem of supply and distribution. When we were asking him he kept looking at Daddy and Daddy kept looking up in the air, and that was when we saw his beard was held on with elastic.

"When we told him about this," Richard continued, "he said we were very bright youngsters and he had to admit that he was only one of Santa's deputies in disguise, sent to say Merry Christmas to all the boys and girls because Santa himself was so rushed with toy-making. He said that Santa didn't even tell *him* how he worked the trick, it was a Top Secret, but he did know that Santa had lots of com-puters and things and that the old boy believed in keeping right up to date science-wise. So we didn't have to worry about our toys coming, all that would be taken care of, he said.

"He was a very nice man," Richard concluded, "and didn't mind when we spotted his disguise and asked all the questions. He even gave us a couple of small presents on account."

As he finished Richard couldn't help wondering if that deputy had told everything he knew—he had looked very uncomfortable during some of the questions. Richard thought that it was a great pity that he couldn't listen to what everybody was thinking instead of just the kids in his gang. If only they knew where that secret cavern was.

"I know," said Liam suddenly. "I found it."

Everybody was asking questions at once then, and they were talking instead of just thinking. Where was it and had he seen Santa and was my train-set there and what were the toys like . . . ? In his mind Richard thundered, "Quiet! You'll wake my Daddy! And I'll ask the questions." To Liam he said, "That's great! How did you find it?"

One of Liam's abilities—one shared by Greg and Buster, and to a lesser degree by the girls—was of thinking about a place he would like to be and then going there. Or to be more precise, going to one of the places that were most like the place he wanted to go. He did not think of where so much as what he wanted—a matter of environment rather than geography. He would decide whether the place should have night, day, rain, sunshine, snow, trees, grass or sand and then think about the fine details. When his mental picture was complete he would go there, or they all—with the exception of Richard—would go there. Liam and Greg had found lots of lovely places in this way, which the gang used when they grew tired of playing in each other's backyards, because once they went to a place they always knew how to go back to it.

This time Liam had been trying for ice caverns with toys and reindeer stalls in them and had got nowhere at all. Apparently no such place existed. Then he started asking himself what would a place look like if it had to make and store things, and maybe had to send them out to people fast.

The answer was machinery. It mightn't be as noisy or dirty as the factory his Daddy had taken him to in Derry last summer, but there would have to be machinery.

But there might not be toys—they might not have been made or arrived yet. And if, as Richard had suggested, reindeer and sleighs were no longer in use, then they were out of the picture as well. And the ice cavern, now, that would be a cold place for Santa to work and if he turned on a heater the walls would melt, so the cavern might not be made of ice. What he was left with was a large underground factory or storehouse either at or somewhere near the North Pole.

It wasn't a very good description of the place he was looking for, but he found it.

In Liam's mind was the memory of a vast, echoing corridor so big it looked like a street. It was clean and brightly lit and empty. There was a sort of crane running along the roof with grabs hanging down, a bit like the ones he had seen lifting coal at the docks only these were painted red and yellow, and on both sides of the corridor stood a line of tall, splendid, unmistakable shapes. Rockets.

Rockets, thought Richard excitedly: *that was the answer, all right!* Rockets were faster than anything, although he didn't quite see how the toys would be delivered. Still they would find that out easily now that they knew where the secret cavern was.

"Did you look inside them for toys?" Greg broke in, just ahead of the others asking the same question.

Liam had. Most of the rockets were filled with machinery and the nose had sort of sparkly stuff in it. All the ones he had looked at were the same and he had grown tired of floating about among the noses of the rockets and gone exploring instead. At the other end of the corridor there was a big notice with funny writing on it. He was standing in front of it when two grown-ups with guns started running at him and yelling nonsense words. He got scared and left.

When Liam finished, the girls began congratulating him and the hole in the chest of his sweater grew bigger. Then Greg tried to cut him down to size again by stating, "They weren't nonsense words. What the guards yelled at you, I mean. If you could remember better how they sounded I could tell you what they said . . ."

Just when things were getting exciting, Richard thought impatiently, another argument was going to start about what were nonsense words and what weren't. Buster, Liam and himself could make themselves understood to each other whether they were speaking or thinking, but when any of the others spoke aloud it was just nonsense. And they said the same thing about words Richard, Liam and Buster spoke aloud. But the funny thing was that Loo, Mub and Greg couldn't understand what each other said, either.

Richard had an idea that this was because they lived in different places, like in the pictures he had studied in his Daddy's *National Geographic* magazines. He had tracked down Liam's place from some of those pictures—Liam lived in a fishing village on the North Irish coast. Why they spoke a funny, but recognizable, form of American there Richard didn't know. Loo and Mub were harder to pin down; there were a couple of places where the people had slanty eyes or had dark brown skin and black curly hair. Greg was the hardest because he didn't have any special skin or hair or eyes. His folks wore furry hats in winter, but that wasn't much to go on . . .

"What do we do now, Richard?" Liam broke in. "Keep thinking about the cavern, huh? Not your Daddy's old books."

For a moment Richard thought into himself, then he opened his mind and asked, "How much time have you all got?"

Mub said it was near her dinner-time. Greg had just finished breakfast and was supposed to be playing in the shed for the next three or four hours. Loo's time was about the same as Greg's. Liam thought it was nearly breakfast time, but his mother didn't mind if he stayed in bed these cold mornings. And Buster, like Richard, had practically the whole of the night to play around in.

"Right," he said briskly when all the reports were in. "It looks like the cavern Liam found isn't the right one—

the rockets don't have toys in them. Maybe it's a place for sending toys out, but they haven't arrived from Santa's workshop yet. That workshop is the place we're looking for, and it shouldn't be hard to find now that we know the sort of place to look for—an underground place with rockets."

His thoughts became authoritative as he went on. "You've got to find these underground places and see what goes on in them. We can't be sure of anything we've been told about them, so there might be a lot of secret caverns. When you find one try not to let anybody see you, look around for toys and see if you can get to the office of the man in charge of the place. If it's Santa or he looks like a nice man, ask him questions. And remember to say please and thank you. If he's not a nice man, or if there's nobody there, try to find out things whatever way you can. Everyone understand?"

Everybody thought, "Yes."

"Okay then. Greg will go to the cavern Liam found, because he can understand what the people say there. Liam and Buster will look for caverns on their own. But remember, once you see that a place doesn't have toys in it, leave and look somewhere else. Don't waste time. Mub and Loo will stay here and be ready to help if you need them, they can't go to new places as easily as you men can."

Richard's mouth felt suddenly dry. He ended, "All right, take off."

Buster flicked out of sight in the middle of a "Wheee-e-e" of excitement. Liam held back for a moment thinking, "But why do they have guards in the caverns?" To which Greg replied, "Maybe to protect the toys against juvenile delinquents. I don't know what they are exactly, but my Daddy says they steal and break things, and if I had kept that tractor I took from the shop I would grow up to be one." Then Liam and Greg quietly disappeared. Loo and Mub began gathering up Buster's teddybear and toys. They floated into Buster's cot with them and started to play houses.

Richard got into bed and lay back on his elbows. Buster was the member of the gang most likely to get into trouble so he listened in for him first. But his brother was in a place where each rocket was held out level by a little crane instead of standing straight up. The sound of voices and footsteps echoed about the place in a spooky fashion, but his brother had not been spotted. Buster reported that he had looked into the noses of the rockets and they were filled with a lot of junk and some stuff which sparkled and frightened him away.

The stuff didn't sparkle really, of course, but Buster had a talent for looking through things—like brick walls and engine casings—and when he looked into the rocket nose in that way the stuff sparkled. Like the electric wiring at home, he thought, only worse. There were no toys or any sign of Santa, so he was going to try some other place. Richard switched to Greg.

Greg was in the cavern originally found by Liam. Two of the guards were still talking about seeing a boy in pajamas. Greg was going to look around some more and then try another place. Liam's report was much the same, right down to the stuff in the rocket noses which made him afraid to go too close. Richard stopped listening to them and began thinking to himself.

Why had the caverns guards in them? To protect the toys against damage or theft, as Greg had suggested? But where were the toys? The answer to that question was, some of them were in the shops . . .

A bit of conversation between his mother and father, overheard yesterday when they were in one of the shops, popped suddenly into his mind. Richard hadn't known exactly what was going on because he had been watching to see that Buster didn't knock over anything. Daddy had asked his mother if she would like something—beads or a shiny brooch or something—for Christmas. Mummy had said, "Oh John, it's lovely but . . ." Then a man from behind the counter had come up to Daddy, said a few words and gone away again. Daddy had said, "Okay." Then Mummy had said, "But John, are you sure you can afford it? It's robbery, sheer robbery! These storekeepers are robbers at Christmas time!"

Guards all over the place, Greg's theory, and storekeepers who were robbers at Christmas time. It was beginning to make sense, but Richard was very worried by the picture that was forming.

Loo and Mub had the cot pillow and the teddybear floating in the air above the cot, with Buster's broken truck doing a figure-of-eight between them. But they were being careful not to make a noise so Richard did not say anything. He began listening in for the others again.

Buster had found another cavern, so had Liam. Greg had gone through three more—they had all been small places and plainly not what the gang was looking for. All reported rockets with the same puzzling load, no sign of toys and no Santa. And so it went on. Richard's eyes began to feel heavy and he had to sit on the edge of the bed again to keep from falling asleep.

Mub was lying in Buster's cot being a sick Mummy and Loo was kneeling beside her being the Nurse. At the same time they had taken the truck apart and now a long procession of parts was in orbit around the pillow and teddybear. Richard knew they would put the truck together again before they went home, and probably fix it, too. He wished that he could do something useful like that, and he began to wonder if Loo could move people, too.

When he mentioned the idea to her she stopped being a Nurse long enough to do some experiments. Richard tried as hard as he could to stay sitting on the edge of his bed, but Loo forced him to lie flat on his back. It was as if a big, soft cushion was pushing against his arms and chest. When he tried to prop his elbows behind him, other cushions pushed his arms out straight. After he had been forced to lie flat three times, Loo told him she wanted to go back to playing Nurse. She didn't like this other game because it made her head hurt.

Richard went back to listening to the searchers again. Buster was working on his fourth cavern, Liam and

Greg on their seventh and ninth respectively. The sudden
speeding up of the search was explained by the fact that
they no longer walked from place to place inside the caverns, they just *went*. Tired legs, Richard discovered, had
been the reason for them all thinking of this time-saving
idea. It seemed to get the guards all excited, though. Everywhere the gang went there were guards who got excited—
it was hard to stay hidden with so many guards about—
but they had not stayed anywhere long enough to be
caught. They had found lots of rockets but no sign of a
toy workshop, or Santa.

Richard was now pretty sure that the guards were soldiers. In some of the caverns they wore dark green uniforms with black belts and red things on their shoulders,
and only Greg could understand the nonsense words they
said. In another place, the cavern Liam had searched
where you could hear planes taking off, they'd had blue-
gray uniforms with shiny buttons and rings on their sleeves
and Liam had been able to understand them. Then in a
lot of other caverns they had been dressed like that picture
of Daddy downstairs, taken when he had been working in
a place called Korea.

But where was *Santa?*

During the next three hours the search still failed to
reveal his whereabouts. Mub went home for her breakfast
and Loo for her dinner, both with orders to come back
tomorrow night or sooner if Richard called them. Liam
had another two hours before his mother expected him
out of bed. Greg had to break off for dinner

But he was back to searching caverns again within half
an hour, and it was then that Richard noticed something
funny about the reports that were coming back. It was as
if he was seeing the same caverns twice—the same red-
painted cranes, the same groupings of rockets, even the
same guards' faces. The only explanation he could think
of was that caverns were being searched which had been
searched before.

Quickly he told the gang of his suspicions and opened
his mind to receive and relay. This meant that Buster,

Greg and Liam knew everything that was in each other's minds having to do with the search, including the total number of caverns found up to that time together with their identifying characteristics. Knowing this they would no longer be in danger of going over ground already searched by another member of the gang. Richard then told them to go looking for new caverns.

They tried, and couldn't find one.

Altogether they had uncovered forty-seven of them, from *big* underground places with hundreds of rockets in them down to small places with just a few. And now it seemed plain that this was all the caverns there were, and there was *still* no trace of Santa Claus.

"We've missed something, gang," Richard told them worriedly. "You've got to go back to the biggest caverns again and look around some more. This time ask questions—"

"B-but the guards run at you and yell," Greg broke in. "They're not nice men."

"No," Liam joined in, "they're scary."

Buster said, "I'm hungry."

Richard ignored him and said, "Search the big caverns again. Look for important places, places where there are lots of guards. Find the boss and ask *him* questions. And don't forget to say please and thank you. Grown-ups will give you practically anything if you say please. . . ."

For a long time after that nothing happened. Richard kept most of his attention on Buster, because his brother had a tendency to forget what he was looking for if anything interesting turned up. Buster was becoming very hungry and a little bored.

His next contact with Liam showed the other hiding behind a large metal cabinet and looking out at a big room. Three walls of the room were covered from floor to ceiling with other cabinets, some of which made clicking, whirring noises and had colored lights on them. The room was empty now except for a guard at the door, but it had not always been that way. In Liam's mind Richard could see the memory of two men in the room who had talked and then left again before Liam could ask them questions. They had been wearing blue-gray uniforms and one of them had had gold stuff on his cap. Liam had remembered every word they said, even the long ones which he didn't understand.

The cabinets with the flashing lights on them were called a Director-Computer, and it worked out speeds and Tradge Ectories so that every rocket in this cavern, and in about twenty others just like it, would be sent to the spot it was meant to go and hit it right on the button. It would tell hundreds and hundreds of rockets where to go, and it would send them off as soon as there was a blip. Liam didn't know what a blip was, however. Did Richard?

"No," said Richard impatiently. "Why didn't you ask one of the guards?"

Because the man with the gold stuff on his cap had told the guard that the situation was getting worse, that there were reports from all over of bases being Infil Trated, and that some sort of Halloo Sinatory weapon was being used because the guards had insisted that the saboteurs were not adults. He had said trust them to play a dirty trick like this just before Christmas, and he had told the guard to kill any unauthorized personnel trying to enter the computer room on sight. Liam didn't know what an unauthorized personnel was, but he thought it might mean him. And anyway, he was hungry and his mother would be expecting him down from bed soon and he wanted to go home.

"Oh, all right," said Richard.

Maybe it was a sleigh and reindeer he used in Daddy's young days, he thought excitedly, *but* now it is rockets. And computers *to tell them where to go, just like the deputy Santa told us!*

But why were the guards being told to kill people? Even unauthorized personnel—which sounded like a very nasty sort of people, like juvenile delinquents maybe. Who was pulling what dirty trick just before Christmas? And where were the toys? In short, who was lousing up his and everyone else's Christmas?

The answer was becoming clearer in Richard's mind, and it made him feel mad enough to hit somebody. He thought of contacting Greg, then decided that he should try to find out if he could fix things instead of just finding out more about what had gone wrong. So he called up Loo and Mub, linked them to each other through his mind, and spoke:

"Loo, do you know the catapult Greg keeps under his mattress? Can you send it here without having to go to Greg's place to look for it?"

The grubby, well-used weapon was lying on Richard's bed.

"Good," he said. "Now can you send it b—"

The catapult was gone.

Loo wasn't doing anything special just then and wouldn't have minded continuing with the game. But it wasn't a game to Richard, it was a test.

"Mub, can you do the same?"

Mub's Daddy was at work and her mother was baking. Mub was waiting to lick the spoon with the icing sugar on it. A little absently she replied, "Yes, Richard."

"Does it make your heads tired?" he asked anxiously.

Apparently it didn't. The girls explained that it was hard to make people, or pussycats, or goldfish move because live things had minds which kind of pushed back, but dead things didn't have anything to push back with and could be moved easily. Richard told them thanks, broke away, then made contact with Greg.

Through Greg's eyes and mind he saw a large desk and two men in dark green uniforms behind it—one standing behind the other, an older and bigger man who was sitting down. Greg was in a chair beside the desk and only a few feet away from the bigger man.

"Your name is Gregor Ivanovitch Krejinski," said the big man, smiling. He was a nice big man, a little like Greg's Daddy, with dark gray hair and lines at the corners of his eyes. He looked like he was scared of Greg but was trying to be nice anyway. Greg, and through him the watching Richard, wondered why he should be scared.

"And you say your parents have a farm not far from a town," the big man went on gently. "But there are no farms or towns such as you describe within three hundred miles of here. What do you say to that, Little Gregor?

"Now suppose you tell me how you got here, eh?"

That was a difficult question. Greg and the other members of the gang didn't know how they got to places, they just went.

"I just . . . came, sir," said Greg.

The man who was standing lifted his cap and rubbed his forehead, which was sweating. In a low voice he spoke to the big man about other launching bases which had been similarly penetrated. He said that relations with the other side had been almost friendly this past year or so, but it was now obvious that they had been lulled into a sense of false security. In his opinion they were being attacked by a brand new psychological weapon and all firing officers should be ready with their finger on the big red button ready for the first blip. The big man frowned at him and he stopped talking.

"Well, now," the big man resumed to Greg, "if you can't say how you came, can you tell me why, Gregor?"

The big man was sweating now, too.

"To find Santa Claus," said Greg.

The other man began to laugh in a funny way until the big man shushed him and told him to phone the Colonel, and told him what to say. In the big man's opinion the boy himself was not a threat but the circumstances of his appearance here were cause for the gravest concern. He therefore suggested that the base be prepared for a full emergency launch and that the Colonel use his influence to urge that all other bases be similarly prepared. He did not yet know what tactic was being used against them, but he would continue with the interrogation.

"Now, son," he said, returning to Greg, "I can't tell you how to find Santa Claus exactly, but maybe we could do a trade. You tell me what you know and I'll tell you what I know."

Richard thought the big man was very nice and he told

Greg to find out all he could from him, then he broke away. It was time he checked on Buster again.

His brother was just on the point of revealing himself to a man sitting in a small room with lots of colored lights around the walls. There was a big glass screen on one wall with a white line going round and round on it, and the man was bent forward in his chair, holding his knees tightly with his hands. He was chewing.

"Feeties . . . ?" asked Buster hopefully.

The man swung round. One hand went to the gun at his belt and the other shot out to stop with one finger on a big red button on his panel, but he didn't push it. He stared at Buster with his face white and shiny and his mouth open. There was a little piece of chewing gum showing on his teeth.

Buster was disappointed; he had thought the man might have been eating cakes of toffee. Chewing gum wasn't much good when you were *hungry*. Still, maybe if he was polite the man might give him some anyway, and even tell him where Santa Claus was.

"How do'oo doe," he said carefully.

"F-fine thanks," said the man, and shook his head. He took his finger off the big red button and pushed another one. He began talking to somebody:

"Unauthorized person in the Firing . . . No, no, I don't have to push the button . . . I know the orders, dammit, but this is a kid! About three, w-wearing pajamas. . . ."

A few minutes later two men ran in. One was thin and young and he told the man at the panel to keep his blasted eyes on the screen in case there was a blip instead of gawking at the kid. The other one was big and broad and very like the man who had asked Greg questions—except he had on a tie instead of a high, tight collar. The second man looked at Buster for a long time, then got down on one knee.

"What are you doing here, sonny?" he said in a funny voice.

"Looking for Santa," said Buster, looking at the man's pockets. They looked empty, not even a hanky in them.

Then, on Richard's prompting, he added, "What's a . . . a blip?"

The man who was standing began to speak rapidly. He said that this was some sort of diversion, that guards at bases all over had been reporting kids, that the other side was working up to some sort of sneak punch. And just when everybody thought relations were improving, too. Maybe this wasn't a kid, maybe this was a child impersonator . . .

"Impersonating a three-year-old?" asked the big man, straightening up again.

All the talk had not helped Richard much and he was getting impatient. He thought for a minute, then made Buster say, "What's a blip . . . *please!*"

The big man went to the one who was sitting in front of the screen. They whispered together, then he walked toward Buster.

"Maybe we should T-I-E his H-A-N-D-S," said the thin man.

In a quiet voice the big man said, "Contact the General. Tell him that until further notice I consider it advisable that all launching bases be placed in Condition Red. Meanwhile I'll see what I can find out. And call Doc, we might as well check on your child impersonation theory."

He turned away from the now open locker with a candy bar in his hand, stripping off the wrapping as he added, "Don't they teach you psychology these days?" And to Buster he said, "A blip is a teeny white mark on a screen like that man is watching."

Buster's mind was so full of thinking about the candy bar that it was hard for Richard to make him ask the proper questions. *Ask him what* makes *a blip?* he thought furiously at his brother—why were the minds of grown-ups impossible to get into! and eventually he got through.

"A rocket going up," said the big man; then added crossly, "This is ridiculous!"

"What makes a rocket go up?" prompted Richard.

The man who was watching for blips was holding his knees tightly again. Nobody was talking to him but he said, "One way is to push a big red button . . ." His voice sounded very hoarse.

Watching and listening through his brother's mind Richard decided that he had heard and seen enough. For some time he had been worried about the safety of Greg and Liam and Buster—all the talk of shooting, and the way the guards looked so cross at just a few children who weren't doing any harm. Richard had seen people get shot lots of times on television, and while he hadn't thought much about what being dead meant, getting shot had looked like a very sore thing. He didn't want it happening to any of his gang, especially now when he was sure that there was no reason to go on with the search.

Santa had hid out somewhere, and if what Richard suspected was true, he couldn't blame him. *Poor Santa,* he thought

Quickly Richard called off the search. He thought he knew what was going on now, but he wanted to think about it some more before deciding what to do. Almost before he had finished Buster was back in his cot, still working on the candy bar. Richard made his brother give him half of it, then he got into bed himself. But not to sleep.

Mub and Loo had never seen any of the caverns yet so he had to attend to that chore first. Using the data available in the three boys' minds he was able to direct the girls to all forty-seven places with no trouble at all. The girls were seen a couple of times but nothing happened— they were just looking, not asking questions. When he was sure they understood what they had to do Richard let them go home, but told them to start practicing on rocks and things outside his window. After that he lay on his side and looked out at the moonlit desert.

Small rocks and big boulders began to move about. They arranged themselves into circles and squares and stars, or built themselves into cairns. But mostly they just changed places with each other too fast for Richard to see. Fence posts disappeared leaving the wire sagging but unbroken and bushes rose into the air with the ground undisturbed beneath them and every root intact. After an hour of it Richard told them to stop and asked them if they were *sure* it didn't make their heads tired.

They told him no, that moving dead things was easy.

"But you'll have to work awful fast . . ." Richard began.

Apparently it didn't matter. Just so long as they knew where everything was they could move it just like *that*, and Mub sent a thought of her Daddy snapping his fingers. Relieved, Richard told them to put everything out on the desert back the way it had been and to start getting to know the other places he had told them about. They went off joyfully to mix the gang's business with their own pleasure.

Richard became aware of movements downstairs. It was nearly breakfast time.

Since the early hours of the morning Richard had been sure he knew what had gone wrong with the Christmas business, and the steps the gang must take to put matters right again—or as near right as it was possible to put them. It was a terrific responsibility for a six-year-old, and the trouble was that he hadn't heard the grown-ups' side of it. What he intended doing could get him into bad trouble if his Daddy found out—he might even get beaten. Richard's parents had taught him to respect other people's property.

But his Daddy was usually a bit dopey at breakfast time. Maybe he would be able to ask some questions without his Daddy asking too many back.

"Daddy," he said as he was finishing his cereal, "d'you know all those rockets Santa has in his secret caverns at the North Pole? And the stuff in the nose of them that you're not allowed to go near . . . ?"

His Daddy choked and got cross and began talking to his mother. He said that he would never have taken this out-of-the-way job if he hadn't been sure that Richard's mother, being an ex-schoolteacher, could look after the children's education. But it was quite obvious that she was forcing Richard far too much and he was too young to be told about things like rocket bases. To which his mother replied that his Daddy didn't believe her when she told him that Richard could read the *National Geographic*— and not just pretend to read them—and even an odd who- dunit. Sure she had taught him more than a normal six- year-old but that was because he could take it—she wasn't doing a doting mother act, Richard really was an excep- tionally bright boy. And *she* hadn't told him about rocket bases, he must have got it from a magazine or some- thing . . .

And so it went on. Richard sighed, thinking that every time he asked a complicated question his mother and father started arguing about him between themselves and ignoring his question completely.

"Daddy," said Richard during a lull, "they're big peo- ple's toys, aren't they?"

"Yes!" his father snapped. "But the big people don't want to play with them. In fact, we'd be better off without them!" Then he turned and went back to arguing with their mother. Richard excused himself and left, thinking at Buster to follow him as soon as he could.

So the big people didn't want their toys, Richard thought with grim satisfaction. That meant the gang was free to go ahead.

All that day Richard listened in on Loo and Mub. The girls were fast but there was an awful lot to do so he set Greg and Liam to helping them—the boys could move things, too, but not as fast as the girls. But everybody had been awake for so long they began to fall asleep one by one. When it happened to Buster and Richard their mother thought they were taking sick and was worried, but both of them were up as fresh as ever when their father came home so she didn't mention it. And that night there was another meeting of the gang in the bedroom.

"We'll dispense with the Minutes of the last Meeting," Richard began formally, then opened his mind to all of them. Up until then the gang had been acting on orders, although from the things they had been doing they must have guessed what he intended, but now they *knew*. He gave them all the pieces of the puzzle and showed them how it fitted together.

The evasions of their parents, the overflowing toy stores and the computers which could direct a rocket to any spot in the world. A strangely uncomfortable deputy Santa—they must have had some kind of hold over him at the store—and secret caverns guarded by angry soldiers and storekeepers who were robbers. And juvenile delinquents, and a Santa Claus who couldn't be found because he must have run away and hidden himself because he was ashamed to face the children and tell them that all their toys had been stolen.

Obviously the juvenile delinquents had raided Santa's toy caverns and cleaned them out, leaving only big people's toys which the adults themselves no longer wanted—this explained why Santa's guards were so mad at everybody. Then the stolen toys had been sent to the storekeepers, who were probably in cahoots with the delinquents. It was as simple as that. Santa just would not be coming around this Christmas and nobody would get any toys, unless the gang did something about it . . .

". . . We're going to see that the children get *something*," Richard went on grimly. "But none of us is going to get what he asked for. There is no way of telling which one of all those hundreds of rockets is meant for any one of us. So we'll just have to take what comes. The only good thing is that we're going to make Christmas come three days early.

"All right, gang, let's get started."

Buster returned to the room where he had been given candy the night before, the room with the man who watched a screen with a white line going round on it. But he stayed hidden this time—he was merely acting as the gang's eyes. Then Mub and Loo, linked to the distant room through Buster's and Richard's minds, began to move the grown-up who sat before the screen. More precisely, they moved his hand and arm in the direction of the big red button.

But the grown-up didn't want to push the button and

make blips. He struggled to pull back his hand so hard that Loo complained that it was hurting her head. Then they all got together—Liam, Greg, Buster and the girls—and concentrated. The man's finger started moving toward the button again and he began to shout to somebody on the radio. Then he drew his gun with the other hand and hit his arm with it, knocking it away from the button. He was being very, very naughty.

"Why don't we push the button," Greg asked suddenly, "instead of making the grown-up push it?"

Richard felt his face going red, *he* should have thought of that. Within a second the big red button drove down into the bottom of its socket.

The Early Warning systems were efficient on both sides. Within three minutes all forty-seven missile bases had launched or were launching their rockets. It was an automatic process, there were no last-minute checks, the missiles being maintained in constant readiness. In those same three minutes orders went out to missile-carrying submarines to take up previously assigned positions off enemy coasts, and giant bombers screamed away from airfields which expected total annihilation before the last one was off. Like two vast, opposing shoals of fish the missiles slid spaceward, their numbers thinned—but only slightly—by the suicidal frenzy of the anti-missiles. The shoals dispersed and curved groundward again, dead on course, to strike dead on target. The casualty and damage reports began coming in.

Seventeen people injured by falling plaster or masonry; impact craters twenty feet across in the middle of city streets; tens of thousands of dollars and pounds and rubles worth of damage. It was not long before urgent messages were going out to recall the subs and bombers. Before anything else was tried the authorities had to know why every missile that had been sent against the enemy, and every missile that the enemy had sent against them, had failed to explode.

They also wanted to know who or what had been making rocket base personnel on both sides do and see things which they didn't want to. And why an examination of the dud missiles revealed the shattered and fused remains of train sets and toy six-shooters, and if this could have any possible connection with the robberies of large toy stores in such widely separate places as Salt Lake City, Irkutsk, Londonderry and Tokyo. Tentatively at first both sides came together to compare notes, their intense curiosity to know what the blazes had *happened* being one thing they had in common. Later, of course, they discovered other things . . .

That year Christmas came with the beginnings of a lasting peace on Earth, although six members of a young and very talented gang did not appreciate this. The toys which they had put in the noses of the rockets to replace the sparkly stuff—which they had dumped in the ocean because the grown-ups didn't want it—had failed to reach them. They had been worrying in case they had done something very wrong or been very bad. They couldn't have been *very* bad, however, because Santa came just as they had been told he would, on a sleigh with reindeer.

They were asleep at the time, though, and didn't see it.

A MIRACLE OF RARE DEVICE

by Ray Bradbury

from *Playboy*

As yet, no one has quite defined the kind of force inherent in the mind of man or measured its extent. The borderlines between wish, dream, thought and (presumed) reality appear to be so fluid that the very pressure of attention focused on them is enough to shift their courses. Yet these varieties of experience are stable by comparison with the *enabling* qualities: concepts like "will power," "suggestibility," "self-confidence," "creativity," even "aptitude" or "intelligence."

That these interior energizers do exist in differing degree in different persons is apparent. For some of them, we have rough indirect measurement techniques (measuring not the quality itself, but its effects); and we have recently acquired a considerable catalogue of "engineering" techniques for the suppression, stimulation or manipulation of these forces. But as to *what* they are, or *how* they work . . . ?

On a day neither too mellow nor too tart, too hot nor too cold, the ancient tin lizzie came over the desert hill traveling at commotion speed. The vibration of the various armored parts of the car caused road-runners to spurt up in floury bursts of dust. Gila monsters, lazy displays of Indian jewelry, took themselves out of the way. Like an infestation, the Ford clamored and dinned away into the deeps of the wilderness.

In the front seat, squinting back, Old Will Bantlin shouted, "Turn off!"

Bob Greenhill spun-swung the lizzie off behind a billboard. Instantly, both men turned. Both peered over the crumpled top of their car, praying to the dust they had wheeled up on the air.

"Lay down! Lay low! Please . . ."

And the dust blew slowly down.

Just in time.

"Duck!"

A motorcycle, looking as if it had burnt through all nine rings of Hell, thundered by. Hunched over its oily handle bars, a hurricane figure, a man with a creased and most unpleasant face, goggled and sun-deviled, leaned on the wind. Roaring bike and man flung away down the road.

The two old men sat up in their lizzie, exhaling.

"So long, Ned Hopper," said Bob Greenhill.

"Why?" said Will Bantlin, "why's he always tailing us?"

"Willy-William, talk sense," said Greenhill. "We're his luck, his Judas goats. Why should he let us go, when trailing us around the land makes him rich and happy and us poor and wise?"

The two men looked at each other, half-in, half-out of their smiles. What the world hadn't done to them, thinking about it had. They had enjoyed thirty years of nonviolence together, in their case meaning nonwork. "I feel a harvest coming on," Will would say, and they'd clear out of town before the wheat ripened. Or, "Those apples are ready to fall!" So they'd stand back about three hundred miles so as not to get hit on the head.

Now Bob Greenhill slowly let the car, in a magnificent controlled avalanche, drift back out on the road.

"Willy, friend, don't be discouraged."

"I've been through 'discouraged,' " said Will. "I'm knee-deep in 'accepting.' "

"Accepting what?"

"Finding a treasure chest of canned beans one day and no can opener. Finding a thousand can openers next day and no beans."

Bob Greenhill listened to the motor talking to itself like an old man under the hood, sounding like sleepless nights and rusty bones and well-worn dreams.

"Our bad luck can't last forever, Willy."

"No, but it sure tries. You and me sell ties and who's across the street ten cents cheaper?"

"Ned Hopper."

"We strike gold in Tonopah and who registers the claim first?"

"Old Ned."

"Haven't we done him a lifetime of favors? Aren't we overdue for something just ours, that never winds up his?"

"Time's ripe, Willy," said Robert, driving calmly. "Trouble is, you, me, Ned never really decided what we wanted. We've run through all the ghost towns, see something, grab. Ned sees and grabs, too. He don't want it, he just wants it because *we* want it. He keeps it till we're out of sight, then tears it up and hang-dogs after us for more litter. The day we really know what we want is the day Ned gets scared of us and runs off forever. Ah, hell." Bob Greenhill breathed the clear fresh-water air running in morning streams over the windshield. "It's good anyway. That sky. Those hills. The desert and—"

His voice faded.

Will Bantlin glanced over. "What's wrong?"

"For some reason . . ." Bob Greenhill's eyes rolled, his leathery hands turned the wheel slow, ". . . we got to . . . pull off . . . the road . . ."

The lizzie bumped on the dirt shoulder. They drove down in a dusty wash and up out and suddenly along a dry peninsula of land overlooking the desert. Bob Greenhill, looking hypnotized, put out his hand to turn the ignition key. The old man under the hood stopped complaining about insomnia and slept.

"Now, why did you do *that?!*" asked Will Bantlin.

Bob Greenhill gazed at the wheel in his suddenly intuitive hands. "Seemed as if I had to. Why?" He blinked up. He let his bones settle and his eyes grow lazy. "Maybe only to look at the land out there. Good. All of it been here a billion years."

"Except for that city," said Will Bantlin.

"City?" said Bob.

He turned to look and the desert was there and the distant hills the color of lions and far out beyond, suspended in a sea of warm morning sand and light, was a kind of floating image, a hasty sketch of a city.

"That can't be Phoenix," said Bob Greenhill. "Phoenix is ninety miles off. No other big place around . . ."

Will Bantlin rumpled the map on his knees, searching. "No . . . no other town."

"It's coming clearer!" cried Bob Greenhill, suddenly.

They both stood absolutely straight up in the car and stared over the dusty windshield, the wind whining softly over their craggy faces.

"Why, you know what that is, Bob? A mirage! Sure, that's it! Light rays just right, atmosphere, sky, temperature. City's the other side of the horizon somewhere. Look how it jumps, fades in and out. It's reflected against that sky up there like a mirror and comes down here where we can see it! A mirage, by gosh!"

"That *big?*"

Will Bantlin measured the city as it grew taller, clearer in a shift of wind, a soft far whirlabout of sand.

"The granddaddy of them all! That's not Phoenix. Not Santa Fe or Alamogordo, no. Let's see. It's not Kansas City—"

"That's too far off, anyway—"

"Yeah, but look at those buildings. Big! Tallest in the world. Only one place like that in the world."

"You don't mean—New York?"

Will Bantlin nodded slowly and they both stood in the silence looking out at the mirage. And the city was tall and shining now and almost perfect, in the early morning light.

"Oh, my," said Bob, after a long while. "That's fine."

"It is," said Will.

"But," said Will, a moment later, whispering, as if afraid the city might hear, "what's it doing three thousand miles from home, here in the middle of Nowhere, Arizona?"

Bob Greenhill gazed and spoke. "Willy, friend, never question nature. It just sits there and minds its knitting. Radio waves, rainbows, northern lights, all that, heck, let's just say a great big picture got took of New York City and is being developed here, three thousand miles away on a morn when we need cheering, just for us."

"Not just us." Will peered over the side of the car. "Look!"

There in the floury dust lay cross-hatchings, diagonals, fascinating symbols printed out in a quiet river of traveling.

"Tire marks," said Bob Greenhill. "Lots of cars pulled off here."

"For what, Bob?" Will Bantlin leaped from the car, landed on the earth, tromped it, turned on it, knelt to touch it with a swiftly and suddenly trembling hand. "For what, for what? To see the mirage? Yes, sir! To see the mirage!"

"So?"

"Boy Howdy!" Will stood up, thrummed his voice like a motor. "Brrrummm!" He turned an imaginary wheel. He ran along a tire track. "Brrrummm! Eeeee! Brakes on! Robert-Bob, you know what we *got* here?! Look East! Look West! This is the only point in miles you can pull off the highway and sit and stare your eyes out!"

"Sure, it's nice people have an eye for beauty—"

"Beauty, my socks! Who *owns* this land?"

"The state, I reckon . . ."

"You reckon wrong! You and me! We set up camp, register a claim, improve the property and the law reads it's *ours* . . . right?"

"Hold on!" Bob Greenhill was staring out at the desert, and the strange city there. "You mean you want to . . . *homestead a mirage?!*"

"Right, by zingo! Homestead a mirage!"

Robert Greenhill stepped down and wandered around the car looking at the tire-treaded earth.

"Can we *do* that?"

"*Do* it? Excuse my dust!"

In an instant, Will Bantlin was pounding tent pegs in the soil, stringing twine.

"From here to here, and here to here, it's a gold mine, we pan it; it's a cow, we milk it; it's a lakeful of money, we swim in it!"

Rummaging in the car, he heaved out cases and brought forth a large cardboard which had once advertised cheap cravats. This, reversed, he painted over with a brush and began lettering.

"Willy," said his friend, "nobody's going to pay to see any darned old—"

"Mirage? Put up a fence, tell folks they can't see a thing, and that's just their itch. There!"

He held up the sign.

> SECRET VIEW MIRAGE.
> THE MYSTERIOUS CITY.
> *25¢ per car. Motor bikes a dime.*

"Here comes a car. Watch!"

"William—"

But Will, running, lifted the sign.

"Hey! Look! Hey!"

The car roared past, a bull ignoring the matador.

Bob shut his eyes so as not to see Will's smile wiped away.

But then—a marvelous sound.

The squeal of brakes.

The car was backing up! Will was leaping forward, waving, pointing.

"Yes, sir! Yes, ma'am! Secret View Mirage! The Mysterious City! Drive right in!"

The tread marks in the simple dirt became numerous, and then, quite suddenly, innumerable.

A great boll of heat-wafted dust hung over the dry peninsula where in a vast sound of arrivals, with braked wheels, slammed doors, stilled engines, the cars of many kinds from many places came and took their places in a line. And the people in the cars were as different as people can be who come from four directions but are drawn in a single moment by a single thing, all talking at first, but growing still at last at what they saw out in the desert. The wind blew softly about their faces, fluttering the hair of the women, the open shirt collars of the men. They sat in their cars for a long time, or they stood on the rim of the earth, saying nothing, and at last one by one turned to go.

As the first car drove back out past Bob and Will, the woman in it nodded happily.

"Thanks! Why, it *is* just like Rome!"

"Did she say 'Rome' or 'home'?" asked Will.

Another car wheeled toward the exit.

"Yes, sir!" The driver reached out to shake Bob's hand. "Just looking made me feel I could speak French!"

"French!?" cried Bob.

Both stepped forward swiftly as the third car made to leave. An old man sat at the wheel, shaking his head.

"Never seen the like. I mean to say, fog and all, Westminster Bridge, better than a postcard, and Big Ben off there in the distance. How do you *do* it? God bless. Much obliged."

Both men, disquieted, let the old man drive away, then slowly wheeled to look out along their small thrust of land toward the growing simmer of noon.

"Big Ben?" said Will Bantlin. "Westminster Bridge? Fog?"

Faintly, faintly, they thought they heard, they could not be sure, they cupped their ears, wasn't that a vast clock striking three times off there beyond land's rim? Weren't foghorns calling after boats and boat horns calling back on some lost river?

"Almost speak French?" whispered Robert. "Big Ben? Home? Rome? *Is* that Rome out there, Will?"

The wind shifted. A broiling surge of warm air tumbled up plucking changes on an invisible harp. The fog almost solidified into gray stone monuments. The sun almost built a golden statue on top of a breasted mount of fresh-cut snow marble.

"How—" said William Bantlin, "how could it change? How could it be four, five cities? Did we *tell* anyone what city they'd see? No. Well, then, Bob, *well!*"

Now they fixed their gaze on their last customer who stood alone at the rim of the dry peninsula. Gesturing his friend to silence, Robert moved silently to stand to one side and behind their paying visitor.

He was a man in his late forties with a vital, sunburned face, good, warm, clear-water eyes, fine cheekbones, a receptive mouth. He looked as if he had traveled a long way around in his life, over many deserts, in search of a particular oasis. He resembled those architects found wandering the rubbled streets below their buildings as the iron, steel and glass go soaring high to block out, fill an empty piece of sky. His face was that of such builders who suddenly see reared up before them on the instant, from horizon to horizon, the perfect implementation of an old, old dream. Now, only half-aware of William and Robert beside him, the stranger spoke at last in a quiet, an easy, a wondrous voice, saying what he saw, telling what he felt:

". . . *In Xanadu . . .*"

"What?" asked William.

The stranger half-smiled, kept his eyes on the mirage, and quietly, from memory, recited.

"In Xanadu did Kubla Khan
A stately pleasure-dome decree:
Where Alph, the sacred river, ran
Through caverns measureless to man
Down to a sunless sea . . ."

His voice spelled the weather and the weather blew about the other two men and made them more still.

"So twice five miles of fertile ground
With walls and towers were girdled round . . .
And there were gardens bright with sinuous rills,
Where blossomed many an incense-bearing tree;
And here were forests ancient as the hills,
Enfolding sunny spots of greenery . . ."

William and Robert looked off at the mirage and what the stranger said was there, in the golden dust, some fabled Middle East or Far East clustering of minarets, domes, frail towers risen up in a magnificent sift of pollen from the Gobi, a spread of river stone baked bright by the fertile Euphrates, Palmyra not yet ruins, only just begun, newly minted, then abandoned by the departing years, now shimmered by heat, now threatening to blow away forever.

The stranger, his face transformed, beatified by his vision, finished it out:

> *"It was a miracle of rare device,*
> *A sunny pleasure-dome with caves of ice . . ."*

And the stranger grew silent.

Which made the silence in Bob and Will all the deeper.

The stranger fumbled with his wallet, his eyes wet.

"Thank you, thank you."

"You already paid us," said William.

"If I had more, you'd get it all."

He gripped William's hand, left a five-dollar bill in it, got in his car, looked for a last time out at the mirage, then sat down, started the car, idled it with wonderful ease, and, face glowing, eyes peaceful, drove away.

Robert walked a few steps after the car, stunned.

Then William suddenly exploded, flung his arms up, whooped, kicked his feet, wheeled around.

"Hallelujah! Fat of the land! Full dinner pails! New squeaky shoes! Look at my fistfuls!"

But Robert said, "I don't think we should take it."

William stopped dancing. "What?"

Robert looked steadily at the desert.

"We can't ever really own it. It's way out there. Sure, we can homestead the land, but . . . We don't even know what *that* thing is."

"Why, it's New York and—"

"Ever *been* to New York?"

"Always wanted. Never did."

"Always wanted, never did." Robert nodded slowly. "Same as them. You heard: Paris. Rome. London. And this last man. Xanadu. Willy, Willy, we've got hold of something strange and big here. I'm scared we won't do right by it."

"Well, we're not keeping anyone out, are we?"

"Who knows? Might be a quarter's too much for some. It don't seem right, a natural thing handled by unnatural rules. Look and tell me I'm wrong."

William looked.

And the city was there like the first city he had seen as a boy when his mother took him on a train across a long meadow of grass early one morning and the city rose up head by head, tower by tower to look at him, to watch him coming near. It was that fresh, that new, that old, that frightening, that wonderful.

"I think," said Robert, "we should take just enough to buy gas for a week, put the rest of the money in the first poor box we come to. That mirage is a clear river running, and people coming by thirsty. If we're wise, we dip one cup, drink it cool in the heat of the day and go. If we stop, build dams, try to own the whole river . . ."

William, peering out through the whispering dust wind, tried to relax, accept.

"If you say so."

"I don't. The wilderness all around says."

"Well, I say *different!*"

Both men jumped and spun about.

Half up the slope stood a motorcycle. Sitting it, rainbowed with oil, eyes goggled, grease masking his stubbly cheeks, was a man of familiar arrogance and free-running contempt.

"Ned Hopper!"

Ned Hopper smiled his most evilly benevolent smile, unbraked the cycle and glided the rest of the way down to halt by his old friends.

"You—" said Robert.

"Me! Me! Me!" Ned Hopper honked his cycle horn three times, laughing loud, head back. "Me!"

"Shut up!" cried Robert. "Bust it like a mirror."

"Bust *what* like a mirror?"

William, catching Robert's concern, glanced apprehensively out beyond at the desert.

The mirage flurried, trembled, misted away, then hung itself like a tapestry once more, on the air.

"Nothing out there! What you guys up to?" Ned peered down at the tread-marked earth. "I was twenty miles on, today, when I realized you boys was hiding back behind. Says to myself, that ain't like my buddies who led me to that gold mine in '47, lent me this cycle with a dice roll in '55. All those years we help each other and now you got secrets from friend Ned. So I come back. Been up on that hill half the day, spying." Ned lifted binoculars from his greasy jacket front. "You know I can read lips? Sure! Saw all the cars zip in here, the cash. Quite a show you're running!"

"Keep your voice down," warned Robert. "So long."

Ned smiled sweetly. "Sorry to see you go. But I surely respect your getting off my property."

"Yours!" Robert and William cried, caught themselves, and said, in a trembling whisper, "yours?"

Ned laughed. "When I saw what you was up to, I just cycled into Phoenix. See this little-bitty Government paper sticking out my back pocket?"

The paper was there, neatly folded.

William put out his hand.

"Don't give him the pleasure," said Robert.

William pulled his hand back. "You want us to believe you filed a homestead claim?"

Ned shut up the smile inside his eyes. "I do. I don't. Even if I was lying, I could still make Phoenix on my bike quicker'n your jalopy." Ned surveyed the land with his binoculars. "So just put down all the money you earned from two this afternoon, when I filed my claim, from which time on you was trespassing my land."

Robert flung the coins in the dust. Ned Hopper glanced casually at the bright litter.

"The U.S. Government Mint! Hot dog, nothing out there, but dumb bunnies willing to pay for it!"

Robert turned slowly to look at the desert.

"You don't see anything?"

Ned snorted. "Nothing and you know it!"

"But we do!" cried William. "We—"

"Will," said Robert.

"But, Bob!"

"Nothing out there. Like he said." Bob winked.

More cars were driving up now in a great thrum of engines.

"Excuse, gents, got to mind the box office!" Ned strode off, waving. "Yes, sir, ma'am! This way! Cash in advance!"

"Why?" William watched Ned Hopper run off, yelling. "Why are we letting him do this?"

"Wait," said Robert, almost serenely. "You'll see."

They got out of the way as a Ford, a Buick and an ancient Moon motored in.

Twilight. On a hill about two hundred yards above the Mysterious City Mirage viewpoint, William Bantlin and Robert Greenhill fried and picked at a small supper, hardly bacon, mostly beans. From time to time, Robert used some battered opera glasses on the scene below.

William stared at a single bean on the end of his fork. "Tell me again: why? Why every time our luck is good, Ned Hopper jumps out of the earth?"

Robert sighed on the opera-glass lenses and wiped them on his cuff. "Because, friend Will, we are the pure in heart. We shine with a light. And the villains of the world they see that light beyond the hills and say, 'Why, now, there's some innocent, some sweet all-day sucker.' And the villains come to warm their hands at us. I don't know what we can do about it, except maybe put out the light."

"I wouldn't want to do that." William brooded gently, his palms to the fire. "It's just, I was hoping this time was comeuppance time. A man like Ned Hopper, living his white underbelly life, ain't he about due for a bolt of lightning?"

"Due?" Robert screwed the opera glasses tighter into his eyes. "Why, it just struck! Oh, ye of little faith!" William jumped up beside him. They shared the glasses, one lens each, peering down. "Look!"

And William, looking, cried:

"Peduncle Q. Mackinaw!"

"Also: Gullable M. Crackers!"

For far below, Ned Hopper was stomping around outside a car. People gesticulated at him. He handed them some money. The car drove off. Faintly, you could hear Ned's anguished cries.

William gasped. "He's giving money back! Now he almost hit that man there. The man shook his fist at him! Ned's paid him back, too! Look—more fond farewells!"

"Yah-hee!" whooped Robert, happy with his half of the glasses.

Below, all the cars were dusting away now. Old Ned did a violent kicking dance, threw his goggles in the dust, tore down the sign, let forth a terrible oath.

"Dear me," mused Robert. "I'm glad I can't hear them words. Come on, Willy!"

As William Bantlin and Robert Greenhill drove back up to the Mysterious City turnoff, Ned Hopper rocketed out in a screaming fury. Braying, roaring on his cycle, he hurled the painted cardboard through the air. The sign whistled up, a boomerang. It hissed, narrowly missing Bob. Long after Ned was gone in his banging thunder, the sign sank down and lay on the earth where William picked it up and brushed it off.

It was twilight indeed now and the sun touching the far hills and the land quiet and hushed and Ned Hopper gone away, and the two men alone in the abandoned territory in the thousand-treaded dust, looking out at the sand and the strange air.

"Oh, no . . ." said William.

"I'm afraid . . . yes," said Robert.

The desert was empty in the pink gold light of the setting sun. The mirage was gone. A few dust devils whirled and fell apart, way out on the horizon, but that was all.

William let out a huge groan of bereavement.

"*He* did it! Ned! Ned Hopper, come back, you! Oh, dammit, Ned, you spoiled it all! Blast you to Perdition!"

He stopped. "Bob, how can you *stand* there!?"

Robert smiled sadly. "Right now, I'm feeling sorry for

Ned Hopper."

"Sorry!"

"He never saw what we saw. He never saw what any-body saw. He never believed for one second. And you know what? Disbelief is catching. It rubs off on people."

William searched the disinhabited land.

"It *that* what happened?"

"Who knows?" Robert shook his head. "One thing sure: when folks drove in here, the city, the cities, the mirage, whatever, was there. But it's awful hard to see when people stand in your way. Without so much as moving, Ned Hopper put his big hand across the sun. First thing you know, theater's closed for good."

"Can't we—" William hesitated, "can't we open it up again? How? How do you bring a thing like that back?"

They let their eyes play over the sand, the hills, the few lone clouds, the sky emptied of wind and very still.

"Maybe if we just look out the sides of our eyes, not di-rect at it, relax, take it easy . . ."

They both looked down at their shoes, their hands, the rocks at their feet, anything. But at last William mourned. *"Are* we? Are we the pure in heart?"

Robert laughed just a little bit.

"Oh, not like the kids who came through here today, and saw anything they wanted to see, and not like the big simple people born in the wheat fields and by God's grace wander-ing the world and who will never grow up. We're neither the little children nor the big children of the world, Willy, but we are one thing: glad to be alive. We know the air mornings on the road, how the stars go up and then down the sky. Old Ned, he stopped being glad a long time ago. I hate to think of him driving his cycle on the road the rest of the night, the rest of the year . . ."

As he finished this, Robert noticed that William was slid-ing his eyes carefully to one side, toward the desert.

Robert whispered, carefully, *"See* anything . . . ?"

William sighed. "No. Maybe . . . tomorrow . . ."

A single car came down the highway.

The two men glanced at each other. A wild look of hope

flashed in their eyes. But they could not quite bring themselves to fling up their hands and yell. They simply stood
with the painted sign held in their arms.

The car roared by.

The two men followed it with their wishful eyes.

The car braked. It backed up. In it were a man, a woman,
a boy, a girl. The man called out:

"You closed for the night?!"

William said, "It's no use——"

Robert cut in. "He means, 'No use giving us money!'
Last customer of the day, and family. Free! On the house!"

"Thank you, neighbor, thank you!"

The car roared out onto the viewpoint.

William seized Robert's elbow. "Bob, what ails you? Dis-
appoint those kids, that nice family?"

"Hush up," said Robert, gently. "Come on."

The kids piled out of the car. The man and his wife
climbed slowly out into the sunset. The sky was all gold and
blue now, and a bird sang somewhere in the fields of sand.

"Watch," said Robert.

And they moved up to stand behind the family where it
lined up now to look out over the desert.

William held his breath.

The man and wife squinted into the twilight, uneasily.

The kids said nothing. Their eyes flexed and filled with a
distillation of late sunlight.

William cleared his throat. "It's late. Uh—can't see too
well——"

The man was going to reply, when the boy said, "Oh,
we can see—fine!"

"Sure!" The girl pointed. "There!"

The mother and father followed her gesture, as if it
might help, and it did.

"Lord," said the woman, "for a moment I thought—but
now—yes—there it is!"

The man read his wife's face, saw a thing there, borrowed
it, and placed it on the land and in the air.

"Yes," he said, at last. "Oh, yes."

William stared at them, the desert, and then at Robert,

who smiled and nodded.

The faces of the father, the mother, the daughter, the son were glowing now, looking off at the desert.

"Oh," murmured the girl, "is it *really* there?"

And the father nodded, his face bright with what he saw that was just within seeing and just beyond knowing. He spoke as if he stood alone in a great forest church.

"Yes. And, Lord . . . it's beautiful."

William started to lift his head, but Robert whispered, "Easy. It's coming. Don't try. Easy, Will."

And then William knew what to do.

"I," he said, "I'm going to stand with the kids."

And he walked slowly over and stood right behind the boy and the girl. He stood for a long time there, like a man between two warm fires on a cool evening, and they warmed him and he breathed soft and at last let his eyes drift up, let his attention wander easy out toward the twilight desert and the hoped-for city in the dusk.

And there in the dust softly blown high from the land, reassembled on the wind into half-shapes of towers and spires, and minarets, was the mirage.

He felt Robert's breath on his neck, close, whispering, half-talking to himself.

"It was . . . a miracle of rare device . . .
A sunny pleasure-dome with caves of ice . . ."

And the city was there.

And the sun set and the first stars came out.

And the city was very clear, as William heard himself repeat, aloud or perhaps for only his secret pleasure:

"It was a miracle of rare device . . ."

And they stood in the dark until they could not see.

ALL THE SOUNDS OF FEAR

by Harlan Ellison

from *Saint Mystery Magazine*

If the distinction between (some kinds of) "fantasy" and "science fiction" is often elusive, this is in part because of the peculiar function of speculative fiction in general.

S-f, by definition, operates just outside the border of "known" facts. It is most valid and usually most successful when it conducts its explorations in those same areas where advance outposts of scientific research are being established. The proper-science encampment, burdened of necessity with all the heavy equipment of experimental evidence and scholastic proof (not to mention the weight of reputation and respectability), is obviously less mobile than the lone-wolf writer-philosopher, who carries no more baggage than his own perceptions, logic, intuition and imagination. In turn, the usefulness of the scout's early reports will depend as much on the light supplied him by the scattered outposts, as on his own personal equipment. And the farther out he wanders, the more likely will his message be no more than a report of a new wonder glimpsed. This we call fantasy.

"Give me some light!"

Cry: tormented, half-moan half-chant, cast out against a whispering darkness; a man wound in white, arms upflung to roistering shadows, sooty sockets where eyes had been, pleading, demanding, anger and hopelessness, anguish from the soul into the world. He stumbled, a step, two, faltering, weak, the man returned to the child, trying to find some exit from the washing sea of darkness in which he trembled.

"Give me some light!"

Around him a Greek chorus of sussurating voices; plucking at his garments he staggered toward an intimation of sound, a resting place, a goal. The man in pain, the figure of *all* pain, all desperation, and nowhere in that circle of painful light was there release from this torment. Sandaled feet stepping, each one above an abyss, no hope and no safety; what can it mean to be so eternally blind?

Again, "Give me some light!"

The last tortured ripping of the words from a throat raw with the hopelessness of salvation. Then the man sank to the shadows that moved in on him. The face half-hidden in chiaroscuro, sharp black, blanched white, down and down into the grayness about his feet, the circle of blazing white light pinpointing him, a creature impaled on a pin of brilliance, till closing, closing, closing it swallowed him, all gone to black, darkness within and without, black even deeper, nothing, finis, end, silence.

Richard Becker, Oedipus, had played his first role. Twenty-four years later, he would play it again, as his last. But before that final performance's curtain could be rung, twenty-four years of greatness would have to strut across stages of life and theater and emotion.

Time, passing.

When they had decided to cast the paranoid beggar in *Sweet Miracles*, Richard Becker had gone to the Salvation Army retail store, and bought a set of rags that even the sanctimonious saleswomen staffing the shop tried to throw out as unsalable and foul. He bought a pair of cracked and soleless shoes that were a size too large. He bought a hat that had seen so many autumns of rain its brim had bowed and withered under the onslaught. He bought a no-color vest from a suit long since destroyed, and a pair of pants whose seat sagged raggedly, and a shirt with three buttons gone, and a jacket that seemed to typify every derelict who had ever cadged an hour's sleep in an alley.

He bought these things over the protest of the kindly, white-haired women who were *doing their bit for charity*, and he asked if he might step into the toilet for a few moments to try them on; and when he emerged, his good tweed jacket and dark slacks over his arm, he was another man entirely. As though magically, the coarse stubble (that may have been there when he came into the store, but he seemed too nice-looking a young man to go around unshaved) had sprouted on his sagging jowls. The hair had grown limp and off-gray under the squashed hat. The face was lined and planed with the depravities and deprivations of a lifetime lived in gutters and saloons. The hands were caked with filth, the eyes lusterless and devoid of personality, the body grotesquely slumped by the burden of mere existence. This old man, this skid from the Bowery, how had he gotten into the toilet, and where was the nice young man who had gone in wearing that jacket and those slacks? Had this *creature* somehow overpowered him (what foul weapon had this feeble old man used to subdue a vital, strong youth like that)? The white-haired Good Women of Charity were frozen with distress as they imagined the strong-faced, attractive youth, lying in the bathroom, his skull crushed by a length of pipe.

The old bum extended the jacket, the pants, and the rest of the clothing the young man had been wearing, and in a voice that was thirty years younger than the body from which it spoke, he explained, "I won't be needing these, ladies. Sell them to someone who can make good use of them." The voice of the young man, from this husk.

And he paid for the rags he wore. They watched him as he limped and rolled through the front door, into the filthy streets, another tramp gone to join the tide of lost souls that would inevitably become a stream and a river and an ocean of wastrels, washing finally into a drunk tank, or a doorway, or a park bench.

Richard Becker spent six weeks living on the Bowery; in fleabags, abandoned warehouses, cellars, gutters and on tenement roof-tops, he shared and wallowed in the nature and filth and degradation of the empty men of his times.

For six weeks he *was* a tramp, a thoroughly washed-out hopeless rumdum, with rheumy eyes and palsied wrists and a weak bladder.

One by one the weeks mounted to six, and on the first day of casting for *Sweet Miracles,* the Monday of the seventh week, Richard Becker arrived at the Martin Theater, where he auditioned for the part in the clothes he had worn for the past six weeks.

The play ran for five hundred and eighteen performances, and Richard Becker won the Drama Critics' Circle Award as the finest male performer of the year. He also won the Circle Award as the most promising newcomer of the year.

He was twenty-two years old at the time.

The following season, after *Sweet Miracles* had gone on the road, Richard Becker was apprised, through the pages of *Variety*, that John Foresman and T. H. Searle were about to begin casting for *House of Infidels,* the new script by Odets, his first in many years. Through friends in the Foresman and Searle offices, he obtained a copy of the script, and selected a part he considered massive in its potentialities.

The role of an introspective and tormented artist, depressed by the level of commercialism to which his work had sunk, resolved to regain an innocence of childhood or nature he had lost, by working with his hands in a foundry.

When the first night critics called Richard Becker's conception of Tresk, the artist, "a pinnacle of thespic intuition" and noted, "His authority in the part led members of the audience to ask one another how such a sensitive actor could grasp the rough unsubtle life of a foundryworker," they had no idea that Richard Becker had worked for nearly two months in a steel stamping plant and foundry in Pittsburgh. But the make-up man on *House of Infidels* suspected Richard Becker had once been in a terrible fire, for his hands were marked by the ravages of great heat.

After two successes, two conquests of Broadway, two characterizations that were immediately ranked with the most brilliant Shubert Alley had ever witnessed, Richard Becker's reputation began to build a legend.

"The Man Who *Is* 'The Method,'" they called him, in perceptive articles and interviews. Lee Strasberg of the

Actors Studio, when questioned, remarked that Becker had never been a student, but had the occasion arisen, he might well have paid *him* to attend. In any event, Richard Becker's command of the Stanislavski theory of total immersion in a part became a working example of the validity of the concept. No mere scratcher and stammerer, Richard Becker *was* the man he pretended to be, on a stage.

Of his private life little was known, for he let it be known that if he was to be totally convincing in a characterization, he wanted no intrusive shadow of himself to stand between the audience and the image he offered.

Hollywood's offers of stardom were refused, for as *Theatre Arts* commented in a brief feature on Richard Becker:

"The gestalt that Becker projects across a row of footlights would be dimmed and turned two-dimensional on the Hollywood screen. Becker's art is an ultimate distillation of truth and metamorphosis that requires the reality of stage production to retain its purity. It might even be noted that Richard Becker acts in *four* dimensions, as opposed to the merely craftsmanlike three of his contemporaries. Surely no one could truly argue with the fact that watching a Becker performance is almost a religious experience. We can only congratulate Richard Becker on his perceptiveness in turning down studio bids.

The years of building a backlog of definite parts (effectively ruining them for other actors who were condemned to play them after Becker had said all there was to say) passed, as Richard Becker became, in turn, a Hamlet that cast new lights on the Freudian implications of Shakespeare . . . a fiery Southern segregationist whose wife reveals her octaroon background . . . a fast-talking salesman come to grips with futility and cowardice . . . a many-faceted Marco Polo . . . a dissolute and totally amoral pimp, driven by a loathing for women, to sell his own sister into evil . . . a ruthless politician, dying of cancer and senility. . . .

And the most challenging part he had ever undertaken, the re-creation, in the play by Tennessee Williams, of the deranged religious zealot, trapped by his own warring emotions, into the hammer-murder of an innocent girl.

When they found him, in the model's apartment off Gramercy Place, they were unable to get a coherent story of why he had done the disgusting act, for he had lapsed into a stentorian tone of Biblical fervor, pontificating about the blood of the lamb and the curse of Jezebel and the eternal fires of Perdition. The men from Homicide numbered among their ranks a rookie, fresh to the squad, who became desperately ill at the sight of the fouled walls and the crumpled form wedged into the tiny kitchenette; he became violently ill, and was taken from the apartment a few minutes before Richard Becker was led away.

The trial was a manifest sadness to all who had seen him onstage, and the jury did not even have to be sent out to agree on a verdict of insanity.

After all, whoever the fanatic was that the defense put on the stands, he was not sane, and was certainly no longer Richard Becker, the actor.

For Dr. Charles Tedrow, the patient in restraining room 16 was a constant involvement. He was unable to divorce himself from the memory of a night three years before, when he had sat in an orchestra seat at the Henry Miller Theater, and seen Richard Becker, light and adroit, as the comical Tosspot in that season's hit comedy, *Never a Rascal*.

He was unable to separate his thoughts from the shape and form of the actor who had so immersed himself in The Method that for a time, in three acts, he *was* a blundering, maundering, larcenous alcoholic with a penchant for pomegranates and (as Becker had mouthed it onstage) "barratry on the low seas!" Separate them from this weird and many-faceted creature that lived its many lives in the padded cell numbered 16.

At first, there had been reporters, who had come to interview the Good Doctor in charge of Becker's case, and to the last of these (for Dr. Tedrow had instituted restrictions on this sort of publicity) he had said, "To a man like Richard Becker, the world was very important. He was very much a man of his times; he had no real personality of his own, with the exception of that one overwhelming faculty and need to reflect the world around him. He was an actor in the purest sense of the word. The world gave him his personality, his attitudes, his reason and his façade for existence. Take those away from him, clap him up in a padded cell—as we were forced to do—and he begins to lose touch with reality."

"I understand," the reporter had inquired carefully, "that Becker is re-living his roles, one after another. Is that true, Dr. Tedrow?"

Charles Tedrow was, above all else, a compassionate man, and his fury at this remark, revealing as it did a leak in the sanitarium's security policy, was manifest. "Richard Becker is undergoing what might be called, in psychiatric terms, 'induced hallucinatory regression.' In his search for some reality, there in that room, he has fastened on the method of assuming characters' moods he had played onstage. From what I've been able to piece together from reviews of his shows, he is going back from the most recent to the next and the next and so on."

The reporter had asked more questions, more superficial and phantasmagoric assumptions, until Dr. Charles Tedrow had concluded the interview forcibly.

But even now, as he sat across from Richard Becker in the quiet office, he knew that almost nothing the reporter had conceived could rival what Becker had done to himself.

"Tell me, Doctor," the florid, bombastic traveling salesman who was Richard Becker asked, "what the hell's new down the line?"

"It's really very quiet, these days, Ted," the physician replied. Becker had been this way for two months now: submerged in the part of Ted Rogat, the loudmouth philandering protagonist of Chayefsky's *The Wanderer*. For six months before that he had been Marco Polo, and before that the nervous, slack-jawed and incestuous son of *The Glass of Sadness.*

"Hell, I remember one little chippie in, where was it, oh yeah, hell yes! It was K.C., good old K.C., man, she was a *goodie!* You ever been to K.C., Doc? I was a drummer in nylons when I worked K.C. Jeezus, lemme tell ya—"

It was difficult to believe the man who sat on the other side of the table was an actor. He looked the part, he spoke the part, he *was* Ted Rogat, and Dr. Tedrow could catch himself from time to time contemplating the release of this total stranger who had wandered into Richard Becker's cell.

He sat and listened to the story of the flame-hipped harlot in Kansas City that Ted Rogat had picked up in an Armenian restaurant, and seduced with promises of nylons. He listened to it, and knew that whatever else was true of Richard Becker, this creature of many faces and many lives, he was no saner than the day he had killed that girl. After eighteen months in the sanitarium, he was going back, back, back through his acting career, and re-playing the roles, but never once coming to grips with reality.

In the plight and disease of Richard Becker, Dr. Charles Tedrow saw a bit of himself, of all men, of his times and the thousand illnesses to which they were heir.

He returned Richard Becker, as well as Ted Rogat, to the security and tiny world of room 16.

Two months later he brought him back and spent a highly interesting three hours discussing group therapy with Herr Doktor Ernst Loebisch, credentials from the Munich Academy of Medicine and the Vienna Psychiatric Clinic. Four months after that, Dr. Tedrow got to know the surly and insipid Jackie Bishoff, juvenile delinquent and hero of *Streets of Night.*

And almost a year later, to the day, Dr. Tedrow sat in his office with a bum, a derelict, a rheumy-eyed and dissipated vagabond who could only be the skid from *Sweet Miracles,* Richard Becker's first triumph, twenty-four years before.

What Richard Becker might look like, without camouflage, in his own shell, Tedrow had no idea. He was, now, to all intents and purposes, the seedy old tramp with the dirt caked into the sagged folds of his face.

"Mr. Becker, I want to talk to you."

Hopelessness shined out of the old bum's eyes. There was no answer.

"Listen to me, Becker. Please listen to me, if you're in there somewhere, if you can hear me. I want you to understand what I'm about to say; it's very important."

A croak, cracked and forced, came from the bum's lips, and he mumbled, "I need'a drink, yuh go' uh drink fuh me, huh . . ."

Tedrow leaned across, his hand shaking as he took the old bum's chin in his palm, and held it fixed, staring into this stranger's eyes. "Now listen to me, Becker. You've got to hear me. I've gone through the files, and as far as I can tell, this was the first part you ever played. I don't know what will happen! I don't know what form this syndrome will take after you've used up all your other lives. But if you can hear me, you've got to understand that you may be approaching a critical period in your—in your life."

The old bum licked cracked lips.

"*Listen!* I'm here, I want to help you, I want to *do* something for you, Becker. If you'll come out for an instant, just a second, we can establish contact. It's got to be now or—"

He left it hanging. He had no way of knowing *if—what*. And as he lapsed into silence, as he released the bum's chin, a strange alteration of facial muscles began, and the derelict's countenance shifted, subtly ran like hot lead, and for a second he saw a face he recognized. From the eyes that were no longer red-rimmed and bloodshot, Dr. Charles Tedrow saw intelligence peering out.

"It sounds like fear, Doctor," he said.

And, "Good-by, once more."

Then the light died, the face shifted again, and the physician was staring once more at the empty face of a gutterbred derelict.

He sent the old man back to room 16. Later that day, he had one of the male nurses take in an 89-cent bottle of muscatel.

"Speak up, man! What in the name of God is going on out there?"

"I—I can't explain it, Dr. Tedrow, but you'd better— you'd better get out here right away. It's—it's, oh Jee-zus!"

"What *is* it? Stop crying, Wilson, and tell me what the hell is *wrong!*"

"It's, it's number 16 . . . it's . . ."

"I'll be there in twenty minutes. Keep everyone away from that room. Do you understand? Wilson! Do you understand me?"

"Yessir, yessir. I'll—oh Christ—hurry up, Doc . . ."

He could feel his pajama pants bunched around his knees, under his slacks, as he floored the pedal of the ranch wagon. The midnight roads were jerky in the windshield, and the murk that he raced through was almost too grotesque to be a fact of nature.

When he slowed the car into the drive, the gatekeeper threw the iron barrier back almost spastically. The ranch wagon chewed gravel, sending debris back in a wide fan, as Tedrow plunged ahead. When he screeched to a halt before the sanitarium, the doors burst open and the senior attendant, Wilson, raced down the steps.

"This way, th—this way, Doctor Te—"

"Get out of my way, you idiot, I know which direction!" He shoved Wilson aside, and strode up the steps and into the building.

"It started about an hour ago . . . we didn't know what was happ—"

"And you didn't call me immediately? Ass!"

"We just thought, we just thought it was another one of his stages, *you* know how he is . . ."

Tedrow snorted in disgust and threw off his topcoat as he made his way rapidly down the corridor to the section of the sanitarium that housed the restraining rooms.

As they came into the annex, through the heavy glassportaled door, he heard the scream for the first time.

In that scream, in that tormented, pleading, demanding and hopelessly lost tremor there were all the sounds of fear he had ever heard. In that voice he heard even his own voice, his own soul, crying out for something.

For an unnameable something, as the scream came again.

"Give me some light!"

Another world, another voice, another life. Some evil and empty beseeching from a corner of a dust-strewn universe. Hanging there timelessly, vibrant in colorless agony. A million tired and blind stolen voices all wrapped into that one howl, all the eternal sadnesses and losses and pains ever known to man. It was all there, as the good in the world was sliced open and left to bleed its golden fluid away in the dirt. It was a lone animal being eaten by a bird of prey. It was a hundred children crushed beneath iron treads. It was one good man with his entrails in his blood-soaked hands. It was the soul and the pain and the very vital fiber of life, draining away, without light, without hope, without succour.

"Give me some light!"

Tedrow flung himself at the door and threw back the bolt on the observation window. He stared for a long and silent moment as the scream trembled once more on the air, weightlessly, transparently, tingling off into emptiness. He stared, and felt the impact of a massive horror stifle his own cry of disbelief and terror.

Then he spun away from the window and hung there, sweat-drenched back flat to the wall, with the last sight of Richard Becker he would ever hope to see, burned forever behind his eyes.

The sound of his soft sobs in the corridor held the others back. They stared silently, still hearing that never-spoken echo reverberating down and down and down the corridor of their minds:

Give me some light!

Fumbling beside him, Tedrow slammed the observation window shut, and then his arm sank back to his side.

While inside room 16, lying up against the far wall, his back against the soft passive padding, Richard Becker looked out at the door, at the corridor, at the world, forever.

Looked out as he had come, purely and simply.

Without a face. From his hairline to his chin, a blank, empty, featureless expanse. Empty. Silent. Devoid of sight or smell or sound. Blank and faceless, a creature God had never deigned to bless with a mirror to the world. His Method now was gone.

Richard Becker, actor, had played his last part, and had gone away, taking with him Richard Becker, a man who had known all the sounds, all the sights, all the life of fear.

"All the Sounds of Fear" is included in *Ellison Wonderland*, Paperback Library, 1962.

ONE OF THOSE DAYS

by William F. Nolan

from *Fantasy and Science Fiction*

Of course, before you can define "reality," you have to define "sanity." Or do I mean, before you can define "sanity," you must define "reality"?

I knew it was going to be one of those days when I heard a blue-and-yellow butterfly humming "Si, mi chiamano Mimi," my favorite aria from *La Bohème*. I was weeding the garden when the papery insect fluttered by, humming beautifully.

I got up, put aside my garden tools and went into the house to dress. I would see my psychoanalyst at once.

Neglecting my cane and spats, I snapped an old homburg on my head and aimed for Dr. Mellowthin's office in downtown Los Angeles.

Several disturbing things happened to me on the way . . .

First of all, a large stippled tomcat darted out of an alley directly after I'd stepped from the bus. The cat was on its hind legs and carried a bundle of frothy pink blanketing in its front paws. It looked desperate.

"Gangway!" shouted the cat. "Baby! Live baby here! Clear back. BACK for the baby!"

Then it was gone, having dipped cat-quick across the street, losing itself in heavy traffic. Upon drawing in a deep lungful of air, smog-laden but steadying, I resumed my brisk pace toward Dr. Mellowthin's office.

As I passed a familiar apartment house, a third-story window opened and Wally Jenks popped his head over the sill and called down to me. "Hi," yelled Wally. "C'mon up for a little drinkie."

I shaded my eyes to get a clearer look at him. "Hi, Jenks!" I yelled back, and we both grinned foolishly at the old play on words. "On my way to Mellowthin's."

"Appointment?" he queried.

"Spur of the moment," I replied.

"Then time's no problem. Up you come, old dads, or I shan't forgive you."

I sighed and entered the building. Jenks was in 3G, and I decided to use the stairs. Elevators trap you. As I reached the second-floor landing I obeyed an irresistible urge to bend down and place my ear close to the base of the wall near the floor.

"Are you mice still *in* there?" I shouted.

To which a thousand tiny musical Disney-voices shot back: "Damned *right* we are!"

I shrugged, adjusted my homburg, and continued my upward climb. Jenks met me at the door with a dry martini.

"Thanks," I said, sipping. As usual, it was superb. Old Wally knew his martinis.

"Well," he said, all cheer, "how goes?"

"Badsville," I answered. "Care to hear?"

"By all means. Unburden."

We sat down, facing one another across the tastefully furnished room. I sipped the martini and told Wally about things. "This morning, 'bout forty minutes ago, I heard a butterfly humming Puccini. Then I saw a cat carrying what I can only assume was a live baby."

"Human?"

"Don't know. Could have been a cat baby."

"Cat say anything?"

"He shouted 'Gangway!' "

"Proceed."

"Then—on the way upstairs—I had a brief conversational exchange with at least a thousand mice."

"In the walls?"

"Where else?"

"Finish your drinkie," said Jenks, finishing his.

I did so.

"Nother?" he asked.

"Nope. Gotta be trotting. I'm in for a mental purge."

"Well, I wouldn't worry too much," he assured me. "Humming insects, talking felines and odd-ball answering mice are admittedly unsettling. But . . . there *are* stranger things in this man's world."

I looked over at him. And knew he was correct—for old Wally Jenks had turned into a loose-pelted brown camel with twin humps, all stained and worn-looking at the tops. I swallowed.

"See you," I said.

Wally grinned, or rather the camel did, and it was awful. Long, cracked yellow teeth like old carnival dishes inside his black gums. I gave a nervous little half-wave, and moved for the door. One final glance over my shoulder at old Jenks verified the fact that he was still grinning at me with those big wet desert-red eyes of his.

Back on the street I quickened my stride, anxious now to reach Mellowthin and render a full account of the day's events. Only a half-block to go.

Then a policeman stopped me. He was all sweaty inside his tight uniform, and his face was dark with hatred.

"Thought you was the wise one, eh, Mugger?" he rasped in a venom-filled voice. "Thought you could give John Law the finger?"

"But, officer, I don't—"

"Come right along, Mugger. We got special cages for the likes 'a you." He was about to snap a pair of silver cuffs to my wrists when I put a quick knee to his vitals and rabbit-punched him on the way down. Then I grabbed his revolver.

"Here!" I shouted to several passers-by. "This man is a fraud. Killed a cop to get this rig. He's a swine of the worst sort. Record as long as your arm. Blackmail, rape, arson, auto theft, kidnapping, grand larceny, wife-beating and petty pilfering. You name it, he's done it!"

I thrust the revolver at a wide-eyed, trembling woman.

"Take this weapon, lady. If he makes a funny move, shoot to kill!"

She aimed the gun at the stunned policeman, who was only now getting his breath. He attempted to rise.

"OOPS!" I yelled, "he's going for a knife. Let him have it—NOW!"

The trembling woman shut both eyes and pulled the trigger. The cop pitched forward on his face, stone dead.

"May heaven forgive you," I moaned, backing away. "You've murdered an officer of the law, a defender of public morals . . . May heaven be merciful!"

The woman flapped off. She had turned into a heavy-billed pelican. The policeman had become a fat-bellied seal with flippers, but he was still dead.

Hurrying, and somewhat depressed, I entered Dr. Mellowthin's office and told the girl at the desk it was an emergency.

"You may go right in," she told me. "The doctor will see you immediately."

In another moment I was pumping Mellowthin's hand.

"Sit down, boy," he told me. "So . . . we've got our little complications again today, have we?"

"Sure have," I said, pocketing one of his cigars. I noted that it was stale.

"Care to essay the couch?"

I slid onto the rich dark leather and closed my eyes.

"Now—tell me all about it."

"First a butterfly sang *La Bohème,* or hummed it rather. Then a tomcat shot out of an alley with a baby in its paws. Then some mice in an apartment house yelled back at me. Then one of my oldest and dearest friends turned into a camel."

"One hump or two?" asked Mellowthin.

"Two," I said. "Large and scruffy and all worn at the tops."

"Anything else?"

"Then a big, pseudo-English cop stopped me. His dialogue was fantastic. Called me Mugger. Said I was fit for a cage. Started to put cuffs on me. I kneed him in the kishkas and gave his gun to a nice trembly lady who shot him. Then she turned into a pelican and flapped off, and he turned into a seal with flippers. Then I came here."

I opened my eyes and sat up.

I stared at Dr. Mellowthin.

"What's the matter?" he asked, somewhat uneasily.

"Well . . ." I said, "to begin with you have large brown, sad-looking, liquidy eyes."

"And?"

"And I bet your nose is cold!" I grinned.

"Anything else?"

"Not really."

"What about my overall appearance?"

"Well, of course you're covered with long black shaggy hair, even down to the tips of your big floppy ears."

A moment of strained silence.

"Can you do tricks?" I asked.

"A few," Mellowthin replied uncomfortably.

"Roll over!" I commanded.

He did.

"Play dead!"

His liquidy eyes rolled up white and his long pink tongue lolled loosely from his jaws.

"Good doggie," I said. "Nice doggie."

"Woof," barked Dr. Mellowthin softly, wagging his tail.

Putting on my hat I tossed him a bone I'd saved from the garden and left his office.

There was absolutely no getting around it.

This was simply one of those days.

"One of Those Days" is included in *Impact 20*, a collection of Mr. Nolan's short stories, Paperback Library; and has also been reprinted in Charles Beaumont's thrill-chiller anthology, *The Fiend In You*, Ballantine, 1962.

THE DAY REMBRANDT WENT PUBLIC

by Arnold M. Auerbach

from *Harper's Magazine*

. . . And if you are one who feels his grip on "reality" is firm and clear, then how about the gradations of the "non-real"?

Between the extremes of the most solid science fiction and the sheerest fantasy lies a wide range of potential: the probable, the plausible, the possible, and the purely poetic. On yet another literary line (somewhere, askew, intersecting fact, fable, *and* fiction) lies a whole other set of undetermined points and limits. "Unreal," "surreal," "satiric," "silly"—the label depends, I expect, on whether you incline to *Harper's* or to *Mad*, or both. In any case, it is a joy to experience the renascence of the imaginative essay.

By 1967 or so, art collectors had discarded their outmoded aesthetic attitudes. They asked only one stark, logical query about a contemporary artist: Was he a sound, going proposition, with healthy prospects for capital appreciation, or were his assets watery? There were just two schools of modern painting: (1) Growth. (2) Income.

Works of the masters, of course, were no longer on public view. As values soared, thefts at galleries became frighteningly commonplace. It wasn't safe to carry even an etching down 57th Street. After the National Gallery heist, in which a gang of smooth-talking gunmen, posing as Princeton art majors, got away with two Giottos and a Veronese, the government closed down the building and buried its contents in Fort Knox. Private owners hid their canvases in vaults, displaying only reproductions—or, as they became known, "cultured paintings."

The first person to take full advantage of the trend was an enterprising plastics magnate named Godfrey L. Willoughby, who issued stock and sold shares in his collection, incorporating on the Big Board under the name Consolidated Art-Lovers, Inc. (Ticker symbol CAL.)

Willoughby's gimmick was well thought out. His portfolio of canvases was strictly blue-chip: solid, high-grade classicists, several gilt-edge post-Impressionists, and, for frosting, one or two up-and-coming nonobjectivists.

His prospectus was alluring. The collection, currently valued at over a million dollars, would be reappraised from time to time, as Willoughby bought and sold. Any weak sisters on the list would be ruthlessly weeded out. As the canvases went up in value, so would the company's shares. True, there would be no cash dividends. But growth prospects were enormous.

Moreover, at corporate meetings, stockholders, besides a box lunch, would receive beautifully bound financial statements, illustrated with color plates of their holdings, to be distributed through the Book-of-the-Month Club. CAL stock certificates, suitable for framing, would bear a handsome reproduction of the company's prize asset—a small "Christ Driving the Moneychangers from the Temple," attributed to El Greco. All in all, for the discriminating investor seeking cultural as well as financial enrichment, a stake in CAL was certainly preferable to real-estate syndication.

CAL common, issued at 10, jumped to 32, steadied at 27½, and, as *The Wall Street Journal* declared, became "the widows'-and-orphans' art favorite." On the strength of his coup, Willoughby gained national fame, sold his holdings, and entered politics, becoming a leading contender for the Republican Presidential nomination.

A number of other collectors soon imitated his scheme. Investors could choose between General Still Life, Soyer Brothers and Levine, and even The Way-Out Boys, Inc. (Admittedly highly speculative, but a vast profit potential.) All prospered.

Unfortunately, an unhealthy trend developed. Wildcat issues appeared: Nudes Preferred, Crazy Collages. John Canaday, president of the newly formed Art-Stock Ethical Association, cracked down, banishing several offending underwriters. Merrill Lynch, Pierce, Fenner and Parke-Bernet, brokers, published a series of chatty ads, advising caution. Still, the boom continued.

Many analysts blamed the eventual debacle on the Metropolitan Museum of Art, which, after much secret debate, decided to sell shares in "Aristotle Contemplating the Bust of Homer." ("Rembrandt Goes Public" said the *Daily News,* that morning.)

The clamor to buy surpassed even the to-do over Ford's first stock issue. The canvas, now kept in a Monacan bank vault, was valued at over $120 million, with bullish prospects. Everyone wanted a slice of the pie. ACBH, opening at 6, shot to 21½, and within two hours was selling at 63¼, carrying other art issues in its wake.

That same afternoon—the day became known forever as Chiaroscuro Thursday—the bubble burst. The decline began when a number of institutions simultaneously decided to take their profits on ACBH, and sell. A wave of rumors followed. "The insiders are dumping ACBH." "Maybe the trend is to compact Rembrandts." "The art cycle has had it."

Suddenly everyone wanted to get out. Prices crumbled, as the ticker was swamped. Vainly, Canaday pleaded for order. Billy Rose, trying to hold the line, sold his AT&T and poured the proceeds into art issues. Nothing helped. ACBH closed that day at 3¼. Thousands of bellboys, taxi-drivers and other art-lovers lost their savings. Outraged crowds stoned the Dutch embassy. Billy Rose announced that he'd have to go back to producing Aquacades.

Belatedly, the government stepped in. The President declared an Art Holiday. The PSC (Painting and Sculpture Commission) was formed. It forbade all speculation, share-owning, and trading in works of art. Unqualified persons were no longer allowed to become collectors. Speculative investors were diverted to new fields, such as outer-space real estate.

After a while, museums began to take their paintings out of hiding, and people hung them on walls and went back to just looking at them.

MS. FOUND IN A BUS

by Russell Baker

from *The New York Times*

Never has so much been written (and read, and heard, and viewed) with such authenticity, such legalistic adherence to literal truth, and such frequently abused power to misrepresent, as in this age of scientific advertising, computed political propaganda, and "true" "inside" "confidential" story-telling. It is perhaps a predictable reaction on the part of some of the best of our serious journalists, that the caricature (satiric? surreal?) news item is returning to American letters. (At the risk of ignoring some whose work has not come to my attention, I can mention here, besides Mr. Baker's pieces in *The Times*, James Wechsler's and Murray Kempton's occasional columns in the *New York Post*, Pierre Berton's deadpanning in *Maclean's*, and the biweekly spoofsheet, *The Outsider's Newsletter*, put out by the publishers of *Monocle* and devoted entirely to the form.)

From some future best seller's Washington novel, here is a page of manuscript left on the bus to Chevy Chase:

"The President's wasted hand trembled violently as he fought to compose himself for this final confrontation. 'Steady, Prez,' he told himself. 'Got to be steady for this one, Prez.'

"But when he thought again of the treachery of it his body surrendered to a shudder of revulsion. To think that Astrohazy, his own Secretary of State, should be coming here to the White House to demand the surrender of the United States to the Kremlin. It was incredible. He could still not bring himself to accept it. But there was the evidence. Cold, brutal, irrefutable: his own Secretary of State was none other than the mysterious Comrade Ubiquitov, known only to Central Intelligence as 'Number Three in the Politburo.'

"The President's secretary cut across his train of thought. 'Cal Simpkins is here, Mr. President,' she said. She wanted to weep when she saw his ruined face. He's dying, she thought. How can they do this to him? 'Send him in,' said the President wearily.

"He despised Simpkins but knew that of all the Senators on Capitol Hill none would make a more reliable partner in the awful ordeal that lay ahead. Simpkins, he realized, might be a thief, a lecher and a boor, but no other man in Congress loved America more or would fight more fiercely to keep her from going down.

"Simpkins strode into the office with his customary ruthless gait, the familiar cunning smile painted on his handsome solon's face.

" 'Cal,' said the President, 'we've never exactly loved one another.'

"Simpkins let his handsomely insincere features express a noncommittal benign evil. 'There's been bad news, Cal,' the President continued.

" 'I know,' Simpkins said. 'The Chinese Reds have just landed the first death-ray crew on Mars and are threatening to disintegrate Milwaukee Tuesday morning unless we turn NATO over to them. I read it on the ticker just before I left the Capitol.'

" 'No, Cal. I mean really bad news.'

" 'Don't let that worry you, Mr. President. We know the Chairman of the Atomic Energy Commission didn't really die of a fall in the bathtub last week. The word has a way of getting around on the Hill. We knew all along that he'd been threatening to blow up New York unless you agreed to a sneak nuclear attack on Moscow. Some of us kind of admire the way you handled that one, Mr. President.'

" 'Cal,' the President murmured feebly, glaring at Simpkins with steely obsolescent eyes, 'thank God you have the vision to see America clearly.'

" 'Afraid some of us are going to have to make a little

noise about the way you had El Paso blown up without any warning last Monday,' Simpkins said.

" 'Yes, yes,' the President said tiredly. 'I know, but there was no alternative. One of our pilots went berserk and blew up Smolensk and we just had to give it to El Paso to keep the Russians from getting edgy.' The telephone jangled. 'Secretary Astrohazy is here,' said his secretary's voice. Before the line had clicked dead, the office door burst open.

"A glance told the President that his Secret Service bodyguard had been gassed. What stunned him even more was the identity of the woman standing at Astrohazy's side, gas gun in hand. 'Belle Traymore, the arbiter of Washington society!' he gasped.

"Astrohazy uttered a throaty chuckle of gloating and Belle's lascivious eyes crinkled as they hungrily embraced Simpkins with glances darting fire."

Here the manuscript page ends. Will the author please claim it?

THE INSANE ONES

by J. G. Ballard

from *Amazing*

Brunner, White, Bradbury and Ellison have all explored or questioned some area of subjective experience (with custard pie and butterfly riffs, from Aandahl and Nolan, between the choruses). Now Ballard returns to the theme examined by Fitzpatrick and Anderson: the relationship between organized society and individual sanity.

Ten miles outside Alexandria he picked up the coast road that ran across the top of the continent through Tunis and Algiers to the transatlantic tunnel at Casablanca, gunned the Jaguar up to 120 and burned along through the cool night air, letting the brine-filled slipstream cut into his six-day tan. Lolling back against the headrest as the palms flicked by, he almost missed the girl in the white raincoat moving from the steps of the hotel at El Alamein, had only three hundred yards to plunge the car to a halt below the rusting neon sign.

"Tunis?" the girl called out, belting the man's raincoat around her trim waist, long black hair in a left-bank cut over one shoulder.

"Tunis—Casablanca—Atlantic City," Gregory shouted back, reaching across to the passenger door. She swung a yellow briefcase behind the seat, settling herself among the magazines and newspapers as they roared off. The headlamps picked out a United World cruiser parked under the palms in the entrance to the war cemetery, and involuntarily Gregory winced and floored the accelerator, eyes clamped to the rear mirror until the road was safely empty.

At 90 he slacked off and looked at the girl, abruptly felt a warning signal sound again. She seemed like any demi-beatnik, with a long melancholy face and gray skin, but something about her rhythms, the slack facial tone and dead eyes and mouth, made him uneasy. Under a flap of the raincoat was a blue-striped gingham skirt, obviously part of a nurse's uniform, out of character like the rest of her strange gear. As she slid the magazines into the dashboard locker he saw the home-made bandage around the left wrist.

She noticed him watching her and flashed a too-bright smile, then made an effort at small talk.

"Paris *Vogue, Neue Frankfurter,* Tel Aviv *Express—* you've really been moving." She pulled a pack of Del Monte's from the breast pocket of the coat, fumbled unfamiliarly with a large brass lighter. "First Europe, then Asia, now Africa. You'll run out of continents soon." Hesitating, she volunteered: "Carole Sturgeon. Thanks for the lift."

Gregory nodded, watching the bandage slide around her slim wrist. He wondered which hospital she had sneaked away from. Probably Cairo General, the old-style English uniforms were still worn there. Ten to one the briefcase was packed with some careless salesman's pharmaceutical samples. "Can I ask where you're going? This is the back end of nowhere."

The girl shrugged. "Just following the road. Cairo, Alex, you know—" She added: "I went to see the pyramids." She lay back, rolling slightly against his shoulder. "That was wonderful. They're the oldest things on Earth. Remember their boast: *'Before Abraham, I was'?"*

They hit a dip in the road and Gregory's license swung out under the steering column. The girl peered down and read it. "Do you mind? It's a long ride to Tunis. 'Charles Gregory, M.D.—'" She stopped, repeating the name to herself uncertainly.

Suddenly she remembered. *"Gregory!* Dr. Charles Gregory! Weren't you—Muriel Bortman, the President's daughter, she drowned herself at Key West, you were sentenced—" She broke off, staring nervously at the windshield.

"You've got a long memory," Gregory said quietly. "I didn't think anyone remembered."

"Of course I remember." She spoke in a whisper. "They were mad what they did to you." For the next few minutes she gushed out a long farrago of sympathy, interspersed with disjointed details from her own life. Gregory tried not to listen, clenching the wheel until his knuckles whitened, deliberately forgetting everything as fast as she reminded him.

There was a pause, as he felt it coming, the way it invariably did. "Tell me, doctor, I hope you forgive my asking, but since the Mental Freedom laws it's difficult to get help, one's got to be so careful—you too, of course . . ." She laughed uneasily. "What I really mean is—"

Her edginess drained power from Gregory. "—you need psychiatric assistance," he cut in, pushing the Jaguar up to 95, eyes swinging to the rear mirror again. The road was dead, palms receding endlessly into the night.

The girl choked on her cigarette, the stub between her fingers a damp mess. "Well, not me," she said lamely. "A close friend of mine. She really needs help, believe me, doctor. Her whole feeling for life is gone, nothing seems to mean anything to her any more."

Brutally, he said: "Tell her to look at the pyramids."

But the girl missed the irony, said quickly: "Oh, she has. I just left her in Cairo. I promised I'd try to find someone for her." She turned to examine Gregory, put a hand up to her hair. In the blue desert light she reminded him of the madonnas he had seen in the Louvre two days after his release, when he had run from the filthy prison searching for the most beautiful things in the world, the solemn-faced more-than-beautiful thirteen-year-olds who had posed for Leonardo and the Bellini brothers. "I thought perhaps you might know someone—?"

He gripped himself and shook his head. "I don't. For the last three years I've been out of touch. Anyway, it's against the MF laws. Do you know what would happen if they caught me giving psychiatric treatment?"

Numbly the girl stared ahead at the road. Gregory flipped away his cigarette, pressing down on the accelerator as the last three years crowded back, memories he had hoped to repress on his ten-thousand-mile drive ... three years at the prison farm near Marseilles, treating scrofulous farm workers and sailors in the dispensary, even squeezing in a little illicit depth analysis for the corporal of police who couldn't satisfy his wife, three embittered years to accept that he would never practice again the one craft in which he was fully himself. Trick-cyclist or assuager of discontents, whatever his title, the psychiatrist had now passed into history, joining the necromancers, sorcerers, and other practitioners of the black sciences.

The Mental Freedom legislation enacted ten years earlier by the ultra-conservative UW government had banned the profession outright and enshrined the individual's freedom to be insane if he wanted to, provided he paid the full civil consequences for any infringements of the law. That was the catch, the hidden object of the MF laws. What had begun as a popular reaction against "subliminal living" and the uncontrolled extension of techniques of mass manipulation for political and economic ends had quickly developed into a systematic attack on the psychological sciences. Over-permissive courts of law with their condoning of delinquency, pseudo-enlightened penal reformers, "victims of society," the psychologist and his patient all came under fierce attack. Discharging their self-hate and anxiety onto a convenient scapegoat, the new rulers, and the great majority electing them, outlawed all forms of psychic control, from the innocent market survey to lobotomy. The mentally ill were on their own, spared pity and consideration, made to pay to the hilt for their failings. The sacred cow of the community was the psychotic, free to wander where he wanted, drooling on doorsteps, sleeping on sidewalks, and woe betide anyone who tried to help him.

Gregory had made that mistake. Escaping to Europe, first home of psychiatry, in the hope of finding a more tolerant climate, he set up a secret clinic in Paris with six other *émigré* analysts. For five years they worked undetected, until one of Gregory's patients, a tall ungainly girl with a psychogenic stutter, was revealed to be Muriel Bortman, daughter of the UW President-General. The analysis had failed tragically when the clinic was raided; after her death a lavish show trial (making endless play of electric shock apparatus, movies of insulin coma and the testimony of countless paranoids rounded up in the alleyways) had concluded in a three-year sentence.

Now at last he was out, his savings invested in the Jaguar, fleeing Europe and his memories of the prison for the empty highways of North Africa. He didn't want any more trouble.

"I'd like to help," he told the girl. "But the risks are too high. All your friend can do is try to come to terms with herself."

The girl chewed her lip fretfully. "I don't think she can. Thanks, anyway, doctor."

For three hours they sat back silently in the speeding car, until the lights of Tobruk came up ahead, the long curve of the harbor.

"It's 2 A.M.," Gregory said. "There's a motel here, I'll pick you up in the morning."

After they had gone to their rooms he sneaked back to the registry, booked himself into a new chalet. He fell asleep as Carole Sturgeon wandered forlornly up and down the verandas, whispering out his name.

After breakfast he came back from the sea, found a big United World cruiser in the court, orderlies carrying a stretcher out to an ambulance.

A tall Libyan police colonel was leaning against the Jaguar, drumming his leather baton on the windscreen.

"Ah, Dr. Gregory. Good morning." He pointed his baton at the ambulance. "A profound tragedy, such a beautiful American girl."

Gregory rooted his feet in the gray sand, with an effort

restrained himself from running over to the ambulance and pulling back the sheet. Fortunately, the colonel's uniform and the thousands of morning and evening cell inspections kept him safely to attention.

"I'm Gregory, yes." The dust thickened in his throat. "Is she dead?"

The colonel stroked his neck with the baton. "Ear to ear. She must have found an old razor blade in the bathroom. About three o'clock this morning." He headed off toward Gregory's chalet, gesturing with the baton. Gregory followed him into the half light, stood tentatively by the bed.

"I was asleep then. The clerk will vouch for that."

"Naturally." The colonel gazed down at Gregory's possessions spread out across the bedcover, idly poked the black medical bag.

"She asked you for assistance, doctor? With her personal problems?"

"Not directly. She hinted at it, though. She sounded a little mixed up."

"Poor child." The colonel lowered his head sympathetically. "Her father is a first secretary at the Cairo Embassy, something of an autocrat. You Americans are very stern with your children, doctor. A firm hand, yes, but understanding costs nothing. Don't you agree? She was frightened of him, escaped from the American Hospital. My task is to provide an explanation for the authorities. If I had an idea of what was really worrying her . . . no doubt you helped her as best you could?"

Gregory shook his head. "I gave her no help at all, colonel. In fact, I refused to discuss her problems altogether." He smiled flatly at the colonel. "I wouldn't make the same mistake twice, would I?"

The colonel studied Gregory thoughtfully. "Sensible of you, doctor. But you surprise me. Surely the members of your profession regard themselves as a special calling, answerable to a higher authority. Are these ideals so easy to cast off?"

"I've had a lot of practice." Gregory began to pack

away his things on the bed, bowed to the colonel as he saluted and made his way out into the court.

Half an hour later he was on the Benghasi road, holding the Jaguar at 100, working off his tension and anger in savage bursts of speed. Free for only ten days, already he had got himself involved again, gone through all the agony of having to refuse help to someone desperately needing it, his hands itching to administer relief to the child but held back by the insane penalties. It wasn't only the lunatic legislation but the people enforcing it who ought to be swept away—Bortman and his fellow oligarchs.

He grimaced at the thought of the cold dead-faced Bortman, addressing the World Senate at Lake Success, arguing for increased penalties for the criminal psychopath. The man had stepped straight out of the fourteenth-century inquisition, his bureaucratic puritanism masking two real obsessions: dirt and death. Any sane society would have locked Bortman up for ever, or given him a complete brain-lift. Indirectly Bortman was as responsible for the death of Carole Sturgeon as he would have been had he personally handed the razor blade to her.

After Libya, Tunis. He blazed steadily along the coast road, the sea like a molten mirror on the right, avoiding the big towns where possible. Fortunately, they weren't as bad as the European cities, psychotics loitering like stray dogs in the uptown parks, wise enough not to shop-lift or cause trouble, but a petty nuisance on the cafe terraces, knocking on hotel-room doors at all hours of the night.

At Algiers he spent three days at the Hilton, having a new engine fitted to the car, and hunted up Philip Kalundborg, an old Toronto colleague now working in a WHO children's hospital.

Over their third carafe of burgundy Gregory told him about Carole Sturgeon.

"It's absurd, but I feel guilty about her. Suicide is a highly suggestive act, I reminded her of Muriel Bortman's death. Damn it, Philip, I could have given her the sort of general advice any sensible layman would have offered."

"Dangerous. Of course you were right," Philip assured him. "After the last three years who could argue otherwise?"

Gregory looked out across the terrace at the traffic whirling over the neon-lit cobbles. Beggars sat at their pitches along the sidewalk, whining for sous.

"Philip, you don't know what it's like in Europe now. At least five per cent are probably in need of institutional care. Believe me, I'm frightened to go to America. In New York alone they're jumping from the roofs at the rate of ten a day. The world's turning into a madhouse, one half of society gloating righteously over the torments of the other. Most people don't realize on which side of the bars they are. It's easier for you. Here the traditions are different."

Kalundborg nodded. "True. In the villages up-country it's been standard practice for centuries to blind schizophrenics and exhibit them in a cage. Injustice is so widespread that you build up an indiscriminate tolerance to every form."

A tall dark-bearded youth in faded cotton slacks and rope sandals stepped across the terrace and put his hands on their table. His eyes were sunk deep below his forehead, around his lips the brown staining of narcotic poisoning.

"Christian!" Kalundborg snapped angrily. He shrugged hopelessly at Gregory, then turned to the young man with quiet exasperation. "My dear fellow, this has gone on for too long. I can't help you, there's no point in asking."

The young man nodded patiently. "It's Marie," he explained in a slow roughened voice. "I can't control her. I'm frightened what she may do to the baby. Postnatal withdrawal, you know——"

"Nonsense! I'm not an idiot, Christian. The baby is nearly three. If Marie is a nervous wreck you've made her so. Believe me, I wouldn't help you if I was allowed to. You must cure yourself or you are finished. Already you have chronic barbiturism. Dr. Gregory here will agree with me."

Gregory nodded. The young man stared blackly at Kalundborg, glanced at Gregory and then shambled off through the tables.

Kalundborg filled his glass. "They have it all wrong today. They think our job was to further addiction, not cure it. In their pantheon the father-figure is always benevolent."

"That's invariably been Bortman's line. Psychiatry is ultimately self-indulgent, an encouragement to weakness and lack of will. Admittedly there's no one more single-minded than an obsessional neurotic. Bortman himself is a good example."

As he entered the tenth-floor bedroom the young man was going through his valise on the bed. For a moment Gregory wondered whether he was a UW spy, perhaps the meeting on the terrace had been an elaborate trap.

"Find what you want?"

Christian finished whipping through the bag, then tossed it irritably onto the floor. He edged restlessly away from Gregory around the bed, his eyes hungrily searching the wardrobe top and lamp brackets.

"Kalundborg was right," Gregory told him quietly. "You're wasting your time."

"The hell with Kalundborg," Christian snarled softly. "He's working the wrong levels. Do you think I'm looking for a jazz heaven, doctor? With a wife and child? I'm not that irresponsible. I took a master's degree in law at Heidelberg." He wandered off around the room, then stopped to survey Gregory closely.

Gregory began to slide in the drawers. "Well, get back to your jurisprudence. There are enough ills to weigh in this world."

"Doctor, I've made a start. Didn't Kalundborg tell you I sued Bortman for murder?" When Gregory seemed puzzled he explained: "A private civil action, not criminal proceedings. My father killed himself five years ago after

Bortman had him thrown out of the Bar Association."

Gregory picked his valise off the floor. "I'm sorry," he said non-committally. "What hapepned to your suit against Bortman?"

Christian stared out through the window into the dark air. "It was never entered. Some World Bureau investigators saw me after I started to be a nuisance and suggested I leave the States for ever. So I came to Europe to get my degree. I'm on my way back now. I need the barbiturates to stop myself from trying to toss a bomb at Bortman."

Suddenly he propelled himself across the room, before Gregory could stop him was out on the balcony, jack-knifed over the edge. Gregory dived after him, kicked away his feet and tried to pull him off the ledge. Christian clung to it, shouting into the darkness, the lights from the cars racing in the damp street below. On the sidewalk people looked up.

Christian was doubled up with laughter as they fell back into the room, slumped down on the bed, pointing his finger at Gregory, who was leaning against the wardrobe, gasping in exhausted spasms.

"Big mistake there, doctor. You'd better get out fast before I tip off the Police Prefect. Stopping a suicide! God, with your record you'd get ten years for that. What a joke!"

Gregory shook him by the shoulders, temper flaring. "Listen, what are you playing at? What do you want?"

Christian pushed Gregory's hands away and lay back weakly. "Help me, doctor. I want to kill Bortman, it's all I think about. If I'm not careful I'll really try. Show me how to forget him." His voice rose desperately. "Damn, I *hated* my father, I was glad when Bortman threw him out."

Gregory eyed him thoughtfully, then went over to the window and bolted out the night.

Two months later, at the motel outside Casablanca, Gregory finally burned the last of the analysis notes. Christian, clean-shaven and wearing a neat white tropical suit, a neutral tie, watched from the door as the stack of coded entries gutted out in the ashtray, then carried them into the bathroom and flushed them away.

When Christian had loaded his suitcases into the car Gregory said: "One thing before we go. A complete analysis can't be effected in two months, let alone two years. It's something you work at all your life. If you have a relapse, come to me, even if I'm in Tahiti, or Shanghai or Archangel." Gregory paused. "If they ever find out, you know what will happen?" When Christian nodded quietly he sat down in the chair by the writing table, gazing out through the date palms at the huge domed mouth of the transatlantic tunnel a mile away. For a long time he knew he would be unable to relax. In a curious way he felt that the three years at Marseilles had been wasted, that he was starting a suspended sentence of indefinite length. There had been no satisfaction at the successful treatment, perhaps because he had given in to Christian partly for fear of being incriminated in an attack on Bortman.

"With luck, you should be able to live with yourself now. Try to remember that whatever evils Bortman may perpetrate in the future, he's really irrelevant to *your* problem. It was the stroke your mother suffered after your father's death that made you realize the guilt you felt subconsciously for hating him, but you conveniently shifted the blame onto Bortman, and by eliminating him you thought you could free yourself. The temptation may occur again."

Christian nodded, standing motionlessly by the doorway. His face had filled out, his eyes were a placid gray. He looked like any well-groomed UW bureaucrat.

Gregory picked up a newspaper. "I see Bortman is attacking the American Bar Association as a subversive body, probably planning to have it proscribed. If it succeeds it'll be an irreparable blow to civil liberty." He looked up thoughtfully at Christian, who showed no reaction. "Right, let's go. Are you still fixed on getting back to the States?"

"Of course." Christian climbed into the car, then shook Gregory's hand. Gregory had decided to stay in Africa, find a hospital where he could work, and had given Christian the car. "Marie will wait for me in Algiers until I finish my business."

"What's that?"

Christian pressed the starter, sent a roar of dust and exhaust across the compound.

"I'm going to kill Bortman," he said quietly.

Gregory gripped the windscreen. "You're not serious."

"You cured me, doctor, and give or take the usual margins I'm completely sane, more than I probably ever will be again. Damn few people in this world are now, so that makes the obligation on me to act rationally even greater. Well, every ounce of logic tells me that someone's got to make the effort to get rid of the grim menagerie running things now, and Bortman looks like a pretty good start. I intend to drive up to Lake Success and take a shot at him." He shunted the gear change into second, and added, "Don't try to have me stopped, doctor, because they'll only dig out our long weekend here."

As he started to take his foot off the clutch Gregory shouted: "Christian! You'll never get away with it! They'll catch you anyway!" but the car wrenched forward out of his hand.

Gregory ran through the dust after it, stumbling over half-buried stones, realizing helplessly that when they caught Christian and probed down into the past few months they would soon find the real assassin, an exiled doctor with a three-year grudge.

"Christian!" he yelled, choking on the white ash. "Christian, you're insane!"

LEPRECHAUN

by William Sambrot

from *Escapade*

Up to this point, the stories here have been concerned with man in a variety of relationships—with himself, with other individuals, with society as a whole, with the natural environment and with the shifting technological environment.

In this selection, and those that follow, the relationship is with other forms of sentience: terrestrial, alien, mythical, magical. Sometimes the contact is initiated by man; sometimes it is altogether involuntary. Sometimes it educates, sometimes it frightens, sometimes serves only to reflect.

To fully understand what I'm about to tell you, you must know what Ireland is like. Not the Ireland of the big modern cities, but old Ireland. Ireland of the fens and bogs. The Ireland that is still a part of the dim Celtic past, before the Saint himself brought the Cross; when every tree, every stone was possessed of demonic life, and monsters big and small were known to roam the misty nights. That Ireland, deep down in some oldsters, still exists. And it exists, God help us all, very deeply in old Peadar—and what it might have cost us; what wonders have been forever lost to us, I can only speculate. But I cannot find it in my heart to blame old Peadar. He is old but still powerful, like a twisted, weather-hardened tree. There is no malice in the man, but his mind was soddened under the years and the bitter hardships of scratching an existence out of the bog he calls home. His family long dead; too little decent food, too much homemade potato liquor—the fiery poteen that keeps him alive.

Peadar told me his story, twisting his huge hands in

anguish while I looked down at the pitiable thing that lay on the table in his sagging windowless sod hut, while the rain that had fallen in solid leaden sheets for days drummed like a dirge on the roof.

He had heard a sound of approaching thunder (Peadar said) although the rain had fallen for days without thunder. At the same time, the sky had come alight, a flat white sheen, like a brilliant beam reflecting from under low-lying clouds, flickering, but gaining in intensity, brighter, nearer, and that was indeed strange since it was well past sundown.

He heard the rumble, soft at first, then louder, harder, cracking like the passage of an infrequently heard military jet—a long-drawn hiss, a whine, a swelling build-up—and then the shuddering rumble of air closing behind some swiftly moving object.

He'd stumbled to the door, pulling it open in time to see a glowing object slanting down; the light intense over the fens despite the gray rain.

It slipped over the rim of a nearby hill and Peadar saw the steady light hold there, then slowly dim and fade to dull red, and finally, it vanished completely.

His first thought had been—a plane crash, some poor souls killed out there. And lurching to his feet, old Peadar had picked up his kerosene lantern, thrown a coat on and immediately started out, thinking only (and this is in his favor) to help. But slogging through the chilly bog he'd seen nothing, only the unending rain, the wispy tendrils of fog. He paused, listening, looking to the right and left, his rheumy old eyes blinking.

He shook his head. He thought he heard popping and crackling sounds, like metal cooling, shrinking, somewhere close in the murky night, but he couldn't be certain. In fact, his mind began wandering; he turned, wondering why he'd come out here. He plodded about for a while and finally went back to his hut. And when he came inside, blowing out the lantern, shaking the wet from his hat, he heard the odd squeaking sound, and turning, he saw a little creature.

He was tiny, tiny (Peadar said, his voice trembling with yearning). Scarcely two feet high. Dressed in a metallic garment vaguely like a fish-skin—dully shining, with infinitesimal overlapping scales. On his head two insectlike antennae bobbed about, affixed to a small helmet of sorts, fitting snugly, with a glasslike faceplate. The whole very cunningly made. A tiny little man, with sparkling black eyes, bowing courteously to clumsy, gigantic old Peadar.

And seeing the little creature, there beside his poor hearth, in the midst of his poverty—the poverty only the Irish, the very remote fen-dweller can know—Peadar, his mind full of the old, old stories, addled with poteen—Peadar spoke aloud one word, like a pagan incantation: "Leprechaun!"

The creature took a step forward, its miniature arms held up, palms out to Peadar and Peadar waited, breathless.

Catch a Leprechaun, everyone knows, and he must tell you where fabulous fortunes are hidden. But hold him tight until he does; the wee folk are full of wiles and devilment.

The creature's broad-lipped mouth stretched in a shy half-smile; he looked curiously about the shabby hut and saw the old broken cot, the one chair, the smouldering, ill-smelling peat in the fireplace, the jug of poteen on the floor, the mug and tin spoon on the table.

Now it would happen; now the miracles, the treasure troves. Ancient glittering tales crowded Peadar's mind as he stared at the tiny man, waiting.

The little creature made another courteous half-bow, then walked slowly around Peadar, keeping his brilliant sequin eyes on his face, and walked toward the door, moving slowly, and with difficulty, as though walking under great pressure. He walked toward the door, and as he reached the threshold, Peadar came out of his trance—and acted.

He snatched at the little man, crying loudly at him, "No, no. Ah no, you darlin' wee man. You don't go until you grant me my due." He held the wriggling little creature in his great calloused hands, conscious of the amazing lightness of the little thing. Why, he might have been made of thistledown, so little did he weigh. The creature squeaked and made muffled sounds.

Peadar put him on the table, still holding his waist with one big hand. "Now then," said he, "it's here you stay until I see the gold with me own eyes—and don't think you'll escape me. I know the tricks you'll be tryin'."

With the other hand, Peadar hoisted the jug and swallowed an enormous drink of the fiery liquor. He paused, cocking his shaggy head. "Forgive me, now, and where's me manners? Don't I know how you'd like a drop of the poteen?"

Peadar slopped some into the cup, hesitated, peering slant-eyed at the little creature, then he pawed about and came up with the tin spoon. He dipped it into the cup and then held the spoonful of liquor up to the little man's face. The little one remained motionless, watching him quietly.

"Now then, of course," Peadar growled. "Can't take a drop with that contraption on." He put the spoon back in his cracked cup, and then fumbling with one huge thick hand, he worked at the tiny faceplate on the creature's head. As he did so, the creature struggled violently, making mewing sounds, wriggling, but helpless in Peadar's grip. There was a rending sound, and the faceplate opened. Instantly there came a hiss as of escaping gas, a whiff of some indescribable odor, and the creature stiffened. Its struggles weakened, slowed, and ceased. It became limp and dangled like a rag doll in Peadar's powerful grip.

At the same moment, beyond the hut, beyond the nearby hill, somewhere above the bogs, there came a great burst of light and sound, a shrill long-drawn whistling, a clap of thunder that rose up into the rainy night sky, echoing about the low hills, higher and higher, then diminished and was gone.

The little man was motionless in Peadar's grip, and slowly Peadar laid the creature down on the table.

Peadar released him—but the little man didn't vanish; didn't suddenly spring to life and bound away with a laugh at having outwitted a mere mortal. The little man remained motionless, lying on the table in his gleaming little metallic suit, the faceplate swinging idly open, his features rapidly turning blue . . .

It was then Peadar had come for me, stumbling out into the rainy night without hat or jacket, shambling over the bogs, making his way these few miles into the village and to the parish house. He found me waiting, for I, too, had seen the lights in the sky, heard the piercing shriek and rumble that rose up and up until it disappeared into the clouds.

Peadar told me his story, sobbing and babbling, while I looked down at the thing that lay on his table. It had begun to shrivel, shrinking inside its metallic carapace under the impact of an atmosphere it had never been meant—or perhaps had lost the ability—to withstand. The silvery antennae drooped from the helmet, touched, sparked feebly, then turned black and crumbled into ash.

I buried the poor creature in an unmarked grave—for there are some things better left undisturbed. But first I did for it what any priest of old Ireland would do. And afterward, I told Peadar it was good of him to mourn, but better to forget. I left him sitting in his windowless sod hut, with the rain pounding down like the sound of endless muted thunder on the roof.

Peadar would forget, I knew. Lost in the fogs of poteen, it would become just another dim dream for him. But I'll remember. I'll always remember that oddly familiar-looking little face; the peaked eyebrows, the broad mouth, the elfin pointed ears.

I'll remember, and I'll wonder—from what far place had he come—and why? Was he retracing a legend of his own; come to see for himself a land as distant and remote in antiquity to his kind as the legend that had inflamed poor old Peadar was to us? A misty millennium when the little ones, already reaching for the stars, were able to perform wonders the larger, simpler savages who replaced them could only have conceived of as magic?

We'll never know—not now.

But I have a feeling, drawn from some primitive well of memory as deep and old as the race of Celts, that from whatever far place that little creature came, the ground I laid him in, the dark and ancient soil of Ireland, was to him not alien.

CHANGE OF HEART

by George Whitley

from *Fantastic*

Of all the legendary and mythical creatures of earth, the dwellers in the sea—mermaids, monsters, were-seals, sirens—have been among the most consistently intriguing. For many years, it has been generally agreed that the superficial resemblance between dolphins and humans was probably responsible for most mermaid "sightings." Now the most recent evidence suggests that the resemblance is not entirely superficial.

Once, during the Second World War, I depth charged a whale.

Those of us who served in the fast (but not fast enough) well-armed (but not well-armed enough) independently sailing merchant ships were apt to suffer from itchy trigger fingers, were liable to shoot first and to ask questions afterward.

This was such an occasion.

We were homeward bound, running north and east from Bermuda to Liverpool. It was a typical Western Ocean morning—not too cold, for we were in the Gulf Stream and the following half-gale was southwesterly. There was a penetrating, unpleasant drizzle that threatened to turn to fog at any moment. We had no radar, neither were we equipped with asdic. The possession of either instrument would have made us much happier, especially since we knew that a convoy not very far ahead of us had been badly mauled by a wolf pack. But we were not lacking in armament. We mounted a six-inch gun, a twelve pounder, eight Oerlikons, half a dozen light machine guns and our full quota of assorted rocket weapons. And smugly in their racks right aft, three depth charges.

It was my forenoon watch.

I was nervously pacing the bridge, checking the alteration of course every time that the bell of the zig-zag clock in the wheelhouse sounded, making sure that the Oerlikon gunners in the bridge wings were keeping an efficient look-out. With my own binoculars I scanned the heaving grayness ahead and astern, to port and to starboard.

And then I saw it, fine on the port bow, a long dark shape that broke surface briefly in a smother of foam, that was crossing our bows and heading out to starboard. It was, perhaps, half a mile distant. The port Oerlikon gunner saw it too; his weapon hammered suddenly and shockingly, sending a stream of twenty-millimeter tracer shells hosing out over the waves. I ran for the wheelhouse shouting to the helmsman. "Starboard a little! Starboard five degrees! Steady!" I pushed up the plunger switch that actuated the alarm bells, then twirled the calling handle of the sound-powered telephone.

"Six-inch!" I snapped.

"Six-inch here, sir."

"Arm and set depth charges!"

The six-inch guns crew would have closed up by now; there would be somebody to attend to the telephone while the gunner on watch set the charges. There would be somebody to stand by the docking telegraph, which could be used for warlike purposes as well as for its original function, a means of rapid communication when berthing the ship. I made a mental computation, felt rather than reasoned that at our speed we should be, now, right over the submarine. I was dimly aware that the other officers were on the bridge, that the Old Man was standing at my elbow. He did not interfere, but followed me out to the wing of the bridge, to the telegraph.

I jerked the handle to *Let Go*. The bell jangled as the pointer came round to acknowledge the order.

"Submarine?" asked the Captain tersely.

"Yes, sir. She was right ahead when I picked her up. I tried to ram, but she must have dived."

We stared aft, at the turbulence of our wake. And then

there was more than the disturbance created by our racing screws. We saw the surface of the sea boil and break before we felt the hammer blow of the underwater explosion. We saw a geyser of white water—and lifted on it, twisting and turning, the great body. The enormous head, the fluked tail, made recognition instantaneous.

The broken thing fell back into the violently disturbed water, remaining afloat for a few seconds. The sea around it was red with blood.

Then—but it was a long time ago—I felt sorry for that whale.

Now . . .

The war was over, and then there was the Cold War, and there was the Korean War, and there were the various revolutions and the suppressions of revolutions—but we, in the Merchant Navy, soon forgot all that we had ever learned about guns and gunnery, very soon lost the feeling of naked defenselessness that at first afflicted us when we ventured out of port without as much as a light machine gun mounted about the decks. Our status hadn't changed. We were still civilians—but we were no longer civilians expecting to be shot at and equipped with the wherewithal for shooting back.

Time passed, and with its passage came the usual promotions until, not so long ago, I found myself Master of one of the Company's smaller and older vessels, outward bound from the U.K. to New Zealand via the Panama Canal.

Frankly, once the initial worries were behind me I was enjoying the voyage. I had no intention of running "a taut ship"—that phrase, in fact, has always rather repelled me. A happy ship is not necessarily an inefficient one; the so-called taut ship very often is just that. My officers were capable and no lazier than the generality of certificated personnel. As long as things got done, I let them do them in their own way. My attitude, I admit, has rather changed of late. I am apt to be extremely fussy about an efficient look-out. Recently I overheard my disgruntled Third Mate complaining to the Second Mate at the watch relief, "The Old Man's getting worse. He gave me hell because I hadn't seen a blasted porpoise playing about the bows!"

So my not very taut—but quite happy—ship was in mid-Pacific, a little artificial satellite falling down the long orbit between the Gulf of Panama and Auckland. (After all, a Great Circle track could be classed as a surface orbit.) There was the sky, usually cloudless, above us, there was the blue, empty sea all around us. There was the familiar, pleasant ship's routine—the routine that on a long voyage seems to be built around meal times and deck golf times and gin times. There was a well-stocked ship's library, supplemented by the books that I had brought with me. There was the novel—*the* novel—that I was going to write some time when I felt strong enough; at the moment, however, I was enjoying the laziness after years of a more or less strenuous life as Chief Officer far too much to be able to drive myself to break out my portable typewriter and supply of paper.

And then, one fine afternoon, I was awakened from my afternoon sleep by the buzzing of the telephone.

I took the instrument from its rest, said drowsily and irritably, "Captain here."

"Second Officer, sir. I've sighted something ahead and a little to starboard. Looks like a raft."

"I'll be right up," I told him.

I found him on the starboard wing of the bridge, his binoculars focussed on the distant object. I brought my own to bear. It was a raft all right—a roughly constructed affair with a mast from which a tattered rag depended limply. There was a man sprawled at the foot of the mast. I thought that I saw him move. I depressed the lever of the automatic whistle control, heard the deep, organ note go booming out over the gently undulant water. The man heard it too. He tried to stagger to his feet, managed to get to his knees. He clung to the mast with one hand, waved feebly with the other. Then he collapsed.

Meanwhile, my Second Mate had not been idle. I had been faintly conscious of the shrilling of his pocket whistle as he called the stand-by man of the watch. Shortly afterward I realized that the Chief Officer was standing behind me, waiting for orders, and that the Bo's'n was waiting behind him.

There was no need to give any orders really. It was just a nice, uncomplicated rescue job, with weather conditions more in our favor than otherwise. I could have brought the ship right alongside the raft and sent a man down with a gantline to make fast around the castaway—he would obviously have been unable to climb a pilot ladder. But I wasn't sufficiently sure of my abilities as a ship handler; it would have been a cruel irony to crush or overset the flimsy craft and to kill the man at the very moment of rescue.

So I stopped the ship about a quarter of a mile from the raft and lowered and sent away the motorboat, under the Chief Officer. The Mate handled the boat well, laid it alongside the rough platform and then sent two A.B.s to help the man aboard. They had to lift him, to carry him, to pass him over the gunwales into the lifeboat. One of them reboarded, the other one remained on the raft for a minute or so, searching the small area. He found nothing—I could see the gesture that he made with his empty hands—and then rejoined his mates.

I went down to the boat deck when the lifeboat returned. I looked down into the boat as it was rehoisted. The castaway looked more dead than alive. He was bearded, shaggy, emaciated, deeply sunburned. He was naked but for a ragged pair of shorts. A jolt as the gunwale of the boat fouled a plate edge seemed to stir him into consciousness. He started up, looked around wildly. The Mate put out a hand to restrain him. He seized the Mate's hand in his own two claws, hung on to it desperately. The sight could have been ludicrous—but it was somehow frightening.

The boat was brought up to fishplate level and then the winch was stopped. The castaway was lifted and passed inboard—"Light as a bleedin' fevver, 'e is," I heard one of the A.B.s say—and then strapped into the waiting stretcher.

The glaring eyes in the dark brown face—the face that was little more than dry skin stretched over a skull—found mine. "Captain?" he croaked.

"Yes. I am the Captain."

"Must . . . Must tell you. Must warn."

"In a little while," I told him.

"Now," he whispered demandingly. *"Now."*

But I had other things to attend to. I ignored his pleadings, went back to the bridge where I waited until the boat had been swung inboard and secured. I gave the orders that put an end to the interruption to our voyage. Then, with the ship once again on her course and with the engines turning at full speed, I left the bridge to the officer of the watch and went down to the hospital.

We carried no doctor that trip, but it didn't really matter. Given the Medical Guide and a well-stocked medicine chest, the average ship's officer can manage as well as the average G.P.—rather better, perhaps, as he has a deeper understanding of the psychology of merchant seamen.

The Mate, I found, was coping quite well. He had put the man into one of the hospital bunks. He had smeared the cracked lips and the cracked skin of the upper face and body with petroleum jelly. He was holding a cup of hot, sweet tea from which the castaway, propped up with pillows, was sipping slowly. He was saying soothingly, "You can tell your story later. You must get your strength back first . . ."

The man jerked his hand violently so that the tea slopped over the Mate's hand and over the white bed linen. He cried—and already his voice was stronger, was less of a croak—"But this is important. You must be warned. You have radio. You must warn the world!"

Pirates? I wondered. *Russian submarines on the prowl? Little green men from flying saucers?*

"Let him talk," I said.

He turned to stare at me. "Yes, Captain. I'll talk. And you will listen. You must listen. You must. *You must!*" His voice had risen to a scream.

"Yes," I said soothingly. "I'll listen."

I listened—and this is what I heard.

There were six of us (he said). There were six of us, and we were bumming around the islands, picking up the odd parcel of cargo, the occasional deck passenger. She had been a smallish patrol craft during the war, and then she'd been converted into a fishing boat, with refrigeration, so we could always catch and later sell fish when there was nothing else offering. Jimmy Larsen—he'd been in the Navy—was our navigator, and Pete Russo was the engineer, and Bill and Clarry and Des and myself just lent a hand as and when required. It was a good enough life while it lasted.

But it didn't last.

We were making a passage from . . . from . . .

Sorry, I wasn't the navigator, and I could never remember the names of those islands. But it was a French island, a small one, and we had this cargo of government stores. And it doesn't matter much where we were taking it to, because we never got there.

It was a fine morning when it happened. I was at the wheel. Bill and Clarry were sunbaking on the foredeck, Pete was in the engine room, Des and Jimmy were sleeping. I was damn' nearly asleep myself, but I was keeping the lubber's line steady enough on the course.

I heard Bill call out, saw him get to his feet. He was pointing, out to starboard. Clarry got up to look. I looked too. I thought at first that the broken water was indication of a reef—then saw that it was a school of dolphins. Nothing unusual, perhaps—but this was unusual. There was a whale among them. A big fellow. A sperm whale, by the looks of him.

They were heading our way. I didn't worry, neither did the others. Porpoises are friendly brutes. They like to show off their superior turn of speed, like to make rings around even fast ships. And the poor little *Sue Darling* wasn't a fast ship. She may have been, when the Navy had her, but she wasn't now.

She was Jimmy's girl friend in Honolulu, Sue Darling.

Yes, that was her name. You'd better tell her, Captain. But break it gently to her if you can. She was a good kid, and she thought the world of Jimmy.

They were heading our way—and then, as I had known they would, they altered course before they hit us, half of them passing astern, the others passing ahead. But the whale didn't alter course. He was a big brute. There must have been damn' near a hundred tons of him, and he was doing a good twelve knots.

He hit us at speed, right amidships, and that was the end of *Sue Darling*. She was a wooden ship, and she was old, and she just fell to pieces at the impact. The diesels must have gone straight down when the bottom fell out of her, taking Pete Russo with them. We never saw anything of him. I did glimpse Jimmy briefly before he went down. He must have been dead—there was a lot of blood. Something must have hit him, must have smashed his skull in. Des got out of it all right—not that it did him much good in the end. I shall never forget the absurd look of amazement on his face as he woke up to find himself struggling in the water.

The porpoises were all around us, buffeting us with their sleek bodies, making odd grunting noises. At first I thought that they were attacking us. But they weren't. They were herding us to where the dinghy that had been lashed to the ship's cabin top was floating, bottom up. And it seemed—I thought at the time that I was going mad—that those grunting noises were some sort of speech, that they were talking among themselves and trying to tell us something.

They helped us to right the dinghy. Yes, Captain, they helped us. And one of them surfaced under me and gave me a boost as I was trying to struggle over the gunwale. I should have been grateful to the brute, but I wasn't. I was frightened. It was . . . uncanny.

Anyhow, there the four of us were—Bill, Clarry, Des and myself. The four nonspecialists. We were seamen by courtesy only. We were no more than pen-pushers who had heard the call of the islands, who had found a nomadic life in a rickety little island tramp preferable to an existence chained to an office desk. But we were none of us much good at doing things—which, perhaps, was just as well. But the porpoises weren't to know that.

There were no oars in the dinghy. They had fallen out and were drifting with the wreckage of the ship. We argued among ourselves about it, tried to decide which one of us was going to swim from the boat to bring them back. But none of us was keen on going over the side. That water was too . . . too crowded. And for the same reason we weren't keen on using our hands as paddles until we recovered the oars. Suddenly we had become very frightened of the sea and of everything that moved within it.

The porpoises settled the argument. They surrounded the boat—to port, to starboard, astern. I was afraid that the pressure of their bodies would push in the planking. They got under way—and we got under way with them. I don't know what speed we were making—but it was a respectable one. We were soaked by the water slopping in over the bows and the low sides.

We traveled—towed or pushed by the porpoises—all that day, and all of the following night. We traveled all the next day as well, and the day after that. When, in the late afternoon, we saw the island, a blue smudge on the far horizon, we were in a sorry state. It was Clarry who had kept us going. He had read a lot. He was one of those people who read anything and everything. It was Clarry who told us to keep our bodies immersed in the sea water—there was plenty of that—so that our skins could absorb the moisture. It was Clarry who told us to tear buttons from the shorts that were all that we had in the way of clothing, and to suck them. It was Clarry who told us about the old legends concerning porpoises or dolphins that have saved the lives of shipwrecked sailors.

But he never convinced me that those porpoises were really friendly.

It was just at sunset that our dinghy grounded on the sandy beach of the island. It wasn't much of an island—although we were glad enough to tumble out of the boat and to stagger up on to the dry land. It wasn't much of an island, as we were to discover when we got around to exploring it the next day. There were a few palm trees—but either they weren't coconut palms or coconuts weren't in season. There was some low scrub. And that was all.

But I'm getting ahead of myself. We staggered up the beach, as I have said, and then, after we had got some of our strength back, we began to feel thirsty. But there wasn't any water—we never found any then, neither did we find any later. Clarry suggested that we dig—which we did, with our bare hands. The trickle of moisture that oozed through into the holes—after a long, long time—was salt. Clarry said that we should pull the boat well up on to the beach so that it would not drift away during the night; it seemed that we should not be able to stay on the island, there was nothing there to support life.

But the boat was gone. There was no sign of it.

And then we saw a commotion out to sea. It was light enough—the full moon had risen as the sun had set—and we could see the flurry of white water, the leaping bodies. It was the porpoises back again—and this time they were driving before them a shoal of mullet. They chased those fish right up on to the sand where they flopped—energetically at first, then more and more feebly.

"Water," said Clarry.

"Food," croaked Des. "Food—if you don't mind eating raw fish. But where is the water?"

"In the fish," said Clarry. "In the flesh of the fish. You always have to take salt with fried fish, don't you? The body fluids are practically pure fresh water."

These body fluids were fresh water all right—but far from pure, very far from pure. Raw fish is so very much fishier than cooked fish. There was food, and there was water, and we got the revolting mess down somehow, tearing the still living bodies to pieces with our fingers and teeth, spitting out scale and bone and . . . and other things.

And that was the first night on the island.

We slept well enough. Come to that, we slept surprisingly well. When we woke up at sunrise we made our exploration of the tiny island, found nothing that would raise our hopes. But we were alive, and that was something. And then Clarry set us to building a pile of brush for a signal fire. How we were going to light it—in the unlikely event of our sighting a passing ship or aircraft—nobody was quite sure, not even Clarry. It's one thing reading about making fire by friction—getting the necessary technique isn't so easy.

The porpoises came back at mid-morning—about forty of them. There was great splashing and confusion as they pushed something up on to the sand. We ran down to examine it. It was a tangled mass of wreckage—steel wreckage. What paint that remained on it was gray. It may have come from a surface ship, it may have come from a submarine. None of us knew enough about ships to be able to hazard a guess.

Another school of the brutes drove in from the horizon. They were pushing more wreckage—but floating wreckage this time. There were shattered timbers—some of them old and barnacle encrusted, some of them comparatively new. There were planks that could have come from the *Sue Darling*, from her dinghy. Led by Clarry, we waded into the shallows, dragged the wood well inshore. It seemed that the sea beasts had presented us to the wherewithal to construct a raft. (But why had they taken and broken up the dinghy?)

Then all but one of the porpoises retired to seaward. He cruised up and down in the shallow water, pointing with his beak first of all at the steel wreckage, then at the timber. He grunted and he whistled. It seemed that there was a note of exasperation in the sounds that he was making.

Eventually he dived.

"He wanted something," said Bill. "He wanted to tell us something. What did he want to tell us?"

"But he's only an animal," objected Des.

"What are we?" asked Clarry. He said softly, "The history of Man is the history of the tool-making, fire-using animal . . . What must it be like to be intelligent—as intelligent as Man, perhaps—but to have no hands, no tools, no fire?"

"Rubbish," said Des. "Those things aren't intelligent."

"Their brains are as heavy as ours, and as convoluted. Nobody is sure just how intelligent they are. They are at least as intelligent as dogs. *At least . . .*" He stared out to sea, looked worried. "But there could have been changes, mutations. Radiation is supposed to be one of the causes of mutation—if not *the* cause—and there must be large volumes of radioactive water in the Pacific after the various bomb tests. And all the Cetacea—the whales and the porpoises—must be genetically unstable. Think of it—not too long ago, geologically speaking, their ancestors were bear-like mammals, living on dry land. They returned to the sea—and must have been able to adapt themselves to the new conditions—or the old conditions?—rapidly, in a very few generations. And now there's been another mutation, another jump ahead . . ."

"Hogwash," said Des, but his voice failed to carry conviction.

While Clarry talked and we listened, the porpoises returned. We became aware that half a dozen of them were pushing something else through the shallows. It was a large slab of slatelike rock. There were scratchings on its smooth surface. At first they made no sense at all as we studied them after we had pulled the slab ashore. Human artists see things differently from each other and such differences are obvious enough in the finished paintings. An essentially alien but intelligent being will see things differently from a man.

And then, quite suddenly, those pictures made sense. There was a fire—depicted by curly lines—about which stood vaguely manlike figures. There were those same manlike figures engaged upon some sort of work, hitting something with hammers. And then there was a porpoise—the shape of that was more easily recognizable—and then there was a swordfish. But it wasn't a swordfish. It was a porpoise and it was wearing a sort of harness from which the sword projected ahead of it.

Clarry—he was quick on the uptake—started to laugh. He spluttered, "The damned things want us to turn armorer.

They want us to fit them out—for war!"

Well, that was what they wanted.

They kept us fed—and I never want to eat fish again!—and as long as they saw us working they seemed to be satisfied. Oh, we never did get around to making fire—although it would have been a pity to have burned the timber that we were supposed to use for firewood. We had other ideas about that timber.

We used stones for tools at first—there was a rocky outcrop at the center of the island—and managed to knock conveniently shaped hunks of iron from the jagged wreckage of the submarine or whatever it was. And with these crude hammers we knocked the nails out of the timbers—and knocked the same nails back in again as we constructed the raft. We were cunning enough to do this inshore, well out of the reach of prying eyes. (At times I thought that the seabirds had become intelligent too, would report what we were doing to our captors.) And those of us who stayed on the beach put up an impression of busyness. Toward the end, however, the leader of the school—I suppose you could call him that—was getting impatient, was cruising up and down snorting indignantly. Clarry tried to tell him that we were handicapped by having no fire; he pointed to the sun, he pointed to the diminished pile of timber, and then he shook his head violently. Whether or not he got the message across I don't know.

And then the raft was finished. We launched it that night. There was no moon, and the sea was quiet, undisturbed by splashings or snortings. We all clambered aboard the flimsy contraption somehow and the current took us out and away. We knew that our attempt at escape was almost certain death—but we were crazy enough to consider death superior to serfdom to lower animals.

But were we so crazy?

And were those animals so very much lower?

Lower or not—they found us.

They found us at noon, when our spirits were at a low ebb, when we were looking back with regret to the scanty shade afforded by those few poor palms, when we would have sold our souls for a trickle of the fishy water, that we had found so revolting, down our throats.

They found us at noon—and I, I must confess, was glad to see them. When they pushed us back to the island I would be a good boy, I decided. I would try to make a fire. I would try to make one of the sword and harness affairs that they wanted. I would try to turn swords out in dozen lots.

They found us—and the others found them.

They came sweeping in at forty knots or so from the south'ard, great, vicious brutes, in appearance not unlike the creatures milling about our raft but bigger, much bigger, black, with white bellies and with great dorsal fins. They may have been what Clarry called mutants; they may have been killer whales. Whatever they were—they were killers. They drove in like a charge of marine cavalry, heavy cavalry, and as they smashed through the squadrons of our captors the water was reddened with blood. They turned, charged again.

And again.

And then one of them nudged the raft. Des was the first to go, to slide, screaming, into the bloody water. His screams ceased abruptly. Then Bill went as the raft was almost capsized, and then Clarry and I were fighting for the mast, for a firm grip on the shaky pole that could mean salvation. I'm glad about one thing. Clarry was unconscious when he went overboard. I felt like a murderer when I hit him as hard as I did—I am a murderer—but at least he didn't feel those teeth that chipped him in two.

I don't know why they left me. Perhaps they thought there were only three men on the raft. Perhaps they were so well fed that they just didn't bother me. But, quite suddenly, they were gone—and the sea was empty but for the floating fragments east. (The air wasn't empty; the birds were feeding well.)

And that's all. That's all as far as I'm concerned, Captain. When we get to port I'm leaving this ship, and I'm going as far inland as I can get, and I never want to see the sea again. It's up to you, now. You must get the messages out—for your sake, as well as everybody else's. You aren't safe. Those things—as we found out—can control whales. Think of it—think of a hundred-ton whale sent to mash himself in your screws and then, while you're drifting, helpless, a dozen or so of the brutes charging against the plating of your side.

You're not safe.

Nobody's safe.

You must warn . . .

You must . . .

"He's passed out," said the Mate. "He excited himself too much."

I looked at the sleeping man. There was nothing, I hoped, wrong with him beyond exhaustion and the effects of prolonged exposure. His breathing seemed natural enough.

"What did *you* make of it?" I asked.

The Mate put his finger to his forehead, made a circling motion. "Round the bend, sir. Round the bend. Probably his raft was chivvied by porpoises. But all this talk of mutants and such—why, it's straight out of science fiction!"

"So are artificial satellites and rockets to the Moon," I told him.

"They're *different*," he said.

"Detail the cadets to stand a watch in the hospital," I ordered. "And arrange for the watch-keeping officers to look in when they come off watch."

I went back to my quarters and started to draft a radio message. A warning? No—not yet. I had no desire to expose myself to the ridicule showered upon such master mariners as observe sea serpents and then are unwise enough to report it. "Picked up survivor from island trader *Sue Darling*." That would do. That would have to do for the time being.

But a full report would have to be made.

I was still working on that report after dinner. It had not been continuous work—I had gone down to look at the rescued man at frequent intervals, and each time he had been sleeping. But I was working on it when I heard the weird whistlings and snortings drifting in through my open port.

I went out on to the lower bridge.

It was a brightly moonlit night, and I could see that the sea around us was alive with porpoises, with sleek, leaping forms that matched our seventeen knots with ease. Suddenly I felt afraid, found myself scanning the ocean for the telltale spout that would betray the presence of a whale.

There was a shout from aft.

I heard a youthful voice crying, "Stop him! Stop him!"

I ran down the ladder, then to the after end of the boat deck. I saw the castaway standing on the bulwarks, shaking his fists, hurling imprecations at the things in the sea. Then the ship lurched and he overbalanced. He kicked at the ship's side as he fell, so he hit the water well clear of the suction of the screws. It should have been easy enough to pick him up again—especially since the cadet who had been on hospital watch threw him a lifebuoy.

It should have been, but . . .

They say that porpoises will never attack a man in the water. These porpoises could never have heard of the saying. They made a quicker and messier job of their victim than a school of starving sharks would have done.

Somebody with both authority and imagination will read my report in time, I hope. Meanwhile, there are far too many small ships going a-missing, far too many little craft, built of wood, of the type that can be disposed of by one charge of a single whale.

And what was it that the castaway had said?

"You aren't safe. Those things—as we found out—can control whales. Think of it—think of a hundred-ton whale sent to mash himself in your screws and then, while you're drifting, helpless, a dozen or so of the brutes charging against the plating of your sides.

"You're not safe.

"Nobody's safe . . ."

I felt very sorry for the whale that I depth charged all those years ago.

But now . . .

But now I'd feel a lot happier if somebody in authority did something about the situation, if once again I had those horribly lethal ashcans sitting smugly in their racks at the stern.

ANGELA'S SATYR
by Brian Cleeve

from the *Saturday Evening Post*

If there is some rationale for mermaids, or even for leprechauns, there is none *needed* for satyrs. Anyone who has been exposed, even for an evening of parlor-jargon, to the basic concepts of modern psychiatry, is aware of the symbolism of the demi-god-demi-goat.

Angela was innocent of such exposure; but she understood it very well.

The music was like a bird singing, so gentle and so natural that she never noticed it. As light as a dandelion clock floating on the summer air, she stepped down the grassy slope and dipped one bare, golden foot in the stream. The stream gave a little skip and ripple of pleasure and washed her toes with silver.

"Ah," the girl whispered, and pulling her simple peasant's dress over her golden head, she stepped into the water. It came to her knees like a kitten purring. Throwing the red cotton dress onto the grass, she crouched down and began to wash herself. The music that had been impersonally beautiful took a sudden, passionate and distinctly masculine tone.

"Ooh!" screamed the girl and covered herself with water to protect her modesty. For there on the bank, half hidden among the bushes and the long grass, was a man. Or perhaps a boy. She raised herself a little, for after all she might need to run, and it was best to be prepared. Distinctly a boy and, so far as she could see, as naked as she was. A dark-bronze chest, a neck of honey gold like a Greek column and a head so handsome that it made her heart swim. Dark curling hair with subtle flames of red gold buried in its darkness. Eyes green gold and slanting like a cat's. A curved nose with flaring nostrils and the most delicious hint of masculine brutality; and teeth as white as the bite of an apple, glistening with pleased ferocity, or so it seemed to the girl.

"You wouldn't—you wouldn't really—" the girl said in a small, weak feminine voice. The boy tilted his head and raised an eyebrow.

"Wouldn't what?" He had a most curious accent, as if he weren't used to speaking dialect, and she wondered if he was a gentleman's son from the city. She stood up the tiniest bit further and spread out a very small hand to cover as much of her beauty as it could, which wasn't much.

"Who are you?" she whispered, for really in all her eighteen years she had never seen anyone half so handsome and her particular valley in Sicily is a valley of handsome men.

The boy put his homemade pipes to his mouth and blew a nightingale's trill of notes. "My name is Dionisio," he said, "and I am a satyr." And with that he stood up and stepped delicately down the bank toward the water, while the girl, with a little scream of fright, fainted dead away. Because from the hips down Dionisio was covered with shaggy fur, and instead of human feet he had the daintiest pointed silvery hoofs, like a goat.

Squatting down by the water's edge, without wetting more than his fingertips—for satyrs have a constitutional aversion to water—Dionisio caught the girl by her floating hair and drew her gently out of the river.

"How very beautiful," he said. "My mother must have been quite mad."

"Why?" said the girl, who had recovered with really astonishing quickness.

"What is your name?" said Dionisio, stroking back the wet gold hair from her temples and gazing into the dark-violet depths of her eyes.

"Angela," whispered the girl. "Dionisio." Her eyelashes fluttered, and the sunlight laid leaf shadows on her slender neck. "But why do you say your mother was mad?"

"Because she told me to beware of humans, and above all of girl humans. She told me they were unbelievably wicked, depraved and untrustworthy."

"Some of them are," whispered Angela. Her lips parted, her eyelids closed. "You wouldn't—take advantage of me, would you?"

"How?" said Dionisio.

"You wouldn't kiss me?"

"How do you kiss someone?" asked Dionisio, whose mother had been most frightfully strict.

"Like this," said Angela, sliding a golden arm round his bronze shoulders, and planting the softest, warmest, most intoxicating of kisses on his astonished lips.

Dionisio's whole body trembled and tears came to his eyes. "Oh," he cried out when he could make any kind of sound at all, "is that kissing? Is that what I mustn't do?"

"Yes," said Angela.

"I'd better try it, just to make sure I don't do it by mistake," said Dionisio and, pursing up his lips with care, as if to blow the sweetest music into his pipes, he kissed Angela rather lopsidedly on the corner of her adorable mouth.

"You haven't got it right at all," said Angela. "I'd better show you again." And she did.

It shows how slow some learners are that it took her the whole afternoon and a lot of the evening to teach him exactly what it was he mustn't do, and before they were both satisfied that he had it right it was dark. They lay side by side in the warm grass under the huntress moon, whispering occasional things and holding hands.

"So this is love," whispered Dionisio, enchanted. "It *is* fun."

Angela said nothing, but only ran her warm hand through the thickness of his curls. And found just above his forehead two small, blunt horns. Which brought her up with something of a start, for it reminded her that Dionisio was not everything that a lover ought to be. The priest, for example, might look askance at them if they tried to get married. She sat up, stabbed by a further thought.

"You're not married already?" she cried.

"What is married?" asked Dionisio and this of course required a further lengthy explanation. So lengthy, in fact, that they fell asleep at the end of it and slept till dawn. When the first rays of sunlight touched them, Angela woke with the most delicious feeling, stretched her darling self and stepped into the stream as if it were a waiting bath.

"Dionisio!" she called. "Don't wake up, you mustn't look," and to her grave vexation he didn't wake and therefore didn't look. She appeared at her best in the river, and she knew it. Even three years ago, when she was still a child, an artist had surprised her washing her hair in the river and had been so thunderstruck that all the time he was trying to sketch her he kept dropping his pencils and charcoals in the water. Afterward her mother had whipped her soundly for not charging the painter a thousand lire for allowing him to paint her, so she remembered the occasion vividly.

She finished washing herself and came and knelt on the bank, gazing down at the sleeping satyr. Something would have to be done about him, but what? To continue meeting him in secret might have a certain charm, and without doubt there remained many other prohibitions to teach him—dear heaven, the boy knew absolutely nothing, it was terrible—but she could see any number of difficulties that might arise. Yet how to bring him into human society? She touched his silvery hoof, and he twitched in his sleep and flung one arm across his face, shielding his eyes from the growing sunlight. Special shoes? Baggy trousers? A hat to cover his horns? And then she thought of Mamma Zolfa, the witch.

"Wake up!" she cried and tugged his hoof with an impatient hand. "I'm going to get you turned into a human boy. Quick, before there are any people about."

So, holding his hand, she running and he skipping, she led him through dark woods to the desolate valley where Mamma Zolfa had her dilapidated hovel. The witch was having her breakfast of stewed mice and herbs, and was less than pleased at being disturbed. But when she saw Dionisio, she sucked her gums in astonishment. "A satyr!" she croaked. "I haven't seen one of them for nigh on seventy years. I thought they all died off of thirst in the time of the phylloxera blight. Well, well, well, what brings you two to Mamma Zolfa?" She leered at Angela in the most disgusting way.

Her hut was so dark that it was difficult to see anything except the yellow round eyes of her tame owl, and the glow of a little red brazier at the back of the hut, like a tiny doorway to hell. Angela tried to make out Mamma Zolfa's wrinkled, walnut features.

"We want to turn Dionisio into a human boy," she said timidly.

"Why?" said Mamma Zolfa. "Isn't he all right as he is?" And she cackled in the most shameless way, which spoke very badly for any dealings that she might have had with satyrs seventy years before.

"We want to get married," Angela said with a rush, twisting her little hands together. "And you see, the priest—"

"Ha," said Mamma Zolfa, "horns before marriage, eh?" And she cackled again. "It'll be very expensive."

"How much?" said Angela, her voice suddenly quite sharp and, to anyone who knew both of them, surprisingly like her mother's.

"Three drops of blood from your third finger," said Mamma Zolfa, trying to seize Angela's left hand. "Three locks of hair from the left side of your head. And three gold coins from your dowry."

"*Mamma mia,*" said Angela. A coal hissed and flared in the brazier, the hut filled for a fleeting moment with soft red light, and Angela saw it reflected on Dionisio's gleaming shoulder. "All right," she whispered. "But cash on delivery. Turn him first."

The light died in the hut, the owl closed his eyes, and Mamma Zolfa huddled down on the pile of rags that served her for bed and chair, table and wardrobe.

"It may take a bit of time," she said. "I haven't done this for years. And never with a satyr. People into goats. Even goats into people. But a satyr—" She sucked her gums, remembering ancient spells.

The air in the hut grew close as a blanket, black as a cave. The owl flew out with a screech of fear, and mice and rats scuttled in their willow cages.

"Anima perduta—" the old crone began, and the words lost themselves in a tumbling jumble of toothless sounds. She felt on the ground for herbs and dropped a handful of them on the brazier, filling the thick darkness with stinking smoke and a green flame that seemed to give no light. *"Cambia risma satiro!"* she screamed suddenly, and Dionisio gave a great cry of pain. The hut was shaken with the sound of the stamping of his hoofs and with wild frightened bleating. Something butted against Angela's thigh. She screamed in terror and tore her way outside the hut, followed by a very large and very handsome goat.

"Dionisio!" shrieked Angela.

"Mehhhhhhh," bleated the goat and tried pathetically to stand on its hind legs. Mamma Zolfa tottered out into the sunlight.

"Where is Dionisio?" Angela shouted at her. "What have you done with him?" She ran past the old woman, wrenched aside the curtain of rags that sheltered the hut's doorway, filling the filthy hovel with sunlight. But there was no one there. Both women, crone and girl, turned to look at the goat.

"Dionisio!" whispered the girl.

"I must have got the spell wrong," said Mamma Zolfa. "Dear oh dear, my memory's failing me terribly these days. I really ought to retire." And she shook a regretful head.

"You silly old witch!" shrieked Angela. "What are we going to do?"

"There's nothing we can do," said Mamma Zolfa, resignedly. "When it goes wrong like that it's irreversible. Except—"

"Except!" breathed Angela.

"It's ridiculous, really," said Mamma Zolfa, "quite impossible. He has to be kissed on the nose by a real princess, and she has to tell him with complete sincerity that he is the most beautiful goat in the world."

"Oh my heavens!" cried Angela. "Do you know any princesses?"

"No," said Mamma Zolfa, "there seem to be far fewer of them about these days. It's the taxation that kills them." And at that moment, with a terrible cry of anger, anguish, anxiety and antipathy, Angela's mother descended like a fat fury on the scene. In one hand she brandished a switch, in the other a length of rope.

"Strumpet!" she screeched. "Shameless baggage, hussy, harlot! Where were you all night? Where is the villain?" For as softly and secretly as Angela had led Dionisio to Mamma Zolfa's hut, an early laborer had seen her golden head stealing through the woods, and not alone, and having followed the pair at a distance too great to see what Dionisio really was, he had run to tell Angela's mother the distressful news. Hence her furious arrival now. "Where is he?" she roared and, throwing down the rope, she caught her daughter by the hair and began to make the switch dance a tattoo on her back.

Filled with protective rage, Dionisio charged the mother and received a blow with the switch across the skull that nearly blinded him.

"Control your goat, you filthy old wretch," shrieked Angela's mother and gave Dionisio such a kick that he lost all interest in Angela or her mother and lay on his back imagining that he was dead. Angela, twisting out of her mother's grip, fled weeping down the valley. Her mother pursued her, showing a remarkable turn of speed and a deadly accuracy with the switch.

"Meh, meh," croaked Dionisio, coming slightly to his senses.

"Waste not, want not," said Mamma Zolfa, slipping the fallen rope round Dionisio's neck. It was a pity that it was a billy goat; if she could beg the loan of a nanny goat from somewhere, there was no telling what might happen. "All's well that ends well," she said, tying the other end of the rope to a nearby tree. Giving Dionisio another hearty kick to introduce him to the new regime, she went inside the hut to finish her breakfast.

Meanwhile the most extraordinary things had been happening in the nearby city.

The artist who had long ago painted a ravishing picture of Angela bathing in the river had died in an appalling state of insolvency. Whereupon his long-suffering landlady, who was owed at least three weeks' rent, seized his goods and arranged for them to be auctioned.

There were four kettles with holes burned in the bottom, two broken chairs, a bed, a piece of carpet, an enormous number of half-empty tubes of paint, forty-seven camel-hair brushes with most of the bristles missing, thirty-seven paintings of no earthly interest to anyone, and the portrait of Angela. And who should happen to see and buy this totally delightful picture but a television producer! A thin, anxious man who wore dark glasses in bed and lived on pills, he gave one tiny but heartfelt cry of delight when he saw the painting and said, "For me, for me!"

There followed a month of detective work to discover who the model might have been, and on exactly the morning that Angela and her mother arrived in a dead heat at their humble cottage in the Sicilian valley of Zeppo di Fiori, there arrived at their door the most enormous motor car, apparently ninety-four feet long and requiring two chauffeurs, while far in the luxurious scarlet-leather depths of the stern, surrounded by swansdown cushions and crystal cocktail shakers, sat the television producer. He took one look at Angela and, uttering another tiny but heartfelt cry of joy, he said again, "For me! For me!"

Only this time, having Angela's mother to deal with, it cost him a great deal more money than the picture had. It also cost Angela's mother some fatiguing exertions with the switch to persuade Angela that this was in the best interests of all concerned.

"He will feed you like a Christmas pig," coaxed Mamma Angela.

"Dionisio!" Angela wept.

"He will dress you in silks and satins, and you'll have clean underclothes every Sunday!" shouted Mamma Angela.

"I only want my Dionisio!" wailed her daughter.

"You'll have a real bathroom to bathe in and hot water out of a tap and a mirror to see yourself in," screamed Mamma Angela in a paroxysm of impatience, and gave her daughter the switch across a tender place so vigorously that it clinched the argument then and there. So, weeping for Dionisio and sitting gingerly on two swansdown cushions, the golden, gorgeous simplicity of Angela was carried off to the city.

Swallowing four tranquilizing pills at a gulp from a little silver box, the television producer guided Angela into his eighteen-room apartment. Angela stood stunned in the hallway until called to herself by the arrival of a maid in a starched white apron. She dropped a profound curtsy. "My goodness, miss," said the maid, "you mustn't do that. You're to be the mistress here. At least, I expect so." And leading her off to the marble bathroom, she introduced her to the delights of hot water and scented soap, talcum powder and enormous, soft, cuddlesome towels. But even while she lay in the steaming water fragrant with essence of jasmine, Angela sighed, "Dionisio," and wondered what horrible things might be happening to her beloved. For the things that can happen to a goat in a place like Sicily are truly horrendous.

She sighed, "Dionisio," while she was being wrapped in a heavy mandarin dressing gown of raw yellow silk; while her toenails were being pedicured and her fingernails manicured; while her tawny golden hair was being waved and sleeked under the skillful fingers of Madame Hortense and her breathless assistants.

She sighed, "Dionisio," while her elocution teacher strove to remove the rough edges of dialect from her linnet's voice; while her dancing teacher taught her to float like a swan; while a retired duchess taught her to eat as if she had never been hungry in her life and to behave at parties with the degree of insolence and boredom proper to her beauty. "You'll be the success of the season!" wheezed the duchess. "I can't wait to see you!" And poor Angela let the weight of her golden head bend her lily neck and sighed, "Dionisio."

Whenever she saw the twittering arrival of the television producer at one of her lessons, her mind's eye saw behind him the living statue of her satyr, the sunlight filtering through forest leaves to fall in light and shadow on his burnished shoulders, his arching chest, his green and slanting eyes. When at her music lessons her teacher guided her fingers on the piano keys, she heard not "do re mi fa" but the woodland notes of Dionisio's pipes. And when at night she lay on swansdown and drew the blue satin sheets up to her delicately molded chin, the last word she invariably uttered was "Dionisio." Nevertheless, being a human girl, she found some consolations in her situation.

Which could not be said for Dionisio. Alas! Mamma Zolfa had borrowed a nanny goat from a near neighbor who owed her something for a little matter of a love potion. It was not a very pretty nanny goat nor a young one. But it was certainly a great one for the billies, as its owner proudly said. Cackling ferociously, Mamma Zolfa led the abandoned creature back to her hut, and untying Dionisio's rope from the tree, fastened the end round the neck of the nanny, tying the two creatures together with three yards of rope between them and the light of love already burning in the nanny's eyes.

"Unholy matrimony!" cackled Mamma Zolfa and went into her hut to cook some rats for supper.

"Stay away from me!" said Dionisio. "I'm not what you think!"

"Dream goat!" whispered the nanny and made a rush. Dionisio jumped three yards back and the nanny followed him like a ball on a string.

"Help!" bleated Dionisio. "Mamma!"

And so, leap and counterleap, the two creatures—the one driven by terror and the other by unmentionable ambitions —tore up the mountainside, and but for the happy accident by which a sharp edge of rock sliced the rope binding them together, I would never have had the heart to go on telling you this story.

"Free!" shrieked Dionisio.

"Lover, come back!" pleaded the nanny. But she hadn't the speed and, after half an hour of fruitless chase, she gave up and wandered disconsolately home. The wretched Dionisio, so ashamed of his appearance that when he drank from a pool he closed his eyes against his reflection, wandered far and wide, avoiding the haunts of men and beasts and stopping only for necessary snacks of grass. Now and then he would raise his poor bearded goat-face to the indifferent sky and sigh, "Angela! Oh, Angela!" Until one day a laborer, seeing a fine fat goat wandering masterless across the mountainside, captured Dionisio and sold him to a butcher.

Meanwhile the exquisite Angela, stopping all breaths with her beauty, had reached the destiny for which the television producer had spent so much money and time and anxious twittering. She was about to go on his program as question mistress in a panel game. Need I describe the ravishment of the studio audience, the spellbound delight of the panel members, the delirium of the viewers, the superlatives of the critics? Angela caused a furor.

"Television has found its soul!" cried the *Gazetta*. "Angela for President!" pleaded the *Giornale*.

In the largest of his palaces the elderly and lecherous Prince Massimo Grasso wheezed, "Angela for me!" as he gazed oyster-eyed into the thirty-six-inch television screen mounted at the foot of his six-poster bed. "See that it is arranged," he said to a henchman. "If necessary, employ the Mafia. Buy the television studios. Do anything. Just so long as she is here by tonight. I shall even marry her."

And so it was that weeping tears like pearls and looking ethereal in a wedding gown of seventy yards of Bruges lace, poor Angela was led slowly up the aisle by the television producer, while the monstrous prince waited for her at the altar steps, breathing heavily. Reporters from ninety-five countries crammed the cathedral, television cameramen hung like bats from the columns and the organ loft, seven bishops served as acolytes, and an eighth bishop, the prince's first cousin, conducted the ceremony. The local

schoolchildren were given a day's holiday, and the prince
ordered a truly enormous barbecue party to take place on
the palace lawns, to be attended by all his retainers, tenants,
serfs, peasants, debtors, creditors and poor relations. So
enormous did the party promise to be that the butchers'
shops of the city were emptied of every lamb, goat and calf
that they contained, and live animals were obtained from
country butchers for miles around as a reserve supply, to be
led bleating and lowing into the orchard gardens of the
palace. And among these unfortunate beasts was poor
Dionisio. Imagine his feelings as he waited, tethered to an
apple tree, while the scent of barbecued goat drifted toward
him.

"Oh, Angela!" he sighed. "If only I knew that you at
least were happy, I could die consoled."

When what should he hear, high-pitched and unmistakable, but his beloved Angela's scream of fear? For I must
tell you that while the barbecue party was going on, the
prince found himself impatient to relive delights that he
ought to have put sternly behind him many years before.

"My little jujube," he crooned in Angela's ear. "Come
upstairs and we'll look at the pretty fireworks from my
bedroom window."

Yet when they got upstairs, to Angela's surprise she
found that the bedroom windows didn't overlook the
front lawns, but the orchard.

"Where are the fireworks?" cried Angela. "I can't see
any at all."

"I've brought my own!" cackled the prince, and with
that he began chasing poor Angela up and down the
enormous bedroom.

"Help!" screamed Angela in a paroxysm of terror.
"Help!" And this was the cry that Dionisio heard. Bound-
ing against his rope with desperate force, he broke free.

"Angela!" he bleated and, leaping through an open
window, he galloped through the palace searching for his
beloved. Up marble staircases, along shining corridors beneath ancestral portraits and suits of armor, Dionisio
charged to the rescue.

While running as fleet and light as a deer, Angela broke from her pursuer and raced out into the corridor, the puffing prince behind her. And there, at the head of the stairs, Dionisio caught up with them.

"Charge!" bleated Dionisio. And down went his head, up went his tail, thud went his hooves, and his curved and powerful horns caught the prince precisely in the rump, lifting him a yard into the air. Dionisio skidded back onto his haunches as if he had hit a railway buffer, and the prince fell, hit the middle step of the staircase, bounced, and crashed to the marble floor twelve feet below, stone dead.

"Oh, my savior!" cried Angela and, not thinking of Dionisio or of anything else but the frightful fate from which she had just been saved, she threw her arms around the goat's neck, kissed him warmly on his moist nose and said with heartfelt sincerity, "You are the most beautiful goat in the world!"

Whereupon the most astonishing changes began to take place in Dionisio; for, of course, Angela since eleven o'clock that morning had been a real princess and quite by accident had done and said the only things which could rescue Dionisio from his horrid shape. Within moments, before her astonished and delighted eyes, there stood her satyr, her beloved Dionisio, bronzed, beautiful, and with green, slanting eyes filled with love and gratitude and wonder.

What more is there to tell? The prince was buried in a black marble sarcophagus in the cathedral, with an inscription relating how he had been killed tragically on his romantic wedding night by a maddened goat escaped from the barbecue wedding feast. The princess, not noticeably overcome by grief, retired to a large country estate, where soon she married a country fellow unknown to aristocratic society. The two are rarely seen and, when they are, the husband is invariably wearing unfashionably baggy trousers and a high-crowned hat. But they seem very happy.

PUPPET SHOW

by Fredric Brown

from *Playboy*

The visitors from space, if they do come some day, may or may not be even mythically familiar in their form.

Horror came to Cherrybell at a little after noon on a blistering hot day in August.

Perhaps that is redundant; *any* August day in Cherrybell, Arizona, is blistering hot. It is on Highway 89, about forty miles south of Tucson and about thirty miles north of the Mexican border. It consists of two filling stations, one on each side of the road to catch travelers going in both directions, a general store, a beer-and-wine-license-only tavern, a tourist-trap-type trading post for tourists who can't wait until they reach the border to start buying serapes and huaraches, a deserted hamburger stand, and a few 'dobe houses inhabited by Mexican-Americans who work in Nogales, the border town to the south, and who, for God knows what reason, prefer to live in Cherrybell and commute, some of them in Model T Fords. The sign on the highway says, CHERRYBELL, POP. 42, but the sign exaggerates; Pop died last year—Pop Anders, who ran the now deserted hamburger stand—and the correct figure should be 41.

Horror came to Cherrybell mounted on a burro led by an ancient, dirty and gray-bearded desert rat of a prospector who later gave the name of Dade Grant. Horror's name was Garvane. He was approximately nine feet tall but so thin, almost a stick-man, that he could not have weighed over a hundred pounds. Old Dade's burro carried him easily, despite the fact that his feet dragged in the sand on either side. Being dragged through the sand for, as it later turned out, well over five miles hadn't caused the slightest wear on the shoes—more like buskins, they were —which constituted all that he wore except for a pair of what could have been swimming trunks, in robin's-egg blue. But it wasn't his dimensions that made him horrible to look upon; it was his *skin*. It looked red, raw. It looked as though he had been skinned alive, and the skin replaced raw side out. His skull, his face, were equally narrow or elongated; otherwise in every visible way he appeared human—or at least humanoid. Unless you count such little things as the fact that his hair was a robin's-egg blue to match his trunks, as were his eyes and his boots. Blood-red and light blue.

Casey, owner of the tavern, was the first one to see them coming across the plain, from the direction of the mountain range to the east. He'd stepped out of the back door of his tavern for a breath of fresh, if hot, air. They were about one hundred yards away at that time, and already he could see the utter alienness of the figure on the led burro. Just alienness at that distance, the horror came only at closer range. Casey's jaw dropped and stayed down until the strange trio was about fifty yards away, then he started slowly toward them. There are people who run at the sight of the unknown, others who advance to meet it. Casey advanced, slowly, to meet it.

Still in the wide open, twenty yards from the back of the little tavern, he met them. Dade Grant stopped and dropped the rope by which he was leading the burro. The burro stood still and dropped its head. The stick-man stood up simply by planting his feet solidly and standing, astride the burro. He stepped one leg across it and stood a moment, leaning his weight against his hands on the burro's back, and then sat down in the sand. "High gravity planet," he said. "Can't stand long."

"Kin I get water fer my burro?" the prospector asked Casey. "Must be purty thirsty by now. Hadda leave water bags, some other things, so it could carry—" He jerked a thumb toward the red-and-blue horror.

Casey was just realizing that it *was* a horror. At a distance the color combination seemed only mildly hideous, but close up—the skin was rough and seemed to have veins on the outside and looked moist (although it wasn't) and *damn* if it didn't look just like he had his skin peeled off and put back on inside out. Or just peeled off, period. Casey had never seen anything like it and hoped he wouldn't ever see anything like it again.

Casey felt something behind him and looked over his shoulder. Others had seen now and were coming, but the nearest of them, a pair of boys, were ten yards behind him. "*Muchachos,*" he called out. "*Agua por el burro. Un pozal. Pronto.*"

He looked back and said, "What—? Who—?"

"Name's Dade Grant," said the prospector, putting out a hand, which Casey took absently. When he let go of it it jerked back over the desert rat's shoulder, thumb indicating the thing that sat on the sand. "*His* name's Garvane, he tells me. He's an extra something or other, and he's some kind of minister."

Casey nodded at the stick-man and was glad to get a nod in return instead of an extended hand. "I'm Manuel Casey," he said. "What does he mean, an extra something?"

The stick-man's voice was unexpectedly deep and vibrant. "I am an extraterrestrial. And a minister plenipotentiary."

Surprisingly, Casey was a moderately well-educated man and knew both of those phrases; he was probably the only person in Cherrybell who would have known the second one. Less surprisingly, considering the speaker's appearance, he believed both of them.

"What can I do for you, sir?" he asked. "But first, why not come in out of the sun?"

"No, thank you. It's a bit cooler here than they told me it would be, but I'm quite comfortable. This is equivalent to a cool spring evening on my planet. And as to what you can do for me, you can notify your authorities of my presence. I believe they will be interested."

Well, Casey thought, by blind luck he's hit the best man for his purpose within at least twenty miles. Manuel Casey was half Irish, half Mexican. He had a half-brother who was half Irish and half assorted-American, and the half-brother was a bird colonel at Davis-Monthan Air Force Base in Tucson.

He said, "Just a minute, Mr. Garvane, I'll telephone. You, Mr. Grant, would you want to come inside?"

"Naw, I don't mind sun. Out in it all day ever' day. An' Garvane here, he ast me if I'd stick with him till he was finished with what he's gotta do here. Said he'd gimme somethin' purty vallable if I did. Somethin'—a 'lectrononic—"

"An electronic battery-operated portable ore indicator," Garvane said. "A simple little device, indicates presence of a concentration of ore up to two miles, indicates kind, grade, quantity and depth."

Casey gulped, excused himself, and pushed through the gathering crowd into his tavern. He had Colonel Casey on the phone in one minute, but it took him another four minutes to convince the colonel that he was neither drunk nor joking.

Twenty-five minutes after that there was a noise in the sky, a noise that swelled and then died as a four-man helicopter sat down and shut off its rotors a dozen yards from an extraterrestrial, two men and a burro. Casey alone had had the courage to rejoin the trio from the desert; there were other spectators, but they still held well back.

Colonel Casey, a major, a captain and a lieutenant who was the helicopter's pilot all came out and ran over. The stick-man stood up, all nine feet of him; from the effort it cost him to stand you could tell that he was used to a much lighter gravity than Earth's. He bowed, repeated his name and the identification of himself as an extraterrestrial and a minister plenipotentiary. Then he apologized for sitting down again, explained why it was necessary, and sat down.

The colonel introduced himself and the three who had come with him. "And now, sir, what can we do for you?"

The stick-man made a grimace that was probably intended as a smile. His teeth were the same light blue as his hair and eyes.

"You have a cliché, 'Take me to your leader.' I do not ask that. In fact, I *must* remain here. Nor do I ask that any of your leaders be brought here to me. That would be impolite. I am perfectly willing for you to represent them, to talk to you and let you question me. But I do ask one thing.

"You have tape recorders. I ask that before I talk or answer questions you have one brought. I want to be sure that the message your leaders eventually receive is full and accurate."

"Fine," the colonel said. He turned to the pilot. "Lieutenant, get on the radio in the whirlybird and tell them to get us a tape recorder faster than possible. It can be dropped by para— No, that'd take longer, rigging it for a drop. Have them send it by another helicopter." The lieutenant turned to go. "Hey," the colonel said. "Also fifty yards of extension cord. We'll have to plug it in inside Manny's tavern."

The lieutenant sprinted for the helicopter.

The others sat and sweated a moment and then Manuel Casey stood up. "That's a half-hour wait," he said, "and if we're going to sit here in the sun, who's for a bottle of cold beer? You, Mr. Garvane?"

"It is a cold beverage, is it not? I am a bit chilly. If you have something hot—?"

"Coffee, coming up. Can I bring you a blanket?"

"No, thank you. It will not be necessary."

Casey left and shortly returned with a tray with half-a-dozen bottles of cold beer and a cup of steaming coffee. The lieutenant was back by then. Casey put the tray down and served the stick-man first, who sipped the coffee and said, "It is delicious."

Colonel Casey cleared his throat. "Serve our prospector friend next, Manny. As for us—well, drinking is forbidden on duty, but it was 112 in the shade in Tucson, and this is hotter and also is *not* in the shade. Gentlemen, consider

yourselves on official leave for as long as it takes you to
drink one bottle of beer, or until the tape recorder arrives,
whichever comes first."

The beer was finished first, but by the time the last of it
had vanished, the second helicopter was within sight and
sound. Casey asked the stick-man if he wanted more coffee.
The offer was politely declined. Casey looked at Dade
Grant and winked and the desert rat winked back, so
Casey went in for two more bottles, one apiece for the
Civilian terrestrials. Coming back he met the lieutenant
arriving with the extension cord and returned as far as the
doorway to show him where to plug it in.

When he came back, he saw that the second helicopter
had brought its full complement of four, besides the tape
recorder. There were, besides the pilot who had flown it, a
technical sergeant who was skilled in its operation and who
was now making adjustments on it, and a lieutenant-colonel
and a warrant officer who had come along for the ride or
because they had been made curious by the request for a
tape recorder to be rushed to Cherrybell, Arizona, by air.
They were standing gaping at the stick-man and whispered
conversations were going on.

The colonel said, "Attention," quietly, but it brought
complete silence. "Please sit down, gentlemen. In a rough
circle. Sergeant, if you rig your mike in the center of the
circle, will it pick up clearly what any one of us may say?"

"Yes, sir. I'm almost ready."

Ten men and one extraterrestrial humanoid sat in a
rough circle, with the microphone hanging from a small
tripod in the approximate center. The humans were sweating profusely; the humanoid shivered slightly. Just outside
the circle, the burro stood dejectedly, its head low. Edging
closer, but still about five yards away, spread out now in
a semicircle, was the entire population of Cherrybell who
had been at home at the time; the stores and the filling
stations were deserted.

The technical sergeant pushed a button and the tape
recorder's reel started to turn. "Testing . . . testing," he
said. He held down the rewind button for a second and

then pushed the playback button. "Testing . . . testing," said the recorder's speaker. Loud and clear. The sergeant pushed the rewind button, then the erase one to clear the tape. Then the stop button.

"When I push the next button, sir," he said to the colonel, "we'll be recording."

The colonel looked at the tall extra-terrestrial, who nodded, and then the colonel nodded at the sergeant. The sergeant pushed the recording button.

"My name is Garvane," said the stick-man, slowly and clearly. "I am from a planet of a star which is not listed in your star catalogs, although the globular cluster in which it is one of 90,000 stars is known to you. It is, from here, in the direction of the center of the galaxy at a distance of over four thousand light-years.

"However, I am not here as a representative of my planet or my people, but as minister plenipotentiary of the Galactic Union, a federation of the enlightened civilizations of the galaxy, for the good of all. It is my assignment to visit you and decide, here and now, whether or not you are to be welcomed to join our federation.

"You may now ask questions freely. However, I reserve the right to postpone answering some of them until my decision has been made. If the decision is favorable, I will then answer all questions, including the ones I have postponed answering meanwhile. Is that satisfactory?"

"Yes," said the colonel. "How did you come here? A spaceship?"

"Correct. It is overhead right now, in orbit twenty-two thousand miles out, so it revolves with the earth and stays over this one spot. I am under observation from it, which is one reason I prefer to remain here in the open. I am to signal it when I want it to come down to pick me up."

"How do you know our language so fluently? Are you telepathic?"

"No, I am not. And nowhere in the galaxy is any race telepathic except among its own members. I was taught your language for this purpose. We have had observers among you for many centuries—by *we,* I mean the Galactic

Union, of course. Quite obviously, I could not pass as an Earthman, but there are other races who can. Incidentally, they are not spies, or agents; they have in no way tried to affect you; they are observers and that is all."

"What benefits do we get from joining your union, if we are asked and if we accept?" the colonel asked.

"First, a quick course in the fundamental social sciences which will end your tendency to fight among yourselves and end or at least control your aggressions. After we are satisfied that you have accomplished that and it is safe for you to do so, you will be given space travel, and many other things, as rapidly as you are able to assimilate them."

"And if we are not asked, or refuse?"

"Nothing. You will be left alone; even our observers will be withdrawn. You will work out your own fate—either you will render your planet uninhabited and uninhabitable within the next century, or you will master social science yourselves and again be candidates for membership and again be offered membership. We will check from time to time and if and when it appears certain that you are not going to destroy yourselves, you will again be approached."

"Why the hurry, now that you're here? Why can't you stay long enough for our leaders, as you call them, to talk to you in person?"

"Postponed. The reason is not important but it is complicated, and I simply do not wish to waste time explaining."

"Assuming your decision is favorable, how will we get in touch with you to let you know *our* decision? You know enough about us, obviously, to know that *I* can't make it."

"We will know your decision through our observers. One condition of acceptance is full and uncensored publication in your newspapers of this interview, verbatim from the tape we are now using to record it. Also of all deliberations and decisions of your government."

"And other governments? We can't decide unilaterally for the world."

"Your government has been chosen for a start. If you accept, we shall furnish the techniques that will cause the others to fall in line quickly—and those techniques do not involve force or the threat of force."

"They must be *some* techniques," said the colonel wryly, "if they'll make one certain country I don't have to name fall into line without even a threat."

"Sometimes the offer of reward is more significant than the use of a threat. Do you think the country you do not wish to name would like your country colonizing planets of far stars before they even reach the moon? But that is a minor point, relatively. You may trust the techniques."

"It sounds almost too good to be true. But you said that you are to decide, here and now, whether or not we are to be invited to join. May I ask on what factors you will base your decision?"

"One is that I am—was, since I already have—to check your degree of xenophobia. In the loose sense in which you use it, that means fear of strangers. We have a word that has no counterpart in your vocabulary: it means fear of and revulsion toward *aliens*. I—or at least a member of my race—was chosen to make the first overt contact with you. Because I am what you would call roughly humanoid —as you are what I would call roughly humanoid—I am probably more horrible, more repulsive, to you than many completely different species would be. Because to you I am a caricature of a human being, I am more horrible to you than a being who bears no remote resemblance to you.

"You may think you *do* feel horror at me, and revulsion, but believe me, you have passed that test. There *are* races in the galaxy who can never be members of the federation, no matter how they advance otherwise, because they are violently and incurably xenophobic; they could never face or talk to an alien of any species. They would either run screaming from him or try to kill him instantly. From watching you and these people"—he waved a long arm at the civilian population of Cherrybell not far outside the circle of the conference—"I know you feel revulsion at the sight of me, but believe me, it is relatively slight and certainly curable. You have passed that test satisfactorily."

"And are there other tests?"

"One other. But I think it is time that I—" Instead of finishing the sentence, the stick-man lay back flat on the sand and closed his eyes.

The colonel started to his feet. "What in *hell?*" he said. He walked quickly around the mike's tripod and bent over the recumbent extraterrestrial, putting an ear to the bloody-appearing chest.

As he raised his head, Dade Grant, the grizzled prospector, chuckled. "No heartbeat, Colonel, because no heart. But I may leave him as a souvenir for you and you'll find much more interesting things inside him than heart and guts. Yes, he is a puppet whom I have been operating, as your Edgar Bergen operates his—what's his name?—oh yes, Charlie McCarthy. Now that he has served his purpose, he is deactivated. You can go back to your place, Colonel."

Colonel Casey moved back slowly. *"Why?"* he asked.

Dade Grant was peeling off his beard and wig. He rubbed a cloth across his face to remove make-up and was revealed as a handsome young man. He said, "What he told you, or what you were told through him, was true as far as it went. He is only a simulacrum, yes, but he is an exact duplicate of a member of one of the intelligent races of the galaxy, the one toward whom you would be disposed —if you were violently and incurably xenophobic—to be most horrified by, according to our psychologists. But we did not bring a real member of his species to make first contact because they have a phobia of their own, agoraphobia—fear of space. They are highly civilized and members in good standing of the federation, but they never leave their own planet.

"Our observers assure us you don't have *that* phobia. But they were unable to judge in advance the degree of your xenophobia, and the only way to test it was to bring along something in lieu of someone to test it against, and presumably to let him make the initial contact."

The colonel sighed audibly. "I can't say this doesn't relieve me in one way. We could get along with humanoids, yes, and we will when we have to. But I'll admit it's a relief to learn that the master race of the galaxy is, after all, human instead of only humanoid. What is the second test?"

"You are undergoing it now. Call me—" He snapped his fingers. "What's the name of Bergen's second-string puppet, after Charlie McCarthy?"

The colonel hesitated, but the tech sergeant supplied the answer. "Mortimer Snerd."

"Right. So call me Mortimer Snerd, and now I think it is time that I—" He lay back flat on the sand and closed his eyes just as the stick-man had done a few minutes before.

The burro raised its head and put it into the circle over the shoulder of the tech sergeant.

"That takes care of the puppets, Colonel," it said. "And now, what's this bit about it being important that the master race be human or at least humanoid? What is a master race?"

HANG HEAD, VANDAL!

by Mark Clifton

from *Amazing Stories*

There is a certain comfort in the notion that Someone Out There is watching—that some pre-established authority (hopefully benign, but even if not . . .) will stop us from leaping off too soon. But if we continue without interruption, and if our know-*how* continues to keep the lead it has long held over our know-*why* . . .

On our abandoned Martian landing field there hangs a man's discarded spacesuit, suspended from the desensitized prongs of a Come-to-me tower. It is stuffed with straw that was filched, no doubt, from packing cases which brought out so many more delicate, sensitive, precision instruments than we will take back.

None knows which of our departing crew hanged the spacesuit there, nor exactly what he meant in the act. A scarecrow to frighten all others away?

More likely a mere Kilroy-was-here symbol: defacing initials irresistibly carved in a priceless, ancient work of art, saying, "I am too shoddy a specimen to create anything of worth, but I can deface. And this proves I, too, have been."

Or was it symbolic suicide: an expression of guilt so overpowering that man hanged himself in effigy upon the scene of his crime?

Captain Leyton saw it there on the morning of final departure. He saw it, and felt a sudden flush of his usual stern discipline surge within him; and he all but formed the harsh command to take that thing down at once. Find the one who hanged it there: Bring him to me!

The anger—the command. Died together. Unspoken.

Something in the pose of the stuffed effigy hanging there must have got down through to the diminishing person inside the ever-thickening rind of a commander. The forlorn sadness, the dejection; and yes, he too must have felt the shame, the guilt, that overwhelmed us all.

Whether the helmet had fallen forward of its own weight because the vandal had been careless in stuffing it with too little straw to hold its head erect—vandals being characteristically futile even in their vandalism—or whether, instead of the supposed vandal, this was the talent of a consummate artist molding steel and rubber, plastic and straw into an expression of how we all felt—no matter, the result was there.

The Captain did not command the effigy be taken down. No one offered and no one asked if that might be his wish—not even the ubiquitous Ensign perpetually bucking for approval.

So on an abandoned Martian landing field there hangs a discarded spacesuit—the image of man stuffed with straw; with straw where heart, and mind, and soul ought to be.

At the time it seemed a most logical solution to an almost impossible problem.

Dr. VanDam summed it up in his memorable speech before the United Nations. If he were visually conscious of the vault of face blurs in the hushed assembly, this lesser sight did not obscure his stronger vision of the great vaulted mass of shining stars in the black of space.

He may not even have been conscious of political realities, which ever obscure man's dreams. What he said would be weighed by each delegate in terms of personal advantage to be gained for his own status. Second, his words would be weighed again in terms of national interest. Third, what advantage could be squeezed out for the racial-religious-color blocs? At the fourth level of consideration, what advantage to the small nation bloc over the large; or how would his plan enhance the special privileges of the large over the small? Down at the fifth level, could it preserve the *status quo,* changing nothing so that those in power could remain in power, while, at the same time, giving the illusion of progress to confound the ever-clamoring liberals? At the deep sixth level, if one ever got down that far, one might give a small fleeting thought to what might be good for mankind.

If Dr. VanDam even knew that such political realities must ever take precedence over the dreams of science, he gave no sign of it. It was as if all his thought was upon the glory of the stars and the dream of man reaching out to them. It was the goal of reaching the stars that inspired his speech.

"We must sum up the problem," he was saying. "It is simply this. There is a limit to how far we can theorize in science without testing those theories to see if they will work. Sooner or later the theorist must submit to the engineer whose acid test of worth is simply this: 'Does it work?'

"We have always known that the Roman candles we are using for our timid little space flights can take us only to the nearest planets, for there is that inexorable ratio of time to initial thrust. Unless thrust continues and continues, the Mayfly lifetime of man will expire many times over before we can reach the nearest star. Nor will our limited resources fuel ion engines. We must learn how to replenish with space dust gathered along the way.

"To have continuous velocity we must have continuous nuclear power. To have continuous nuclear power, we must have more nuclear tests. Now we believe we know how to take not special ores but ordinary matter, of any kind, and convert it into nuclear power. We believe we can control this. We have this in theory. But the engineer has not tested it with his question, 'Does it work?'

"We cannot make these tests on Earth. For what if it does not work? We dare not use the Moon. Its lighter gravity makes it too valuable a piece of real estate in terms of future star journeys. It will be our busy landing stage; we dare not contaminate it nor risk destroying it.

"We have reached stalemate. On Earth and Moon we

can go on no further without testing. On Earth and Moon we dare not test. Some other testing area must be found.

"Our explorers have brought us conclusive proof that Mars is a dead world. A useless world in terms of life. Useless, too, as a source of minerals, for our little Roman candles can carry no commercial pay load. A useless world for colonization, with air too tenuous for human lungs and water too scarce for growing food. Humans must be housed in sealed chambers, or wear spacesuits constantly. From all practical points of view, a worthless world.

"But invaluable to science. For there, without destroying anything of value to man, we can put our theories to test. We believe we can start a nuclear reaction in ordinary rock and dirt, and keep it under control to produce a continuous flow of power. We believe we can keep it from running wild out of control.

"If the innumerable tests we must run *do* contaminate the planet, or even destroy it slowly, our gain in knowledge will be greater than the loss of this worthless real estate."

There was a stir in the Assembly: something between a gasp of horror and a murmur of admiration at the audacity of man's sacrificing a whole planet to his knowledge. They had not known we were so far along the way.

And then, on second thought, a settling back in satisfaction. It seemed a simple solution to an impossible problem. To take not only VanDam's tests away from Earth, but nuclear testing of every kind! To quell the fears and still the clamoring of the humanists who would rather see man stagnate in ignorance than risk the future to learn. At every level of political reality this might turn to advantage. If there were any who still thought in such terms, it might even be good for mankind generally!

"I am not mystic minded," VanDam continued, when the rustle and murmur had diminished, "but the convenience of this particular planet, located precisely where it is, far enough away that we must have made great progress in science to reach it, and close enough to be ready when we need it for further progress—this seems almost mystical in its coincidence."

(That for the ones who would have to go through the usual motions of obtaining Higher Power approval for doing what they fully intended doing all along.)

"My question: Shall the nations of Earth agree upon our use of this so convenient and otherwise worthless stage placed right where we need it—waiting for us down through all the ages until we should be ready to make use of it?"

Their ultimate response was favorable.

Dr. VanDam did not mention, and the members being only politicians unable to see beyond the next vote or appointment, did not say:

"True, we do have a theory of how to start and continue the slow-burn nuclear conversion of ordinary rock and dirt to energy. What we do not have, as yet, is a way to stop it.

"We *think* that eventually future man will probably find a way to stop the process. We *think* slow burn will not speed up and run out of control to consume an entire planet before we have found a way to stop it. We *think* that future science may even find a way to decontaminate the planet. We *hope* these things.

"But we *know* that the science of nucleonics will be stillborn and stunted to grow no further unless we go on testing. We convince ourselves that even if an entire planet is consumed, it is a worthless planet anyway, and will be worth it."

Yet there was the usual small minority who questioned our right to destroy one of the planets of the solar system. There is always such a minority, and as always, the rest of the world, intent on turning what it intended to do anyway into the Right-Thing-To-Do, was able to shout them down.

Anyway, the consequences were for future man to face. Or so we thought.

I say we, because I was one of the members of Project Slow-Burn. Not that I'm the hero. There wasn't any hero.

Mistaken or not, as it was conceived this wasn't one of those television spectaculars cooked up to convert science into public emotionalism. There was no country-wide search for special photogenic hero-types to front the project.

The reporters, true to their writing tradition of trying to reduce even the most profound scientific achievement to the lowest common denominator of sloppy sentimentalism or avid sensationalism, tried to heroize Dr. VanDam as head of the science side of the project. But he wasn't having any.

"Don't you think, gentlemen," he answered them with acid scorn, "it is about time the public grew up enough to support the search for knowledge because we need it, rather than because they'd like to go to bed with some handsome, brainless kook you've built up into a hero?"

This response was not likely to further the cause of journalism.

They tried to lionize Captain Leyton, as head of the transport side of it; but his remarks were even more unprintable.

They never got down far enough through the echelons of status to reach me. I was Chief of Communications, which is just another way of saying I was a television repairman with headaches. Not that it would have done them any good.

There isn't one thing about me that fits the sentimental notions of what a hero should be. I'm not even a colorful character. If I'm expert in my job it's only because I learned early what any lazy man with an ounce of brains also learns—that life goes easier for the expert than for the ignorant. Which is not exactly the hero attitude the public likes to hear, but true all the same.

I did have an advantage which qualifies me to tell this tale.

Supervision nowadays sits on its duff in an office, surrounded by television monitors showing them every phase of their responsibilities, and punches buttons when some guy tries to goof off or starts lousing up the operation.

Somebody has to maintain the system and check the

same monitors. I saw everything of importance that happened.

That's the only way I come into the yarn at all. I didn't start out a hero type. I didn't turn into one. I just watched what happened; and I got sick at my stomach along with everybody else. And now I slink away, sick and ashamed, and not understanding even that, along with the rest. Not heroes—no, none of us.

From the first this was intended and conducted as a genuine scientific project, a group effort, with each man's ego subdued to serve the needs of the whole. No special heroes emerging to show up the rest of the dopes. None of the usual stuff of romantic fiction was supposed to happen—those unusual dangers, horrible accidents, sudden frightful emergencies so dear to the little sadistic hearts of readers and viewers.

So far as I know, nobody beat up anybody with his fists, nor gunned anyone down, which is the usual, almost the only, fictional way yet found by the humanists for coping with life problems.

We assembled the mastership on the Moon base from parts which were Roman candled up, a few pieces at a time, from too heavily gravitied Earth.

The yelps of pain from taxpayers reached almost as high. It was one thing to wash the hands of the vexing problem of nuclear testing by wanting it shifted out to Mars. It was something else to pay for the project.

Against the Moon's lighter gravity we eventually were space-borne with no more than the usual fight between power thrust and inertia, both physical and psychological.

Without touching that precious reserve of fuel which we hoped would bring us back again, we were able to build up so much speed that it took us only a month to reach Mars. No point in showing, because nobody would care, how the two dozen of us were cramped in the tiny spaces left by the equipment and instruments we had to carry.

Construction and maintenance had done their job properly, and, for once, inspection had actually done its job, too. We were able to reverse properly at the right time, and soft-cushion powered our way down into a Martian plain eastward of a low range of hills.

Surely everybody has watched the documentaries long enough to have some idea about the incredibly hostile surface of Mars: the too thin air, which lets some stars shine through even in daytime; the waterless desert; the extremes of temperature; the desolation. . . .

Ah, the desolation! The terrifying desolation!

Moon surface is bad enough; but at least there is the great ball of Earth, seeming so near in that airless world that one has the illusion of being able to reach out and almost touch it, touch home, know home is still there, imagine he can almost see it.

"See that little tip of land there on the east coast of the North American continent? That's where I live!"

"Yeah," somebody answers. "And who is that guy walking through your front door without knocking while you're away?"

Sometimes it seems that close.

On Mars, Earth is just another bright spot in the black night sky; so far away that the first reaction is one of terrible despair, the overpowering conviction that in all that vast hostility a man will nevermore see home; nor know again the balmy twilight of soft, moist summer; nor feel the arms of love.

Explorers had not lied. Nothing, anywhere, could be more worthless to man than the planet Mars. Worthless, except for the unique purpose which brought us here.

We dug in beneath the surface.

Now surely, again, everyone has seen so many of the documentaries that it is unnecessary to show us digging out our living quarters and laboratories beneath that merciless plain. We used the displaced powdered rock to form a crude cement, not long lasting but adequate for the time we would be there. With it, we surfaced over our living area. This was not so much to provide a landing field, since most of our journeying would be in individual jet-powered spacesuits, but to help insure against any leakage of air if our inner seals cracked.

To help seal out the killing radiation we intended to let loose—that, too.

We erected Come-to-me towers at each elevator which would lower space-suited men to lower levels where they could go through locks to reach their quarters. One Come-to-me tower for each half dozen men, tuned to the power source of their suits, to bring each man safely back, as truly as a homing pigeon, to guarantee against their becoming lost on that hostile planet; and, in emergency, should one arise, to see that no panic mob ganged up at one lock and died waiting there for entrance to safety while other locks remained idle—the human way of doing things under stress.

We had to finish all that in the first few weeks before any nuclear tests could be started. Anybody whose notions of science are derived from white-frocked actors in television commercials hasn't the vaguest idea of how much back-breaking physical work at the common labor level a genuine scientist has to do.

There was some emotional relief once we had dug in and sealed out the awful desolation of an uncaring universe. (This is the hardest part of reconciling oneself to the science attitude. More comforting to believe even that the universe is hostile than to admit that it simply doesn't care about man, one way or another.) In our sealed quarters we might briefly imagine ourselves working in an air-conditioned laboratory back home.

It helped. It certainly helped.

Not that I seemed to find time for more than exhausted sleeping there. To see what would be going on at the various field sites where tests were to be run meant the cameras had to be installed at those spots. In spite of the purported rigid tests for expedition personnel, my two assistants must have been somebody's nephews. Somehow each installation seemed to require that I be there.

I was there, and usually without some little piece of equipment which would have helped so much, but which had been deleted from the lists we submitted by clerks who were more concerned with making a big showing of how much weight they could eliminate than in helping us.

Somehow we managed.

But I have made a little list of guys I'm going to ferret out and poke in the nose once I get back to Earth. Maybe those Hollywood producers who think the only way to solve a problem is to beat up somebody or gun him down have something, after all. Right on top of that list, in big bold letters, is the spacesuit designer who thinks a man can handle the incredibly fine parts of miniaturized electronic equipment with those crude instruments they give us to screw into the arm ends of spacesuits.

Somehow we managed. Somehow, out of chaos, order came. Somehow tests got made. Sometimes the theories worked; sometimes, more often, there was only the human sigh, the gulp, the shrug, and back to the drawing board.

Big surprise at the end of the first three months. A supply ship landed. Mostly food and some champagne, yet! Stuff the folks back home thought they'd like to have if they were out here. Even some pin-up pictures, as if we weren't already having enough trouble without being reminded. But none of the equipment we'd radioed for in case the taxpayers could forego a drink and a cigarette apiece to raise money for sending it. The public couldn't understand our need for equipment, so they didn't send any. Miracles aren't supposed to need any equipment or effort; they just come into being because people want them.

The packages of home-baked cookies were welcome enough after our diet of hydroponic algae, but I'd still rather have had a handful of miniature transistors.

Some of the guys said they'd have been willing to substitute their cookies for an equal weight of big, buxom blonde; but that's something the cookie bakers probably preferred not to think about.

The little three-man crew of the supply ship promised, as they were taking off for their return journey, they'd tell 'em what we really wanted when they got back, but I doubt the message ever got broadcast over the home and family television sets. Anyway, scientists are supposed to be cold, unfeeling, inhuman creatures who wander around looking noble, wise, and above it all.

In the beginning I'd thought that once I got the heavy work of installation completed, I could do a little wandering around myself, looking wise and noble. No such luck. I'd no more than get set up to show one experiment than it was over; and I'd have to dismantle, move, and set up for another. We'd thought the lighter gravity of Mars, thirty-eight per cent, would make the labor easy. But somehow there was still lifting, tugging, pulling, hauling, cursing.

But then, nobody wants to hear how the scientist has to work to get his miracle. The whole essence is the illusion that miracles can be had without work, that all one needs is to wish.

All right. So we'll get to the miracle.

Now we were finally ready to get down to the real test, the main reason for our coming out to Mars—Project Slow-Burn.

VanDam chose a little pocket at the center of that little cluster of hills to our West—that little cluster of hills everybody has seen in the pictures radioed back to Earth.

We didn't know it at the time, but that little cluster of hills was causing quite an uproar among archeologists back home. No archeologists had been included in the expedition, and now they were beating their breasts because from the pictures those hills looked mighty artificial to them. There was too much of a hint that the hills might once have been pyramids, they said, incredibly ancient, perhaps weathered down eons ago when the planet was younger, before it had lost so much of its atmosphere, but maybe still containing something beneath them.

We didn't hear the uproar, of course. Administration deemed it unnecessary for us to bother our pretty little heads about such nonsense. In fact the uproar never got outside the academic cloister to reach the public at all. Administration should have listened. But then, when does man listen to what might interfere with his plans and spoil something?

We got all set to go in that little pocket at the center of the hills. The spot was ideal for us because the hill elevations gave us an opportunity to place our cameras on their tops to focus down into the crater we hoped would appear.

A whole ring of cameras was demanded. The physicists seemed to share too much of the public's attitude that all I needed to produce enough equipment was to wish for it. But by stripping the stuff from virtually every other project, I managed to balance the demands of the Slow-Burn crew against the outraged screams of the side-issue scientists.

VanDam's theories worked.

At first it took the instruments to detect that there was any activity; but gradually, even crude human eyes could see there was a hole beginning to appear, deepen and spread—progressively.

It was out of my line, but the general idea seemed to be that only one molecular layer at a time was affected, and that it, in turn, activated the next beneath and to the side while its own electrons and protons gave up their final energy.

The experiment did not work perfectly. The process should have been complete. There should have been no by-product of smoke and fire, no sign to human eyes of anything happening except a slowly deepening and spreading hole in the ground.

Instead there was some waste of improperly consumed molecules, resulting in an increasingly heavy, fire-laced smoke which arose sluggishly in the thin air, borne aloft only by its heat, funneling briefly while it gave up that heat. Then it settled down and contaminated everything it touched. To compound my troubles, of course.

The physicists were griping their guts out because I didn't have the proper infra-red equipment to penetrate the smoke; and somehow I wasn't smart enough to snap my fingers and—abracadabra—produce. Those damned cookie packages instead of equipment! Those damned clerks who had decided what we wouldn't need. My little list was getting longer.

Still, I guess I was able to get a feeble little snap from my fingers. I did manage to convert some stuff, never intended for that purpose, into infra-red penetration. We managed to see down into that smoke- and fire-filled crater.

To see enough.

It was the middle of a morning (somebody who still cared claimed it would be a Tuesday back home) some three basic weeks after the beginning of the experiment. The hole was now some thirty feet across and equally deep, growing faster than VanDam's figures predicted it should, but still not running wild and out of control. Even if it had been, we couldn't have stopped it. We didn't know how.

I was trying to work out a little cleaner fix on the south wall of the crater when that wall disappeared like the side of a soap bubble. My focus was sharp enough to see.

To see down and into that huge, vaulted room. To see the living Martians in that room shrivel, blacken, writhe and die. To see some priceless, alien works of art writhe and blacken and curl; some burst into flame; some shatter unto dust.

That was when the scientists, sitting there watching their monitors with horror-stricken eyes, felt jubilation replaced with terrible guilt.

I, too. For naturally I was watching the master monitors to see that the equipment kept working. I saw it all.

I saw those miniature people, yes people, whole and beautiful, in one brief instant blacken, writhe and die.

Out of the billions of gross people on Earth, once in a generation a tiny midget is born and matures to such perfection in proportion and surpassing beauty that the huge, coarse, normal person can only stare and marvel— and remember the delicate perfection of that miniature being with nostalgic yearning for the rest of his life.

From such, perhaps, come the legends common to all peoples in all ages, of the fairies. Or, eons ago, was there traffic between Earth and Mars? Or even original colonization from Mars to Earth, finally mutating into giants? They were people, miniatures of ourselves.

I saw them there. Perhaps not more than a dozen in that room. But in other rooms? Perhaps in a lacework of underground rooms? A whole civilization which, like ourselves on Mars, had gone underground, sealed themselves in against the thinning atmosphere, the dying planet?

And we had begun the atomic destruction of their planet. We had begun it. We could not stop it. The corrosion keeps growing, spreading.

I saw them die. Somehow I felt their pain.

But I did not die of it.

I carry it with me. I shall always carry it with me.

That's all there is.

In years to come people on Earth, people who did not see what we saw, did not feel the pain and guilt we felt, will wonder at our behavior following that.

Oh there is much to wonder. If there is a civilization, where does their food come from? If they are able to convert rock to food, why are they not able to stop the atomic destruction of their planet we have started? If they are able to fill us with such grief that we can think of nothing but to slink away, like whipped curs caught in vandalism, why didn't they do this before we started the fire we cannot stop?

Oh, there is so much unanswered. People will wonder at the fact that we simply abandoned most of our equipment, the very project itself; that for a sick hour we watched, then, with one accord, without anybody making the decision, we began to withdraw and start for home.

Like small boys, thinking only to vandalize a schoolhouse in their savage glee, discovering it is a shrine.

Or, perhaps in time, we can rationalize it all away. Perhaps so soon as during that long, journey back.

It wasn't our fault, we shall begin to say. They were as much to blame as we. Sure they were!

More to blame! They were more to blame than we!

Why didn't they come out of their holes and fight us? With their fists if they didn't have any guns? *Any* red-bloodied—er, red-blooded—Amuri—well, whatever they are—ought to have enough guts to come out and fight, to defend home, flag and mother!

We'll probably get around to that. It's the normal attitude to take after vandalism. It's the human way.

But as of now, our only thought is to slink away.

On our abandoned Martian landing field there hangs a man's discarded spacesuit, suspended from the desensitized prongs of a Come-to-me tower. It is stuffed with straw filched, no doubt, from packing cases which brought out so many more delicate, sensitive, precision instruments than we take back.

Although we have not been entirely irresponsible in our head-long flight back home.

We do bring back some of what we took out: the more valuable of the instruments. We have been most selective in this.

The only coarse, insensitive, unfinished instrument we bring back—is man.

MARS PROBE: REPORT IN TRIPLICATE

It has been the custom of this *Annual* to present at least one seriously speculative article each year. This time, in honor of the Year of the Venus Probe, we bring you instead SF's own Mars Probe—a selection of the best available advance reports on the Number One planetary prospect for a Terran home-away-from-home.

Herewith, one travelogue and two chapters of Martian history . . .

EARTHLINGS GO HOME!
by Mack Reynolds

from *Rogue*

Time was when a freewheeling bachelor could take off for Lhasa or Timbuktu and upon his return expect to have a conversation piece he could trade on for at least a few months. You know the scene: star attraction at the cocktail parties, bright young things hanging on your words, the other single males standing around looking bleak. You had it made.

Now everybody's been everywhere. Mention your trip to China and three guys yawn and say, yeah, wasn't it awful when the air-conditioning went on the blink at the Peiping Hilton in August. A world traveler is about as unique as an automobile in downtown Manhattan.

Which brings us to the point. You got to get out of the

world, man. There's still so few space travelers, it's all but a monopoly. Suppose the next time you're at a party and the conversation drags, you gaze contemptuously at the 99-to-1 Martini you're drinking and drop a nonchalant bit such as, "When I was on Mars, I got smashed on Canal Coolers. Now there's a *dry* drink. They make it from woji and dehydrated water."

There's this place and that place, in space, but if you're this freewheeling type we're talking about, you'll be choosing Marsport for your vacation, a combination sin city and bargain paradise that'd be hard to equal. Let's start at the beginning.

Spaceship is the only means of transport that can be recommended, and so far as cost is concerned it doesn't make much difference—Pan-Planets Spacelines or Soviet Spaceways. You can't afford either. And don't jump to the conclusion that we're recommending stowing away. The last such case we heard of, a youth hosteler named Elmer Hung, hid himself in a nook too near the rocket tubes. He was eventually discovered when a ship's officer noticed a bunch of Martian stevedores whomping up some barbecue sauce and became suspicious.

No, the only way is to utilize this new system of *Travel Now . . . let your grandchildren pay later*. Which is sort of a combination of the government's deficit spending now and letting posterity pick up the tab, and the old airline system of Travel Now, Pay Later. The loan companies pick your grandchildren, rather than your children, working on the theory that you're probably already so far in debt your kids won't be able to pay it off.

There's not much to say about space travel. The faster you travel, the more boring it becomes. Stroll five miles and you'll probably see a great deal, have an experience or so, meet somebody interesting, and the trip will take possibly two hours. Spend two hours driving along a highway in your car and you'll cover up to two hundred miles, see damn little but the road, and have no experiences whatsoever, you hope, since about the only thing that could happen would be a flat tire or a wreck. Spend the same two hours in a jet aircraft and you'll get halfway across the country and aside from a moment of take-off and one of landing, you'll see nothing except possibly the magazine the stewardess gives you to kill time.

So, okay, in a spaceship you have butterflies in the tummy during count-down and blast-off, and then you sit around doing nothing and with nothing to see except space, of which there is a lot, until you get to your destination. So it's boring.

The boredom ends once you set down in Marsport. Gentlemen, let's face reality. Things are *different* on Mars. If you think you've seen some strange items during your travels such as stand-up bathtubs in Japan, sexual mores in Scandinavia, food in England, politics in South America, forget about them. Till you've hit Marsport, you've seen nothing out of the way.

First things first. You'll want a pad. Unless you can sleep suspended by your knees, something like a bat, you'd better choose an Earth-side type hotel. We believe in adapting to local custom, but somehow Earthlings just don't get the hang of Martian beds.

If you're on a shoestring, you might try the Marsport Young Men's Christian, Hebrew, Moslem, Zen Buddhist and Reformed Agnostic Association. Without going into details, *all* Earth-side religions have combined their resources to open this hotel. It isn't as confusing as you'd first think. The Moslems take over the chapel on Friday, the Hebrews on Saturday, the Christians on Sunday, the Buddhists on Tuesday and the agnostics go to hell in their own way, all week long.

We'll mention in passing here, because this, being a rundown on high life in Marsport, wouldn't usually deal with religion at all, that Earth-side missionaries have a rough row to hoe on Mars, no matter what denomination. It's not that the Martians aren't religious. That is, they believe that Mars was created by a god, or gods, and that all things that live on Mars were also so created. But there the similarity ends to Earth-side religions. Instead of worshipping their gods, they sort of *ignore* them. They adopt a sort of hurt, reproachful attitude toward divinity. Kind of a why-did-you-have-to-do-this-to-us approach. They work on the theory that if the gods had to get onto this creating kick, they could have done it better.

If your budget isn't as tight as all that, you'll probably do as well at the Accelerated Motel as any place. No, that isn't a typesetter's or proofreader's mistake. It isn't the Excelsior Hotel, but the Accelerated Motel, and if you'll stick with us for a moment we'll point out that in spite of the fact that you haven't a car with you on Mars, the Accelerated might still be the best hostelry for you. It's not always in town, of course, but you can usually time your activities so that you can pick it up on the way through.

The fact of the matter is that the climate is so brutally hot in midday and so brutally cold at night that the owners of the Accelerated Motel met the situation by keeping on the move. In short, the establishment is motorized, and keeps in the twilight zone. Of course, this might not be practical on Earth, what with stronger gravity and international boundaries, but, like we keep telling you, Mars is different. Happily, since the Accelerated is Earth-side owned, you'll be able to use American exchange and there'll be no problem there. However, this brings us to the Martian monetary system. They don't have any.

Earthling economists of every hue, including Marxists, are still in a condition of shock trying to make some sort of sense of the Martian means of exchange, but they don't seem to be getting very far. Martian historians will admit that some thousands of years ago they did use money on Mars but that it didn't work out so well. In fact, it caused a lot of trouble. It seems as though some people wanted to acquire unreasonably large amounts of the stuff and that led to all sorts of disagreeableness. So the Martians discontinued it.

Anticipating some of your questions, and admitting that we, ourselves, are none too clear, we can only say that it *seems* as though from the earliest youth each Martian simply puts everything he ever buys on the cuff. When he's eventually lived his life out and is laid to rest, the fiscal authorities settle it all up, deducting from the earnings of his lifetime everything that he spent.

Yes, yes, we know. You're saying, "Suppose his tab totals up to more than he earned?" And we can only say, repeating all over again that Mars is different, that in that case they wake him up and make him work out the difference. It seems that medicine is a science that is very advanced among the Martians.

Happily, this money problem isn't going to affect you much since you'll be paying off to Earth-side concerns for your hotel, food, drinks and such.

And anticipating, once again, a matter that you'll undoubtedly bring up at this point, we can only say that in spite of what you now think, you will *not* want to eat the native food and will *not* want to drink the native drinks. True enough, a few of the Martian dishes are such that you can sample them as prepared in your Earth-side type hotel, and adapted to your Earthling palate.

For instance, there's the dish they call the Cold Tamale, undoubtedly because visually it somewhat resembles the famed Mexican food. However, instead of being well laced with red chili peppers, the Martian version has a sort of *reverse* pepper, which, instead of burning your mouth, cools it to the point where you spit icicles, a very disconcerting experience the first time you sample the dish.

But it is not in food that you run into your greatest hazard in items Martian. Their drink can be even more startling, given Earthling tastes.

High on the list of Martian potables is woji, which is, uh, let us say, expanded, rather than distilled, from a strange berry that contracts in the deserts of Mars. Note that we said contracts rather than grows. We won't go into the biological aspects of Martian plant life at this point, but it is possibly this factor that leads to the strange effects of drinking woji.

Briefly, when you take your first drink of the lapis lazuli-colored stuff, it gives you one hell of a hangover, which only decreases slightly on your next drink. Your mouth feels like the proverbial bottom of a bird's cage, your head is splitting, you feel like tossing your cookies, you don't give a damn if school keeps or not. Why enumerate? You have one hell of a hangover, period. It helps to take another slug and then another, but only partially. Altogether, you might put away as much as a pint, before stumbling off to bed, feeling as lousy as you ever have in your life.

The question you are now asking is, "Then why drink woji at all?"

And the answer is, when you wake up in the morning you feel swell. The stuff contains an ingredient something like a reverse alcohol. You get the hangover first, and then feel fine the next morning. It takes getting used to. But woji is for peasants. It's somewhat the equivalent of beer on Earth. The drink of the gods, given the Martian viewpoint, is nig, and the fact that it's gin spelled backwards has no significance since nig is more like champagne than anything else.

The truth of the matter is that you get high on nig. No, no, don't misunderstand. We mean literally high. And in that lies the difficulty with the delicious stuff.

You take your first glass of nig and a pleasant glow goes through you and you rise about two inches off the floor. It seems that one of nig's ingredients has an antigravity effect that has to be experienced to be believed. You have a bit of trouble at first but soon get the hang of it and maintain equilibrium. Two drinks and you're about two feet off the floor, but things are still fairly well under control. Three, and you're about six feet high and have various difficulties reaching down to the bar for further refreshment. However, this is just as well because that's the danger point. Thin air makes helicopters impractical on Mars and it can be tedious rescuing some two-bottle man who has overindulged.

Once organized, you're going to want to do some sightseeing and if you've read the tourist literature, you'll probably want to take a look at some of the famous Martian caverns which make the Mammoth Cave of Kentucky pale into insignificance. One thing, though, that the tourist pamphlets fail to mention, you're going to have to watch out for dugg. Which is another one of these deals that's hard to believe if you've never been off Earth before. It's a rather strange substance, very bothersome to those who stay over long in Martian caves and caverns. After an hour or so you start growing stalactites at a shockingly fast pace, from your nose, ears, chin, fingers, and, if by strange chance you happen to be nude, other extremities.

This being nude bit isn't as unlikely as you might think since the climate, lack of humidity, and so forth is such that clothing isn't the item on Mars that it is on Earth. In fact, the girls run about on their day-by-day duties in the equivalent of bikinis. This is balanced by the fact that when they go out onto the beach they get themselves all done up in what amounts to Mother Hubbards to protect themselves from the sun.

The beaches are impressive on Mars. You've never seen such beaches. In fact, we should say, such beach. Because all Mars is a beach. The trouble is, there's no water to go with it.

Which brings us to one phenomenon you're going to have to see before leaving Marsport. The great deposits, in the deepest depressions of what were once long eons past the oceans of Mars, of dehydrated water. Nothing like it is to be found on Earth. In fact, there's been some discussion of importing the stuff to be used in agriculture in such spots as the Sahara and Gobi Deserts. Dry water, as it's sometimes called, would have various advantages. For one thing, it can be carried around very handily in burlap bags. It's also been considered for washing animals, such as cats, which don't like to get wet.

There's just one aspect of living-it-up on Mars that we haven't dealt with thus far and approach with a certain trepidation. We speak now of Martian women. In America of recent years there has been a great relaxing of censorship. In fact, what with Henry Miller's novels, the pocketbooks to be found on every magazine rack, not to speak of the delectable pin-ups which now have no difficulties in Uncle Sam's mails, it's just about a thing of the past. How-

ever, at this point we're stymied. We simply can't run the
chance of losing this magazine's mailing privileges by describing just *how* Martian girls differ from Earth-side girls
and what it leads to . . .

Oh, yes. Just one last item. Don't pay any attention to
the EARTHLINGS GO HOME! signs you'll see written all over
the walls. These Martians have no sense of gratitude. After
liberating the planet, Earth has been granting them aid
for twenty years until now their whole economy is on the
skids.

THE MARTIAN STAR-GAZERS

by Frederik Pohl

from *Galaxy*

Recent researches into the surviving documents of the Old
Race of Mars have provided insights into the morals and
manners of these quaint, extinct creatures who at one time
were the only outpost of intelligent life in our Solar System. Three-fingered, cleft of chin, addicted to carrying umbrellas in the early stages of their long history, these Martian humanoids have represented a considerable mystery,
both as to their way of life and its abrupt and disastrous
end—so recently in time.

Our new studies make it possible to understand many
of the questions, including the answer to the greatest question of all: What killed the Martian race in its prime, only
some four centuries ago?

As we know, the Martian civilization, unlike that of
Earth, arose in its southern hemisphere. This had far-
reaching consequences. As on Earth an entire mythology

grew around the North Star and its attendant circumpolar constellations, so it was on Mars, with its clearer air and consequent sharper view of the Milky Way and other nebulosities.

On Mars, of course, it was the South Star that was the "hub" of their heaven—rather, would have been, had there been a "South Star."

Unfortunately, at the Martian South Celestial Pole there is no star of significant magnitude. The pole itself is located roughly midway between the quite unimportant stars *mu* Velae and *iota* Carina, in a tentacled patch of the Milky Way shaped rather like a three-fingered hand with opposed thumb. The pole itself is located near the palm of the hand.

This resemblance to a hand had unfortunate effects on the Martian mythos. It was called, in their dialects, either The Clutch or Ol' Grabby, and it came to be a prime tenet of Martian psychoanthropology that the heavens were out to get them.

The southerly constellation known to us as Crucis (The Southern Cross) lies astride this extension, at about the position of a wrist. In Martian nomenclature this constellation was called The Cuffs; and in their mythology it was regarded as the manacle which kept Ol' Grabby from seizing and destroying their planet. In this view the Greater and Lesser Magellanic Clouds were considered to be Ol' Grabby's eyes, known as The Peepers. And the matching extension of the Milky Way coming from what we know as the constellations of Pyxis, Puppis and Monoceros was called Ol' Grabby's Other Mitt.

The Martians believed that Ol' Grabby's Other Mitt was trying to open The Cuffs and that, if this were done, Ol' Grabby would crush and rend every living Martian and all their works.

The bright southern stars Canopus and Achernar also played a part in this construction. We know that nearly all Martian creatures were hairless and hornless; the only exception is a small and venomous beast much feared by the Martians. It was an additional source of dread to the Martians that Canopus and Achernar were considered to be horns of the head of which The Peepers were the eyes.

With a night sky composed principally of the features of a demon, it is no wonder that Martian efforts came to be devoted largely to getting out of its sight. This accounts for the markedly subterranean quality of their architecture—explaining why their great cities were never seen by telescopic observation from Earth—and also for the fact that all adult Martians carried umbrellas. This feature of the Martian culture puzzled areologists for many years. (Even in historic times Mars was not noted for its rain.) It is now established that these were carried only out of doors and at night, to conceal the carrier from the hungry gaze of The Peepers.

This in turn accounts, at least in part, for the tremendous expansionist spread of the Martian culture northward at about the beginning their Second Millennium. "Go north, young Martian!" was a familiar Martian injunction for centuries. (Perhaps an additional consideration was the relative mildness of the seasons in the northern hemisphere of Mars. Its axial tilt is such that the northern hemisphere is tipped away from the Sun at closest approach, toward it at farthest. Mars therefore has a warmer winter and cooler summer in the north.)

When at last the Martian civilization had re-rooted itself in the north it was discovered that a Pole Star did exist for them.

It was not a very bright star, nor is it particularly close to our own Polaris (due to the difference in axial tilt between Mars and Terra). It is a star about midway between the star Caph in Cassiopeia and the bright star Deneb (which forms one of the points of the famous terrestrial Summer Triangle).

The Martian North Pole Star is, in fact, what we call *delta* Cephei, the fourth brightest star in the northerly constellation of Cepheus. To the casual observer it is a star of no great interest. But it repays dividends on closer study, even with the naked eye. Delta Cephei is a variable star. It flickers like a candle, waxing and waning quite visibly, at fairly short intervals. It is, in fact, a cepheid variable, and the one after which the whole class of cepheids was named.

A Pole Star is, of course, in a favorable position to become the center of astronomical legends, as it is visibly the hub on which the heavens rotate. To the Martians, already uneasy in their cosmological views, it was a source of considerable psychic discomfort to have their northerly heavens swing around a star as unstable as *delta* Cephei. (Our *own* Polaris, of course, is itself a variable—but a less conspicuous one, partly innately, partly because it has fewer near-by stars to serve as comparisons.) Delta Cephei's regular rise and fall in brightness reminded the Martians of the even breathing of a sleeper; and in their language it was named Sleeper, or sometimes The Drowsy One.

The other northerly constellations were thought to be more friendly, on the whole, than the demon-haunted sky of the south. (One major exception is the Andromeda Nebula, which we shall discuss in its place.) The stars we know as Mira Ceti (another famous variable), Fomalhaut and Denebola, along with other stars and the Praesepe Nebula, lying as they did more or less along the plane of the Martian Celestial Equator, were known as The Picket Fence, a heavenly fortification erected to keep Ol' Grabby in his southerly domain. Two of the brightest stars in the Fence (which we know as Betelgeuse and Bellatrix, in the constellation of Orion) were called The Gates.

By a coincidence, the constellation of Orion itself had long been thought to be the outline of a giant—as it is on Earth, Orion being the name of the mighty Heavenly Hunter (whose companions are the Greater and Lesser Dogs: Canis Major, with Sirius, and Canis Minor, with Procyon). However, the Martians, their culture arising in the southern half of their planet, had at first viewed Orion in the position we would consider upside-down.

In Earthly eyes, The Gates (Betelgeuse and Bellatrix) are considered to be the shoulders of the giant. Saiph and

Rigel, to the south, are his feet. The three stars in a row in the center of the constellation are Orion's Belt. And the lesser stars, with the Great Nebula in Orion, which dangle below the Belt are called Orion's Sword.

From the south-oriented Martian view the giant had no feet. Rigel and Saiph became his shoulders. The Belt was still the Belt; but as the projection downward was, from their point of view, a projection upward, the stars in the Sword of Orion were ignored; and the Great Nebula (now falling somewhere on the giant's chest, at about the position of a heart) was called The Bloody Wound.

The story associated with the constellation was one of danger and tragedy. Ol' Grabby, before being manacled, had lashed out and caught the giant (who was called The Guardian) a deadly blow near the heart. The Guardian was dying. When he died, the northward-moving Martians considered, Ol' Grabby would find The Gates undefended. And then the way would be clear for him to move north after them.

But meanwhile, The Picket Fence stood, and the other northerly constellations were thought to provide valuable secondary defenses.

On Earth it is easy to see the difference in naming customs between northern and southern constellations. The northern skies, first viewed and first mapped by preastronomical shepherds and nomads, have complicated and devious legends. (As the constellations themselves are complicated and difficult to see—at least when viewed in the light of their supposed resemblances to hares, whales, hunting dogs or swans.) But the southern skies of Earth were named by exploring seafarers. They saw the skies in terms of ships—wherefore such southern terrestrial constellations as The Keel, The Compasses, The Telescope, The Net and so on. (Indeed, the southern sky was at first seen as almost a single constellation—Argo, the Ship—of which most of the presently renamed constellations are the parts.)

An analogous effect occurred on Mars. The northern constellations were named on a larger plan.

Ol' Grabby and his various parts, although they dominated the sky, had been only a few of more than a score of southern constellations for the Martians. But of our Earthly northern constellations (there are more than two dozen of them), the Martians made only a few.

Our Summer Triangle, the points of which are the stars Deneb, Altair and Vega, actually takes in five constellations. The Martians considered it one. They called it The Axe, the sharp blade coming to a point at Altair in the south; and it was their weapon to strike at Ol' Grabby in the event that he should somehow break through The Picket Fence at the point in the year's parade of constellations when The Gates and their Guardian were out of the nighttime sky.

Such northern nebulosities as The Pleiades, the Hyades and Messier 31, the Great Nebula in Andromeda, gave the Martians pause. Conditioned to think of star clusters, nebulae and the like as somehow inimical—the parts of Ol' Grabby; the deadly Bloody Wound of The Guardian—they could not well assign friendly roles to these astronomical objects. Pleiades and Hyades were considered to be drops of blood shed by The Guardian in his battle, and the legend arose that once Ol' Grabby had broken through The Gates, to the point in the sky marked by these star clusters, and was repulsed only as The Guardian's dying act.

Our Big Dipper (Ursa Major) became for them The Armored Car, a stately and powerful military patrol wheeling through the skies. (As, indeed, in Britain on Earth the same constellation was once called Charles's Wain, or Wagon.) The Little Dipper was a smaller armored car, patrolling backward through the sky, Polaris first.

The triangle formed by Aldebaran, Capella and the twin stars of Castor and Pollux, located near The Guardian's spilled blood, just above The Gates, became The Tank Trap, a fortified line of defense behind which The Guardian could retreat if Ol' Grabby drove him from The Gates.

Our constellation of Aries, along with Mirach, Alpheratz and Algenib from other constellations, became The Pit. The Pit lay just above Mira Ceti, the variable star in The Picket Fence; when Mira Ceti waned the Fence was weakened; if then Ol' Grabby broke through, The Pit might trap him and half his attack.

Most reassuring of all, our Cassiopeia, the wobbly "W" that swings around the Pole Star, swung also around theirs. (Polaris, however, lies above the "W". The Sleeper lies to its right.) The deeply cleft Martian chin gave their closed mouths some of the appearance of a "W"—and they chose to look on Cassiopeia as The Smile.

This was, beyond doubt, a favorable sign. Yet the cryptic Sleeper lay just beside The Smile, and below it the ominous, Ol' Grabby-like fuzziness that we call the Great Nebula in Andromeda. The likeness to the Orion Nebula (different as they are in reality, one an external galaxy, the other a mere patch of glowing gas) could not escape notice. Messier 31 was called The Other Wound. The Sleeper smiled in his sleep, yet he too had been hurt. Perhaps he too would be angry if he woke.

We know that the last surviving Martian perished in a planet-wide death a bare four centuries ago. And we know, finally, why.

The Third, Fourth, Fifth and Sixth Millennia of the Martian planetary civilization proceeded in a cultural stasis like nothing so much as our own Ancient Egypt. Perhaps it was for similar reasons: a hostile, near-desert environment, with seasons strongly marked by the annual flooding of the Nile, the annual melting of the Martian polar icecaps. No doubt, too, social causes were involved beyond this. We do not yet know all of the social factors involved; but we know that the Martian theocracy grew, blossomed—and froze.

Nearly all of Mars now lived in the northern hemisphere. Ol' Grabby was no longer a nightly sight for every Martian. But his worship—more accurately, his propitiation—

was the official state religion. And his image, picked out in precious stones, decorated every public building.

Yet in the Martian mind Ol' Grabby must have receded somewhat as a figure of public terror. We know that the custom of carrying umbrellas by night fell into disuse. They are found everywhere in the abandoned southern Martian cities, but hardly exist in the more recent cities of the north. Ol' Grabby was merely the official property of the theocracy. They interpreted his moods; they ordered acts for his appeasement.

So lingered the long afternoon of the Martian civilization, until the year which in our Earthly calendar is called 1572 A.D.

The Sleeper, it should be pointed out, lies itself at the edge of a northerly stream of the Milky Way (whose southerly projections, we recall, were the hands of Ol' Grabby). An uneasy sort of convention had come to exist that this branch of the Milky Way was indeed a part of Ol' Grabby's body, or perhaps a limb of another Ol' Grabby, but that as long as The Sleeper slept there was no danger.

In 1572 A.D. (our reckoning) The Sleeper awoke.

This was the year of the great nova in Cassiopeia—which appeared to Martians as well as to pre-Elizabethan terrestrials. It was no ordinary nova; was not, indeed, a nova at all. Tycho, who observed it (it is often called Tycho's Star in his honor) was stricken with its enormous brightness, dimming the rest of the sky. It was that rare celestial event, a supernova, the total destruction of a star.

Brightest object in the sky, it mushroomed above the closed mouth of The Smile. It looked like an eye—it was an eye, was the Eye of The Sleeper, cried the frantic, panicky mobs that swarmed around the Martian cities. Ol' Grabby—or one like him—had wakened and found them at last; The Sleeper no longer slept. In the terror and riot of those few days of the flaring of Tycho's Star a planet died at its own hands. It was suicide. Nine-tenths of the Martian race killed itself, through fear; and the few remaining could not long survive.

So ends the story of the Martian star-gazers. *Requiescat in pace*. It is a tragic and ironic story, a world destroying itself. How superior we Terrestrials, in our greater wisdom, are well entitled to feel.

PLANETARY EFFULGENCE

by Bertrand Russell

from *Fact and Fiction*

Science in Mars had been making extraordinarily rapid progress. The territory of Mars was divided between two great Empires, the Alphas and the Betas, and it was their competition, more than any other one cause, which had led to the immense development of technique. In this competition neither side secured any advantage over the other. This fact caused universal disquiet, since each side felt that only its own supremacy could secure the future of life. Among the more thoughtful Martians, a feeling developed that security required the conquest of other planets. At last there came a day when the Alphas and the Betas, alike, found themselves able to despatch projectiles to Earth containing Martian scientists provided with means of survival in a strange environment. Each side simultaneously despatched projectiles, which duly reached their terrestrial target. One of them fell in what the inhabitants of Earth called "The United States," and the other in what they called "Russia." To the great disappointment of the scientists, they were a little too late for many of the investigations which they had hoped to make. They found large cities, partially destroyed; vast machines, some of them still in operation; storehouses of food; and large ships tossing aimlessly on stormy seas. Wherever they found such things, they also found human bodies, but all the bodies were lifeless. The Martian scientists, by means of their super-radar, had discovered that on Earth, as in Mars, power was divided between two factions which, on Earth, were called the A's and the B's. It had been hoped that intercourse with the curious beings inhabiting Earth might add to Martian wisdom. But, unfortunately, life on Earth had become extinct a few months before the arrival of the projectiles.

At first the scientific disappointment was keen; but before very long cryptologists, linguists, and historians succeeded in deciphering the immense mass of record accumulated by these odd beings while they still lived. The Alphas and the Betas from Mars each drew up very full reports on what they had discovered about Tellurian thought and history. There was very little difference between the two reports. So long as each of the two factions remained unidentified, what A said about itself and about B was indistinguishable from what B said about itself and about A. It appeared that, according to each side, the other side wanted world dominion and wished all power to be in the hands of heartless officials whom the one side designated as bureaucrats and the other as capitalists. Each side held that the other advocated a soulless mechanism which should grind out engines of war without any regard to human happiness. Each side believed that the other, by unscrupulous machinations, was endeavouring to promote world war in spite of the obvious danger to all. Each side declared loudly: "We, who stand for peace and justice and truth, dare not relax our vigilance or cease to increase our armaments, because the other side is so wicked." The two Martian reports, drawn up by the Alphas and the Betas respectively had similarities exactly like those of the A's and B's whom they were describing. Each ended up with a moral to its government. The moral was this: "These foolish inhabitants of Earth forgot the obvious lesson that their situation should have taught them, namely, that it is necessary to be stronger than the other side. We hope that the government to which we are reporting will learn this salutary lesson from the awful warning of the catastrophe on our sister planet."

The governments of the Alphas and the Betas, alike, listened to the reports of their Tellurian experts and, alike, determined that their faction should be the stronger.

A few years after this policy had been adopted by both the Alphas and the Betas, two projectiles reached Mars from Jupiter. Jupiter was divided between the Alephs and the Beths, and each had sent its own projectile. Like the Martian travelers to Earth, the Jovian travelers found life in Mars extinct, but they soon discovered the two reports which had been brought from Earth. They presented them to their respective governments, both of which accepted the Martian moral with which the two Martian reports had ended. But as the rulers of the two rival states of Alephs and Beths were finishing the drawing up of their comments, each had a strange, disquieting experience. A moving finger appeared, seized the pen from their astonished hands, and, without their co-operation, wrote these words: "I am sorry I was so halfhearted at the time of Noah. (Signed) Cosmic President." These words were deleted by the censor on each side and their strange occurrence was kept a profound secret.

"Planetary Effulgence" is included in *Fact and Fiction*, George Allen & Unwin Ltd. (London), 1961; Simon and Schuster (New York), 1962.

DEADLY GAME

by Edward Wellen

from *If*

Meanwhile, back on Earth . . .

Deep in the dusk of the wood Jess Seely saw the beast's pupils shine.

He had been careful of every footfall and of every shift of his shotgun as he made his way through the forest. But they had got wind of him, they had been on his trail from the instant he stepped into the wood, they were all around him now. The eyes vanished, but he could hear soft scurryings.

Move quietly and keep your eyes open: that was the first lesson he had learned and the best. He moved still deeper into the wood, years of woodcraft in every move. The years had slowed him. But the experience gained in those same years had made every move tell. He heard soft scurryings. They were stalking him. How would they try to get him this time?

He let the shotgun dangle carelessly so the barrels threatened himself.

Would that tempt one of them—a squirrel?—to leap from a limb, aiming to strike at the trigger and set off the shot? No, he saw it now. They had something else in wait just ahead. A deadfall.

Only at the last fraction of a second did his sweep of eye take in the one bit of beaver track they had failed to brush away.

He walked slowly on, straining for sign of trip wire. It would be a length of vine; he should spot it by its dying color. He should, but he did not. He frowned. Was he guessing wrong? Then he spotted it—a length of living vine, one end still rooted, the other wrapping the trunk of a great spruce in a neat knot. The spruce itself seemed untouched, at first sight. They had plastered the gnawings back in place, but to his eyes—now that he knew what he was looking for—there stood out enough difference between the living wood and the dead to show the big bite they had taken out of the base of the tree. He admired their sense of balance. His lightest brush against the vine would bring the tree crashing down on him.

To raise—then dash—their hopes, he tried to keep from letting on he had seen the setup and went on without breaking stride—then he lengthened and lifted his step at the last to miss triggering the trip wire by a hair. A silence, then a small chatter of disappointment.

He kept on. Under the talking foliage of quaking aspen he made out other sounds. Soft scurryings. What would they have waiting ahead? A noose? No, poison-tipped thorns.

The rustle of leaves gave warning. He whirled aside. One of them—a raccoon?—loosed a bent branch of hawthorn. The branch whipped at him and the wicked spikes barely missed his flesh. The branch was still trembling when he raised his shotgun but the raccoon—he felt sure it was a raccoon and smiled, remembering the first of them, Bandido—had vanished. Yet he had to make the futile gesture so those watching would not know the gun bore no load. He eyed the wicked spikes and again smiled. On each tip a sticky smear held a thick powdering. The powder would be dried leaves of foxglove. Or had they found something better? He smiled again at more chatter of frustration.

But he sharpened his senses as he pushed on. He stopped where the going grew suddenly easy. They had cleared a path; it invited him to bypass a tangle of underbrush. He looked to see that the overarching boughs did not hold loops of vine ready to drop, and took the path. Nothing. But there had to be something. He pushed on, then slowed, smelling dampness that was not the dankness of mold.

Ahead, the trail widened into a clearing. In the center of

the clearing lay a patch of spongy ground that could be lethal quagmire. Yet the tracks of a big woodchuck led straight across the patch, promising the ground would hold. Something about the tracks gave Jess Seely pause. They had a dainty, yet dragging, look.

He read faint tracks on either side of the patch and knew what had taken place. Not one but three woodchucks had crossed the clearing together, abreast, almost in step. Two had kept to the solid ground on either side of the bog, each holding in its jaws one end of a fallen tree limb. The big woodchuck in the middle had ridden with the bulk of his weight on that support, making footprints without sinking into the mire.

Jess Seely smiled and skirted the patch.

He wondered vaguely why the chatter he heard now seemed to be chatter not of frustration but of expectation. He had no time for more than vague wonder at that, and at the sudden hush. The ground—not ground but a covering of dirt over a wickerwork of branches—gave under him. His hands flung up, the gun shot out of his grip. He fell.

His coming to was an in-and-out thing, pulsing awareness, intermitting dream.

The pit was deep. They were good at digging. They had patience. He nodded, and blacked out.

He came to again. He lay crumpled, a leg bent strangely under him. He was helpless, but they would not come right away. They would not trust him, they would wait to make sure he was not playing helpless. Then they would come.

They had patience.

He tightened himself against the pain. This was what he had worked toward, and in any case it would have been useless to have regrets. He had no regrets. He had been a good game warden. He lapsed into unconsciousness again, smiling.

The wait was long and he knew he had passed through a spell of delirium. There was a timeless moment when it seemed to him he came aware in the past, reliving the start of it. That had been the time when, feeling a gnawing helplessness, seeing the day coming when he would no longer be there to save them from his fellow man, he caught that poacher. The poacher was too busy to sense his approach, busy cursing some animal that had once again sprung the trap and made off with the bait.

He knew, in that long-ago day, that it would be wasting time to haul the man into court. The local justice of the peace would let him off with a mild rebuke. So Jess Seely booted the man out of the wood, baited and reset the trap and lay in wait.

At last a large raccoon nosed into view, picked up a piece of twig in a forepaw and reached cautiously to stick it into the trap. The trap snapped shut its grin on nothing. The raccoon was about to make off with the bait when Jess Seely remembered to move. He aimed his hypodermic gun and shot the raccoon to sleep. He carried the raccoon home—and that was the start of Jess Seely's private, unauthorized and top-secret psychological testing laboratory.

The raccoon made an auspicious first subject, quickly mastering all sorts of release mechanisms to escape from puzzle boxes and to win rewards, learning to fit pegs into holes and to tie knots. The one stupidity was Jess Seely's. He had grown fond of the raccoon—Bandido—and he had let Bandido sense that. It was lucky Jess Seely had realized that at this early stage, or the whole thing would have gone for nothing. He had to break Bandido of his liking. He forced himself to set about coldly instilling in Bandido hate and fear of man—any man.

Only when he felt sure he had brought that about did he free Bandido. He tagged Bandido and released him into the wild, then hunted other promising subjects. There was only one Bandido. Jess Seely did not give any of the others a name.

He did not dare.

He rigged more and more sophisticated release mechanisms, and in time was graduating animals that were able to disarm any trap safely and, before making off with the bait, move the trap, reset it and conceal it so the original setter of the trap would step into it. Other than a shot from a trapper who thought the resetting was his doing, Jess

Seely had little trouble with poachers after that.

At mating seasons he used his capture-gun again to bring together the brightest of his subjects. And in thirty years, thanks to training and selective breeding, the wildlife under his protection had learned to deal with all traps, set out sentries, string alarm wires across trails, toss stones to mislead hunters and put hounds out of action and, with earth or urine, fight fire.

Now he was clear in his mind and he felt a humble pride. He had set out to teach them to guard their preserve, to save themselves. He had done a good job of this. He had taught them well. He heard them coming closer to the rim of the pit. Now he saw their eyes.

He fixed on one face. Old Bandido! But that couldn't be. Old Bandido was long dead. This was a son or a grandson or a great-grandson. In a sense they were all children of Jess Seely.

No matter. They would have no pity on him. He had taught them well indeed, he thought smiling.

SUBCOMMITTEE

by Zenna Henderson

from *Fantasy and Science Fiction*

I have pointed out, in connection with other stories here, two major themes of contemporary s-f (science/speculative fantasy/fiction): the examination of the mind of man; and the relationships between mankind and the constantly changing man-made environment. The question raised by the writers, of course, is: What will man make of himself?

Fitzpatrick, Anderson, Aandahl and Ballard all touched on the theme —most of them with little optimism. The next (and last) three stories in the book strike three very different, but all hopeful, notes.

First came the sleek black ships, falling out of the sky in patterned disorder, sowing fear as they settled like seeds on the broad landing field. After them, like bright butterflies, came the vivid-colored slow ships that hovered and hesitated and came to rest scattered among the deadly dark ones.

"Beautiful!" sighed Serena, turning from the conference room window. "There should have been music to go with it."

"A funeral dirge," said Thorn, "Or a requiem. Or flutes before failure. Frankly, I'm frightened, Rena. If these conferences fail, all hell will break loose again. Imagine living another year like this past one."

"But the conference won't fail!" Serena protested. "If they're willing to consent to the conference, surely they'll be willing to work with us for peace."

"Their peace or ours?" asked Thorn, staring morosely out the window. "I'm afraid we're being entirely too naïve about this whole affair. It's been a long time since we finally were able to say, 'Ain't gonna study war no more,' and made it stick. We've lost a lot of the cunning that used to be necessary in dealing with other people. We can't, even now, be sure this isn't a trick to get all our high command together in one place for a grand massacre."

"Oh, no!" Serena pressed close to him and his arm went around her. "They couldn't possibly violate—"

"Couldn't they?" Thorn pressed his cheek to the top of her head. "We don't know, Rena. We just don't know. We have so little information about them. We know practically nothing about their customs—even less about their values or from what frame of reference they look upon our suggestion of suspending hostilities."

"But surely they must be sincere. They brought their families along with them. You did say those brights ships are family craft, didn't you?"

"Yes, they suggested we bring our families and they brought their families along with them, but it's nothing to give us comfort. They take them everywhere—even into battle."

"Into battle!"

"Yes. They mass the home craft off out of range during battles, but every time we disable or blast one of their fighters, one or more of the home craft spin away out of control or flare into nothingness. Apparently they're just glorified trailers, dependent on the fighters for motive power and everything else." The unhappy lines deepened in Thorn's face. "They don't know it, but even apart from their superior weapons, they practically forced us into this truce. How could we go on wiping out their war fleet when, with every black ship, those confounded posy-colored home craft fell too, like pulling petals off a flower. And each petal heavy with the lives of women and children."

Serena shivered and pressed closer to Thorn. "The conference must work. We just can't have war any more. You've got to get through to them. Surely, if we want peace and so do they—"

"We don't know what they want," said Thorn heavily. "Invaders, aggressors, strangers from hostile worlds—so

completely alien to us—How can we ever hope to get together?"

They left the conference room in silence, snapping the
button on the door knob before they closed it.

"Hey, lookit, Mommie! Here's a wall!" Splinter's five-
year-old hands flattened themselves like grubby starfish
against the greenish ripple of the ten-foot vitricrete fence
that wound through the trees and slid down the gentle
curve of the hill. "Where did it come from? What's it for?
How come we can't go play in the go'fish pond any more?"

Serena leaned her hand against the wall. "The people
who came in the pretty ships wanted a place to walk and
play, too. So the Construction Corps put the fence up for
them."

"Why won't they let me play in the go'fish pond?" Splinter's brows bent ominously.

"They don't know you want to," said Serena.

"I'll tell them, then," said Splinter. He threw his head
back. "Hey! Over there!" He yelled, his fists doubling
and his whole body stiffening with the intensity of the
shout. "Hey! I wanta play in the go'fish pond!"

Serena laughed. "Hush, Splinter. Even if they could
hear you, they wouldn't understand. They're from far, far
away. They don't talk the way we do."

"But maybe we could play," said Splinter wistfully.

"Yes," sighed Serena. "Maybe you could play. If the
fence weren't there. But you see, Splinter, we don't know
what kind of—people—they are. Whether they would
want to play. Whether they would be—nice."

"Well, how can we find out with that old wall there?"

"We can't, Splinter," said Serena. "Not with the fence
there."

They walked on down the hill, Splinter's hand trailing
along the wall.

"Maybe they're mean," he said finally. "Maybe they're
so bad that the 'struction Corps had to build a cage for
them—a big, big cage!" He stretched his arm as high as

he could reach, up the wall. "Do you suppose they got tails?"

"Tails?" laughed Serena. "Whatever gave you that idea?"

"I dunno. They came from a long ways away. I'd like a tail—a long, curly one with fur on!" He swished his miniature behind energetically.

"Whatever for?" asked Serena.

"It'd come in handy," said Splinter solemnly. "For climbing and—and keeping my neck warm!

"Why aren't there any other kids here?" he asked as they reached the bottom of the slope. "I'd like *somebody* to play with."

"Well, Splinter, it's kind of hard to explain," started Serena, sinking down on the narrow ledge shelving on the tiny dry water course at her feet.

"Don't esplain then," said Splinter. "Just tell me."

"Well, some Linjeni generals came in the big black ships to talk with General Worsham and some more of our generals. They brought their families with them in the fat, pretty ships. So our generals brought their families, too, but your daddy is the only one of our generals who has a little child. All the others are grown up. That's why there's no one for you to play with." I wish it were as simple as it sounds, thought Serena, suddenly weary again with the weeks of negotiation and waiting that had passed.

"Oh," said Splinter, thoughtfully. "Then there *are* kids on the other side of the wall, aren't there?"

"Yes, there must be young Linjeni," said Serena. "I guess you could call them children."

Splinter slid down to the bottom of the little water course and flopped down on his stomach. He pressed his cheek to the sand and peered through a tiny gap left under the fence where it crossed the stream bed. "I can't see anybody," he said, disappointed.

They started back up the hill toward their quarters, walking silently, Splinter's hand whispering along the wall.

"Mommie?" Splinter said as they neared the patio.

"Yes, Splinter?"

"That fence is to keep them in, isn't it?"

"Yes," said Serena.

"It doesn't feel like that to me," said Splinter. "It feels like it's to shut me out."

Serena suffered through the next days with Thorn. She lay wide-eyed beside him in the darkness of their bedroom, praying as he slept restlessly, struggling even in his sleep —groping for a way.

Tight-lipped, she cleared away untouched meals and brewed more coffee. Her thoughts went hopefully with him every time he started out with new hope and resolution, and her spirits flagged and fell as he brought back dead-end, stalemate and growing despair. And in between times, she tried to keep Splinter on as even a keel as possible, giving him the freedom of the Quarters Area during the long, sunlit days and playing with him as much as possible in the evenings.

One evening Serena was pinning up her hair and keeping half an eye on Splinter as he splashed in his bath. He was gathering up handfuls of foaming soap bubbles and pressing them to his chin and cheeks.

"Now I hafta shave like Daddy," he hummed to himself. "Shave, shave, shave!" He flicked the suds off with his forefinger. Then he scooped up a big double handful of bubbles and pressed them all over his face. "Now I'm Doovie. I'm all over fuzzy like Doovie. Lookit, Mommie, I'm all over—" He opened his eyes and peered through the suds to see if she was watching. Consequently, Serena spent a busy next few minutes helping him get the soap out of his eyes. When the tears had finally washed away the trouble, Serena sat toweling Splinter's relaxed little body.

"I bet Doovie'd cry too, if he got soap in his eyes," he said with a sniff. "Wouldn't he, Mommie?"

"Doovie?" said Serena. "Probably. Almost anyone would. Who's Doovie?"

She felt Splinter stiffen on her lap. His eyes wandered away from hers. "Mommie, do you think Daddy will play with me a-morrow?"

"Perhaps." She captured one of his wet feet. "Who's Doovie?"

"Can we have pink cake for dessert tonight? I think I like pink—"

"Who's Doovie?" Serena's voice was firm. Splinter examined his thumbnail critically, then peered up at Serena out of the corner of his eye.

"Doovie," he began. "Doovie's a little boy."

"Oh?" said Serena. "A playlike little boy?"

"No," Splinter whispered, hanging his head. "A real little boy. A Linjeni little boy." Serena drew an astonished breath and Splinter hurried on, his eyes intent on hers. "He's nice people, Mommie, honest! He doesn't say bad words or tell lies or talk sassy to his mother. He can run as fast as I can—faster, if I stumble. He—he—" His eyes dropped again. "I like him—" His mouth quivered.

"Where did—how could—I mean, the fence—" Serena was horrified and completely at a loss for words.

"I dug a hole," confessed Splinter. "Under the fence where the sand is. You didn't say not to! Doovie came to play. His Mommie came, too. She's pretty. Her fur is pink, but Doovie's is nice and green. All over!" Splinter got excited. "All over, even where his clothes are! All but his nose and eyes and ears and the front of his hands!"

"But Splinter, how could you! You might have got hurt! They might have—" Serena hugged him tight to hide her face from him.

Splinter squirmed out of her arms. "Doovie wouldn't hurt anyone. You know what, Mommie! He can shut his nose! Yes, he can! He can shut his nose and fold up his ears! I wish I could. It'd come in handy. But I'm bigger'n he is and I can sing and he can't. But he can whistle with his nose and when I try, I just blow mine. Doovie's nice!"

Serena's mind was churning as she helped Splinter get into his night clothes. She felt the chill of fear along her forearms and the back of her neck. What to do now? Forbid Splinter's crawling under the fence? Keep him from possible danger that might just be biding its time? What would

Thorn say? Should she tell him? This might precipitate an incident that—

"Splinter, how many times have you played with Doovie?"

"How many?" Splinter's chest swelled under his clean pajamas. "Let me count," he said importantly and murmured and mumbled over his fingers for a minute. "Four times!" he proclaimed triumphantly. "One, two, three, four whole times!"

"Weren't you scared?"

"Naw!" he said, adding hastily, "Well, maybe a little bit the first time. I thought maybe they might have tails that liked to curl around people's necks. But they haven't." Disappointed. "Only clothes on like us with fur on under."

"Did you say you saw Doovie's mother, too?"

"Sure," said Splinter. "She was there the first day. She was the one that sent all the others away when they all crowded around me. All grownups. Not any kids excepting Doovie. They kinda pushed and wanted to touch me, but she told them to go away, and they all did 'cepting her and Doovie."

"Oh, Splinter!" cried Serena, overcome by the vision of his small self surrounded by pushing, crowding Linjeni grownups who wanted to 'touch him.'

"What's the matter, Mommie?" asked Splinter.

"Nothing, dear." She wet her lips. "May I go along with you the next time you go to see Doovie? I'd like to meet his mother."

"Sure, sure!" cried Splinter. "Let's go now. Let's go now!"

"Not now," said Serena, feeling the reaction of her fear in her knees and ankles. "It's too late. Tomorrow we'll go see them. And Splinter, let's not tell Daddy yet. Let's keep it a surprise for a while."

"Okay, Mommie," said Splinter. "It's a good surprise, isn't it? You were awful surprised, weren't you?"

"Yes, I was," said Serena. "Awful surprised."

Next day Splinter squatted down and inspected the hole

under the fence. "It's kinda little," he said. "Maybe you'll get stuck."

Serena, her heart pounding in her throat, laughed. "That wouldn't be very dignified, would it?" she asked. "To go calling and get stuck in the door."

Splinter laughed. "It'd be funny," he said. "Maybe we better go find a really door for you."

"Oh, no," said Serena hastily. "We can make this one bigger."

"Sure," said Splinter. "I'll go get Doovie and he can help dig."

"Fine," said Serena, her throat tightening. *Afraid of a child,* she mocked herself. *Afraid of a Linjeni—aggressor —invader,* she defended.

Splinter flattened on the sand and slid under the fence. "You start digging," he called. "I'll be back!"

Serena knelt to the job, the loose sand coming away readily to her scooping hands, so readily that she circled her arms and dredged with them.

Then she heard Splinter scream.

For a brief second, she was paralyzed. Then he screamed again, closer, and Serena dragged the sand away in a frantic frenzy. She felt the sand scoop down the neck of her blouse and the skin scrape off her spine as she forced herself under the fence.

Then there was Splinter, catapulting out of the shrubbery, sobbing and screaming, "Doovie! Doovie's drowning! He's in the go'fish pond! All under the water! I can't get him out! Mommie, Mommie!"

Serena grabbed his hand as she shot past and towed him along, stumbling and dragging, as she ran for the goldfish pond. She leaned across the low wall and caught a glimpse, under the churning thrash of the water, of green mossy fur and staring eyes. With hardly a pause except to shove Splinter backward and start a deep breath, she plunged over into the pond. She felt the burning bite of water up her nostrils and grappled in the murky darkness for Doovie—feeling again and again the thrash of small limbs that slipped away before she could grasp them.

Then she was choking and sputtering on the edge of the pond, pushing the still struggling Doovie up and over. Splinter grabbed him and pulled as Serena heaved herself over the edge of the pond and fell sprawling across Doovie.

Then she heard another higher, shriller scream and was shoved off Doovie viciously and Doovie was snatched up into rose-pink arms. Serena pushed her lank, dripping hair out of her eyes and met the hostile glare of the rose-pink eyes of Doovie's mother.

Serena edged over to Splinter and held him close, her eyes intent on the Linjeni. The pink mother felt the green child all over anxiously and Serena noticed with an odd detachment that Splinter hadn't mentioned that Doovie's eyes matched his fur and that he had webbed feet.

Webbed feet! She began to laugh, almost hysterically. Oh, Lordy! No wonder Doovie's mother was so alarmed.

"Can you talk to Doovie?" asked Serena of the sobbing Splinter.

"No!" wailed Splinter. "You don't have to talk to play."

"Stop crying, Splinter," said Serena. "Help me think. Doovie's mother thinks we were trying to hurt Doovie. He wouldn't drown in the water. Remember, he can close his nose and fold up his ears. How are we going to tell his mother we weren't trying to hurt him?"

"Well," Splinter scrubbed his cheeks with the back of his hand. "We could hug him—"

"That wouldn't do, Splinter," said Serena, noticing with near panic that other brightly colored figures were moving among the shrubs, drawing closer—"I'm afraid she won't let us touch him."

Briefly she toyed with the idea of turning and trying to get back to the fence, then she took a deep breath and tried to calm down.

"Let's play-like, Splinter," she said. "Let's show Doovie's mother that we thought he was drowning. You go fall in the pond and I'll pull you out. You play-like drowned and I'll —I'll cry."

"Gee, Mommie, you're crying already!" said Splinter, his face puckering.

"I'm just practicing," she said, steadying her voice. "Go on."

Splinter hesitated on the edge of the pond, shrinking away from the water that had fascinated him so many times before. Serena screamed suddenly, and Splinter, startled, lost his balance and fell in. Serena had hold of him almost before he went under water and pulled him out, cramming as much fear and apprehension into her voice and actions as she could. "Be dead," she whispered fiercely. "Be dead all over!" And Splinter melted so completely in her arms that her moans and cries of sorrow were only partly make-believe. She bent over his still form and rocked to and fro in her grief.

A hand touched her arm and she looked up into the bright eyes of the Linjeni. The look held for a long moment and then the Linjeni smiled, showing even white teeth, and a pink, furry hand patted Splinter on the shoulder. His eyes flew open and he sat up. Doovie peered around from behind his mother and then he and Splinter were rolling and tumbling together, wrestling happily between the two hesitant mothers. Serena found a shaky laugh somewhere in among her alarms and Doovie's mother whistled softly with her nose.

That night, Thorn cried out in his sleep and woke Serena. She lay in the darkness, her constant prayer moving like a candle flame in her mind. She crept out of bed and checked Splinter in his shadowy room. Then she knelt and opened the bottom drawer of Splinter's chest-robe. She ran her hand over the gleaming folds of the length of Linjeni material that lay there—the material the Linjeni had found to wrap her in while her clothes dried. She had given them her lacy slip in exchange. Her fingers read the raised pattern in the dark, remembering how beautiful it was in the afternoon sun. Then the sun was gone and she saw a black ship destroyed, a home craft plunging to incandescent death and the pink and green and yellow and all the other bright furs charring and crisping and the patterned materials curling before the last flare of flame. She leaned her head on her hand and shuddered.

But then she saw the glitter of a silver ship, blackening and fusing, dripping monstrously against the emptiness of space. And heard the wail of a fatherless Splinter so vividly that she shoved the drawer in hastily and went back to look at his quiet sleeping face and unnecessarily to tuck him in.

When she came back to bed, Thorn was awake, lying on his back, his elbows winging out.

"Awake?" she asked as she sat down on the edge of the bed.

"Yes." His voice was tense as the twang of a wire. "We're getting nowhere," he said. "Both sides keep holding up neat little hoops of ideas, but no one is jumping through, either way. We want peace, but we can't seem to convey anything to them. They want something, but they haven't said what, as though to tell us would betray them irrevocably into our hands, but they won't make peace unless they can get it. Where do we go from here?"

"If they'd just go away—" Rena swung her feet up onto the bed and clasped her slender ankles with both hands.

"That's one thing we've established." Thorn was bitter. "They *won't* go. They're here to stay—like it or not."

"Thorn—" Rena spoke impulsively into the shadowy silence, "Why don't we just make them welcome? Why can't we just say, 'Come on in!' They're travelers from afar. Can't we be hospitable—"

"You talk as though the afar was just the next county—or state!" Thorn tossed impatiently on the pillow.

"Don't tell me we're back to that old equation—Stranger equals Enemy," said Rena, her voice sharp with strain. "Can't we assume they're friendly? Go visit with them—talk with them casually—"

"Friendly!" Thorn shot upright from the tangled bedclothes. "Go visit! Talk!" His voice choked off. Then dangerously calmly he went on. "Would you care to visit with the widows of our men who went to visit the friendly Linjeni? Whose ships dropped out of the sky without warning—"

"Theirs did, too." Rena's voice was small but stubborn. "With no more warning than we had. Who shot first? You must admit no one knows for sure."

There was a tense' silence, then Thorn lay down slowly, turned his back to Serena and spoke no more.

"Now I can't ever tell," mourned Serena into her crumpled pillow. "He'd die if he knew about the hole under the fence."

In the days that followed, Serena went every afternoon with Splinter, and the hole under the fence got larger and larger.

Doovie's mother, whom Splinter called Mrs. Pink, was teaching Serena to embroider the rich materials like the length they had given her. In exchange, Serena was teaching Mrs. Pink how to knit. At least, she started to teach her. She got as far as purl and knit, decrease and increase, when Mrs. Pink took the work from her, and Serena sat wide-mouthed at the incredible speed and accuracy of Mrs. Pink's furry fingers. She felt a little silly for having assumed that the Linjeni didn't know about knitting. And yet, the other Linjeni crowded around and felt of the knitting and exclaimed over it in their soft, fluty voices as though they'd never seen any before. The little ball of wool Serena had brought was soon used up, but Mrs. Pink brought out hanks of heavy thread such as were split and used in their embroidery, and, after a glance through Serena's pattern book, settled down to knitting the shining brilliance of Linjeni thread.

Before long, smiles and gestures, laughter and whistling, were not enough. Serena sought out the available tapes— a scant handful—on Linjeni speech and learned them. They didn't help much since the vocabulary wasn't easily applied to the matters she wanted to discuss with Mrs. Pink and the others. But the day she voiced and whistled her first Linjeni sentence to Mrs. Pink, Mrs. Pink stumbled through her first English sentence. They laughed and whistled together and settled down to pointing and naming and guessing across areas of incommunication.

Serena felt guilty by the end of the week. She and Splinter were having so much fun and Thorn was wearier and wearier at each session's end.

"They're impossible," he said bitterly, one night, crouched forward tensely on the front edge of his easy chair. "We can't pin them down to anything."

"What do they want?" asked Serena. "Haven't they said yet?"

"I shouldn't talk—" Thorn sank back in his chair. "Oh what does it matter?" he asked wearily. "It'll all come to nothing anyway!"

"Oh, no, Thorn!" cried Serena. "They're reasonable human—" she broke off at Thorn's surprised look. "Aren't they?" she stammered. "Aren't they?"

"Human? They're uncommunicative, hostile aliens," he said. "We talk ourselves blue in the face and they whistle at one another and say yes or no. Just that, flatly."

"Do they understand—" began Serena.

"We have interpreters, such as they are. None too good, but all we have."

"Well, what are they asking?" asked Serena.

Thorn laughed shortly. "So far as we've been able to ascertain, they just want all our oceans and the land contiguous thereto."

"Oh, Thorn, they couldn't be that unreasonable!"

"Well I'll admit we aren't even sure that's what they mean, but they keep coming back to the subject of the oceans, except they whistle rejection when we ask them point-blank if it's the oceans they want. There's just no communication." Thorn sighed heavily. "You don't know them like we do, Rena."

"No," said Serena miserably. "Not like you do."

She took her disquiet, Splinter, and a picnic basket down the hill to the hole next day. Mrs. Pink had shared her lunch with them the day before, and now it was Serena's turn. They sat on the grass together, Serena crowding back her unhappiness to laugh at Mrs. Pink and her first olive with the same friendly amusement Mrs. Pink had shown when Serena had bit down on her first *pirwit* and had been afraid to swallow it and ashamed to spit it out.

Splinter and Doovie were agreeing over a thick meringued

lemon pie that was supposed to be dessert.

"Leave the pie alone, Splinter," said Serena. "It's to top-off on."

"We're only testing the fluffy stuff," said Splinter, a blob of meringue on his upper lip bobbing as he spoke.

"Well, save your testing for later. Why don't you get out the eggs. I'll bet Doovie isn't familiar with them either."

Splinter rummaged in the basket and Serena took out the huge camp salt shaker.

"Here they are, Mommie!" cried Splinter. "Lookit, Doovie, first you have to crack the shell——"

Serena began initiating Mrs. Pink into the mysteries of hard-boiled eggs and it was all very casual and matter of fact until she sprinkled the peeled egg with salt. Mrs. Pink held out her cupped hand and Serena sprinkled a little salt into it. Mrs. Pink tasted it.

She gave a low whistle of astonishment and tasted again. Then she reached tentatively for the shaker. Serena gave it to her, amused. Mrs. Pink shook more into her hand and peered through the holes in the cap of the shaker. Serena unscrewed the top and showed Mrs. Pink the salt inside it.

For a long minute Mrs. Pink stared at the white granules and then she whistled urgently, piercingly. Serena shrank back, bewildered, as every bush seemed to erupt Linjeni. They crowded around Mrs. Pink, staring into the shaker, jostling one another, whistling softly. One scurried away and brought back a tall jug of water. Mrs. Pink slowly and carefully emptied the salt from her hand into the water and then up-ended the shaker. She stirred the water with a branch someone snatched from a bush. After the salt was dissolved, all the Linjeni around them lined up with cupped hands. Each received—as though it were a sacrament—a handful of salt water. And they all, quickly, not to lose a drop, lifted the handful of water to their faces and inhaled, breathing deeply, deeply of the salty solution.

Mrs. Pink was last, and, as she raised her wet face from her cupped hands, the gratitude in her eyes almost made Serena cry. And the dozens of Linjeni crowded around, each eager to press a soft forefinger to Serena's cheek, a thank-you gesture Splinter was picking up already.

When the crowd melted into the shadows again, Mrs. Pink sat down, fondling the salt shaker.

"Salt," said Serena, indicating the shaker.

"*Shreeprill,*" said Mrs. Pink.

"*Shreeprill?*" said Serena, her stumbling tongue robbing the word of its liquidness. Mrs. Pink nodded.

"*Shreeprill* good?" asked Serena, groping for an explanation for the just finished scene.

"*Shreeprill* good," said Mrs. Pink. "No *shreeprill,* no Linjeni baby. Doovie—Doovie—" she hesitated, groping. "One Doovie—no baby." She shook her head, unable to bridge the gap.

Serena groped after an idea she had almost caught from Mrs. Pink. She pulled up a handful of grass. "Grass," she said. She pulled another handful. "More grass. More. More." She added to the pile.

Mrs. Pink looked from the grass to Serena.

"No *more* Linjeni baby. Doovie—" She separated the grass into piles. "Baby, baby, baby—" she counted down to the last one, lingering tenderly over it. "Doovie."

"Oh," said Serena, "Doovie is the last Linjeni baby? No more?"

Mrs. Pink studied the words and then she nodded. "Yes, yes! No more. No *shreeprill,* no baby."

Serena felt a flutter of wonder. Maybe—maybe this is what the war was over. Maybe they just wanted salt. A world to them. Maybe—

"Salt, *shreeprill,*" she said. "More, more, more *shreeprill,* Linjeni go home?"

"More, more, more *shreeprill,* yes," said Mrs. Pink. "Go home, no. No home. Home no good. No water, no *shreeprill.*"

"Oh," said Serena. Then thoughtfully, "More Linjeni? More, more, more?"

Mrs. Pink looked at Serena and in the sudden silence the realization that they were, after all, members of enemy camps flared between them. Serena tried to smile. Mrs. Pink looked over at Splinter and Doovie who were happily

sampling everything in the picnic basket. Mrs. Pink relaxed, and then she said.

"No more Linjeni." She gestured toward the crowded
landing field. "Linjeni." She pressed her hands, palm to
palm, her shoulders sagging. "No more Linjeni."

Serena sat dazed, thinking what this would mean to
Earth's High Command. No more Linjeni of the terrible,
devastating weapons. No more than those that had landed—
no waiting alien world ready to send reinforcements when
these ships were gone. When these were gone—no more
Linjeni. All that Earth had to do now was wipe out these
ships, taking the heavy losses that would be inevitable, and
they would win the war—and wipe out a race.

The Linjeni must have come seeking asylum—or demanding it. Neighbors who were afraid to ask—or hadn't
been given time to ask. How had the war started? Who
fired upon whom? Did anyone know?

Serena took uncertainty home with her, along with the
empty picnic basket. *Tell, tell, tell,* whispered her feet
through the grass up the hill. *Tell and the war will end.*
But how? she cried out to herself. By wiping them out or
giving them a home? Which? Which?

Kill, kill, kill grated her feet across the graveled patio
edge. *Kill the aliens—no common ground—not human—
all our hallowed dead.*

But what about *their* hallowed dead? All falling, the
flaming ships—the home-seekers—the dispossessed—the
childless?

Serena settled Splinter with a new puzzle and a picture
book and went into the bedroom. She sat on the bed and
stared at herself in the mirror.

But give them salt water and they'll increase—all our
oceans, even if they said they were no good. Increase and
increase and take the world—push us out—trespass—
oppress—

But their men—our men. They've been meeting for over
a week and can't agree. Of course they can't! They're
afraid of betraying themselves to each other. Neither knows

anything about the other, really. They aren't trying to find out anything really important. I'll bet not one of our men knows the Linjeni can close their noses and fold their ears. And not one of the Linjeni knows we sprinkle their life on our food.

Serena had no idea how long she sat there, but Splinter finally found her and insisted on supper and then Serena insisted on bed for him.

She was nearly mad with indecision when Thorn finally got home.

"Well," he said, dropping wearily into his chair. "It's almost over."

"Over!" cried Serena, hope flaring, "Then you've reached—"

"Stalemate, impasse," said Thorn heavily. "Our meeting tomorrow is the last. One final 'no' from each side and it's over. Back to blood-letting."

"Oh, Thorn, no!" Serena pressed her clenched fist to her mouth. "We can't kill any more of them! It's inhuman— it's—"

"It's self-defense," Thorn's voice was sharp with exasperated displeasure. "Please, not tonight, Rena. Spare me your idealistic ideas. Heaven knows we're inexperienced enough in warlike negotiations without having to cope with suggestions that we make cute pets out of our enemies. We're in a war and we've got it to win. Let the Linjeni get a wedge in and they'll swarm the Earth like flies!"

"No, no!" whispered Serena, her own secret fears sending the tears flooding down her face. "They wouldn't! They wouldn't! Would they?"

Long after Thorn's sleeping breath whispered in the darkness beside her, she lay awake, staring at the invisible ceiling. Carefully she put the words up before her on the slate of the darkness.

Tell—the war will end.

Either we will help the Linjeni—or wipe them out.

Don't tell. The conference will break up. The war will go on.

We will have heavy losses—and wipe the Linjeni out.

Mrs. Pink trusted me.

Splinter loves Doovie. Doovie loves him.

Then the little candle-flame of prayer that had so nearly burned out in her torment, flared brightly again and she slept.

Next morning she sent Splinter to play with Doovie. "Play by the goldfish pond," she said. "I'll be along soon."

"Okay, Mommie," said Splinter. "Will you bring some cake?" he asked slyly. "Doovie isn't a-miliar with cake."

Serena laughed. "A certain little Splinter is a-miliar with cake, though! You run along, greedy!" And she boosted him out of the door with a slap on the rear.

"Bye, Mommie," he called back.

"Bye, dear. Be good."

"I will."

Serena watched until he disappeared down the slope of the hill, then she smoothed her hair and ran her tongue over her lips. She started for the bedroom, but turned suddenly and went to the front door. If she had to face even her own eyes, her resolution would waver and dissolve. She stood, hand on knob, watching the clock inch around until an interminable fifteen minutes had passed—Splinter safely gone—then she snatched the door open and left.

Her smile took her out of the Quarters Area to the Administration Building. Her brisk assumption of authority and destination took her to the conference wing and there her courage failed her. She lurked out of sight of the guards, almost wringing her hands in indecision. Then she straightened the set of her skirt, smoothed her hair, dredged a smile up from some hidden source of strength and tiptoed out into the hall.

She felt like a butterfly pinned to the wall by the instant unwinking attention of the guards. She gestured silence with a finger to her lips and tiptoed up to them.

"Hello, Turner. Hi, Franiveri," she whispered.

The two exchanged looks and Turner said hoarsely, "You aren't supposed to be here, Ma'am. Better go."

"I know I'm not," she said, looking guilty—with no effort at all. "But, Turner, I—I just want to see a Linjeni." She hurried on before Turner's open mouth could form a word. "Oh, I've seen pictures of them, but I'd like awfully to see a real one. Can't I have even one little peek?" She slipped closer to the door. "Look!" she cried softly. "It's even ajar a little already!"

"Supposed to be," rasped Turner. "Orders. But Ma'am, we can't—"

"Just one peek?" she pleaded, putting her thumb in the crack of the door. "I won't make a sound."

She coaxed the door open a little farther, her hand creeping inside, fumbling for the knob, the little button.

"But, Ma'am, you couldn't see 'em from here anyway."

Quicker than thought, Serena jerked the door open and darted in, pushing the little button and slamming the door to with what seemed to her a thunder that vibrated through the whole building. Breathlessly, afraid to think, she sped through the anteroom and into the conference room. She came to a scared skidding stop, her hands tight on the back of a chair, every eye in the room on her. Thorn, almost unrecognizable in his armor of authority and severity, stood up abruptly.

"Serena!" he said, his voice cracking with incredulity. Then he sat down again, hastily.

Serena circled the table, refusing to meet the eyes that bored into her—blue eyes, brown eyes, black eyes, yellow eyes, green eyes, lavender eyes. She turned at the foot of the table and looked fearfully up at the shining expanse.

"Gentlemen," her voice was almost inaudible. She cleared her throat. "Gentlemen." She saw General Worsham getting ready to speak—his face harshly unfamiliar with the weight of his position. She pressed her hands to the polished table and leaned forward hastily.

"You're going to quit, aren't you? You're giving up!" The translators bent to their mikes and their lips moved to hers. "What have you been talking about all this time? Guns? Battles? Casualty lists? We'll-do-this-to-you-if-you-do-that-to-us? I don't know!" she cried, shaking her head tightly, almost shuddering. "I don't know what goes on at high level conference tables. All I know is that I've been teaching Mrs. Pink to knit, and how to cut a lemon pie——" She could see the bewildered interpreters thumbing their manuals. "And already I know why they're here and what they want!" Pursing her lips, she half whistled, half trilled in her halting Linjeni, "Doovie baby. No more Linjeni babies!"

One of the Linjeni started at Doovie's name and stood up slowly, his lavender bulk towering over the table. Serena saw the interpreters thumbing frantically again. She knew they were looking for a translation of the Linjeni "baby." Babies had no place in a military conference.

The Linjeni spoke slowly, but Serena shook her head. "I don't know enough Linjeni."

There was a whisper at her shoulder. "What do you know of Doovie?" And a pair of earphones were pushed into her hands. She adjusted them with trembling fingers. Why were they letting her talk? Why was General Worsham sitting there letting her break into the conference like this?

"I know Doovie," she said breathlessly. "I know Doovie's mother, too. Doovie plays with Splinter, my son—my little son." She twisted her fingers, dropping her head at the murmur that arose around the table. The Linjeni spoke again and the earphones murmured metallically. "What is the color of Doovie's mother?"

"Pink," said Serena.

Again the scurry for a word—pink—pink. Finally Serena turned up the hem of her skirt and displayed the hem of her slip—rose-pink. The Linjeni sat down again, nodding.

"Serena," General Worsham spoke as quietly as though it were just another lounging evening in the patio. "What do you want?"

Serena's eyes wavered and then her chin lifted.

"Thorn said today would be the last day. That it was to be 'no' on both sides. That we and the Linjeni have no common meeting ground, no basis for agreement on anything."

"And you think we have?" General Worsham's voice cut gently through the stir at the naked statement of thoughts and attitudes so carefully concealed.

"I know we do. Our similarities so far outweigh our differences that it's just foolish to sit here all this time, shaking our differences at each other and not finding out a thing about our similarities. We are fundamentally the same —the same—" she faltered. "Under God we are all the same." And she knew with certainty that the translators wouldn't find God's name in their books. "I think we ought to let them eat our salt and bread and make them welcome!" She half smiled and said, "The word for salt is *shreeprill*."

There was a smothered rush of whistling from the Linjeni, and the lavender Linjeni half rose from his chair and subsided.

General Worsham glanced at the Linjeni speculatively and pursed his lips. "But there are ramifications—" he began.

"Ramifications!" spat Serena. "There are no ramifications that can't resolve themselves if two peoples really know each other!"

She glanced around the table, noting with sharp relief that Thorn's face had softened.

"Come with me!" she urged. "Come and see Doovie and Splinter together—Linjeni young and ours, who haven't learned suspicion and fear and hate and prejudice yet. Declare a—a—recess or a truce or whatever is necessary and come with me. After you see the children and see Mrs. Pink knitting and we talk this matter over like members of a family— Well, if you still think you have to fight after that, then—" she spread her hands.

Her knees shook so as they started downhill that Thorn had to help her walk.

"Oh, Thorn," she whispered, almost sobbing. "I didn't think they would. I thought they'd shoot me or lock me up or—"

"We don't want war. I told you that," he murmured. "We're ready to grab at straws, even in the guise of snippy females who barge in on solemn councils and display their slips!" Then his lips tightened. "How long has this been going on?"

"For Splinter, a couple of weeks. For me, a little more than a week."

"Why didn't you tell me?"

"I tried—twice. You wouldn't listen. I was too scared to insist. Besides, you know what your reaction would have been."

Thorn had no words until they neared the foot of the hill, then he said, "How come you know so much? What makes you think you can solve—"

Serena choked back a hysterical laugh. "I took eggs to a picnic!"

And then they were standing, looking down at the hole under the fence.

"Splinter found the way," Serena defended. "I made it bigger, but you'll have to get down—flat."

She dropped to the sand and wiggled under. She crouched on the other side, her knees against her chest, her clasped hands pressed against her mouth, and waited. There was a long minute of silence and then a creak and a grunt and Serena bit her lips as General Worsham inched under the fence, flat on the sand, catching and jerking free halfway through. But her amusement changed to admiration as she realized that even covered with dust, scrambling awkwardly to his feet and beating his rumpled clothing, he possessed dignity and strength that made her deeply thankful that he was the voice of Earth in this time of crisis.

One by one the others crawled under, the Linjeni sandwiched between the other men and Thorn bringing up the rear. Motioning silence, she led them to the thicket of bushes that screened one side of the goldfish pond.

Doovie and Splinter were leaning over the edge of the pond.

"There it is!" cried Splinter, leaning perilously and pointing. "Way down there on the bottom and it's my best marble. Would your Mommie care if you got it for me?"

Doovie peered down. "Marble go in water."

"That's what I said," cried Splinter impatiently. "And

you can shut your nose—" he put his finger to the black, glistening button, "and fold your ears." He flicked them with his forefinger and watched them fold. "Gee!" he said admiringly, "I wish I could do that."

"Doovie go in water?" asked Doovie.

"Yeah," nodded Splinter. "It's my good taw and you won't even have to put on swimming trunks—you got fur."

Doovie shucked out of his brief clothing and slid down into the pond. He bobbed back up, his hand clenched.

"Gee, thanks." Splinter held out his hand and Doovie carefully turned his hand over and Splinter closed his. Then he shrieked and flung his hand out. "You mean old thing!" yelled Splinter. "Give me my marble! That was a slippy old fish!" He leaned over, scuffling, trying to reach Doovie's other hand. There was a slither and a splash and Splinter and Doovie disappeared under the water.

Serena caught her breath and had started forward when Doovie's anxious face bobbed to the surface again. He yanked and tugged at the sputtering, coughing Splinter and tumbled him out onto the grass. Doovie squatted by Splinter, patting his back and alternately whistling dolefully through his nose and talking apologetic sounding Linjeni.

Splinter coughed and dug his fists into his eyes.

"Golly, golly!" he said, spatting his hands against his wet jersey. "Mommie'll sure be mad. My clean clothes all wet. Where's my marble, Doovie?"

Doovie scrambled to his feet and went back to the pond. Splinter started to follow, then he cried. "Oh, Doovie, where did that poor little fish go? It'll die if it's out of the water. My guppy did."

"Fish?" asked Doovie.

"Yes," said Splinter, holding out his hand as he searched the grass with intent eyes. "The slippery little fish that wasn't my marble."

The two youngsters scrambled around in the grass until Doovie whistled and cried out triumphantly, "Fish!" and scooped it up in his hands and rushed it back to the pond.

"There," said Splinter, "now it won't die. Looky, it's swimming away!"

Doovie slid into the pond again and retrieved the lost marble.

"Now," said Splinter, "watch me and I'll show you how to shoot."

The bushes beyond the two absorbed boys parted and Mrs. Pink stepped out. She smiled at the children and then she saw the silent group on the other side of the clearing. Her eyes widened and she gave an astonished whistle. The two boys looked up and followed the direction of her eyes.

"Daddy!" yelled Splinter. "Did you come to play?" And he sped, arms outstretched, to Thorn, arriving only a couple of steps ahead of Doovie who was whistling excitedly and rushing to greet the tall lavender Linjeni.

Serena felt a sudden choke of laughter at how alike Thorn and the Linjeni looked, trying to greet their offspring adequately and still retain their dignity.

Mrs. Pink came hesitantly to the group to stand in the circle of Serena's arm. Splinter had swarmed up Thorn, hugged him with thoroughness and slid down again. "Hi, General Worsham!" he said, extending a muddy hand in a belated remembrance of his manners. "Hey, Daddy, I'm showing Doovie how to play marbles, but you can shoot better'n I can. You come show him how."

"Well—" said Thorn, glancing uncomfortably at General Worsham.

General Worsham was watching the Linjeni as Doovie whistled and fluted over a handful of bright colored glassie marbles. He quirked an eyebrow at Thorn and then at the rest of the group.

"I suggest a recess," he said. "In order that we may examine new matters that have been brought to our attention."

Serena felt herself getting all hollow inside, and she turned her face away so Mrs. Pink wouldn't see her cry. But Mrs. Pink was too interested in the colorful marbles to see Serena's gathering, hopeful tears.

THE PIEBALD HIPPOGRIFF

by Karen Anderson

from *Fantastic*

It could be a distant future. It could be an altogether different world. It is, of course, sheer make-believe—but while I am not certain whether the fantasy is Mrs. Anderson's or Johnny's, I am quite sure it is the kind of let's-pretend that has the most to do with the uniqueness of man and with his greatest potential.

The edge of the world is fenced off stoutly enough, but the fence isn't made that will stop a boy. Johnny tossed his pack and coil of rope over it and started climbing. The top three strands were barbed wire. He caught his shirt as he went over, and had to stop for a moment to ease himself off. Then he dropped lightly to the grass on the other side.

The pack had landed in a clump of white clover. A cloud of disturbed bees hung above, and he snatched it away quickly lest they should notice the honeycomb inside.

For a minute he stood still, looking out over the edge. This was different from looking through the fence, and when he moved it was slowly. He eased himself to the ground where a corner of rock rose clear of the thick larkspur and lay on his belly, the stone hard and cool under his chin, and looked down.

The granite cliff curved away out of sight, and he couldn't see if it had a foot. He saw only endless blue, beyond, below, and on both sides. Clouds passed slowly.

Directly beneath him there was a ledge covered with long grass where clusters of stars bloomed on tall, slender stalks.

He uncoiled his rope and found a stout beech tree not too close to the edge. Doubling the rope around the bole, he tied one end around his waist, slung the pack on his back, and belayed himself down the cliff. Pebbles clattered, saxifrage brushed his arms and tickled his ears; once he groped for a hold with his face in a patch of rustling ferns.

The climb was hard, but not too much. Less than half an hour later he was stretched out on the grass with stars nodding about him. They had a sharp, gingery smell. He lay in the cool shadow of the world's edge for a while, eating apples and honeycomb from his pack. When he was finished he licked the honey off his fingers and threw the apple cores over, watching them fall into the blue.

Little islands floated along, rocking gently in air eddies. Sunlight flashed on glossy leaves of bushes growing there. When an island drifted into the shadow of the cliff, the blossoming stars shone out. Beyond the shadows, deep in the light-filled gulf, he saw the hippogriffs at play.

There were dozens of them, frisking and cavorting in the air. He gazed at them full of wonder. They pretended to fight, stooped at one another, soared off in long spirals to stoop and soar and stoop again. One flashed by him, a golden palomino that shone like polished wood. The wind whistled in its wings.

Away to the left, the cliff fell back in a wide crescent, and nearly opposite him a river tumbled over the edge. A pool on a ledge beneath caught most of the water, and there were hippogriffs drinking. One side of the broad pool was notched. The overflow fell sheer in a white plume blown sideways by the wind.

As the sun grew hotter, the hippogriffs began to settle and browse on the islands that floated past. Not far below, he noticed, a dozen or so stood drowsily on an island that was floating through the cliff's shadow toward his ledge. It would pass directly below him.

With a sudden resolution, Johnny jerked his rope down from the tree above and tied the end to a projecting knob on the cliff. Slinging on his pack again, he slid over the edge and down the rope.

The island was already passing. The end of the rope trailed through the grass. He slithered down and cut a piece off his line.

It was barely long enough after he had tied a noose in the end. He looked around at the hippogriffs. They had shied away when he dropped onto the island, but now they stood still, watching him warily.

Johnny started to take an apple out of his pack, then changed his mind and took a piece of honeycomb. He broke off one corner and tossed it toward them. They fluttered their wings and backed off a few steps, then stood still again.

Johnny sat down to wait. They were mostly chestnuts and blacks, and some had white stockings. One was piebald. That was the one which, after a while, began edging closer to where the honeycomb had fallen. Johnny sat very still.

The piebald sniffed at the honeycomb, then jerked up its head to watch him suspiciously. He didn't move. After a moment it took the honeycomb.

When he threw another bit, the piebald hippogriff wheeled away, but returned almost at once and ate it. Johnny tossed a third piece only a few yards from where he was sitting.

It was bigger than the others, and the hippogriff had to bite it in two. When the hippogriff bent its head to take the rest Johnny was on his feet instantly, swinging his lariat. He dropped the noose over the hippogriff's head. For a moment the animal was too startled to do anything; then Johnny was on its back, clinging tight.

The piebald hippogriff leaped into the air, and Johnny clamped his legs about convulsed muscles. Pinions whipped against his knees and wind blasted his eyes. The world tilted; they were rushing downward. His knees pressed the sockets of the enormous wings.

The distant ramparts of the world swung madly, and he seemed to fall upward, away from the sun that suddenly glared under the hippogriff's talons. He forced his knees under the roots of the beating wings and dug heels into prickling hair. A sob caught his breath and he clenched his teeth.

The universe righted itself about him for a moment and he pulled breath into his lungs. Then they plunged again. Wind searched under his shirt. Once he looked down. After that he kept his eyes on the flutter of the feather-mane.

A jolt sent him sliding backward. He clutched the rope with slippery fingers. The wings missed a beat and the hippogriff shook its head as the rope momentarily checked its breath. It tried to fly straight up, lost way, and fell stiff-winged. The long muscles stretched under him as it arched its back, then bunched when it kicked straight out behind. The violence loosened his knees and he trembled with fatigue, but he wound the rope around his wrists and pressed his forehead against whitened knuckles. Another kick, and another. Johnny dragged at the rope.

The tense wings flailed, caught air, and brought the hippogriff upright again. The rope slackened and he heard huge gasps. Sunlight was hot on him again and a drop of sweat crawled down his temple. It tickled. He loosened one hand to dab at the annoyance. A new twist sent him sliding and he grabbed the rope. The tickle continued until he nearly screamed. He no longer dared let go. Another tickle developed beside the first. He scrubbed his face against the coarse fibre of the rope; the relief was like a world conquered.

Then they glided in a steady spiral that carried them upward with scarcely a feather's motion. When the next plunge came Johnny was ready for it and leaned back until the hippogriff arched its neck, trying to free itself from the pressure on its windpipe. Half choked, it glided again, and Johnny gave it breath.

They landed on one of the little islands. The hippogriff drooped its head and wings, trembling.

He took another piece of honeycomb from his pack and tossed it to the ground where the hippogriff could reach it easily. While it ate he stroked it and talked to it. When he dismounted the hippogriff took honeycomb from his hand.

He stroked its neck, breathing the sweet warm feathery smell, and laughed aloud when it snuffled the back of his neck.

Tying the rope into a sort of hackamore, he mounted again and rode the hippogriff to the pool below the thunder and cold spray of the waterfall. He took care that it did not drink too much. When he ate some apples for his lunch, the hippogriff ate the cores.

Afterward he rode to one of the drifting islands and let his mount graze. For a while he kept by its side, making much of it. With his fingers, he combed out the soft flowing plumes of its mane, and examined its hoofs and the sickle-like talons of the forelegs. He saw how the smooth feathers on its forequarters became finer and finer until he could scarcely see where the hair on the hindquarters began. Delicate feathers covered its head.

The island glided further and further away from the cliffs, and he watched the waterfall dwindle away to a streak and disappear. After a while he fell asleep.

He woke with a start, suddenly cold: the setting sun was below his island. The feathery odor was still on his hands. He looked around for the hippogriff and saw it sniffing at his pack.

When it saw him move, it trotted up to him with an expectant air. He threw his arms about the great flat-muscled neck and pressed his face against the warm feathers, with a faint sense of embarassment at feeling tears in his eyes.

"Good old Patch," he said, and got his pack. He shared the last piece of honeycomb with his hippogriff and watched the sun sink still further. The clouds were turning red.

"Let's go see those clouds," Johnny said. He mounted the piebald hippogriff and they flew off, up through the golden air to the sunset clouds. There they stopped and Johnny dismounted on the highest cloud of all, stood there as it turned slowly gray, and looked into dimming depths. When he turned to look at the world, he saw only a wide smudge of darkness spread in the distance.

The cloud they were standing on turned silver. Johnny

glanced up and saw the moon, a crescent shore far above.

He ate an apple and gave one to his hippogriff. While he chewed he gazed back at the world. When he finished his apple, he was about to toss the core to the hippogriff, but stopped himself and carefully took out the seeds first. With the seeds in his pocket, he mounted again.

He took a deep breath. "Come on, Patch," he said. "Let's homestead the moon."

HOME FROM THE SHORE
by Gordon R. Dickson

from *Galaxy*

And, finally, one possible future in which man might actually make careful use of *all* the knowledge he has gained: adapting self and environment both in a uniquely conscious evolution.

Well it was about four in the afternoon. You know how it is that time of day at Savannah Stand, with most of the day-charter flyers back in the ranks. All the hanging around and talking and the smell of cigarette smoke on the air, and the water stains drying back to the pale color of the concrete from the flyers that have just been washed down. You know what a good time of day that is.

Well, it was maybe a few minutes after four. Everybody was kidding about how the *Nu-Ark* was just about ready to split apart in the air and her pilot never know the difference. We were talking like that when somebody spotted a fare down at the far end of the ranks. He came up along the line, a big young tourist in a flower-patterned Thousand-Islands shirt hanging outside his pants, walking across the water stains already fading out like the cigarette smoke in the sun and looking into faces under the shadows of the ducted fans as he passed. He came on down and stopped at last by the *Nu-Ark* and hired her. And they took off east out over the ocean.

"One to five, in beers," said the pilot of the *Squarefish* as we watched them shrink down in the distance, "one of the fans comes off before he gets back here."

"That's a bad luck bet," said the pilot of the *Slingalong*. "Don't none of you take him up on that." Nobody did, either.

"You got no sense of humor," said the *Squarefish* pilot.

It was one of those hot bright days in late July, clear as a bell. About twelve miles offshore aboard the *Nu-Ark* they felt the motors to both fans quit, stutter a moment and then take up their tale again, perhaps not just as smoothly as before. But the pilot said nothing and the passenger said nothing. They had not said a word in each other's direction since leaving the Stand. They had not even looked at each other.

The pilot was sitting by himself up front. The passenger stood in back. They were in different sections of the flyer, which was like a metal shoebox in shape between the fans, and divided up near the front by a steel partition with a narrow doorway in it just back of the pilot seat. The whole flyer had a light, flat-tasting stink of lubricating oil from the fans all through it. It vibrated to the hard working of the fans so that anything touched sent a quiver from the finger ends up to the elbow. Up in front of the partition there was just room for the pilot, his control bar and instruments, and a wide windscreen looking forward. In the bigger part of the box behind was the passenger, six bolted-down seats and luggage racks in the space behind the seats.

The racks were forest-green like the walls, with a permanent color that had been fused into them. The two side walls had a couple of windows apiece. All the seats, which were overstuffed and with arm and headrests, were covered in an imitation tan leather that still looked as good as the day it had been put on at the factory. Only the brown color of the floor had been scratched and worn clear down to silver streaks of metal by the sand tracked in from the beach, which gritted and squeaked underfoot at every step.

With only an occasional little noise from the sand, the passenger stood by one of the windows looking north in the back section, staring out and down at the sea. To his left, back the way they had come, the shoreline where the land ended and the ocean began was sharp and as definite as if someone had drawn it in sand-colored ink. To his right and northeast, the sea was blue-gray from this height, smoke-colored, corrugated and unmoving, stretching miles without end to the horizon, and lost there. There was no doubt about the shoreline. But the distant horizon line where ocean met sky was no line at all. The still, blue-gray waters lifted to the far emptiness until they were lost in it. No one could have said for sure where the one ended and the other began.

The sky, on the other hand, that went to meet the sea, was a pale thin blue with only a small handful of white clouds about thirty miles off and at twenty thousand feet. Right from the moment of take-off, the passenger had seen that the pilot of the *Nu-Ark* never looked at the clouds. He kept his eyes only on the indefinite horizon. Glancing over now, the passenger saw by the back of a head showing above the headrest of the pilot seat that the pilot was still at it. It looked to the passenger as if the pilot was so used to the sky that he no longer noticed it. He did not notice the vibration, the faltering of his fans or the stink of oil. Likewise, he seemed used to the look of the sea. But the far-off and strange part of things that was the horizon drew all the attention of his eyes.

They were brown, his eyes, the passenger remembered. A little bloodshot. Set in a middle-aged tropical face tanned and thickened into squint lines around the corners of the eyes. Just then the pilot spoke, without turning.

"Keep straight on out?" he said.

The passenger went tight at the sound of the voice, jerking his eyes back to the pilot seat. But the black, straight hair of the pilot showed unmoving against the tan imitation leather. The passenger hooked a thumb into the neck opening of his bright-printed sports shirt. With one quick downward jerk of the thumb he unsealed the closure and the shirt fell open.

"Straight on out," he said. He shrugged off the shirt and reached for the belt closure of his green slacks. "Another four or five minutes, this heading."

"Ten, twelve miles," said the pilot. "All right."

The black-haired portion of his head that was showing tilted forward. The passenger could see him finally leaning toward the sea. Looking, no doubt, for a vee of wake, a squat triangle of sail, some dark boat-shape.

"Who do you think's out here now—" he began.

He had started turning his head to look back as he spoke. As his eyes came around to see the passenger undressing, he moved with unexpected quickness, letting go of the control bar and swinging himself and his pilot seat all the way around. The flyer shuddered briefly as it went into autopilot. The passenger ripped off his slacks and stood up straight in only khaki-colored shorts. They looked at each other.

The look on the pilot's face had not changed. But now the passenger saw the brown eyes come to sharp focus on him. He stood balanced and waiting.

The only thing he was afraid of now was that the pilot would not look closely enough. He was afraid the pilot might see only a big young man in his early twenties. A young man with a strong-boned body muscled like a wrestler, but with a square, open and too easy-going sort of face. Then he saw the pilot's eyes flicker to the three blue dots tattooed on his bare right collarbone, and after that drop to the third finger of his right hand which showed a ring of untanned white about its base. The eyes came back up to his face then. When he saw their expression had still not changed, he knew that that one fear, at least, he could forget.

"I guess," said the pilot, "you know who's out there after all."

"That's right," he said. He continued to stand, leaving the next move up to the pilot. Six inches from the pilot's still left hand was the small, closed door of a map compartment. In there would probably be a knife or gun. The pilot himself was big-boned and thick-bodied. The years had put a scar above one eyebrow and broken and enlarged three knuckles on his right hand. These were things that had caused the pilot to be picked by him for this taxi-job in the first place. He had trusted a man like the pilot of the *Nu-Ark* not to go off half-cocked.

"So you seen a space bat," said the pilot now, still watching him. The name came out sounding odd in the Southern accent; but for a moment it hit home and the pilot blurred before his eyes as tears jumped in them. He blinked quickly; but the pilot had not moved. Once again he remembered how slow land people were to cry. The pilot would not have been figuring that advantage.

"We all did," he said.

"Yeah," said the pilot. "Your picture was on the news. Johnny Joya, aren't you?"

"That's right," he said.

"Ringleader, weren't you?"

"No," said Johnny. "There's no ringleaders with us."

"News said so."

"No."

"Well, they did."

"They don't know."

The pilot shrugged. He sat still for a second.

"All right," he said. "They still got a reward out for you bigger than on any the rest of the Cadets."

They held still for another little moment, watching each other. The flyer bored on through the air, automatically holding its course. Johnny stood balanced. He was thinking that he had picked this pilot because the man was like him. It might be they were too much alike. It might be that the pilot had too much pride to let himself be forced, in spite of the squint lines and broken knuckles and knowing now what his chances would be with someone like Johnny. If it was that, the pilot would need some excuse, or reason.

Easily, not taking his eyes off the pilot, Johnny reached down and picked up his slacks. From one pocket he searched out something small, circular and hard. Holding it outstretched in his fingers, he took two steps forward and offered it to the pilot.

"Souvenir," he said.

The pilot looked down at it. It was a steel ring with a crest on it showing what looked like a mailed fist grasping at a star.

Two words—*ad astra*—were cut in under the crest.

"Souvenir," said Johnny again.

The pilot looked it over for a long second, then slowly reached out two of the fingers with the broken knuckles and tweezered it between the ends of them, out of Johnny's grasp. He turned it slowly over, first one way and then the other, looking at it.

He said, "Once I would've wanted one like that." He lifted his eyes to Johnny. "I don't understand. Nobody does."

"It looks that way to us, too," he answered, not moving. "We don't understand Landers."

"Yeah," said the pilot. He turned the ring again. "Well, you was the one that was there. You all go home, all you sea kids?"

"It's not our job," he said. "Fill your Space Academy with your own people."

"Yeah," said the pilot, almost to himself. Slowly he folded in the fingers holding the ring, until it was covered and hidden in the grasp of his fist. He put the fist in his pocket and when it came out again he no longer held the ring. "All right. Souvenir." He turned back to the controls. "How much on out?"

"About a mile now."

The pilot took hold of the control bar. The flyer dropped. The surface of the sea came up to meet them, becoming more blue and less gray as it approached. From high up it had looked fixed and unmoving, but now they could see there was motion to it. When they got close indeed, they could see how it was furrowed and all in action, so that no part of it was the same as any other, or stayed the same.

Johnny put one palm to the ceiling and pressed upward. He stood braced against the angle of their descent, looking past the bunched-up muscles of his forearms at the jacketed back of the pilot and the approaching sea.

"How can you tell?" asked the pilot, suddenly. "You know where we are now?"

"About eight-one, fifty west," said Johnny, "by about thirty-one, forty north."

The pilot glanced at his instruments.

"Right on," the pilot said. "Or almost. How?"

"Come to sea," he answered. "Your grandchildren'll have it." His eyes blurred suddenly again for a second. "Why the hell you think they wanted us for their Space Program?"

"No," said the pilot, not turning his head, "leave me out of it." A moment later he leaned toward the windscreen. "Something in the top of the water, there."

"That's it," said Johnny. The flyer dropped. It came down on the surface and began to rock and move with the ceaseless motion of the waves. The ducted fans were unexpectedly still. Their thrumming had given way to a strange silence broken by the slapping of the waves against the flyer's underbody and small creakings of metal.

"Well, look there!" said the pilot.

He leaned forward, staring out through the windscreen. The flyer had become surrounded by a gang of stunting dolphin and seal. A great, swollen balloon of a fish—a guasa—floated almost to the surface alongside the flyer and gaped at it with a mouth that opened like a lifting manhole cover. Johnny slipped full-eye contact lenses into place and stripped off the shorts. In only the lenses and an athletic supporter, he picked up the small sealed suitcase he had brought aboard and opened the side door of the flyer, just back of the partition on the right. The pilot turned his seat to watch.

"Here—" he said suddenly. He reached into his pocket, brought out the Academy ring and held it out to Johnny. Johnny stared at him. "Go ahead, take it. What the hell, it don't mean anything to me!" Slowly, Johnny took it, hesitated, and slid it back on his right third finger to carry it. "Good luck."

"All right," said Johnny. "Thanks." He turned and tossed the suitcase out the door. Several dolphins raced for it, the lead one taking it in his almost beakless mouth. He was larger and somewhat different from the others.

"You going very deep there?" asked the pilot as Johnny stepped down on to the top of the landing steps, whose base was in the waves.

"Twenty . . ." Johnny glanced at the gamboling sea-creatures. "No, only about fifteen fathoms."

The pilot looked from him to the dolphins and back again.

"Ninety feet," said the pilot.

Johnny went down a couple of steps and felt the soft warmth of the sun-warmed surface waters roll over his feet. He looked back at the pilot.

"Thanks again," he said. He hesitated and then held out his hand. The pilot got up from his seat, came to the flyer door and shook. In the grip of their hands, Johnny could feel the hard calluses of the man's palm.

"It's what you call Castle-Home, down there?" said the pilot as they let go.

"No," said Johnny. "It's Home." On the last word he felt his vocal cords tighten and he was suddenly in a hurry to be going. "Castle-Home's—something else."

He let go of the doorpost of the flyer and stepped down and out into the ever-moving waves.

The ones that had come up to meet him—the seals, the dolphins, the guasa—went down with him. He saw the color of the under-waters, green as light behind a leaf-shadowed window. And he spread his arms with the gesture of the first man who ever stood on a hilltop watching the easy soaring of the birds. He swam downward.

The salt water was cool and simple and complete around him, after all the chills and sweatings of the land. In the stillness he could feel the slow, strong beating of his own heart driving the salt blood throughout his body. He felt cleaned at last from the dust and dirt of the past four and a half years. He felt free at last from the prison of his clothing.

Down he swam, his heart surging slowly and strongly. Around him, a revolving circus act of underwater, free-flying aerialists leaped and danced—ponderous guasa, doe-eyed harp seals, bottle-nosed and common dolphins. And the one large Risso's dolphin, with the suitcase in his mouth, circling closest.

Johnny clicked fingernails and tongue at the Risso's

dolphin. It was a message in the dolphin code that the Risso's knew well. *"Baldur . . . Baldur the Beautiful . . ."* The twelve-foot gray beast rolled almost against him in the water, offering the trailing reins of the harness.

He caught first one rein, then the other, and let himself be towed down, no longer pivot man to the group but a moving part of it.

Seconds later, there was light below them, brighter than the light from above. They were coming down into the open hub of a large number of apartments, mostly with transparent walls, sealed together into the shape of a wheel. People poured out of the apartments like birds from an aviary. They clustered around him, swept him down and pushed him through the magnetic iris of an entrance. His ears popped slightly and he came through walking into a large, air-filled room surrounding a pool. The dolphins, the seals and the guasa broke water in the pool in the same second. People crowded in after him, swarmed around him, shouting and laughing.

In a second the room was over-full. There was no spare space. A tall, lean young man, Johnny's age, looking like Johnny, climbed up on a table holding a sort of curved, long-necked banjo. Sitting crosslegged, he flashed fingers over the strings, ringing out wild, shouting music. Voices caught up the tune. A song—one Johnny had never heard before—beat at the walls.

> *Hey, Johnny! Hey-a, Johnny!*
> *Home, from the shore!*
> *Hey-o, Johnny! Hey, Johnny!*
> *To high land, go no more!*
>
> *Long away, away, my Johnny!*
> *Four long years and more!*
> *Hey-o, Johnny! Hey, Johnny!*
> *Go high land, no more!*

They were all singing. They sang, shouting it, swaying together, holding together, laughing and crying at the same time. The tears ran down their clean faces.

Johnny felt the arms of those closest to him, hugging him. Those who could not reach to hold him, held each other. The song rose, canted, wept. It would be one of his lean cousin's songs, made up for the occasion of his homecoming. He did not know the words. But as he was handed on, slowly from the arms of one relative or friend to the next, he was caught up, at last, in the music and sang with the rest of them.

He felt the tears running down his own cheeks, the easy tears of his childhood. There was a great feeling in the room. It was the *nous-nous* of his people, of The People, the People of the Sea in all their three generations. He was caught up with them in the moment now and sang and wept with them. They were moved together in this moment of his returning, as the oceans themselves were moved by the great currents that gave life and movement to their waters. The roadways of the seal, the dolphin, and now the roadways of his people. The Liman, the Kuroshio, the Humboldt Current. The Canary, the Gulf Stream in which they were now this moment drifting north. The Labrador.

For four years he had been without this feeling. But now he was Home.

Gradually the great we-feeling of the People in the room relaxed and settled down into a spirit of celebration. The song of his homecoming shifted to a humorous ballad— about an old man who had a harp seal, which wouldn't get out of his bed. Laughter crackled among them. Long-necked green pressure bottles and a variety of marinated tidbits of seafood were passed from hand to hand. The mood of all of them settled into cheerfulness, swung at last to attention on Johnny. Quiet welled up and spread around the pool, quenching other talk.

Sitting now on the table that his cousin Patrick with the banjo had vacated, he suddenly noticed their waiting. He had his arm around the shoulders of a round-breasted, brown-haired, slight girl who sat leaning against him on the table, her head in the hollow of his shoulder. He had been looking down at her without talking, trying to see what difference four years had made in her. He saw something, but he could not put his finger on just what it was. Like all the sea-people, she was free; although he wondered if the Landers had appreciated the difference between that, and their own legal ways, when they had set all the Cadets from the sea down as unmarried. But still, she was free; and he had not even been certain that he would find her still here with his family and friends' Group when he came back.

She sat up and moved aside now, to let him sit up. Her eyes glanced against his for a moment and once more he thought he saw a new difference between her now and the girl he remembered. But what it was still stayed hidden to him. He turned and looked out at the people. They were all quiet now, sitting on chairs or hassocks or cross-legged on the floor and looking at him.

"I suppose you've all heard it on the news," he said.

"Only that it was something about the space bats," said the voice of Patrick beneath him. Johnny leaned forward and peered over the edge of the table. Patrick sat cross-legged there, the banjo upright between his knees with the long neck sloping over his shoulder, his head leaning against it with the edge pressing into his cheek. He winked up at Johnny. The wink was the same wink Johnny remembered, but it put creases in Patrick's lean face he had never seen there before. Without warning, Patrick's face looked as Johnny had seen it on the jacket of a tape of Patrick's Moho Symphony, in a music department ashore. At the time Johnny had thought the picture was a bad likeness.

He winked back and straightened up.

He said, "The space bats were the final straw. That's all, actually."

"Were they big, Johnny?"

It was a child's voice. Johnny looked and saw a boy seated cross-legged almost at the foot of the table, his eyes full open, his lips a little parted, all his upper body leaning forward. He was one who had evidently been born into the Joya Group since Johnny left. Johnny did not know his name.

"The one I saw would have weighed about six ounces

down here on Earth." He spoke to the boy as he would have spoken to any of the rest, regardless of age. "But—it was a good quarter mile across."

The boy drew in so deep a breath his shoulders lifted. When he let it out again his whole body shuddered.

"A quar-ter *mile!*" he whispered.

"A quarter mile," said Johnny, remembering. "A quarter mile. Like a silver curtain waving in the current of an offshore tide. That's how it looked to me."

"You helped catch it?" said Emil Joya, who was an uncle both to Johnny and his cousin Patrick with the banjo.

Johnny looked up.

"No," he said. "They took the senior class, which was mostly made up of us sea people, out beyond Mars to observe. We just watched." He hesitated a second. "They said it'd be something some of us would be doing some day. Part of a project to find out how the space bats make it between the stars, if they do. And how to duplicate the process."

"I don't quite understand," said Emil, his heavy gray brows frowning in his square rock of a face.

"The Space Project people think the space bats can give up a secret of a practical way to drive our own ships between the stars at almost the speed of light."

"And you caught this one?" said Patrick, beneath the table.

"We watched," said Johnny. "It didn't try to escape. Men on space scooters walled it about with a net of charged particles. Then, all of a sudden, it seemed to understand. And it died."

"You killed it!" said the boy.

"Nobody killed it," said Johnny. "It died by itself. One minute it was there, waving like a silver curtain, and then the color started to go out of it. It fell in on itself. In just a moment it was nothing but a gray rag in the middle of the net."

He stopped talking. There was a second or two of silence in the small-Home crowded with sea people.

"And seeing that made you leave the Academy?" asked Patrick's voice.

"No," said Johnny. He drew a breath as deep as the boy had drawn. "After we came back from the observation cruise, we had to write reports. We wrote them separately; but afterward we found we'd all written the same thing, we sea-Cadets. We wrote that the space bats killed themselves when they were captured because they couldn't bear being trapped." He breathed deeply again. "We wrote that it would never work this way. The bats would always die. The project was a blind alley."

"And then?" said Patrick.

"Then the CO commended us for the excellence of our reports." Johnny laughed a little. "And the next week we sea-Cadets were all scheduled for some more of their psychiatric explorative examinations—to determine the causes of our emotional reactions, as they called them, to the capture of the bat."

Once more no one said anything.

"It doesn't make sense," said Patrick at last.

"Not to us, it doesn't," said Johnny. "To a Lander it makes very good sense. They never wanted us sea people as people in the first place. When they asked our third generation men to enlist as Academy Cadets, they only wanted those parts of us they could make use of—our faster reaction times, our more stable emotional structure—our gift of reckoning location and distance and the new instincts living in the sea has wakened in us . . ." Johnny's voice trailed off. He thumped softly on the table by his knee with one knotted fist, staring at the blank wall opposite, until Sara Light, the girl beside him, took his fist gently in her hands and cushioned it to stillness.

"We were like the space bats to them," said Johnny after a bit. "Time and again they'd proved it to us. I called a meeting of the other class representatives—I was Senior Class Rep. Jose Polar for the freshmen sea-Cadets, Martin Connor for the second year group, Mikros Palamas for the juniors. We decided there was no use trying any longer.

We went back and told the men in our own class. The next weekend, when we were allowed passes, we all took our rings off and headed as best we could for our own Homes."

He stopped speaking and sat looking across the unvarying surface of the wall.

They swarmed all over him for a second time. But they quieted down soon, the more so as Patrick's banjo did not join them. When it was still again Patrick spoke from under the table.

"You were the one who called the meeting, Johnny?"

"It was me," said Johnny. "I was Senior Representative."

"That's true," said Patrick. A faint E minor chord sounded from the strings of his banjo as if he had just happened to shift his grip on the neck of it. "That's why news has been calling you the ringleader. But you had no choice, I suppose."

"No," said Johnny.

"It'll be a hard thing for them to swallow."

"Perhaps," said Johnny. "I've lived with them four years, and they swallow different than us, Pat. We see and think different than they do. We have instincts already they don't have—and who knows what the next generations will be like? But they're not ready to admit our difference. And until they do, we can't live on dry land with them."

For a second it seemed as if Patrick would not say anything more. Then they heard a faint chord from his banjo again.

"Maybe," said Patrick, "maybe. But we all started with coming from high land in the beginning. A hundred thousand generations of men ashore, and only three or four in the sea. All the history, the art, the music . . . We can't cut ourselves off from that."

His voice stopped.

"We won't," said Emil. He stood up from the chair in which he was sitting. The rest of the people began to rise, too. "We'll be going to Castle-Home, shortly. And Castle-Home will straighten it out with the Closed Congress ashore, the way they've always done before. After all, we're a free people here in the sea. There's no way they can make us do for them against our will."

The people nearest the exit irises were already slipping out. Beyond the transparent front walls of the small-Home they were leaving. The encompassing waters were already darkening toward opaqueness. By ones and severals, saying good night to Johnny, they melted away toward their own small-Homes in the Joya Group's wheel.

Johnny found himself alone by the pool.

He looked about for Sara, but he could not see her. As he stepped toward the iris leading to the inner part of the small-Home unit, she came out of it. He reached out to her, but she avoided his grasp and took his hand. Puzzled, he let her lead him through the eye-baffling shimmer of the iris.

Beyond it he found not one bedroom, but two. Another iris led to a further sleeping room. But in this first area, a single bed was against a well at the foot of which a small nightlight glowed.

On the bed under a light cover, his face dug sideways into the softness of a pillow, dampened by his open-breathing mouth, was a small interloper. It was the boy who had spoken up earlier to ask about the space bats.

Politeness was for all ages among the sea people. Johnny stepped to the bed and reached down to shake gently a small bare shoulder and wake him to the fact that he was in the wrong small-Home. But Sara caught Johnny's hand; and when he looked down into her face he found it luminous with an emotion he did not know.

"Tomi," she said. "His name's Tomi. He's your son, Johnny."

Johnny stared at her. They had talked to and written each other across the distance between them these last four and a half years, and never once had she mentioned a child. Among the People, this was her right, if she wished. But somehow Johnny had never thought that with him a woman—and particularly Sara—

He forced his gaze away from her watching face, back down to the boy. His son slept the heavy slumber of childhood's exhaustion.

Slowly he sank on his knees by the bedside, drawing his hand out of Sara's grasp. A chill ran through him. He felt the heavy muscles of his stomach contract. In the small white glow of the nightlight reflected from the palely opaque walls, Tomi slumbered as if in a world remote, not only from land and sea and all the reaches of space, but from all things outside this one small room. He breathed without a sound. His chest movements were almost invisible, his skin fine to the point of translucency. The chill in Johnny spread numbness through all his body and limbs, and his neck creaked on stiff tendons.

He reached out slowly. With what seemed an enormous, creased and coarse-skinned fingertip, he traced the slight line of an eyebrow on the boy. The brown, fine hairs were crisp to his touch. An abrupt flush of emotion rushed through him, burning away the chill like a wave of fever. He felt clumsy and helpless; and a wild desire prompted him to gather the boy in his arms and, holding him tightly, snarl above him at all the forces of the universe. Wrung and bewildered, Johnny turned his face up to Sara.

"Sara!" It was almost a wail of despair from his lips.

She knelt down beside him and put her arms around him and the boy, together. He clung to her and the sleeping youngster; and the boy, half-waking, roused and held to them both.

And so they held together, the three of them, there in the glow of the nightlight.

It was the hurricane season. One big wind had begun its march north on the day Johnny left the Academy. On the fourth day of his return, it hammered the ocean surface above the Joya Home into spume and dark, tall masses of leaning water. It battered Georgia and the North Carolina shore.

The Joya Home slipped down to twenty fathoms depth and dwelt there in calm, green-blue silence. No effect of the howling, furious borderland between air and water reached down here to the bright wheel-shaped Home, away up in the middle of the ocean universe. The People of the Joya group hardly thought about what was happening above. In their swim-masks or small-Homes, they breathed the atmosphere made for them out of the water elements. They ate and drank of bounty the living ocean supplied. When they reached Castle-Home would be time enough to think about replacing any of the large, complex items of equipment that only the automatories of Castle-Home could supply. Now they were concerned only with the fact of Johnny's being home; and the planning of a party.

But their laughter and their voices were not the pleasure to Johnny that they thought. He told himself he had been too long away. He thought less of their plans and more of the wind and water storming overhead. He felt an urge to leave them. To put on mask and fins and swim up to the surface and feel it for himself. But he held back—a little ashamed of how it would look, at this time, for him to sneak off from the rest of his people.

He tried his hand at the charts showing the currents at various depths, a work the Joya group traded for credit against other needed things supplied through Castle-Home. But they no longer seemed important. The third generation did not need them, with their new instinct for location and direction. The older generations would be gone in a few years. And the Landers would have all the use of them.

He could not work, and he could not relax. Sara still seemed to him to be holding back something from him, something he should know. They were both older and it was not the same between them. She had never explained not telling him about Tomi; and the boy did not call him Daddy, but Johnny.

On the fourth morning a call came to rescue him. It was a phone call from Chad Ridell, Chief of Staff for one of the four Castle-Homes about the sea waters of the world. Ridell's Castle-Home was nearest, only about four hundred miles north of where the Joya Home drifted now.

"This time," he said, "we're going to have to form a

Council to talk to the Closed Congress." Chad was second-generation. His lean, fifty-four-year-old face had lines more suited to someone of the first generation. "They're as worked up ashore about this as they were about the whaling industry. Maybe more. I thought we'd eventually have elections, with each ten Homes electing a representative. But for now, I'm simply bespeaking about twenty or so people I think are pretty sure of being elected."

"Patrick, you mean?" said Johnny.

"For one," said Chad. "Because his music's made him known and respected on shore. You, for one of the representatives of the Cadets."

Johnny nodded.

"You'll come as quickly as you can, Johnny?"

"Yes. Patrick too. I'm sure. All of us, I think," said Johnny.

They broke their phone connection and Johnny went to tell the others. Within an hour, the Joya Home was beginning to break into the small-Home sections that made it up. Each small-Home sent an electric current through its outer shell, and the plastic of that shell "remembered" a different shape, changing into an outline like that of a supersonic aircraft. Together, the altered small-Homes turned north at a speed of ninety knots, under the thrust of individual drive units that used a controlled hydrogen fusion process to produce high-pressure steam jets. They drove through the still waters for Castle-Home.

Five hours later, reunited in wheel-shape, the Joya Home trembled into position and locked down atop a column of nine other previously arrived Homes. Johnny, who was acting pilot for the Home, locked the controls and turned from them.

Tomi said, "Why didn't Mommy wait while you did that?"

Johnny looked down. The small face, in which Johnny often found himself searching for a resemblance to himself, looked up at him across a gulf of years.

"Her own folks' Home may be here," Johnny said. "She wanted to find out."

"Grandpa," said Tomi. "And Grandma Light."

"Yes," Johnny said.

"They're my Grandpa and Grandma. They're not yours." The boy stood with feet apart. "Why didn't *she* take me to see my Grandpa and Grandma Light?"

Johnny looked out the wide transparency before him at the blue waters and the ten-Home upright columns of Castle-Home. "I think she wants us to become better acquainted."

Tomi scowled.

"What's 'acquainted'?"

"We aren't acquainted," said Johnny. He looked back at the boy.

"What," said Tomi, "is ac-*quaint*-ed, I say!"

"Acquainted," said Johnny. "Acquainted's what you are with your mother."

Tomi looked hard at him.

"She's *my* mother," he said at last.

"And you're my son." Johnny gazed at the boy. He was square-shouldered, solid and thick. His eyes were not brown like Sara's but blue like Johnny's. But their blueness was as transparent and unreflective as a pane of glass.

Johnny said suddenly, "Did your mother ever take you to see the corral at a Castle-Home?"

"Uhh-uh!" Tomi shook his head slowly from side to side. "She never took me."

"Get your mask and fins on, then," said Johnny. "I'll take you."

Outside the small-Home entrance iris, they found Baldur waiting with Sara's bottle-nosed dolphin, Neta, and Neta's half-grown pup, Tantrums.

"Not now, Tantrums!" Tomi shoved the five-foot pup aside and reached toward Baldur; but Baldur evaded the boy, spiraling up on Johnny's far side. Tomi muttered something and grabbed at the reins of the harness on Neta, who let him take them willingly.

"No," said Johnny. The mutter had barely reached his ears over the underwater radio circuit built into the swim masks. If they had been relying on voice-box communica-

tion from mask to mask through the water it would not
have reached him at all. But he felt it was time to settle
this matter. "Baldur is not your dolphin."

Tomi muttered once more. This time it was truly unin-
telligible, but Johnny did not need to understand the words
in this case.

"Our sea-friends pick us, not we them," said Johnny.
"Baldur picked me many years ago. While I was gone he
let you use him, but now I'm back. You'll have to let
him do what he wants."

Tomi said nothing. Letting the dolphins pull them, they
headed across the top of Castle-Home through three fathoms of water to a far area of open water where yellow
warning buoys stood balanced at various depths. Neta
jerked the reins suddenly from Tomi and, herding Tantrums ruthlessly before her, headed home.

"Bad Neta!" shouted Tomi through his voice-box. "Bad
dolphin!"

"No, careful dolphin," said Johnny. "What do yellow
buoys stand for?"

"Danger," muttered Tomi. He glanced at Baldur and
grumbled again.

"Don't blame the dolphin," said Johnny. "If Sara were
here, Neta wouldn't leave her even for Tantrum's sake.
It's nothing against you. Some day you'll have your own
dolphin for a sea-friend, and it'll stick with you."

"Won't!" muttered Tomi. "I don't want scared little
dolphins! A great, great, big space bat, that's what I'll
get!"

"Suit yourself," said Johnny. "Well, that's the corral,
beyond the buoys there and for four miles out. Want to go
in?"

Tomi's face mask jerked up sharply toward his father.
"Pass the yellow . . .?"

"As long as I'm with you. Well?" Tomi kicked himself
forward.

"Let's go in, Johnny."

"All right. Stay close now." Johnny led the way. Tomi

crowded him. Baldur hesitated, then spurted level with them.

They swam forward for thirty or forty feet. Tomi gradually forged ahead. Then, suddenly, he went into a flurry of movement, flipped around and swam thrashingly back into Johnny.

"Daddy!" He clung to Johnny's right arm and chest. *"Killers!"*

Johnny put his left arm instinctively around the boy. Holding him, Johnny could feel the abrupt and powerful surge of his own heart and the warmth of blood cresting out through his own body.

"It's all right," Johnny said. "They're muzzled."

Tomi still clung. The warmth racing through Johnny came up against a different, powerful pressure that seemed to spread out and down from behind his ears.

"Look at them," he said. Tomi did not move. The pressure moved further out and downward. He put his hands around the small waist and overpowered the boy's grip, turning him around. He held his son out, facing the killer whales.

For a second, as he turned him, Tomi had gone rigid through all his body. Now the rigidity began to go out of him. He stared straight at the looming shape of the nearest killer whale with the open basket-weaving of the enormous muzzle covering the huge head. Johnny's fingers pressed about the light arch of childish ribs; but he felt no shiver or tremble. He was aware of Baldur quivering in the water at his back; but between his hands there was only stillness.

The boy relaxed even more. He hung, staring at the great, dim shape just ahead. After a second his hands went to Johnny's hand and he pushed Johnny's grip from his waist. He swam a few strokes forward.

Johnny felt the hard beating of his own heart against the pressure in his brain. He was tense as a strung bow himself; and his heart beat with the hard, proud rhythm of a man forging a sword for his own carrying. Without warning he remembered the striped gold length of a Siberian tiger lying in his cage outdoors at the zoo ashore in San Diego.

And the small, dancing figure of a ruby-throated humming-bird which floated from some nearby yellow tulips, in through the gleaming bars of the cage. It had hesitated, then, hovering on the blurred motion of its wings, moved driftingly toward the great head and sleepy eye of the tiger that watched it advancing.

Johnny looked about him.

At first there had been only the one killer to be seen. Now, like long boxcar length resolving out of the green dimness, other ponderous, dark-backed shapes were making their appearance without seeming to exert any effort of swimming. It was as if they coalesced, and came drifting close under some magnetic influence. They approached side-ways. Through the open-work of the muzzle about the one now drifting, rising toward him on his left, Johnny could see the murderously cheerful mouth, the dark intelligent watching of the eye.

The eye, dark and reflective, approached Johnny, growing as it came. Behind it lay the large cetacean brain, and a mind close to Johnny's own. But that mind was a stranger, self-sufficient. Staring now into the approaching eye, Johnny thought he caught there his own sea-image. And it came to him then that it was for something like this he had advised the Cadets' return. It was for something like this that he had brought his son to the killer's pen.

Very mighty, ignorant of domination, moved by deep instincts to act to an end unseen but surely felt, the reflecting eye of the killer whale looked out on an unending liquid universe where there were no lords, no chains, nor any walls. Through this universe only the dark tides of instinct moved back and forth. For the killer whale as for the people, now, those dark tides spoke with a voice of certainty. To listen to that voice, to follow the path it told of, setting aside all things of the moment, all pity, all fear of life or death—it was this knowledge Johnny saw reflected in the killer's eye. In those dark tides, movement, there was neither wife nor child, nor friend nor enemy—but only truth and what the mind desired. First came survival. After that what the individual chose to accept. That was the truth, the secret and the truce of the dark tides.

And that was why, thought Johnny over the strong beating of his heart, that it had been safe to bring his son to this place. His son was of the sea. In this place was the truce of the sea, and in that truce he was safe.

"Daddy!"

Tomi's voice shouted suddenly in Johnny's earphone, in the close confines of the mask and over the sound of the bubbling exhaust valve.

"Daddy! Look at me!"

Johnny jerked around in the water. Twenty feet from him and a little higher in the water, Tomi was violating one of the oldest knowledges of the people—that the quicksilver members of the dolphin family hated to be held or clung to by any but their oldest friends. Like a boy on a Juggernaut, Tomi rode high on the shoulder area of the first killer whale.

"—Tomi," said Johnny. He felt neither beating, nor pressure now. Only a wide, hollow feeling inside him. He kept his voice calm.

"Uh-huh!" Tomi kicked carelessly with the heels of his swim fins against the great swelling sides of the killer. Five feet ahead and below him, the dark eye there looked like a poker player's through an opening in the muzzle. It gazed steadily on Johnny. The great flukes of the killer, capable of smashing clear through the side of a small rowboat, hung still in the water. Johnny thought of the truce, of the primitive sense of fun to be found in all the dolphins, the savage humor of the killer whales.

"Tomi," he said, surprised at his own calmness, "it's time to go home."

"All right." Surprisingly without argument, Tomi kicked free of the twenty-five-foot shape and swam down towards his father. For a moment Johnny saw the boy beating by the muzzle where the dark eye watched, and then he was swimming freely toward Johnny.

Johnny turned and they swam together toward the edge of the corral. Baldur shot on ahead.

"Tomi—" said Johnny; and found words did not come

easily. He started again. "I should have warned you not to get close to them. Killers aren't like dolphins—"

"He's going to be my sea-friend, I think," said Tomi, kicking vigorously through the water.

"Tomi," said Johnny, "killers don't make friends like dolphins."

"Then why does he keep coming after me, Daddy?"

Johnny's head jerked around to look back over his shoulder. A dozen feet behind them, the basket shape of a killer whale's muzzle was gliding through the water. At that moment the yellow buoys loomed before them, and they passed through. Here the killer should stop following. But he came on through with them.

"Tomi," said Johnny quietly. "You see the iris in the wall there?"

"I see it," said Tomi, looking ahead to the side of Castle-Home.

"When I tell you to, in just a minute when we get close, I want you to start swimming for it. And don't look back. You understand? I want you to swim as fast as you can and not stop."

The sudden wild clangor of an alarm bell broke through his words, racketing through the water all around them and over Castle-Home. And a buzzer sounded in the earphones of their mask-radio circuit.

"All bespoke members of the Council, this is Chad Ridell speaking," said the voice of the Chief of Staff of Castle-Home. "Please come to the Conference Room at once. All members—" Chad's voice repeated the request twice more.

"Daddy!" said Tomi, as the voice stopped. Johnny turned swiftly to him. "Look, Daddy." Johnny followed the boy's pointing finger and saw the waters behind them empty and still. "My killer's *gone!*"

"Never mind," said Johnny automatically. "We've got to streak for home now." He caught up a rein from Baldur and handed another rein to Tomi.

When the two of them entered their own small-Home again, Sara was back.

"Mommy! Mommy, listen!" Tomi ripped off his mask. "We went in the corral with the killers. And I made friends with one and rode on his back and he followed us but the bell scared him—"

Sara's face flashed up to stare into Johnny's. Her eyes were wide, her nose pinched, the skin over her cheekbones tight and pale. There was an abruptly white look to her eyes.

"I've got to go—" said Johnny. He pulled on his mask and hurried out of the small-Home.

He saw he was late as he stepped into the conference room. About twenty of the people were already there. They were seated in a semicircle near the far end of the green-walled room, around the broadcast image of a small middle-aged man, standing, in gray slacks and Lander jacket. Johnny recognized him. It was Pul Vant, Secretary-Advocate for the Closed Congress, governing body of the grouped nations of the land.

Johnny came up quietly and took a seat. His cousin Patrick was among those already there, as were two other representatives of the ex-Cadets—Mikros Palamas and Tom Loy. Besides these, he recognized Chad Ridell, and Toby Darnley of the Communications Dome, here at Castle-Home. And Anna Marieanna, a dark-haired woman of the second generation, startlingly beautiful still in her forties and in spite of the fact her left hand was gone at the wrist. She smiled at him across the semicircle, and he smiled back briefly.

". . . ringleaders," Pul Vant was saying.

"I tell you," Ridell interrupted. "There are no ring-leaders among the people."

"Very well. Setting that aside then—" Vant gestured neatly with his hands as he talked. He had the smooth movements of an actor. "I'm trying to explain to you what the Space Program and the Academy can mean to a fron-tierless people ashore." He went on talking. It was an old argument, one Johnny had heard before. He looked around the semicircle, noting the difference of his people from this little man of the land. Anna Marieanna was not the only one marked by the sea among the older generations; and in his own generation the very structure of mind and body was different. Different from the Landers. Already they were starting to use the same words to mean different things on each side. And the dangerous thing was they did not realize the difference was there in their words.

"Now," Vant was saying, "the Congress is ready to make the same offer. To take you in as a full member nation . . ."

"No," said Chad.

"You understand," Vant said, "we can't have six million people without even a government holding seventy-point-eight per cent of the world's surface area. You can't do that."

"We've been doing it," said Chad. "We intend to keep on."

Vant lifted his hands and let them drop.

"I'm sorry," he said. "There's nothing I can do then, I just explain the situation, that's all my job is. You know, historically, the tail's never been let to wag the dog very long." He ran his eyes around the semicircle. They met Johnny's eyes, paused for a second, then passed on. "If the rest of the Cadets'll come back voluntarily . . . Otherwise, public opinion's going to get out of hand." He looked at Chad. "We don't *want* to declare war on you."

"No," said Chad. "You don't want that."

Vant waved an easy hand and disappeared. The people rose and began to shove their chairs back to make a full circle, breaking out at the same time into a clatter of conversation. Johnny found himself next to Chad.

"He talked like they caught some of us?" Johnny said. Chad looked at him.

"Yes," he said. "A hundred and twenty-nine didn't make it to the sea. They're holding them at Congress Territory on Manhattan. He said they may be tried as deserters."

"Deserters?" Johnny stopped shoving his chair.

"Why should they?" he heard Toby Darnley, of the Communications Dome of Castle-Home, his slightly shrill voice rising over the others. "Why should they give in at all? We can't give in to them. We can't let them put a leash around our necks. But we can't let them put those boys before a firing squad, either." Glancing across the room, Johnny saw Toby's small, square face was rigid and dark. "What is there we can do?"

Beside Johnny, Chad sat down. The circle was formed now. Johnny saw he was the only one standing. For some reason, following the shock of what he had just heard, he found his mind filled by a memory of the eye of the killer whale, as he had seen it watching through the openings in the muzzle. The dark eye, hidden of meaning, and steady. In the same moment something moved in him. It suddenly seemed to him that he felt the actual presence of the hundred and twenty-nine prisoner Cadets, as he had felt Tomi between his hands.

"We can save them," he said. "We can go rescue our own people."

They all stared at him. The roomful of people were silent. Though the four walls of the room barred all about him, he felt the eye of the killer whale through them upon him, steadily watching.

Only Patrick said no to the idea. But when the rest of the council all voted for it, he said nothing more. He sat without talking, watching Johnny. After a little while he left them to their planning.

The sea people could always move at a moment's notice. In an emergency they could almost dispense with the notice. Three hours later, a spindle-shaped formation of small-Homes in their craft-shape bored due west through the brilliant blueness of the hundred-fathom depth toward the New York shore. Before them, a vibratory weapon on low broadcast power herded the sealife from their path. Their speed was a hundred and seventy knots.

Piloting the lead craft, Johnny stood alone at the controls. The small-Homes behind held nearly five hundred men, almost every one of the ex-Cadets who had been in Castle-Home at the time. The small-Homes were supplied with automatic controls. The ex-Cadets had explosives, the radio equipment built into their masks and take-apart sonic rifles and vibratory weapons of the sort the people used for sea-hunting. The element of surprise was on their side, they thought they knew where the prisoners were being held in Congress Territory, and they had a plan.

In the lead craft, alone, facing the empty, luminous waters showing through the transparent wall before him, Johnny felt detached from the speed of their movement. All sound was damped out and there were no signposts to gauge by, only the strange blue twilight of a hundred fathoms down that had so fascinated Beebe in his first bathysphere descent a hundred years before. It glowed through the transparent forward wall to wrap Johnny in the unreal feeling of a dream. He, the sea, the ex-Cadets behind him—even the destination to which they were all hurtling—seemed ghostlike and unreal.

The sound of footsteps behind him, in the small-Home where he was supposed to be alone, jerked him around sharply.

"Patrick!" he said.

Patrick, dressed like all the ex-Cadets in black, elastic cold-water skins, swim mask and fins, came like some shuffling monster out of the rear dimness of the small-Home to stand beside Johnny.

"I stowed away," said Patrick. He was looking out at the blue.

"But why? You were against this, weren't you?" Johnny peered at him. Patrick slowly turned his head, but the apparently brilliant blue was so dim that Johnny could not make out the expression on Patrick's face.

"Yes," said Patrick. "I had to. It's true, you know, Johnny. You're a ringleader."

"Ringleader?" Johnny leaned toward him, but still he could not make out the look on Patrick's face.

"Yes," said Patrick. "Just like you were at the Academy. You decide something on your own. And then you always push it through."

"What did I push through?" Johnny let go the controls.

On automatic, independent, the craft bored on, leading the formation.

"This." Pat's voice changed. "Johnny," he said. "Johnny, turn back."

"But we have to do this," said Johnny. "Why can't you see that, Pat? We've already broken off from the Landers. We're different."

"You think you're different," said Patrick.

"I know it. So do all the third generation. You know it, Pat." He peered again, unsuccessfully. "You want to make me personally responsible for all this?"

"Yes," said the blur of Patrick's face. "For a war we can't win."

"It's not war yet," said Johnny.

"It's war. War with the land. I wish I could stop you, Johnny."

Johnny stood for a second.

"If you feel like that, Pat, why'd you come along?"

Pat laughed, a queer, choking sort of laugh. "I knew you wouldn't turn back. I had to ask you, though."

He turned and walked back, away. In the dimness, his outline seemed to melt, rather than go off. Left alone, Johnny felt the blue illumination as if it shone coldly through him.

Once he and Patrick had been as alike in their thoughts as twin brothers. They had gone off on months-long expeditions, alone with their dolphins and sonic rifles, living off the open sea like dolphins themselves. Now, in this new dimness, he could not even call clearly to mind his cousin's face. What he remembered was overlaid by the picture of Patrick that had been on the Moho tape in the music store ashore.

Johnny turned back to the controls, and put his mind to the coming work.

Off Jones beach, they left the small-Homes. Half of these they put together in a mock-up of one of the large Lander deep-sea subs, resting in the Brooklyn Navy Yard a handful of miles away. This and the smaller ships were sent off on automatic controls, to rendezvous with the expedition later in the East River alongside Congress Territory. Individually, Patrick and Johnny among them, they dispersed and headed shoreward—to emerge at last in the early evening of a hot July day, among the Lander swimmers and skin-divers of the crowded beach.

Johnny bought Lander throwaway clothes and changed into them in a pullman dressing-room above the beach. His disassembled sonic rifle and his swim mask with its radio were tucked in under his belt. He headed in to Manhattan.

The first step toward rescuing the prisoners was so completely without incident it was almost dull. Congress Territory covered a full twenty-block area running south from where the old Queensboro bridge had been. It was a show place, beautifully terraced and landscaped, and quite open. At midnight, Johnny reached the broad boulevard entrance at the north end and saw Mikros and Tom Loy come up to him.

"All clear?" Johnny asked.

"All clear," said Mikros. His big face under its black hair was grinning. Tom Loy looked a little pale under the lights of the Manhattan dome, but steady enough. Johnny himself felt a little as he had felt facing the killer whales with Tomi.

"Move everybody in, then," Johnny said. They went in. Half an hour later, without being stopped, they were spread out around the plaza, surrounded by office buildings, that lay before the old U. N. Secretariat. The pool in the plaza was black and still.

"What if they aren't in the blast shelter under the Secretariat Building?" Tom Loy asked. He had asked it twice before.

"Where else could they hold a hundred and twenty-nine men?" asked Johnny. "But if they aren't, we'll just have to search." He took Tom and a dozen of the ex-Cadets. They went in the Secretariat Building, down the regular escalators, to a special old fashioned, mechanical elevator in a sub-basement. They went down this; and it let them out all at once into a guardroom filled with Closed Congress soldiers, half-dressed and wholly unready to fight.

The soldiers submitted without protest. They were lined
up and disarmed. The inner doors to the blast shelter were
broken open and the captured ex-Cadets poured out.

"That's good," said Johnny to Tom Loy. "Now, we'll get
them upstairs as quickly as we can."

He was turning back to the elevator—when the dull,
heavy sound of a sonic explosion from above rattled the
elevator in its shaft.

For a second no one moved. Then Johnny snatched his
swim mask out of his pocket, thumbed the controls and
spoke into his radio mike.

"Mikros?" he said. "What happened?"

Mikros's voice was suddenly blurred by the buzzing of a
distorter. "Soldiers up in the buildings!"

"Take charge," said Johnny to Tom Loy. He ran for the
elevator, rode it up, then ran up the humming escalators to
the ground floor.

The present-day ground floor of the Secretariat was
fronted by a conservatory lush with flowers, trees and other
plants. Looking through its foliage, Johnny saw most of
the dome lights were out over the place. In the dimness,
the sea people had taken cover where they could behind
hedges and ornamental trees surrounding the pool. From
the buildings on three sides of the plaza military gunfire was
reaching for them.

Mike was not to be seen. The springing of the trap had
evidently caught him somewhere outside. The ventilation
was off; and smoke, drifting out of the building on Johnny's
right, was thickening and fogging the air in layers that did
not move. Water had been splashed out of the pool, darkening a terrace as if the building itself was bleeding. Otherwise, there was no blood to be seen, for the sonic and vibratory weapons wounded and damaged internally.

The distorter, set going to make any bounce-echo sighting mechanism of a sonic rifle useless, buzzed eerily in the
heads of all. It sang in Johnny's inner ear like a noise heard
in high fever. As he looked about the plaza he saw, here
and there, bodies of the sea people, lying still.

Up toward the front of the conservatory, behind a lemon

tree in a wooden tub, one of the ex-Cadets crouched suddenly, putting his forehead to the pavement. Johnny ran and knelt down beside him. But when he put his hand on the boy's shoulder, the other went over on one side and lay still with a little trickle of blood showing at the corner of his mouth. It was one of the freshman class. His eyes were closed and his skin showed nearly as finely transparent as Tomi's had been in his sleep. Johnny stared at him, for he could not even now remember the other's name.

"Johnny—" said someone. He looked up and saw Tom Loy. "We're all upstairs."

"Yes." Johnny climbed automatically to his feet. He glanced along the Secretariat's front to the sort of alley between buildings that led to the East River. No soldiers blocked it yet. "Everybody out. Tell Mike." The smoke was thick around them now. "You come with me."

He led the way in a dash to the corner of the Secretariat building at the alley's entrance. They knelt there and burrowed with their hands in the soft earth of a flower bed. Tom packed a number of the yellow cubes of explosive jelly that they used for deep-sea mining into the hole. Sea people hurried, staggered by them through the smoke.

"Are they all out?" asked Johnny, setting the radio detonator.

"All out, Mike?" Tom asked in open speech into his radio mike.

"All but me." Johnny, putting on his mask, heard Mikros's voice over the distorter in his earphone. "I'll be along in a—"

The swelling impact of another sonic explosion shuddered through the square. Johnny looked and saw Tom's lips move, but he heard nothing. They were deafened. Johnny waved Tom on toward the river; and Tom leaped up, then ran off through the smoke.

Johnny waited. Mikros did not appear. There was no more time. Johnny turned and ran, pressing the detonator transceiver. Behind him the smoke billowed and swirled in an explosion he could not hear. He ran for the river.

"All over, into the water," he shouted into his mike; but

he could not even hear himself. He felt an unexpected fear. If they could not hear him . . .

But then he reached the balcony, fifty feet above the river; and all was going well. The unhurt ex-Cadets were going over feet-first. The wounded were being slid down escape chutes of plastic. The small-Homes and the imitation Lander sub were waiting in the water below. He could see little of this in the smoke, but he knew it was so. Suddenly he seemed to hook in on a network of awareness. It was as it had been when he had stood in the conference room and felt the hundred and twenty-nine prisoners as if he held them like Tomi, between his hands. In this emergency some new instinct of the third generation was taking over; and they were all a unit.

"Keep moving," he said automatically. He felt they heard him. Then he realized it was his own numbed hearing beginning to clear. A little moving air off the river cleared the smoke from the balcony. Only Tom Loy was standing with him. He motioned Tom over, then turned to go himself. Then he felt one of the people still coming from the direction of the plaza.

"Mike," he said, turning. But then the one coming broke into the clear air of the balcony, and it was not Mikros, but Patrick with a soldier's vibratory rifle in his hands. "You, Pat?" said Johnny, staring. Suddenly it broke on him. "*You* told them about us!"

Pat stopped a few feet from him. The rifle he held wavered, pointing at Johnny. Then, with a sort of sob, Patrick threw the gun from him, grabbed Johnny, stooped and threw him back over the balcony. Johnny turned instinctively like a cat in the air. And the water smashed hard against him.

He caught himself, readjusting his mask, six feet under. Below him he saw the small-Homes waiting. He turned and swam down to them.

"Don't hang to your father," said Sara to Tomi, when Johnny was once more back in the small-Home with them.

"But—"

"Not now," Sara said. "They're waiting for him in the

Conference Room. Daddy just came by for a minute, and we have to talk. Go swim outside."

Tomi hesitated, standing on one foot, face screwed up.

"You go!" said Sara. Her voice had a hard note in it Johnny had never heard before. Tomi's eyes went wide and he left.

Johnny watched him go numbly. The Lander subs had chased them out into open sea. The decoy they had made out of the small-Homes had drawn them off. On automatic controls, it had led the subs three miles deep to the Atlantic ooze and then blown itself up, taking at least one sub with it. A Lander sub carried over two hundred men. There had been more than a hundred of the ex-Cadets who had not come back.

Riding home after that in the rest of the small-Homes, those that returned had begun to sing *"Hey, Johnny!"* And the song had spread over the radio circuit from ship to ship until they all sang. Johnny had turned his face to the rushing blue beyond the transparent wall of his craft to hide the fact he could not sing along with them.

Patrick's voice had sounded again in his ears. *"You're a ringleader—"*

"—I've got to talk to you about Tomi," Sara was saying.

"Now?" he said dully. His real reason for detouring by here on his way to the Conference Room was that he had wanted to hide for a few moments. At the sound of his son's name he shivered unexpectedly. The dark eye of the killer whale had come back to his mind. But now it gazed without change and without pity on the still shape of the young ex-Cadet he had seen die in the conservatory, ashore.

"I've never told you why I didn't let you know about you having a son, all these years. Do you know why?"

"Why?" He focused on her with difficulty. "No—no, I don't." He became aware, for the first time, that her face was stiff and pale. "Sara, what is it?"

"I didn't tell you," she said as if she were reciting a lesson, "because I didn't want him to be like you."

He thought of Patrick and the men who were now dead.

"Well," he said, "I don't blame you."

"Don't *blame* me!" Without warning she began to cry. It was not the easy, relief-giving sorrow of the people. Her tears were angry. She stood with them running down her cheeks and her fists clenched, facing him. "I knew what you were like when I fell in love with you! I knew you'd always be going and pushing things through. No matter what it cost, no matter who it hurt. You say things and people do them—it's something about you! And you just take it all for granted."

He put his hands on her to soothe her, but she was as hard as a rock.

"But you weren't going to kill my baby!" she thrust at him. "I was going to hide him—keep him safe, so he'd never know what his father was like and want to go and be like him. And go away from me, too, without thinking of anything but what he personally wanted to do, and get himself killed all for nothing."

"Sara—" he said.

"And then you came back. And he told me all about that business in the killer whale corral. And then I knew it was no use. No use at all. Because he was just like you. He was born just like you, and there was nothing I could do to protect him, no matter what I did. My baby . . ." and with that, at last she broke down. All the hardness went out of her; and he held her to him as she cried.

For a moment or two he thought the crisis was over. But she stiffened again and pulled away from him.

"You've got to make me a promise," she said, wiping her eyes.

"Of course," he said.

"Not of course. You listen to what I want. You make me a promise that if anything happens to me, you'll take care of him. You'll keep him safe. Not the way you would —the way I'd keep him safe. You promise me."

"Nothing's going to happen to you."

"Promise me!"

"All right," he said. "I promise I'll take care of him the way you would."

She wiped her eyes again. "You'd better go now. They'll be waiting for you. Oh, wait." She turned and hurried from him, back into the bedroom. She came back in a second with a tangle of smashed plastic and dangling wires.

"Patrick left it for you," she said. "He said you'd understand."

Numbly he took the ruined banjo.

When he finally reached the Conference Room, it was full of Council members.

"It's war," said Chad Ridell, looking at him bleakly. "We got their declaration an hour after you landed at Jones Beach. And an hour before one of our gull-cameras picked up this."

He touched a button on his chair. The end of the room blanked out. Johnny saw a gull's-view image of the Atlantic sea-surface in the cold, gray-blue light of early dawn. His sea-instinct recognized the spot as less than a hundred miles south.

"Look," said Chad. There was a flicker in the sky, and a hole yawned suddenly huge and deep in the ocean's face. For a moment the unnatural situation lasted. And then leaping up through the hole moved a fist of water. It lifted toward the paling sky of dawn like a mountain torn from the ocean floor; and a roar like that of some huge, tortured beast burst on the Conference Room.

The fist stretched out into a pillar, broke and disintegrated. A cow biscay whale drifted by on her side, trying to turn over, blood running from the corner of her mouth.

"Sonic explosion," said Johnny. "Big enough for all Castle-Home."

"They meant that declaration of war," said Chad.

"But why bomb empty ocean?" Johnny said.

"Castle-Home was there three hours ago," put in Tom Loy, who was standing close by Chad. "They must have spotted us from a satellite and thought we were still close. We can stay deep from now on, though."

Johnny nodded. Castle-Home had been at a hundred fathoms when the expedition had come back. He remembered what he was carrying.

"No," he said, "even that won't work." He handed the tangle of broken plastic and wires to Chad, who stared at it, blankly.

"It's Patrick's banjo," said Johnny. "Pat went in with us. He was the one who tipped off the Congress soldiers so that they laid that trap in the plaza for us. He's on their side now."

"But Patrick—" Tom Loy stared at him across Chad. "Patrick's third generation! He can find Castle-Home as well as any of us."

"That's right," said Johnny.

"But I don't understand it!" Chad got up abruptly from his chair. He faced Johnny. "Why Patrick—Patrick of all people?"

"I don't know," said Johnny. "He thinks we're wrong to fight the land. It's what he believes, I guess." He shrugged his shoulders unhappily. "Maybe I was wrong."

"You don't believe that," said Tom.

"No, I guess not." Johnny tried to smile at Tom. "At any rate, the only thing that seems to make sense to me, now, is for me and anyone else who wants to come with me to give ourselves up to them." He glanced at Chad. "If they get what they call ringleaders, maybe—"

Cutting through what he was going to say, came the sudden, brazen shrieking of the alarm bell.

"Missile!" cried a voice from the wall speaker of the room. "This is the Communications Dome. Missile approaching! Missile—"

A sound too great to be heard folded all around them. Johnny felt himself picked up and carried away at an angle upward. He ducked away from the ceiling, but the ceiling was no longer there. For a second, still moving, he was in a little box of air, with water all around him. Then the water closed in on him, he felt himself seeming to fly apart in all directions, and he lost track abruptly of what was going on.

. . . At some time later when he came back to his senses, he and the world about him were moving very fast. He was rushing through the water in the black suit of cold-water skins he had never taken off and his mask was over his face, in position. Baldur was with him. He had hold of the dolphin's reins and Baldur was towing him swiftly through debris-strewn water at about the fifteen-fathom depth. They came at last to Johnny's own small-Home, sheared almost in half and floating loggily in the surrounding water.

The pool entrance was missing. Neta, Sara's dolphin, was frantically trying the impossible feat of entering the small-Home through the air-iris, all unmindful of Tantrums beside her. Johnny pushed her aside and dove through himself.

Across the room, beyond the pool, he saw Sara lying on a couch covered by a drape. Tomi was sitting huddled with his knees together on a hassock beside the couch. Johnny ran around the pool and dropped on his knees by the couch.

"My mommy's not feeling good," Tomi said.

Johnny looked at Sara. The world, which had been moving so fast about him, slowed and stopped. All things came to an end, and stopped.

Sara lay still, on her back. There was a little blood dried at the corners of her mouth. Her eyes were not quite closed. They looked from under her eyelids at nothing in particular and her cheeks seemed already sunken in a little under her high, cold cheekbones.

He stared down at her and a slow and terrible chill began to creep gradually through him. He could not take his eyes off her still face. Slowly he began to shiver. The shivers increased until he shuddered through his whole body and his teeth chattered. He saw Tomi coming toward him with arms outstretched to put them around his father. And suddenly Johnny broke the spell holding him and shoved the boy back, away from him, so hard he staggered.

"Stay away from me!" Johnny shouted. The room tilted and spun around him. The eye of the killer whale rushed abruptly like death upon him through the wall behind the couch, and he fell forward into roaring nothingness.

When he came back after this, it was to find Tomi clinging to him and sobbing. Johnny awoke as somebody might

who had been asleep for a long night. The great gust of
feeling that had whirled him into unconsciousness was
gone. He felt numbed and coldly clear-headed. Automatically he soothed Tomi. Reflexively he went about the small-
Home, pulling out a sea-sled and loading it with clothing,
medical supplies, weapons and other equipment for living
off the sea.

When it was loaded he took it outside and left Tomi,
now also dressed in cold-water skins, fins and mask, to
harness Baldur to it. He himelf went back inside.

He set straight the drape over Sara and stood a little
while looking down at her body. Then he detached the
governor from the small-Homes heating element and went
back outside. Together, he and Tomi watched as the small-
Home caught fire inside.

Collapsing inward, as its walls melted, it sank away from
them, a flickering light into dark depths, with Neta and her
pup circling bewilderedly down after it.

"Where are we going?" said Tomi, as Johnny handed a
rein to Tomi and took one himself.

"Where you'll be safe," said Johnny. He put the boy's
other hand on a rail of the sled.

"All by ourselves?" said Tomi.

"Yes." Johnny broke off suddenly. Inside Tomi's mask,
he saw the boy pale and frowning, the way Sara had been
used to frown. Something moved in Johnny's guts. "All
right," he said; but he did not say it to Tomi.

He touched the radio controls of his mask with his
tongue, turning the circle of reception up to full. A roar of
conversations sounded like surf in his ears.

"This is Johnny Joya," he said into the mike. "Are there
any Council members listening?" The surf-sound of voices
roared on unchanging. "This is Johnny Joya speaking. Are
there any Council members who can hear me?"

There seemed no change in the sound coming into his
earphone. He turned to Tomi, shrugging. And then the
roar began to diminish a little. It slackened. "This is Johnny
Joya," he said. "Are there any Council members listening?"

The voices dwindled, faded and disappeared. Silence

roared instead in his earphone. From far away, blurredly, a single voice spoke.

"Johnny? Johnny, is that you? This is Tom Loy. Johnny, we're the only Council members left. I found the room. None of the rest got out." Tom hesitated. "Johnny, can you hear me? Where are you?"

"North of you," said Johnny. "And swimming north." There was a cold, clean, dead feeling in him, like a man might experience after an amputation when the pain was blocked. "I'm taking my son, my dolphin and sea-camping equipment and I'm heading out."

"Heading out?"

"Yes," said Johnny.

He touched the rein and moved it and Baldur began to swim, pulling the sled and the two humans with it. Through the rushing gray-blue water, Johnny saw the young arm and hand of Tomi in its black sleeve clinging to the sled rail; and he remembered Patrick's arm, older and larger, seen in the same position. "The rest of you should do the same thing."

"Head out?" Tom's voice faded for a second in the earphone. "Out into the sea without small-Homes?"

"That's right," said Johnny. He watched Baldur sliding smoothly through the water. "Castle-Home is gone. By this time the other Castle-Homes are probably gone, too. We're Homeless, now. Everybody might as well face that."

"But we're going to have to build new Homes."

"We can't," said Johnny. "With Patrick helping, the Landers'll just go on destroying them."

"But we've got to have Homes!"

"No," said Johnny. A strap on the sled was working loose. He reached forward automatically and unbuckled it. "That's what the Landers think. But they're wrong. Everyone of the third generation and lots of the second have lived off the sea without Homes, for the fun of it. We can do it permanently. We can take care of the older people, as well, if they want."

"But," Tom's voice came stronger in the earphone for a second, "we'll be nothing but a lot of water-gypsies!" He fell silent, as if he had suddenly run out of words.

"No," said Johnny. He pulled the strap tight and buckled it again. It held well this time. "Our Homes were something we brought to the sea from the land. Sooner or later we were bound to leave them behind and live like true people of the sea. The Land's just pushed us to it a little early." He checked the other straps. They were all tight. "I'm only telling you what I think. That's what I'm doing."

There was a long moment of rushing silence in the earphone. Then Tom's voice called out.

"Johnny! You aren't leaving us?"

"Yes," said Johnny.

"But some day we'll be carrying the fight back to the Landers. We need you to plan for then. We need you—"

"No!" The word came out so harshly that Johnny saw Tomi flinch alongside him and stare in his direction. "I've helped too much already. Get someone else to make your plans!"

He felt Tomi's eyes reach into him. He reached himself for calmness. For a moment he had almost come back to life, but now the safe feeling, the cold, clean, dead feeling, took him over once again.

"No," he said, more quietly. "You don't want my help, Tom. And besides, my wife is dead and I made her a promise to keep our boy safe. That's all the job I have now. I wouldn't take any other if I could. If you'll take a last piece of advice, though, you'll all scatter the way I'm doing. Spread out through the seas, we'll be safe." He turned off his mike, then turned it on. "Good-by, Tom," he said. "Good-by, people. Good luck to you all."

Tom's voice spoke again, but Johnny no longer listened. He picked up the rein turned Baldur's head a little to the northeast, along the water road of the North Atlantic Current. He shut his mind to all the past.

Baldur responded smoothly. He swam easily and not too fast, in the graceful underwater up and down weaving motion of the dolphin that brought him occasionally to the surface to breathe. In the earphone, the perplexed conversations picked up once more.

Johnny did not listen. He felt emptied of all emotion. Of sorrow, of bitterness, of fear of anger. He looked ahead and northward into a future as wide and empty as the Arctic waters. Only the wild wastes of the endless oceans were left now to the people of the sea. They would gather at Castle-Home no more

He thought that he had no more feeling left in him; and that this was a good thing. And then, in his earphone, he heard one of the parting people begin to sing:

Hey, Johnny! Hey-a, Johnny!
Home from the shore . . .

And the voices of others of the people took it up, joining in. The earphone echoed to a spreading chorus.

Hey-o, Johnny! Hey, Johnny!
To high land go no more!

The song blended in many voices. It reached through the cold, dead feeling of amputation in him to the awareness that had come as he stood in the Conference Room and felt the beating lives of the hundred and twenty-nine prisoners as if he held them in his hands.

It took hold of him as he had been taken hold of, in the moment of perception that had linked him with the other ex-Cadets as, deafened and smoke-blinded, they made their escape into the East River. He had cut himself loose from his people. But he saw now he could not escape them. No, never could he escape them, any more than a molecule of water, in its long journey by sky and mountain and field and harbor-mouth, could escape its eventual homecoming to the salt sea. And the knowledge of this, discovered at last, brought a sort of sad comfort to him.

He opened his mouth to sing with them; but—as in the small-Home returning from Manhattan Island—he found the words would not come. He held to the sled, listening. About him, three fathoms of water pressed against his passage. Baldur swam strongly to the north. The Atlantic Drift was carrying them east and north and in time they would come to the Irminger Current, swinging north between the Iceland coast and the Greenland shore . . . he, his son, and his dolphin.

Baldur swam strongly, as if he could sense the purpose of their going. Behind, in his earphone, Johnny could hear the voices of the singers beginning to fade and dwindle as they moved out of range. The number of their voices lessened and became distant.

The sun was going down. The three of them broke surface for a moment and the cloud-heavy sky above was darkening gray. Soon it would be full dark, and somewhere in the black water under the stars they would camp and sleep. Tomi held without a word to the sled. The dolphin swam with strength to the north and east. Behind, the last voices were failing, until only one still sounded, faintly in the earphone:

Long away, away, my Johnny!
Four long years and more.
Hey-o, Johnny! Hey, Johnny!
Go to land, no more.

And still the three of them swam to the north, under a gray sky that was like a road, and forever-flowing.

"Home from the Shore" is a slightly revised section of Mr. Dickson's new novel, *The Space Swimmers*, scheduled for publication in the late spring of 1964 by Doubleday & Company, Inc.

SUMMATION:
SF, 1962

by Judith Merril

What hath God wrought?

It was, of course, the telegraph. And the sentiment, in 1844, was probably the only predictable (perhaps the only permissible) available response.

Yet what was significant about the telegraph was precisely the fact that God had not wrought it. It was not—like fire, the wheel, the arch, or even the telescope—a new way to use, understand, or control some "natural" phenomenon. It was, specifically, a human creation: a synthesis—a putting together—of already-known facts about the God-given (natural) world, to form a *new thing*, visualized and constructed by natural (God-given) human intelligence.

This was the glittering dawn of the Age of Synthesis, the beginning of man's technological self-consciousness. In two short, fabulous generations, the founders of modern engineering and applied science (Faraday, Henry, Morse, Bessemer, Pasteur, Mendel, Perkin, for instance) took hold of the great discoveries of the past two centuries (the great Age of Analysis—Galileo, Harvey, Leeuwenhoek, Newton, Lavoisier, to name a few) and pointed the way for mankind to remake his own world to suit his own images.

What hath man wrought?

This was the true marvel of Mr. Morse's demonstration of "instantaneous" long-distance communication. And it was this kind of miracle, man-made, that generated in imaginative writers the new kind of exploratory fantasy that became "science fiction."

The Wonderful Invention (literary), in its earliest phase, was almost always a machine or a formula, and it functioned in one of the precisely defined areas of natural science: physics, chemistry, medicine or biology. It was not until the Darwinian explosion (or, more broadly, the philosophic eruption that included Marx-Engels, Darwin-Wallace and Freud) that the concept of *process* really developed: the idea that a new way of doing things, or even of looking at things, might change the world as readily as a new machine; and the corollary, that any successful innovation is not merely physical, but social as well.

What hath the machine wrought?
This was the wonder that brought about what is generally called "modern science fiction"—the school that started with Wells and Verne, Chesterton, Kipling and Forster. And, of course, implicit in their approach (as in the whole notion of *process*) was the kind of speculative work that constitutes most of the best of s-f today, where the Invention, as such, is often dropped from the middle, and the field of exploration becomes man himself.

What have man's inventiveness, man's civilization, man's knowledge and technology, done to man? What *is* man, to have done these things? What roads may lead to what Norbert Wiener calls "the human use of human beings"?

I have before me two statements on contemporary s-f, from the past year's crop of critical writings. One is from *Time* magazine's first essay at reviewing this anthology. The other is from an introduction by Frederik Pohl to Theodore R. Cogswell's short story collection, *The Wall Around the World.*

Time discusses the *Seventh Annual SF* under the heading, "Outpaced by Space," in a tone of sanctimonious mourning that represents a dubiously pleasant change from that publication's usual snide, sniping attitude toward s-f in general. This time, *Time* seemed almost to approve of the stories—as stories. It was the lack of "science fiction" that disturbed the reviewer. "Science fiction," he concludes unhappily, "will have to take a breather until neutrinos, wave mechanics and information theory grow familiar enough to be clothed in human terms."

I do not choose to quibble with anyone's definition of this most ambiguous of labels. If what the folks at *Time* want is human stories about neutrinos and wave mechanics, they may well have to hold their breaths for a bit (although with a bit more academic knowledge of information theory on their part, they might have recognized the information-theory stories in the *Seventh Annual*). It is not, basically, unreasonable to equate "science fiction" with the man-in-the-street's idea of "science"; it is only inaccurate. Mr. Pohl's semantics are somewhat closer to today's intellectual realities:

" 'Science' is, after all, knowledge. The term for any given science is a 'discipline'—what distinguishes science from non-science is an attitude. The gadgets, the cybernetic brains and space-drives, are only hardware that transmute into practice the knowledge obtained by methodical investigation . . . . It is the *study* that is science (or isn't science), not the subject matter. So with science fiction; it is not the subject matter that determines whether or not it qualifies, but the manner in which it is written. You can write a science-fiction story about ghosts as well as you can write one about rockets . . . ." And the specifying quality, for Mr. Pohl, of a work handled "*as* science fiction" is "by the application of brainpower, by investigating the causes and the consequences."

I find the Pohl approach a good deal more useful than that of *Time;* it still leaves, to my mind, an area of the literature unclassified. Obviously, "A Miracle of Rare Device" is fantasy; as clearly, "The Circuit Riders" is science fiction. But what about "Seven-Day Terror" or "Such Stuff" or "The Unfortunate Mr. Morky"? The "attitude" of science is clearly implicit in them all; the detail-work is absent, in each case, to varying degrees; the seriously speculative (studying) approach is present in all.

For my part, I do not care whether you, or he, or the editor in that corner, or the reviewer in the other, call them "science fiction" or not. They are—like all the material considered for inclusion in this *Annual* —examples of the broad field of S (for speculative) F (for fantasy, fiction, or fact), SF: the literature of the disciplined imagination.

The progress of this broad field took some interesting turns in 1962. Last year, I spoke of an observable trend toward the absorption of s-f in general into the mainstream of literature. This year, in apparent contradiction, there was a notable return (as reflected in the sources listed in this volume) of serious speculative fiction to the specialty magazines. (If one includes in this phrase the "*Playboy*-type" men's magazines, which *make* a specialty of s-f, there are very few other sources mentioned at all.) Most of the imaginative literature in general fiction media during the year was "straight fantasy" of either the adventure-horror or light-whimsey types.

In the face of this surface reversal of the trend, there were some less obvious, but more deep-rooted, evidences of its continuation. Most notable, probably, was the re-emergence, in popular publications, of the speculative essay. There were serious and provocative articles on Whatnext-in-science? in virtually every major national magazine sometime during the year (with an especially exciting series by Arthur C. Clarke in *Playboy,* scheduled for book publication soon, I believe). An annual predictive piece, serious or humorous, has come to be a New Year's item with a large number of publications. And of course there has been the happy comeback of the hoax article: the satiric or fanciful pseudo-news that falls halfway between fact and fantasy.

The other signs are mostly more subtle, but they continue to add up. I do not recall, for instance, that Walter Kerr ever mentioned s-f, or its attitudes, in his book, *The Decline of Pleasure*—but Mr. Kerr is a regular contributor (of excellent light verse) to the magazine, *Fantasy and Science Fiction*, and presumably a regular reader as well; it shows, in his critique. Richard McKenna, whose *Sand Pebbles* made publishing history last year, not only started as a writer of s-f (and we point with pride to the inclusion of his first published story, "Casey Agonistes," in this anthology four years ago), but has attempted whenever possible to assert his origins. ("I think science fiction is capable of being very serious literature," he wrote to one newspaper in an effort to correct the oversights of an interviewer; "in a very real sense my novel is science fiction, the science being anthropology. My primary thematic insight for it came to me in a course on theory of ritual.")

And then there is the continued creeping acceptance by the academic world. I found out last year, for instance, that William Golding's *Lord of the Flies* has become standard classroom reading in many high schools—and found it out when a local high school invited me to speak to several English classes in connection with their reading of it— to speak on "writing in general and science fiction in particular." Earlier in the year, a local lecture series "On Existence" was initiated with a dramatic reading of a science-fiction story. Most intriguing of all was the brochure sent to me by a friend who teaches at a Midwestern state teachers college, a piece of literature pushing their summer sessions, with a cover that announced: "1962 Professors—Mosquitoes, Gyros, Sculpture, Science Fiction!"

I want to take this opportunity to express my deep obligation to a number of people whose assistance (of several kinds) eased the work on this book greatly: Richard Wilson, Hans Santesson and Anthony Boucher, for suggestions on inclusions; Dr. Clayton Rawson (of the Witchdoctors' Club, Society of the Friends of Lizzie Borden, Anti-Gas Chamber League, and Association for the Preservation of the Rational) for the use of his exclusive facilities; Ann Pohl and Karen Emden for emergency secretarial help; Virginia Kidd, Ken Ross, and Chris Farlekas, for many kinds of assistance; and above all, Barbara Norville, for encouragement and assistance far beyond the call of editorial duty.

Judith Merril
Milford, Pennsylvania, 1963

BOOKS

by Anthony Boucher

There's life in the old girl yet.

Just when the muse of science fiction seems to have settled down into drab retirement, she suddenly decides to emerge with all of her old charm and sparkle, and we are once more enthralled.

By late November, when the accounts of the publishing year have normally been settled, 1962 seemed as dull a year for s-f in book form as any of its recent predecessors—a year in which even Eric Frank Russell could produce an unfortunate book (a misguided expansion of his splendid 1951 novella, *And Then There Were None)* and Clifford Simak a poor one. The gems of the year appeared to be such skillful and entertaining, but basically overfamiliar, interplanetary tales as Poul Anderson's *After Doomsday* (Ballantine) and H. Beam Piper's *Little Fuzzy* (Avon).

And then, in a happy rush, came a pentad of creatively satisfying novels, original in concept and in tone: Leonard Wibberley's *The Mouse on the Moon* (Morrow), a worthy lunar companion to *The Mouse That Roared;* Robert Sheckley's Candidesque *Journey Beyond Tomorrow* (Signet; serialized as *The Journey of Joenes);* John D. MacDonald's wacky and bawdy *The Girl, the Gold Watch & Everything* (Gold Medal); the lusty historico-satiric *Joyleg* (Pyramid) by Avram Davidson (his first novel) and Ward Moore; and above all Philip K. Dick's *The Man in the High Castle* (Putnam's), a serious consideration of life in the world of an Axis victory in World War II which is at once an *If*-novel to rank beside *Bring the Jubilee* and one of the strongest bridges to date between s-f and the "mainstream" novel.

One comparably exciting s-f novel had appeared earlier in the year in the juvenile field, when Madeleine L'Engle made her s-f debut with *A Wrinkle in Time* (Ariel); and the veteran of juveniles-to-please-adults, Andre Norton, sustained her high reputation with *The Defiant Agents* (World).

In exploration of s-f's often more rewarding past, anthologies were unusually frequent in 1962, and of unusually high quality. Isaac Asimov collected *The Hugo Winners* of the past (Doubleday), and Kingsley Amis (with Robert Conquest), Groff Conklin, Clifton Fadiman, Damon Knight and Frederik Pohl all contributed well-researched and intelligently patterned collections which added to critical and historical understanding of the field.* Of particular interest and novelty even to the specialist were two volumes of *Soviet Science Fiction* (Collier), which can reassure us that we are at least winning the Spacefiction Race—though these often naïve and primitive Russian stories do preserve something of the "sense of wonder" which our sophistication too frequently loses.

Outstanding among collections by individual authors were the long-overdue first assemblies of stories by Avram Davidson (*Or All the Seas with Oysters*, Berkley) and Katherine MacLean (*The Diploids*, Avon).

Two all but unique events of 1962 were the publication of a s-f play (William Golding's dazzlingly Shavian *The Brass Butterfly* in Mentor's *The Genius of the Later English Theater*) and a volume of s-f humor (Grendel Briarton's outrageous *Through Time and Space with Ferdinand Feghoot*, Paradox).

There were happy signs of a breaking away from strict ghettoization in the appearance of a number of stories of fantasy, and even of strict science fiction, in "mainstream" collections by Robert Lowry, Muriel Spark, Mark Van Doren and especially Jorge Luis Borges, whose *Labyrinths* (New Directions) and *Ficciones* (Grove) contain some of the year's most stimulatingly unclassifiable fictions. A further token of declassification was the publication of three admirable novels of the supernatural in the mystery-suspense form: Charity Blackstock's *A House Possessed* (Lippincott), Arthur Calder-Marshall's *The Scarlet Boy* (Harper) and Mark McShane's *Seance* (Crime Club)—and with their closely reasoned approach to problems of the paranormal, these are, I suppose, as much science fiction as a good deal of the contents of *Analog*.

In all-out nonscientific fantasy of terror, the book of the year was Ray Bradbury's *Something Wicked This Way Comes* (Simon and Schuster)—less substantial than one might have hoped from Bradbury's long-awaited first full-sized novel, but cne hell of a melodramatic chiller. The old-fashioned, but still highly viable ghost story was well represented by Russell Kirk's collection, *The Surly Sullen Bell* (Fleet)—which was advertised by Pacifica Radio, when Mr. Kirk read excerpts, as *The Surly Southern Belle*, which is possibly more frightening.

Spectrum, edited by Kingsley Amis and Robert Conquest (Harcourt; abridged Berkley, 1963); *Great Science Fiction by Scientists*, edited by Groff Conklin (Collier); *The Mathematical Magpie*, assembled and edited by Clifton Fadiman (Simon and Schuster); *A Century of Science Fiction*, edited by Damon Knight (Simon and Schuster; reprinted Dell, 1963); *The Expert Dreamers*, edited by Frederik Pohl (Doubleday).

HONORABLE MENTIONS

Abbreviations:

    Amz   Amazing Stories
    Anal   Analog Science Fact & Science Fiction
    Fant   Fantastic Stories of Imagination
    F&SF   Fantasy and Science Fiction
    Gal   Galaxy
    If   Worlds of If Science Fiction
    NW   New Worlds Science Fiction (British)
    SciF   Science Fantasy (British)

VANCE AANDAHL "Darfgarth," *F&SF*, Jul.;
    "Adam Frost," *Playboy*, Apr.
BRIAN W. ALDISS "Tyrant's Territory," *Amz*, Mar.;
    "A Pleasure Shared," *Rogue*, Dec.
POUL ANDERSON "Escape from Orbit," *Amz*, Oct.;
    "Progress," *F&SF*, Jan.;
    "Epilogue," *Anal*, Mar.
CHRISTOPHER ANVIL "Gadget vs. Trend," *Anal*, Oct.
SAM & JANET ARGO "Hail to the Chief," *Anal*, Oct.
ROBERT ARTHUR "Garvey's Ghost," *F&SF*, Apr.
J. G. BALLARD "The Watch Towers," *SciF*, Jun.;
    "The Singing Statues," *Fant*, Jul.
STEPHEN BARR "Tybalt," *If*, Mar.
JAMES & VIRGINIA BLISH "On the Wall of the Lodge," *Gal*, Jun.
J. F. BONE "Pandemic," *Anal*, Feb.
CARL BRANDON "Stanley Toothbrush," *F&SF*, Jul.
R. BRETNOR "Dr. Birdmouse," *Fant*, Apr.
ROSEL GEORGE BROWN "Fruiting Body," *F&SF*, Aug.
JOHN BRUNNER "Father of Lies," *SciF*, Apr.
ALGIS BUDRYS "The Rag and Bone Men," *Gal*, Feb.
DAVID R. BUNCH "The Reluctant Immortals," *If*, Nov.

ALAN BURNS "Pixy Planet," *NW,* Apr.

TERRY CARR "Hop-Friend," *F&SF,* Nov.

MILDRED CLINGERMAN "Measure My Love," *F&SF,* Oct.

THEODORE R. COGSWELL "Prisoner of Love," in *The Wall Around the World* (Pyramid, 1962)

GHISLAIN DE DIESBACK "The Toys of Princes," *Mademoiselle,* March 1962

ROGER DEE "Rough Beast," *Anal,* Mar.

MIRIAM ALLEN DEFORD "The Akkra Case," *Amz,* Jan.

LESTER DEL REY "Thunder in Space," *Amz,* Jun.

GORDON R. DICKSON "Three-Part Puzzle," *Anal,* Jun.; "Roofs of Silver," *F&SF,* Dec.

THOMAS M. DISCH "The Double Timer," *Fant,* Oct.

JACK EGAN "World Edge," *Amz,* Nov.

DJINN FAINE "Daughter of Eve," *F&SF,* Jun.

JULES FEIFFER "The Lonely Machine," *Playboy,* Dec.

JACK FINNEY "Where the Cluetts Are," in *I Love Galesburg in the Springtime* (Simon and Schuster, 1963)

ERIC FRAZEE "Noselrubb, the Tree," *F&SF,* May.

H. B. FYFE "The Talkative Tree," *If,* Jan.

DANIEL F. GALOUYE "A Silence of Wings," *Fant,* Feb.

H. L. GOLD "What Price Wings?," *F&SF,* Aug.

RON GOULART "Nor Iron Bars a Cage," *Fant,* Oct.

JOSEPH L. GREEN "The Colonist," *NW,* Aug.

STEVE HALL "Weekend Trip," *SciF,* Oct.

EDMOND HAMILTON "The Stars, My Brothers," *Amz,* May.

LEE HARDING "Birthright," *NW,* Jun.

JIM HARMON "The Place Where Chicago Was," *Gal,* Feb.; "Always a Qurono," *Gal,* Aug.; "The Depths," *F&SF,* Dec.

LARRY M. HARRIS "Sword of Flowers," *Fant,* Aug.

FRANK HERBERT "Mindfield," *Amz,* Mar.

PHILIP E. HIGH "The Psi Squad," *NW,* Jan.

JOHN JAKES "The Protector," *Amz,* May.

RAYMOND F. JONES "The Great Gray Plague," *Anal,* Feb.

COLIN KAPP "Lambda 1," *NW,* Dec.

KEITH LAUMER "Cocoon," *Fant,* Dec.; "Retief of the Red-Tape Mountain," *If,* May.

FRITZ LEIBER "The Secret Songs," *F&SF,* Aug.

MURP˙V LEINSTER "Imbalance," *Fant,* Dec.

LEONARD LOCKHARD "The Professional Approach," *Anal,* Sep.

MAGNUS LUDENS "The Long Silvery Day," *Gal,* Apr.

JONATHAN BLAKE MACKENZIE ". . . Nor Iron Bars . . . ," *Anal,*
    May.

ROBERT S. MALCOLM "A Free Fall, Free for All," *Gent,* Aug.

FELIX MARTI-IBAÑEZ "Senhor Zumbeira's Leg," *F&SF,* Dec.

JUDITH MERRIL "The Shrine of Temptation," *Fant,* Apr.

MORRIS NAGEL "Serpent in Paradise," *NW,* Sep.

H. C. NEAL "Who Shall Dwell," *Playboy,* Jul.

DAVID NEWMAN "Three Fables for the Post-Atomic Age,"
    Esquire, Apr.

JOHN NOVOTNY "Snug as a Bug," *The Dude,* Nov.

ROBERT PRESSLIE "One Foot in the Door," *NW,* Aug.;
    "Lucky Dog," *NW, Nov.*

TOM PURDOM "The Warriors," *Amz,* Jun.

FRANCIS G. RAYER "Variant," *NW,* Aug.

KIT REED "The New You," *F&SF,* Sep.

MACK REYNOLDS "Mercenary," *Anal,* Apr.;
    "Subversive," *Anal,* Dec.

DAVID ROME "Meaning," *NW,* Dec.

MARIA RUSSELL "The Deer Park," *F&SF,* Jan.

WILLIAM SAMBROT "Control Sonambule," in *Island of Fear,*
    (Permabooks, 1963)

JAMES H. SCHMITZ "Watch the Sky," *Anal,* Aug.

JACK SHARKEY "A Matter of Protocol," *Gal,* Aug.

JOHN SHEPLEY "The Kit-Katt Klub," *F&SF,* Apr.

CORDWAINER SMITH "The Ballad of Lost C'Mell," *Gal,* Oct.

EDWARD SOREL *Moon Missing* (Simon and Schuster, 1963)

JAMES STAMERS "E Being," *If,* Mar.

THEODORE STURGEON "When You Care, When You Love," *F&SF,*
    Sep.

THOMAS BURNETT SWANN "The Sudden Wings," *SciF,* Oct.

THEODORE L. THOMAS "The Weather Man," *Anal,* Jun.

E. C. TUBB "Worm in the Woodwork," *Anal,* Jan.

SYDNEY VAN SCYOC "Shatter the Wall," *Gal,* Feb.

JACK VANCE "Gateway to Strangeness," *Amz,* Aug.

KURT VONNEGUT, JR. "2 B R O 2 B," *If,* Jan.

GEOFFREY WAGNER "Autogeddon," *Fant,* Oct.

EDWARD WELLEN "Flashback," *Amz,* Apr.

DON WESTLAKE "Look Before You Leap," *Anal,* May.

LEONARD WIBBERLEY "The Man Who Lived On Water," *Saturday
    Evening Post* Mar. 28.

GAHAN WILSON   "Horror Trio," *Playboy*, Jun.
ROBERT F. YOUNG   "Jonathan and the Space Whale," *F&SF*, Mar.;
          "The Star Fisherman," *Fant*, Jun.;
          "Plane Jane," *Fant*, Sep.
ROGER ZELAZNY   "Passion Play," *Amz*, Aug.